KEEPING secrets

KEEPING
Secrets

A Novel

BINA BERNARD

Arcade Publishing • New York

Arcade Publishing books may be purchased in bulk at special discounts for sales promotion, corporate gifts, fund-raising, or educational purposes. Special editions can also be created to specifications. For details, contact the Special Sales Department, Arcade Publishing, 307 West 36th Street, 11th Floor, New York, NY 10018 or arcade@skyhorsepublishing.com.

Arcade Publishing® is a registered trademark of Skyhorse Publishing, Inc.®, a Delaware corporation.

Visit our website at www.arcadepub.com.

10 9 8 7 6 5 4 3 2 1

Library of Congress Cataloging-in-Publication Data is available on file.

Cover design by Walter Bernard
Interior designed by Natalia Olbinski

Print ISBN: 978-1-951627-30-0
Ebook ISBN: 978-1-951627-57-7

Printed in the United States of America

Children begin by loving their parents;
as they grow older they judge them;
sometimes they forgive them.

—Oscar Wilde,
The Portrait of Dorian Gray

Shaped by actual events, this novel is dedicated to all
survivors living with their scars, and to my granddaughters,
Scarlett Dorothy Lindgren and Orly Olympia Lindgren,
who make me feel hopeful about the future!

PROLOGUE

Poland, January 1945

HIS BREATH FORMED PUFFY CLOUDS. The only sound he heard was the crackling noise his shoes made as he walked over the crisp snow. If he had not been warmed by the anticipation of seeing Lena, the freezing cold Polish winter would have made him shiver. When he saw the iron gate off in the distance, he quickened his pace, his heart racing.

The young nun who greeted him as she opened the heavy gate made no eye contact but seemed cordial. She led him to the office of the Mother Superior. He smiled as he remembered the sound he and Lena had made walking these same glistening hard wood floors four years before. Inside the office, he stopped smiling when the face he expected to see was not there. Instead a much younger woman with a stern expression sat behind the desk.

"I'm here to see the Mother Superior," he said, expecting to be ushered into the proper room.

"I am the Mother Superior," Sister Marianna said firmly, and gestured for him to take a seat.

"I've come to get Lena!" he said and sat down on the chair in front of her desk, clutching the wooden arms so tightly his knuckles turned white.

"I know the other Mother Superior understood that I brought Lena to the orphanage temporarily, until someone in her family was able to care for her. Her father was supposed to get her back after the war. But since he died fighting with the Underground, her aunt, her mother's sister, wants to raise her," he said, reiterating the story he had given the former Mother Superior. Even with this new nun in charge they had to give Lena back to her family, he thought, and relaxed.

Then he heard, "I'm sorry. Lena is not here. There are no children here, and have not been for some years."

Stunned, he stared blankly into space and thought about the last time he saw Lena's sad little face framed by cascading blonde curls.

"Where is she?" His question barely audible.

"I don't know," Sister Marianna said forcefully.

"How can that be?"

"The children were moved years before I came here, and the orphanage records were destroyed by a fire," she answered.

"What do I tell the family?"

The Mother Superior sighed. "I will try to find out what happened to Lena, but I'm sure she was placed in a good home," Sister Marianna said as she began ushering him out.

Outside the howling wind blew the mounds of snow. The gate shut behind him, and he leaned against it for support. Paralyzed.

2

PART I

1

New York, May 1976

HANNAH STONE WAS TROUBLED. Friday closings at *Weekend* magazine, where she worked as a staff writer, were notoriously chaotic, but she always managed to keep her anxiety level mid-meter. This Friday was different. The one weapon in her survival arsenal she always depended on, her ability to do her job well no matter what was going on in her life, had failed her.

"What is this supposed to be?" the managing editor shouted. Hannah had walked into Betty's office for an assessment of the draft she'd left in her in-box early that morning. Before Hannah could answer, Betty handed the marked-up manuscript back to her and announced, "I expect a publishable piece by three o'clock. Go!"

Clutching the rejected manuscript as she walked back to her cubicle, Hannah squeezed her eyes tight to keep the tears in check. Betty's dismissal of her profile of Rosalynn Carter was painful, but it was not her only problem that morning. Her parents were about to resurface and Robert, her Robert, was far away. Back at her desk, she sat there for a few minutes, swaying from left to right in her swivel chair.

"Get a grip and get to work," she finally told herself.

Hannah reached for one of a half dozen cold coffee containers languishing on her desk as she started to read Betty's comments. She broke out laughing when she realized she was about to take a sip of a substance that seemed to be growing penicillin. Her laughter lifted her spirits. A resolute Hannah was ready to start over.

Fingers poised on the home keys, eyes closed as if in prayer, she was determined to salvage her lackluster interview with the possible next First Lady, while anxiously waiting for the call announcing her parents' safe arrival at LaGuardia Airport.

When her mother had mentioned in one of their weekly chats that they were coming back to New York a month early so her father could see a heart specialist, Hannah didn't believe that was the real reason for their return. She herself had been trying to get him to see a cardiologist for years.

"Why should I take another doctor's opinion?" was his answer. "I've forgotten more about medicine than most of them will ever know!"

Did the great Dr. Harry Stone suddenly change his mind? Not likely, Hannah thought. Why were they coming back? She suspected her casual comment that Robert was staying at the cottage in Amagansett might be why. Whatever the reason, their impending return made Hannah's body stiffen and she mentally reached for some Maalox. Hannah loved her parents, but their unspoken demands almost cut off her air supply. Only while they were away in Eastland Village could she breathe freely. Once a week Hannah willingly listened to her mother's complaints. And with twelve hundred miles separating them, she could easily maintain the fiction that the coldness between her and her father did not exist. While they were in New York, she attributed the pain she saw etched on both their faces to her missteps. Hannah assumed guilt the way a sponge soaked up water.

At three o'clock when she checked her watch and her rewrite was still not ready for Betty's critical eyes, Hannah's anxiety

6

level spiked. Several times she reached for the box of Marlboro cigarettes in her purse. Having resisted each temptation, she congratulated herself mentally. After Hannah had interviewed a young woman battling lung cancer, she decided to test the strength of her willpower to curb a pack-a-day habit. Without committing to stop smoking, she wanted to see how long she could go without lighting up. "I can take one whenever I want," she assured herself. The unopened box of Marlboros had waited in her purse for three months. Although the butt-filled ashtrays were gone, the books and everything in her office still reeked of stale cigarette smoke.

While Hannah kept her cigarettes handy, the M&Ms in the large glass apothecary jar next to the phone now served as a substitute.

"Am I simply choosing diabetes over cancer?" Hannah joked to herself, as she noted how quickly the M&Ms were disappearing. She was eating them by the handful, carefully selecting the red ones to help her fight her writer's block.

Hannah loved working on a magazine, even though defending story ideas at the weekly editorial meeting was a blood sport. While the staff walked into the conference room with the enthusiasm of lambs going to the slaughter, Hannah, clipboard in one hand and coffee cup in the other, insisted, "What's not to like? Free glazed doughnuts for everybody." She sat in the same seat around the oval conference table and waited until the editor said a variation of, "You're up Hannah. Since we don't have time to hear your hundred ideas, just give us your Top 10." That always brought laughter from the staff, and a grinning Hannah started making her pitch.

She preferred writing profiles rather than covering headline grabbing events. "I like to let people tell why they do what they do," Hannah explained. She had often fantasized about interviewing her father to figure him out.

On late nights waiting for their stories to close, when she wasn't sleeping on the floor in her cubicle, Hannah enjoyed hanging out with her fellow writers, drinking jug wine, and contemplating such existential questions as Why do doctors and nurses wear their hospital scrubs in the street? and Who exactly prefers a glass half-empty to a glass half-full? Ostensibly a willing participant in these gab sessions, Hannah always kept some distance. For her any conversation, no matter how trivial, was equivalent to a championship chess match. It was exhausting! Before Hannah uttered a word in jest or as part of a serious exchange, she had to know what the last gambit would be. She envied people who did not mentally calculate all the possible consequences of any words they uttered or action they planned to undertake. A self-described information junky, Hannah stored important and trivial tidbits in her brain bank to be retrieved as needed. Facts were her protective armor. She never thought she had to know everything, but Hannah had to know what she didn't know. That gave her a chance to figure out how to get answers before anyone knew she didn't have them. For Hannah it was always, No Mistakes Allowed.

When her mother phoned at 4:30, all the red M&Ms were gone and Hannah was still struggling.

"Welcome home," she said in her best cheerleader voice. "How was the flight?"

"Fine. There were so many people in wheelchairs you'd think we were on a flight to Lourdes." Molly Stone chuckled.

It cheered Hannah that her mother seemed to be in good spirits. She was grateful that she did not mention Robert. Hannah felt the stiffness in her neck soften.

"Sorry I can't take off early today and help you get settled," she said. Trying to explain her predicament, Hannah added, "I'm having trouble with my Rosalynn Carter story, it's . . ."

Molly interrupted. "You met Rosalynn Carter? Next week she and Jimmy Carter are making a campaign stop at Eastland Village. Too bad I won't get to meet them, but I'm glad to be back," she said, still cheerful.

"Great. Let me finish writing and I'll come by later to welcome you properly." Hannah hoped she could keep her word. "Give my best to Dad," she said, signing off.

Hannah was glad her parents had not expected her to pick them up at the airport. Still she felt guilty because she had never made the offer. Sometimes feeling guilty was Hannah's trade-off for doing what she wanted.

At 10:30 when her mother called again, the apothecary jar was empty and Hannah was putting the final touches on her story.

"You're still there," Molly said, surprised.

"Of course. I told you I was working late and would come by afterwards." Hannah was defensive.

"Well, we're going to bed. It's been a long day. Can you come tomorrow? Your father is anxious to see you."

"Sorry about tonight, Mom. I'll come for breakfast. Really, I'm having trouble . . ."

"I understand," she cut her off. Hannah couldn't decide if her mother was truly being understanding, or miffed thinking she'd been ignored. After a tough week Hannah hoped the weekend would not be tougher. She sighed and crossed her fingers. The fact that she still had not figured out the real reason for her parents' early return gnawed at her. And Hannah dreaded having to explain Robert's living in Amagansett.

They had had some reservations about the marriage to begin with. A definite red flag for Molly was the fact that Robert was divorced and had a child. Surprisingly his not being Jewish never seemed to be an issue. Hannah knew a possible break up was the last thing her parents would want. Harry and Molly Stone did not adjust easily to change. Their version of "Be careful what you wish for!" was "Stick with what you have, what you might get could be worse."

That night when Hannah opened the door to her apartment she headed straight for the bedroom and fell, spread-eagle, on the bed. I'll just rest for five minutes, then go into the shower, Hannah thought. She woke up Saturday morning still in her street clothes, something she had not done since college.

Hannah stripped, dragged herself into the shower, got dressed in record time and, armed with assorted bagels and cream cheese from Zabar's, and the morning newspaper, arrived at her parents' Upper

West Side apartment by 10:30, absolutely determined to make their reunion pleasant.

Seconds after Hannah rang the bell, the door to the apartment swung open and her mother flung her arms around her even before she had set both feet inside.

"It's so good to be home," Molly said.

"You look great, Mom!" Hannah said as she loosened her mother's grip.

"Thank you." Molly grinned, and patted her perfectly coiffed hairdo with her beautifully manicured hand. How does she keep that flaming red nail polish from chipping, Hannah wondered, as she looked down at her own scruffy nails. Molly pulled her daughter toward the living room. Nothing changed here, Hannah mused as she looked around the apartment she hadn't seen in eight months.

When she glanced into the living room where her father was asleep on the sofa, Hannah held her breath. She was visibly shaken seeing his frail body engulfed by down cushions.

Who is that man? Hannah thought.

* * *

Dr. Harry Stone, née Hershel Stein, was one of the lucky ones: a Jew who survived World War II in Poland by passing himself off as a Gentile. With the help of his Polish friends and the money he amassed from his thriving medical practice in Krakow, Harry secured false identity papers for his wife, his daughter Hannah, and himself.

Secure with his new documents in his breast pocket, he had brazenly walked out of the Krakow Jewish Quarter and boarded a train for Warsaw. There, as Dr. Bronisław Bieliński, he became an actor in a dangerous drama. His masquerade was aided by his straight nose, light brown hair and green eyes, which did not fit the Jewish stereotype. However, his circumcision branded him a Jew. Harry ingeniously fashioned a foreskin out of skin-tone artist wax to camouflage that. But he was always mindful that his ruse could not pass a close inspection.

A mere accusation of "JEW!" by a potential extortionist demanding money put him in jeopardy. On several occasions, instead of paying, Harry threatened his would-be blackmailer.

"Yes, let's stop that German officer over there and see if he believes a thug like you or the doctor who fixed his sprained wrist last week!" he bluffed. But more often Dr. Bieliński paid and immediately moved his office or residence to another part of Warsaw, depending at which venue the encounter occurred.

In 1944 after the Polish Underground failed to liberate Warsaw, the Germans packed the few Polish men left alive onto trains heading to concentration camps. Dr. Bronisław Bieliński was one of them. With his medical bag under his arm, he stationed himself along the edge of the boxcar. Just as the train slowed down around a curve, he jumped off. A young German soldier spotted him, pulled the emergency cord and stopped the train. At gunpoint he forced Harry back aboard. A few miles later, feeling he had nothing to lose, Harry jumped again. This time the same soldier waved him on. A grateful Harry waved back.

Harry often wondered what that young German would have done if he had known he was letting a Jew go free. Luck was with him. He felt invincible then.

Being a survivor was a burden Harry Stone could not shake. It wasn't his fault the retreating Germans burned down entire buildings in Warsaw with his relatives hidden inside. Still he was haunted by those deaths. He grieved for those he hadn't saved. Those he left behind. Time did not heal those wounds. His new life in America could not make up for what he lost.

* * *

Hannah always believed her father was indestructible. The figure she saw now tossing and turning on the sofa bore little resemblance to the formidable man Harry once was. His gaunt face and graying brown hair made him look much older than his sixty-eight years. My God, he's really sick, Hannah mouthed the words to herself. She glanced around the apartment again. Nothing had changed, except Harry.

"Let him sleep," Molly said, bringing a finger to her lips. "He didn't have a good night."

Still holding Hannah's hand, she led her into the kitchen.

"I didn't realize how sick Dad was," Hannah said.

"I told you on the phone many times!" an aggrieved Molly almost shouted.

Over her fresh-brewed coffee and Hannah's bagels and cream cheese, Molly finally expected to get the sympathy she deserved from her daughter. "You have no idea what it was like for me this winter!"

"Mom, you say the same thing every year," Hannah said impatiently, before she caught herself and grinned, hoping to pass her comment off as a joke.

Hannah knew her father was difficult. After almost forty years of marriage it couldn't be a surprise to her mother. Hannah didn't know what her mother expected her to say. She didn't want to be pulled into a conspiracy against Harry. Hannah obviously had enough issues with her father. She didn't need to take on her mother's as well.

"Believe me, he was never this bad. It's easy for you to minimize what I've been through. You were in New York leading a normal life. I was a prisoner in Eastland Village!"

Hannah rolled her eyes. "That's a little melodramatic, don't you think?"

"No! I was there. I lived it. Those dance trophies we won last year were the only reminders I had of what our life used to be like. Your father wouldn't go anywhere and wouldn't let me go out either. I've been his prisoner this whole winter."

While Hannah believed her mother never missed an opportunity to dramatize her situation, always exaggerating her own suffering, she decided to let her vent and not argue.

"I'm used to his nightmares and the fact that Mr. Personality turned into Mr. Sourpuss once we were alone and he had no one to charm, but this winter . . . I don't know what happened to him. Maybe it's his heart. Maybe he thinks something bad would happen to me if I'm out of his sight . . ." her voice trailed off.

"Forget about this winter, Mom," Hannah said, hoping to cut short her mother's complaints. But Molly was not ready to give up the floor.

"Last week I thought he'd brought on a heart attack for sure because of something one of our neighbors said to him. We got into the elevator just before the door closed. We each had two shopping bags. I gave him the light one and I carried the heavier bags. Morris from downstairs was inside. I smiled at him, but when your father just stared at the floor, Morris grinned and said, 'Can't look me in the eye, Harry? What are you up to? Hiding some dark secret?' Instead of just laughing off his comments, like everyone else, your father stared straight ahead. I could see the veins at the side of his neck were popping out."

Molly was enjoying having her daughter's full attention. Finally! She patted Hannah's hand and continued her story. "I was relieved when Morris got off on the third floor. Your father didn't say a word until we were inside our apartment. Then he became a crazy person. He started shouting, 'Why? Why did Morris say what he said? Who does he work for?' I didn't even get a chance to put away the groceries."

Hannah nodded, but made no comment.

"I reminded him Morris was retired. Your father ignored me. He kept yelling, 'He worked for immigration or the IRS. I'm sure he worked for the government!' I pleaded with him to calm down. He insisted Morris implied he was a criminal, hiding a secret. When I said nobody is interested in Harry Stone, he screamed, 'You're naive! People can accuse you of anything they want!' and flared his nostrils."

"I'm sorry it was so hard for you, Mom." Hannah hugged her mother.

Molly was happy to have her daughter's sympathy at last.

"Your father never acted like that before. If someone invited us out he made me lie and say *I* was sick!"

"Look at him Mom, he's not in good shape."

"Everybody at Eastland has something wrong!"

"But no one wants to be around people when they don't feel well," Hannah argued.

"It's not just his health, Hannah. It's his mind, too," Molly insisted. "Believe me, he's not the same."

"Maybe he just doesn't like Eastland Village anymore."

"What's not to like?" Molly demanded, as if not liking Eastland Village was another reason to question Harry's sanity. "It's paradise!

The best entertainers come to our huge clubhouse. Rosalind Kind, Julius LaRosa, Red Buttons. We have a movie almost every night. You can go swimming, play shuffleboard, tennis! There's even a nine-hole golf course. Your father could have taken up golf, like other doctors. I could have a bridge game as often as I wanted. Each morning we had breakfast on the terrace and looked out at the canal. At sundown, we'd go for a leisurely walk around the village. What else could we possibly need for retirement?" Molly asked.

Hannah heard her mother out, but she wasn't sure how to evaluate the situation. Her father was clearly in poor physical condition, but she didn't know how to gauge his mental state. For now all she wanted was to make her mother feel better.

"Mom, you're back in New York. Dad's finally agreed to see a specialist. Everything is going to be fine," she reassured her. "Wait and see. Things will change."

Molly smiled and Hannah was pleased. But it wasn't what Hannah said that put a smile on her mother's face. Rather in her mind, Molly was passing the burden of taking care of Harry on to Hannah. She'd suffered all winter, put up with his irrational mood swings and bad dreams. Now it was Hannah's turn.

Hearing the phone ring, Molly quickly ran into the entryway to answer so Harry wouldn't be awakened. Her friend Rachel's cheerful voice made Molly feel her situation was improving.

From her vantage point in the kitchen, Hannah saw her mother gesturing animatedly and congratulated herself. That was not so hard. All I have to do is listen and not argue.

Hannah was pouring herself a second cup of coffee, when she realized her mother had her coat on, preparing to leave. Before she could voice an objection, Molly was at the door about to waltz out.

"I'm going to meet Rachel," Molly whispered. "I'll be back in a couple of hours. If you and your father get hungry, there are cold cuts in the refrigerator." She closed the door behind her.

Hannah stayed in the kitchen reading the paper. Periodically she tiptoed down the two steps into the sunken living room to check on her father. She hoped their first conversation would not be a confrontation. But whenever Hannah and Harry were together a fight was inevitable. It was as if an unidentified power propelled them into battle, and they were each defenseless against its force. Their verbal outbursts seemed to be the only thing that pierced the coldness between them.

* * *

As Hannah was growing up, no matter what specialty Molly prepared, kopytka, *the Polish potato dumplings she loved, stuffed cabbage, lamb chops, or Swedish meatballs, their Bronx apartment became a war zone some time during the meal. The three of them would sit down to eat in silence. At opposite ends of the table Harry and Hannah stared at their plates, until Molly, determined to lift the tension, would smile and start some meaningless chatter.*

"So, how was school today, Hannah?" she'd ask, thinking that was a safe enough subject to bring up.

"Fine."

"Have you done your homework?" Like a good lawyer, Molly already knew the answer.

"Yes."

"If you've finished your homework so fast, they're not giving you enough work to do," Harry interjected, and they were off.

"I do as much as I'm told to do."

"You should be more ambitious!"

"I'm ambitious enough."

"Not if you do the least amount expected of you!"

With each retort their verbal volleys intensified. As Harry raised his voice another decibel, Hannah followed his example.

"I do everything my teachers expect of me. I get no complaints from them!"

"What do they care? You're not their daughter!"

Hoping to end it, Molly would put her finger to her lips. "Sha! Both of you, please, no more fighting," she'd beg. Sometimes she succeeded, and the fight was a mere skirmish. More often she could do nothing but let the fight run its course.

On those occasions when Hannah would run away from the table crying, Molly chased after her and pleaded with her daughter to come back and apologize to her father.

"I have nothing to apologize for," Hannah always insisted, hurt that her mother never took her side. After such a blow-up even when Molly did get Hannah back to the table, she steadfastly refused to apologize. Silence and cold stares prevailed between Hannah and Harry for the remainder of the meal. Often father and daughter did not speak to each other for the rest of the evening, sometimes longer.

Hannah dreaded their shouting matches. But even when there was no fight in progress, there was always tension in the Stones' apartment.

"Hannah, remember to say 'Hello' when your father comes home and don't fight with him," Molly coached her daughter daily.

"I'm not the one who starts the fights," Hannah insisted.

Molly sighed and hoped for the best. Like a referee in a Frazier-Ali boxing match, Molly's role was to keep Harry and Hannah from killing each other.

Once a verbal outburst did become physical. In the middle of the argument Harry screamed: "Is this why I saved your life? So you could fight with me?" and Hannah yelled back, "I don't know why you saved my life! I never asked you to!"

Hearing those words, Harry lashed out. The smack, as his open palm collided with Hannah's cheek, shocked all of them. A contrite Harry immediately reached out to comfort Hannah but he was too late. Fearing he was about to strike again, Molly swooped her out of his reach, into another room. That night while she was in bed with the light on, against her father's dictates, Hannah heard her parents arguing for a long time. She could not make out their conversation. After that incident, for several weeks, Harry and Hannah spoke to each other only when absolutely necessary.

A truce was in effect when her parents entertained. Usually the only child present, Hannah enjoyed sitting with the men after the meal while the women helped Molly in the kitchen. To her surprise, at such gatherings, her father would allow her to pontificate unchallenged about politics. Once after a rousing discussion in which Hannah participated, Abe Beigleman pulled Harry aside. She overheard him say, "Your little Hannah has some head on her shoulders."

She was amazed to hear a smiling Harry proudly reply, "I know!"

Hannah wanted to believe that her father loved her. After all, *I am his only child. Puzzled by his iciness, she plaintively asked, in the midst of one of their minor skirmishes, "Why don't you love me?"*

Harry shouted back in genuine disbelief, "How can you even ask such a question? We're one of the few families that survived. We're a miracle!"

Sadly neither Harry nor Hannah seemed capable of experiencing the joy of being part of that miracle. Hannah sometimes wondered if things would have been better between them if she'd gone to medical school, as he had wanted.

Over the years, their fights morphed into debates. Harry and Hannah found themselves on opposite sides of almost any subject: hemlines, headlines, movies, drugs, drug companies, restaurants. Even if there was no basis for disagreement, a heated debate ensued. In April 1968, when the Columbia students took over campus buildings and declared themselves social revolutionaries with a laundry list of demands, Hannah listened as Harry ridiculed them and their tactics.

"These kids think they're revolutionaries. That's a laugh. They have no idea what it means to fight for something. To risk your life! They think taking over a building, while incidentally depriving other students of an education, and issuing a list of demands, including amnesty for their unlawful take-over, makes them bona fide revolutionaries! Ha! They're hooligans who want to get their demands met without risking even the skin off their snot noses. They want to see themselves on television and their names in The New York Times, *that's all," Harry said, expecting Hannah to take the opposite view. And she didn't disappoint.*

"These kids are trying to make the establishment see things differently, they're trying to bring about some social changes. They're idealists, Dad. They think they can make a difference," Hannah argued. But her opinion of the student takeover was not very different from Harry's. Still she could not help but come to their defense. It was her family's version of, "The enemy of my enemy is my friend."

* * *

When she heard Harry's voice, Hannah rushed into the living room. He was thrashing around on the sofa, his body contorted.

He seemed to be calling out for someone named Lena. Hannah gently shook her father, trying to end his disturbing dream. Harry squinted at first, and then opened his eyes wide. Seeing her blurry image without his glasses, he reached up with an unsteady hand to touch her face.

"Lena, Lena," he said softly.

Hannah patted her father's bony hand. She forced herself to ignore the slight she felt for being mistaken for someone Harry seemed to feel more affection toward than he'd shown her over the years.

"Wake up, Dad. You're home," she said.

Hearing Hannah's voice, Harry blinked several times, to force his eyes into focus. He seemed confused.

"It's Hannah, Dad. You're in New York."

He looked around the living room, trying to reorient himself as he reached for his glasses on the nearby table.

"You're home, Dad."

Harry nodded, put his glasses on, and sat up.

"Who is Lena?" Hannah asked matter-of-factly, when Harry seemed to have regained his bearings.

As he started to reply, Molly opened the door to the apartment.

"I'm back," she called out, and armed with packages, headed into the kitchen.

Once he heard his wife's voice, Harry stopped talking. Hannah realized her father did not want to discuss Lena with Molly home. She recalled a terrible fight her parents had had years ago. While she tried to do homework in her room, she heard them shouting. Since her mother rarely raised her voice to her father, Molly's shouts stayed with her. When the door to the apartment slammed shut behind Harry, Hannah rushed out of her room. Before she had a chance to say anything, Molly yelled at her.

"I don't know why your father didn't marry that slut he was sleeping with in medical school? He should have married her and left me alone!"

Hardly a thought a mother should be sharing with her fourteen-year-old daughter, Hannah thought in retrospect. Could that be

Lena? Had to be. Hannah was relieved Harry hadn't answered her. Lena is not my business. That is between Molly and Harry.

While her mother busied herself in the kitchen, Hannah stayed in the living room with her father. She picked up a magazine from the coffee table, sat down in the easy chair opposite him and braced herself for their inevitable fight. She was unprepared when instead of flaring his nostrils as he usually did addressing her, her father smiled broadly and almost pleaded, "Hannah, come, come. Sit here next to me."

Molly's words reverberated in Hannah's brain. "Your father never acted like that before!" Noting Harry's poor physical condition, Hannah wondered, Does Dr. Stone think he's dying and finally wants to make up for all our past battles?

Confused, and with some apprehension, Hannah obliged. As she sat down, Harry reached out and gently stroked her cheek. She flinched.

"*Ja cię kocham, ja cię kocham,*" Harry said as he put his arms around her.

Hannah was stunned. Not only did he hold her tighter than she thought he'd be able to from the looks of him, but Hannah could not remember the last time her father had held her. He kept repeating, "*Ja cię kocham,*" as he gently rocked her back and forth.

"*Ja cię kocham też,*" she said in Polish without even thinking. Hannah had not spoken a word of Polish in years. They had stopped speaking Polish long ago so Harry and Molly could practice their English. Father and daughter had stopped saying "I love you" to each other a long time ago, too.

The scene in the Stone apartment that afternoon was most unusual. While Molly was serenading herself with Polish songs as she cooked in the kitchen, Harry and Hannah were in the living room, not sniping at each other as they usually did, and now even speaking in Polish. But most surprising, they were talking about a subject that had always been taboo for Hannah.

When Harry asked, "What do you remember about our life in Poland?" Hannah took a deep breath and hesitated. She usually derailed any conversation on that subject. Unlike her parents, Hannah didn't want to look back. She saw herself as the end product of her history and that was all she was willing to present to the world. Hannah Stone McCabe was someone she had willed into existence. As best as she could, she was determined to shield that self. She did not wish to deny her past, only to keep it out of view. Not many people knew that Hannah had not been born in the United States. And that's how she preferred it.

Robert had only the sketchiest idea of how she had survived the war. He never pressed her for details. Occasionally during dinner at her parents' house, when Harry brought up anything to do with the war, Robert listened with great interest and asked questions. Seeing her daughter grimace was always a signal for Molly to redirect the conversation. If she wasn't successful and Harry kept on talking, invariably Hannah would start clearing the table or just leave the room.

Even in therapy, the war years went largely unexamined. "You have to stop burying your feelings about that experience. You were a happy child. You were sent away. You had to feel abandoned. Let the rage out. Be angry! Be sad!" No matter how hard Dr. Kahn tried to make her talk about Poland, Hannah resisted. She was willing to dissect and analyze problems at work, current relationships, but refused to deal with anything having to do with the war. Hannah kept those memories stored in her subconscious marked DO NOT DISTURB. As she saw it, the protective layer that had formed over those psychic wounds allowed her to heal slowly. Now only an invisible scab remained. Hannah didn't want to risk disturbing the old wounds. Fearing they would reopen and never heal again.

While she couldn't explain her father's sudden burst of affection toward her, Hannah knew she didn't want to do anything that might jeopardize his new warmth. If Harry wanted to go down memory lane for a bit, she was willing to go along. Overriding her usual trepidations, she decided to answer his question.

"My memories are pretty spotty," Hannah lied. "Not something I like to think about," she added, truthfully. "I remember Grandma

Sonia and Grandpa Jakob. I used to play in their store, behind the bookcases," she said, and paused.

Hannah bit her lip and started to wring her hands. A weak smile appeared on her face as she pictured herself, not quite three years old, standing on the counter in her grandparents' bookstore, reciting limericks her grandmother had taught her.

"Whenever a customer came in, Grandma Sonia put me up on the counter, and watched, proudly, as I performed," she said.

Suddenly, in a childlike voice, Hannah started to recite her favorite limerick about pears, apples, and plums:

> *Wpadła gruszka do fartuszka,*
> *a za gruszką dwa jabłuszka.*
> *A śliweczka wpaść nie chciała,*
> *bo śliweczka niedojrzała.*

The image of her grandmother's beaming face broadened Hannah's smile. But soon the tears flowed, and she stopped talking. Seeing Hannah blot her cheeks with the back of her hand, Harry took out his handkerchief and gently wiped her tears. As she let her limp body lean against her father's boney frame, he kissed the top of her head, and pressed for more:

"Do you remember . . . any of your playmates?"

Hannah shook her head.

"What else do you remember?" he prodded, patting her hand.

Although Hannah would have preferred changing the subject, the pleased look on her father's face made her answer his question.

"I remember your father. He walked with a cane. It had a silver handle that was always polished. He was very tall, and had a long gray beard. He never smiled. He scared me."

"I think he scared me, too," Harry confided. "Not when I was grown up. But when I was a child," he added, smiling. "Anything else?"

She searched her mind for happy images.

"Uncle Leo's wedding. There was music and dancing."

"That's right!" His look of approval kept Hannah talking. She made herself revisit that celebration. A fleeting image of a little girl dancing flashed through her mind, and vanished.

"I think I got sick at the wedding," she said.

"No. Not you. But . . . " Harry stopped mid-sentence. For a few moments father and daughter sat in silence. Harry tenderly stroked Hannah's hair.

"Do you remember how you got your Polish name?" he asked.

"Only half and half," Hannah said cryptically. "I always assumed I was named after my big wooden doll, Zofia. I affectionately called her Zosia. When you got the false papers for me I became Zofia. But I never knew how you picked my last name, No-wa-kow-ska." She enunciated the name syllable by syllable, giving each equal weight. Now Hannah let her mind wander back in time.

* * *

The morning they sent her away, it was still dark outside when her mother put Hannah, half asleep, on the double bed in their master bedroom. The small lamp on the mahogany night table provided the only light. Hannah rubbed her eyes as her mother and Grandma Sonia began to dress her. Nearby, her father and Grandpa Jakob watched. The silky down quilt felt good against her bare bottom and she smiled. Everyone else in the room looked glum. Once she was dressed, Sonia removed the Star of David from around Hannah's neck and replaced it with a shiny gold cross. "You will be safe now," she said as she cupped the child's face in both hands, and kissed the top of her head.

Sonia was wearing her sky-blue wool sweater with a gold zipper on the breast pocket. Whenever her grandmother picked her up wearing that sweater, Hannah would playfully open and close the zipper as Sonia hummed, pretending the zipper was making music. Their duet made them both laugh. In her grandmother's arms that morning, Hannah tinkered with the zipper as usual, and Sonia hummed as usual. But this time there was no raucous laughter from Sonia. "I love you," she whispered solemnly and squeezed the child so tight Hannah had trouble breathing.

* * *

Hannah's memories rebelled, refusing to be repressed. She spoke in a flat, halting voice.

"The morning I was sent away, everyone was watching me. Nobody smiled. You told me your friends, Ela and Janek Wyszyński, were going to take me on a trip to Kielce . . . to stay with a nice Polish family they knew. I never could remember the name of those people," Hannah muttered under her breath. "You said they were going to care for me for a while. I was to be a good girl and do what I was told . . . ."

Through tear-filled eyes, Hannah looked around her parents' familiar living room, seeing only color and blur. But she no longer needed Harry's questions to keep her talking.

As her grandmother's solemn face appeared before her, Hannah's voice began to crack. "I didn't understand Grandma . . . was saying goodbye. I remember how smooth her cheek was. During the war . . . when I was alone . . . and scared I used to rub my earlobe. It reminded me of her cheek. It made me feel safe."

Sitting next to her father, her head resting on his shoulder as he gently wiped her tears with his now damp handkerchief, Hannah felt closer to him than ever before. Clearly, reliving the past brought them together in a way she could not have imagined an hour ago. What amazed her even more was that it felt natural for them to be talking about a time that had been off limits all these years, and Hannah no longer wanted to change the subject.

"Do you remember being in Kielce?" Harry asked.

"I cried a lot then, too. Expecting the perfect child you probably told them they were getting, they were unprepared to deal with me. I wouldn't eat. I talked only to their dog. And I prayed to the Black Madonna. Remember? Mother gave me a framed picture of the Madonna, who would watch over me."

Hannah let out a chuckle. "That's how the patron saint of Poland became my personal protector. Every night I begged the Madonna to take me back home."

* * *

In Kielce, the room Hannah slept in was narrow and dark. Her bed was wedged between two mahogany bookcases. With the embossed navy wallpaper and burgundy Oriental rug that covered the dark floor the room was too grown-up for a child. The small window at the far end was so high she could not look out.

A weepy Hannah spent her days curled up on a chaise on the balcony off the living room talking to their collie, Sasha. She regaled her canine friend with stories about her family, particularly her grandmother. "When I go home, I will send you a big ball to chase," she promised. "My grandmother has many toys in her store that you would like to play with." Sasha proved to be her faithful companion.

* * *

"I don't think I stayed with those people very long. I remember I finally stopped crying when Ela came to get me. I thought the Madonna had answered my prayers. I thought I was going home," Hannah said.

"There was no home for you to go back to. By then I was living in Warsaw. So was Mother," Harry said.

Hannah nodded. "Ela brought me to Warsaw. I remember we went to a hotel near the railroad station. Hotel Polonia, I think. Once she promised I was going to see Mother the next day I went to sleep happy. In the morning she told me I had slept through a bombing. I could hardly believe it."

"That's what saved your life and Ela's that night," Harry said. "She got you out of Kielce fast, before I could arrange for new false identity papers. The couple feared their maid was beginning to suspect they were harboring a Jewish child and might report them to the Gestapo. At the hotel, Ela told the policeman checking identity papers that you were very sick. Luckily he believed her. He assumed only a sick child would sleep through a bombing, and he forgot to ask for the papers you did not have. You were very, very lucky that night." Harry squeezed Hannah's hand.

With her head still resting comfortably on her father's shoulder, Hannah and Harry sat quietly for a time, enjoying their new intimacy. Without any prodding from Harry, suddenly she started talking again.

"The next evening when Mama came to the hotel, she told me we weren't going home, but we had to leave Warsaw. I didn't care where we were going as long as I was going with her. I kept hugging her and kissing her hand." Hannah paused and remembered how happy she was at that moment to be with her mother again, and how that feeling soon changed. "As we were about to leave, Mother gripped my shoulders firmly with both hands and in a stern voice said, 'From now on you must call me Aunt Marta, never Mama!' Seeing the shocked look on my face, Mother said, 'Don't worry, I'll explain later.' As she closed the hotel door, she added, 'No talking in the street!'"

Hannah blinked. "It took a long time before I felt it was safe to talk in the street. Even when we got to New York, seeing people chatting and laughing outside, I was still afraid to do the same. I don't remember when that changed."

* * *

Ela bought the tickets inside the station before the three of them boarded the night train to Skawina. They found an empty compartment and settled in. Hannah took the window seat even though it was pitch dark outside. That night the moon was obscured by clouds and because of the wartime blackouts there were no lights anywhere.

"Best thing to do now is to get some sleep," her mother told her as she folded a coat into a pillow.

Hannah was content. With her body touching her mother, she closed her eyes. When she felt her mother moving away, Hannah opened her eyes a little. She saw Ela asleep on the seat across from her, but standing at the door of their compartment was a German officer. Hannah squeezed her body further away from her mother and pretended to be asleep. She was scared.

"Guten Abend, Fraulein," the officer said to the only person who appeared to be awake.

"Guten Abend," she answered, smiling weakly.

Hannah held her breath. The mere sight of a German officer always meant danger. As he was about to enter the compartment, another soldier appeared. He saluted, whispered something and pointed to the next car. The officer clicked the heels of his shiny boots, and in German said, "We have a sleeper in the next car. Gute Nacht, Fraulein."

Mother and daughter let out a nervous giggle in response to the averted disaster, which awoke Ela. After being told what had happened while she peacefully slept, Ela made the sign of the cross and thanked God for their good fortune. Hannah snuggled next to her mother and fell asleep.

* * *

As Hannah recalled that trip to Skawina, the fear she felt that night washed over her.

"Once again you were lucky." Harry pinched her cheek.

Hannah grinned, remembering her father doing the same thing when she was a toddler.

* * *

The station was deserted when the train pulled into Skawina early in the morning. They walked to the safe house Ela had rented. No one noticed them. As they approached the uninhabited building along the railroad tracks, Hannah tightened her grip on her mother's hand. She thought the house looked haunted. It was dark and cold inside. Once her mother started a fire in the cast iron stove the place seemed less menacing. But it was nothing like home.

"Are we going to be here for long?" Hannah asked, while Ela was out getting some supplies.

"We'll stay until your father finds a safe place for you to live."

Hannah was stunned. She cried out, "Don't you want me anymore? Can't I live with you?"

"Of course I would want you to live with me," her mother assured Hannah, rocking her in her arms. "It hurts me that we can't be together!" Sadly she could not alter their circumstances. She was now Marta Wilakowa, a single woman, working as a live-in housekeeper in Warsaw for a well-to-do family with two daughters, a few years older than her own. There was no room for a child in that arrangement.

Soothed by her mother's touch, Hannah listened intently to her explanation of what had to be. Most important, for them to stay safe, no one could know that they were Jewish. Two months before she was to celebrate her fourth birthday, Hannah was forced to accept the fact that they had to become different people. Her mother had to pretend to be her aunt. The only good news was that both of them would be living in Warsaw. "So I can come see you on my day off," her mother promised. Hannah vowed to be a big girl and keep the family secret.

Before she left, Ela made sure the house was stocked with flour, sugar, potatoes, a little butter, bread, some milk, and a few eggs. Mother and daughter made the most of their reunion. They played games and hugged a lot. Meanwhile Hannah was being prepared for her new life. She learned to say Christian prayers, when to kneel and how to cross herself in church and whenever she walked past one. An apt pupil, Hannah was soon flawlessly reciting her newly-learned prayers as she kneeled at the foot of the bed.

To conserve coal they only fired up the stove during the day. At night, mother and daughter huddled in bed, fully clothed, under the goose down quilt they'd brought with them. In the morning, next to her mother Hannah awakened smiling. Until she was reminded of what was coming.

"Don't forget, once we leave here, you can never call me Mama. In Warsaw, when I leave you with Ela at the train station, please, please, please, no crying."

Hannah could suppress her tears, but she couldn't keep the tightness in her stomach from turning into cramps.

Toward the end of their stay they ran out of coal. A major crisis! They needed it to heat that drafty house in February, and to cook their food. As they watched from the windows, they saw trains loaded with coal speeding by, with chunks falling onto the tracks. When her mother announced she would risk going out under the cover of darkness to pick up some coal, Hannah pleaded to come along. "The two of us can carry more and do it faster!" she reasoned.

Each carrying a bucket, they walked unseen along the tracks. They had filled their buckets and were ready to go back when a watchman appeared out of nowhere. Hannah felt her mother's hand over her mouth as she pushed her under a standing boxcar, and rolled herself next to her. Both of them held their breath waiting for the guard to pass. Hannah bit her lip so hard she drew blood.

After they'd lugged their bounty safely into the house, they celebrated their successful quest, eating a special omelet made from the two eggs they had left. On their last night in Skawina, Hannah tried to stay awake as long as she could, cherishing the closeness with her mother.

The next morning when Ela arrived with identity papers for Hannah, she was reborn as Zofia Nowakowska. At the train station in Warsaw, Hannah, now officially Zosia, watched her mother disappear into the crowd. She did not cry.

Later that day when Ela brought her to live with Aunt Emma, it was Zofia Nowakowska, not Hannah Stein, who curtsied as she was introduced to her new caretaker.

"I'm glad you are a proper Polish girl," were Emma's welcoming words. No hugs followed. Whenever she missed her mother, she thought about their time in Skawina playing silly games under the quilt. In Aunt Emma's apartment she often got under the covers and pretended her mother was there with her. If Emma admonished her for being too raucous, she played in silence. But she never felt like a child again.

* * *

"You had to grow up so fast," Harry said, almost to himself.

Hannah shrugged. "It's not like I had much choice! I think we stayed in Skawina for two weeks. We never ventured out in the daylight. Ela had warned mother that it would be too dangerous."

"Amazing, you remember so much! Not many people remember things as well as you do from such an early age," Harry said.

"Thank God they don't have to," Hannah said, alluding to the punch line of a famous Jewish joke. She wanted to lighten the mood, to return to the present.

But as she looked around the well-appointed living room, a picture in a silver frame on the Steinway baby grand took her back to another time. The strange lighting in the photograph made the little girl with round cheeks and huge saucer-size eyes, dressed in silk pajamas, look unreal.

"That day you took me to the photographer's studio to have this picture taken . . ."

"My God, you remember that? You weren't even two years old!" Harry shook his head.

"After the photographer finished shooting, you told me this was to be our secret. Not to tell anyone."

"It was to be a surprise for your mother," Harry explained.

"I didn't tell anyone. I liked that we had a secret, just the two of us." Hannah thought about how close she had felt to her father. She searched her memory, trying to pinpoint when things between them changed.

That evening, instead of eating in the kitchen as they usually did, Molly set the table in the dining room. It felt like a special occasion even though she did not use her "good dishes"—the white porcelain china with cobalt blue and gold trim that now stood in for the treasured Rosenthal set that had been a wedding present from Molly's parents. Actually, Hannah thought the made-in-Japan American version was a poor substitute, but she was glad her mother hadn't opted for a set of the real thing. Buying anything German was verboten as far as she was concerned. Besides, recreating the past was not part of Hannah's agenda. She preferred the white Russel Wright Iroquois china she picked out the day she signed a lease on her first apartment.

Whenever she recalled her exchange with the salesclerk at Bloomingdale's, Hannah chuckled to herself.

"So when's the wedding day?" the woman asked once Hannah had made her choice.

"There's no wedding date! I don't need a husband to have dishes I like to eat on," Hannah shot back defiantly.

Not sure how to respond at first, the woman finally said: "Good for you!"

Hannah took a bow. She was tempted to confess she'd already treated herself to a set of George Jensen flatware but decided not to.

At dinner everyone was on good behavior. Hannah wondered how long it could last. They started talking politics. Harry confessed that in spite of himself, after reading the excerpt of *Final Days* in the recent issue of *Newsweek*, he really felt sorry for Richard Nixon.

"He's a broken man," Harry said. "He made a mistake. He made a big mistake."

"I felt sorry for Nixon when he rambled on about his mother in his farewell speech to his White House staff," Hannah said. "But I'm not ready to forgive and forget. The Watergate break-in was bad enough, and then the cover-up, and the slush fund and the enemies list? Because of him, and Watergate, people now don't trust the government."

"I'm sure he would give anything for a chance to do the last five years over. He wouldn't make the same mistake this time," Harry said.

"On big things you don't get a second chance! You think he deserves one?" Bracing for a fight, Hannah challenged her father with a wide-eyed stare.

"Everybody deserves a second chance," Harry whispered, more hopeful than sure. "He's a broken man. He lost everything. You have to feel sorry for that."

"He did it to himself."

"I know."

No sparks flew. Maybe we're finally old enough to give up our private war, Hannah thought to herself. While father and daughter agreed to disagree without a fight, Molly remained on the sidelines, happy she didn't have to referee.

When the conversation eventually got around to Harry's failing health, Dr. Stone tried to minimize the seriousness of his situation.

"The pills just aren't working. I probably need new medication, that's all," he said without conviction. "Hannah, you'll have to find a doctor for me. The doctors I know have either closed their practice or moved to warmer climates. Maybe one of those young geniuses you've been trying to get me to see knows of a new wonder drug that will do the trick," he said, and started whistling. Harry often whistled when he was nervous.

"Don't you worry," Molly chimed in. "Hannah will find the right doctor and you'll be better than new." For Molly, denial came naturally. It was a trait that normally infuriated Hannah, but at that moment it seemed comforting.

"I'll get on it first thing Monday morning," Hannah promised.

As those words were out of her mouth, the knot in her stomach hardened. What if he is so sick that no doctor could help him?

Finding a good doctor and getting Harry an appointment was only step one. It was her job to keep Harry alive. She had to find the right doctor. During the war Hannah knew that any misstep on her part could result in death. Logically she no longer believed that. Still she could not rid herself of an almost pathological fear of making a mistake. No Mistakes Allowed continued to be her guiding principle. No mistakes allowed! No mistakes allowed! Hannah repeated in her head. She took a deep breath and wished Robert were there.

CHAPTER

2

BY THE TIME HANNAH and Molly finished their coffee and some of Molly's homemade strudel, Harry was again asleep on the living room sofa, and Hannah was longing to be back in her own apartment. She offered to help Molly clean up, though she knew her mother would insist on doing everything herself. As Hannah reached for her tote and jacket, Molly tried to convince her to spend the night.

"I can't, Mom. I have work to do at home," Hannah lied. She needed a break. This was more of her family than Hannah was used to. "I'll come by tomorrow around noontime. We can relax and read the Sunday papers. Or, if Dad feels well enough, we can go to the movies."

"Okay. Do what you have to do," Molly said, hugging her daughter goodnight. "Give our best to Robert," she added as she closed the door. Molly assumed Robert was away, working out of town. Which was true. Hannah smiled but said nothing. She had decided to put off telling her parents about her situation with Robert for as long as possible. As she pushed the button for the elevator, Hannah let out a laugh at her own expense. She was guilty of the same thing she so often accused her mother of doing. By not acknowledging the rift between herself and Robert to her parents, for the time being at least, it ceased to exist.

Hannah inhaled the warm spring evening air as she walked through the cobblestone courtyard of her parents' complex. Almost in a daze, she turned right on to West 86th Street. She happily joined the parade of people along Broadway, some strolling, others going in and out of restaurants. She didn't know how to explain her father's sudden display of warmth toward her. It was what she'd longed for and never thought would happen. He does love me, after all, she thought.

As she watched the faces passing by, she glimpsed her own reflection in a store window and hardly recognized herself. Hannah looked as if she didn't have a care in the world. Hardly a natural look for her. Her spirits were high. Monday morning I'll start my search for the doctor for Harry. It shouldn't take long to find the right one. Her new optimism seemed to tamp down her fear of making a mistake. But by the time she reached Lincoln Center, Hannah sensed some anxiety seeping in.

She hailed a cab to avoid the crowds rushing out of the theaters. Within twenty minutes she was opening the door to her two-bedroom apartment, a block from Washington Square Park.

Great to be home! she thought, and kicked off her shoes, even before turning on the light. Hannah missed Robert, but she was glad to be back in her own space even without him. Seeing the Amish quilt draped on one wall of the entryway always brought back fond memories of their first weekend away as a couple. They had stopped at a Pennsylvania county fair to eat. Walking around munching on her grilled knockwurst and sauerkraut hero, Hannah was drawn to an auction in progress. They wandered over without any intention of bidding, but when the auctioneer held up a mustard and navy quilt, they looked at each other and nodded. Hannah raised her hand to make an opening bid. Before she realized what was happening, four, then five bids quickly followed, and the auctioneer was saying, "Going once, going twice . . ." As the quilt was about to become the property of the man standing next to Hannah, Robert jumped in with a final bid, and the quilt was theirs.

"That cost so much," she said.

Robert patted her hand. "It was worth it."

This apartment became an amalgam of their life together, and the first place where Hannah lived that didn't feel temporary. Robert was an architect who did not need to be surrounded by stark white walls, tempered glass, and cold chrome. His huge nautical maps on one wall of the sea-foam green living room complemented Hannah's collection of primitive boat paintings above the tufted leather tuxedo sofa that faced the fireplace. Random books and copies of old magazines stacked haphazardly around the apartment added to the lived-in decor. Ayn Rand's Howard Roark would not approve.

"I'm lucky you're an architect who doesn't mind clutter," Hannah often teased Robert. Their second bedroom had a day bed for guests, but Hannah had appropriated most of the space as her home office. The floor-to-ceiling bookcases were packed with books, but also crammed with framed photographs and random treasures. An avid collector, Hannah was clearly on a path to becoming a hoarder. She still had the first check she had ever written, probably squirreled away in one of the boxes destined for the basement storage unit. They had been on the waiting list for a year. For now, Hannah carefully navigated around the warren of boxes to reach her desk.

Hannah could see the red light flickering on her answering machine and pushed the button to retrieve her messages.

"I certainly won't miss these international junkets. Been at it all day. I'm going to hit the sack as soon as I get out of these clothes. Be back on Monday and going straight to Amagansett. Call you when I get in. Miss you." Robert sounded tired but cheerful.

"I miss you, too," Hannah said to her machine, happy to hear his voice. But her smile faded as she thought back to that painful April day, still fresh in her mind, when her marriage appeared to be unraveling.

Hannah had rushed home that day to sign their joint income tax return. As she walked into the darkened apartment, Robert was sitting at the dining room table.

"Why are you sitting in the dark?" she asked, as she took off her jacket. He did not answer. Hannah flipped on the light and went over to hug him. Surprised when he recoiled from her touch, she sat down opposite him.

"How was your day?" Hannah assumed his somber mood was work-related.

"Busy," he said, and shuffled the papers in front of him.

Hannah studied his face. "Something wrong?" she finally asked.

"I'll say there is! When was the last time you did something around the house?" he shouted. Robert's voice sounded unfamiliar.

Shocked by his tone and by his words, Hannah wasn't sure how to respond.

"You like to cook and I like to eat. I'd say that's a perfect arrangement. Don't you agree?" she asked.

Robert just glared. "It's not about the cooking!" he shot back.

"What is it? You do some things. I do others. We have a marriage of equals."

Robert drew a circle in the air with his two index fingers. "We have a marriage of equals, all right. It equals zero! Hannah, face it, we barely see each other. Once your parents get back, all we'll have time for is saying goodnight." Although he softened his tone, Robert avoided making eye contact.

"Your job is just as demanding as mine," Hannah argued. She ignored his reference to Harry and Molly.

"Well I'm willing to do something about that. What about you?"

"Do something about what? I'm not out partying. I'm working. It's a weekly. With the Presidential election, and the Convention here in July, a lot is going on. But things will slow down soon. I promise."

Her promise did not mollify Robert. Instead his body tensed up. With his arms folded across his chest, he rocked back and forth in the chair. He seemed ready to explode. Robert mentally counted to ten, then asked, "You really like things the way they are?"

"Most of the time. If it's not broken, don't fix it," she said, hoping to make him smile. But Robert's lips stayed rigid.

"Well, I don't! I don't like the way things are between us. Maybe the charm of living in New York has worn off. I've put in my time building corporate complexes. I think I'd like to try something smaller. Even do some sculpting again."

Hannah felt her body stiffen. She thought they had the marriage they both wanted. They each had demanding careers, but Hannah thought they were happy.

"You want to leave New York?"

"Maybe."

"I don't want to be a suburban housewife. Besides, you tried that life with Margo, and you were miserable."

"That was different. Hannah, I just want more time for us. You can write anywhere. We can live at the cottage in Amagansett. You can work on a book."

"I don't write books. I'm a reporter. I interview people. I write articles," Hannah said. Suddenly Robert was changing the rules, making her feel she had somehow reneged on their marriage vows.

"You want me to be someone I'm not," she said. He doesn't love me any more, she thought.

"No! I want to spend more time with the person you are. Maybe if we had less pressure from work, you'd get pregnant. I'd like us to have a baby before Christy makes me a grandfather."

"I'm sorry I can't get pregnant," Hannah whispered, almost to herself.

"You're just like your father," Robert blurted out. "Everything has to be your way. You say you want to have a baby, but you won't even consider fertility treatments."

For Hannah, being compared to her father was bad enough, but bringing up her infertility assured Robert a knockout. As soon as he said it, he wished he could take his words back. He knew how vulnerable Hannah felt on both counts. But fueled by his frustration, he made the attack.

Hannah took Robert's verbal assault in silence. For a time she sat frozen. Finally, almost inaudibly, she said: "I stopped taking the pill once we decided to get pregnant."

When Robert first brought up starting a family a month after they celebrated their first wedding anniversary, she didn't feel ready to stop work and concentrate on being a mother. Hannah was not thinking about her biological clock.

"It's too soon," she argued. "You're still trying to improve your relationship with Christy. How is she going to deal with a baby brother or sister?"

"I guess you're right. It's too soon," Robert agreed.

Hannah convinced herself, and him, that they had plenty of time to start a family. Robert and Margo had gotten married because she was three months pregnant. Only twenty-four when Christy was born, he wasn't ready to be a husband, much less a father. Now he wanted another chance to prove to himself that he could be a good dad. Hannah was sure he would be. Secretly she worried about what kind of mother she'd make.

She'd never played house, except the summer she visited her aunt and uncle in Asheville. They introduced her to their teenage next-door neighbor. Unlike Hannah, Mary Ellen had lots of dolls and the two girls spent many hours playing house. In their pretend family, Hannah chose to be the husband who went to work while Mary Ellen stayed home and mothered their doll-children. Adult Hannah was haunted by that memory, fearing it meant she did not want to be a woman.

In therapy it became clear that what Hannah did not want was a life like her mother's. Long before therapy, she chose a role model for herself that was not Molly.

When the round Zenith television appeared in the Stones' Bronx living room in 1950, *The Roy Rogers Show* quickly became her favorite. She pictured herself as Dale Evans, telling the ranch foreman how she wanted things done, and helping chase away rustlers, if they dared to show up. Once she decided she had no interest in riding a horse, Brenda Starr, Girl Reporter, became a more appropriate role model.

After her miscarriage on January 11, 1975, a distraught Hannah was stunned to hear Dr. de Falco say, "At your age it's not unusual to have a miscarriage!"

"I'm thirty-six," she said. Hannah didn't feel old. Why was her body behaving this way?

"After thirty-five your body makes certain adjustments. Don't worry. It doesn't mean you won't be able to have a baby. We'll pinpoint the problem, and then we'll fix it." To reassure her, Dr. de Falco said, "There are drugs available."

Hannah began to hyperventilate. "I'm not taking any drugs!" she yelled at her doctor. "I interviewed the DES daughters and their mothers! When those pregnant women took the Thalidomide pills, their doctors never told them their daughters could be born without limbs and later on develop uterine cancer!"

"You need to calm down, Hannah," Dr. de Falco said. "We have no idea what may need adjusting in your case. We'll do some tests and look at the options."

But her mind was closed. The fear of unintended consequences of any medical treatment paralyzed Hannah. Her guiding principle trumped all logic. No Mistakes Allowed!

Hannah didn't need Robert's accusation to stoke her guilt. Since her miscarriage she viewed her desire to put off trying to get pregnant a BIG MISTAKE. Now she felt doubly guilty because she hadn't realized how unhappy Robert was. Hannah did not present a defense. Instead, she left him sitting at the dining table and locked herself in the second bathroom. She stayed there until she was certain he had gone to sleep.

In bed that night, both made sure their bodies never touched. The next morning, Hannah got up as usual and had the coffee on by the time Robert finished dressing. Her bagel had just popped up in the toaster when Robert came into their tiny kitchen.

"Good morning," Hannah said.

"Morning," Robert answered, pouring himself a cup of coffee.

Neither of them knew how to deal with what had happened the night before.

Without making eye contact, they ate their breakfast at the dining table, but sat a safe distance from each other, rustling the pages of the morning *Times*.

Robert turned on the radio to fill the silence. The frost between them only melted sufficiently to facilitate an exchange of sections of the morning paper, but they did not touch.

Over the next few days, Hannah and Robert gradually began talking, but not about their blowup. Friday morning, when he suggested they go out to dinner that evening, Hannah agreed even though Friday was usually a late night at the magazine.

On the way to Pete's Tavern on Irving Place, Hannah watched a group of mothers pushing strollers in Gramercy Park, and worried about the state of her marriage. She told herself the fact that Robert had picked the restaurant where he had proposed was a positive sign. Or had he picked a public place to announce he was leaving, she wondered, knowing she would not make a scene in a restaurant.

Hannah decided to go with the optimistic version. Pete's Tavern claimed to be the oldest continually operating restaurant in New York, and it was rumored that O. Henry, who had lived nearby at 55 Irving Place, penned "The Gift of the Magi" in its front booth. Until Robert's outburst, Hannah had thought they were as perfectly matched as the fictional Jim and Della Dillingham of O. Henry's story.

When she walked through the door, Hannah saw Robert sitting at their regular table, tapping his fingers. She checked her watch.

"Hi. You did say 6:30? Am I late?" Hannah asked, hoping she wasn't.

"You're on time," he reassured her, and jumped up to hold her chair.

Both of them were nervous. They sat in silence, studying the familiar menu, until the waiter brought the bottle of wine Robert had ordered. With their glasses filled, he raised his to make a toast.

"I've taken a three-month leave," Robert announced. "Let's drink to that!"

Hannah was shocked by his unilateral decision. Her face sagged. She lifted her glass to her lips, but couldn't bring herself to take a sip. When she started to speak, Robert said, "Please, let me finish before you say anything."

Hannah tried to contain her panic as he raced through his speech.

"Evan turned two jobs over to me that were too small for the firm. I met with one couple yesterday. I'm going to build their vacation dream house. Their land is in Amagansett, not far from the cottage. Isn't that perfect? The other client, a painter, has an old farmhouse in the Springs and he needs a studio. I plan to move out to the cottage, while I work on these two projects, and sort things out."

Hannah flinched. Oh my God, he's going to leave me!

"I know I said some hurtful things the other day," Robert continued. "I still believe we have things to work out. But I realize that my dissatisfaction has more to do with my work. In my mind, it got all mixed up with us. Hannah, I need a break. I want to make some changes. Maybe after three months I'll end up missing the city and the big commissions. Or maybe I'll find my niche as a small-time architect. I just want to see how it goes." Having had his say, Robert leaned back in his chair and relaxed.

But the knot in Hannah's stomach hardened. Her palms began to sweat.

"Where does that leave us?" She was afraid to hear his answer.

"You like the beach. You'll come out as often as you can. It'll be like we're dating again. That should bring romance back into our life." He smiled sheepishly.

Hannah opened her mouth to speak, but before she could say anything, Robert continued.

"I don't want to live the way we've been living. I want more than what we have now." Tentatively he reached for her hand. When she didn't pull back, he leaned over to kiss her. Hannah closed her eyes hard to stop her tears, and put her arms around Robert's neck.

"That's okay for the summer. But if you're still living at the cottage in the cold of winter, you'll have to make the trips into New York," Hannah said, hoping to get a laugh.

No laugh from Robert. Instead he said, "Being apart for a while will give both of us a chance to focus on what we want, what kind of life will make us happy."

"Except for our damn schedules, I was happy the way we were," Hannah answered. She couldn't shake the feeling that he was inching toward abandoning her. "Do you see this as a trial separation?"

"No. I see it as an exploration. For both of us."

She sighed. "Well, I guess this is not the worst present you could have given me for my birthday."

"Oh no! What a jerk!" Robert closed his eyes and gave himself a slap on the head. He reached over and squeezed Hannah's clammy hand. "Happy Birthday! I'm so sorry!" he said, and raised his wine glass to toast the occasion.

Hannah forced a smile, and took a sip of wine. At least you didn't flat-out leave me, she thought. But the feeling of uneasiness stayed with her.

What had happened with her father this weekend made Hannah feel hopeful. If Harry and I can be close, anything is possible, she reasoned. Smiling, Hannah pressed the button on her answering machine. Two hang-ups followed, and then Christy's voice blared: "I need some help. I need an editor. You! I have a book report due and a creative-writing assignment. Only you can help me on this one. Pleeezz!"

Hannah decided it was too late to call Christy back. I'll get to her tomorrow, she thought. She hoped Margo would not be the one answering the phone. Robert's ex-wife was positively the last person on the planet she wanted to talk to about the state of her marriage. Margo knew Christy had been spending weekends in Amagansett.

Sorry she'd missed his call, Hannah thought about calling Robert back and reached into her cavernous tote bag for her appointment book.

As she pulled out the well-worn, navy blue faux leather organizer, Hannah saw it as further proof that a bad situation could be reversed. It was a Mother's Day gift from Christy, who had decided Hannah needed a better way to keep track of things than on random scraps of paper at the bottom of her handbag.

Christy was just four years old when Robert and Hannah began dating. Uncomfortable around the child at first, Hannah willingly went on outings to the zoo, museums or lunch at Serendipity when Robert had Christy. But Margo's venom kept poisoning their relationship.

"I don't want that whore anywhere near my child," she'd yell in front of Christy. Although she was too young to understand the meaning of the words, her mother's attitude toward Hannah made the child feel she could ignore anything Hannah said. For a brief time Margo's outbursts put the brakes on Robert and Hannah's dating.

He's not divorced, his kid's a problem. Why do I need this? Hannah thought. For four months, they only talked on the phone and Hannah started seeing other people. But it was too late for her. She realized that she was in love.

Once they got married, Margo's tactics changed. She no longer attacked Hannah personally. Instead, she berated Robert. Margo complained about everything, especially money and religion. Every conversation included a complaint: "Christy and I can't live on the money you give us!" and "I expect you to take Christy to church on Sunday, not to Serendipity."

Hannah watched as Robert held the phone two feet away from his ear, closed his eyes and took the verbal battering.

"How can you not scream back at her?" Hannah asked.

"It wouldn't do any good," he said philosophically. "Besides, I can take it. Let her yell at me and get her anger out. I just don't want her to turn Christy against me."

Hannah did her best to woo Christy. On his weekends, Robert would pick her up early Saturday morning and bring her to the apartment. Hannah always had breakfast ready.

"I'm not hungry," was Christy's usual response.

"You don't have to eat, but your father and I haven't had breakfast yet, so we'll eat."

Invariably, Christy relented and gobbled whatever was available. But everything with Christy started with "No!"

"Is there anything special you'd like to do today?"

"No!"

"Want to go to the park?"

"No!"

"What about riding your bike?"

"No. Mom said it's too dangerous in Manhattan."

"How about going to the bookstore? We'll get something you'd like to read."

"No. Mom said I can only read the books she buys for me."

Their visits became so difficult, Robert looked forward to the weekends when Margo announced Christy was too busy to see him. But with relief came guilt. "I'm a lousy father. I think I'm losing Christy," Robert confided to Hannah.

The first change came when Margo met a man she liked better than tormenting Robert. She turned into a different person, and so did Christy. The boyfriend had a share in a house on Fire Island. That summer Robert and Hannah got to see a lot of Christy.

With Robert's hotel phone number in her hand, Hannah hesitated. But whenever anything special happened to her, he was the person she wanted to tell, and Harry's apparent change of heart toward her was a monumental special event in Hannah's life. For years Robert had listened to her complain about Harry. Now she had something good to tell him. She gave herself permission to make the call. Getting through to Tokyo was not as easy as calling across town. She almost gave up when a sleepy Robert answered the phone.

"'Lo, who is this?" he asked.

"Hannah. Sorry I missed your call."

"Uh huh."

"I just needed to talk to you. Something strange and wonderful has happened."

"Uh huh."

44

"Harry and I . . . we stopped fighting. At least today . . . It was so different. He actually hugged me. Isn't that something? After all these years."

"That's nice."

Once she realized she was talking to someone who was basically asleep, Hannah felt foolish.

"Sorry I disturbed you. Go back to sleep. We'll talk when you get home."

"That's nice . . ." were the last words Hannah heard before she hung up.

She admonished herself. He said he was tired and going to sleep, but Hannah Stone couldn't be put off. Robert's accusation: "You're just like your father!" echoed in her head. Hannah remembered how she had bristled at the comparison.

"You may be right. Maybe I am just like Harry!" Hannah caught her reflection in the mirror. "I'm a crazy person, talking to herself. But that's really your fault, my dear husband, because you are not here with me."

What a day! Hannah thought, heading to her bedroom. But was it a sea change? Hannah was at a loss to explain her own behavior or Harry's. She was as shocked by her willingness to let out those repressed memories, as she was by Harry's changed attitude.

Sometimes, triggered by outside events, memories resurfaced unexpectedly. She remembered the time Robert came home and found her huddled on the sofa, her arms hugging her knees, crying hysterically, staring at the TV.

David Brinkley was reporting the evening news from Vietnam. His mouth was moving but no words reached the McCabe living room. With the sound muted, the images flickering on the TV of casualties lying along the road, while U.S. soldiers rounded up Viet Cong prisoners, marching them away from the camera, seemed to be part of a silent movie, rather than the evening newscast.

"My God, what happened?" Robert asked, worried she'd been in an accident.

"No . . . thing . . . happ . . . end . . ." Hannah rocked back and forth, her chest heaving between breaths. She blotted her wet cheeks with a soggy tissue but the tears continued to flow as she sat hypnotized by the sight of what had been a battlefield hours before.

"What's the matter?" Robert insisted. He sat down next to her and began to massage her neck.

Hannah did not answer, but her body relaxed a little. Still she continued staring at the television.

"Hannah, talk to me," he pleaded.

"I smell them . . . those dead bodies lying along the road," she finally said, her voice almost inaudible. "That smell of decaying flesh. I can still smell it. It won't go away," Hannah said.

Robert did not ask for an explanation. He shut off the TV and held her in his arms. Hannah tried to sink into his chest. Her tears soaked Robert's shirt. She couldn't block out the images, nor the smell, until she fell asleep in his arms.

As she stripped and headed for the shower, Hannah made a mental list of things to do on Sunday: (1) Call Christy back, (2) Do laundry, (3) Revisit M & H. Of the three items on her list, Hannah knew only doing the laundry would be stress-free. Actually it was a chore Hannah enjoyed. She took pride in her skills as a laundress who made difficult stains disappear.

After her hot shower Hannah was still wired. To decompress, she turned on the TV and curled up in bed with a pile of magazines. As pleased as she was by her father's new expression of affection, after a day of reminiscing with Harry, Hannah needed to reconnect with the present, to counter the gravitational pull of the past.

That night when she finally reached REM sleep, Hannah found herself in the middle of a dream that had haunted her nights for nearly twenty-five years. It had receded into history the year after she and Robert were married. Until now.

The dream began on a warm, sunny day, as three-year-old Hannah played by herself in a courtyard. Off in the distance she watched a little girl dancing around a huge musical top that was spinning magically. As Hannah approached the curly-haired blonde, she gestured for her to join in. Soon holding hands, the two danced faster and faster around the top, laughing with pleasure. Suddenly it got very dark and cold. The little blonde girl vanished. Hannah was left alone yelling, "No! No!"

The cries of, "No! No!" awakened Hannah from her deep sleep. Dazed, she looked around the room and instinctively reached across the bed for Robert. His absence woke her up fully. Hannah sat up and clutched Robert's pillow.

The dream's sudden reappearance unnerved Hannah. Not again, she thought and shook her head, hoping to flush the dreaded dream from her subconscious forever. Hannah had spent many sessions with Dr. Kahn attempting to decipher the meaning of the dream.

One of Dr. Kahn's explanations was: "It's about separation anxiety, very common. You're afraid if you care about someone, that person will leave you."

Remembering how anxious she was when Robert first told her he was moving to Amagansett, Hannah accepted that interpretation for the dream's return.

In bright green neon the clock on the night table said it was 3:30. Hannah turned up the TV volume and hoped the hum of the infomercial about beauty creams would lull her back to sleep. To drown out her troubling dream, years ago she had gotten into the habit of falling asleep with the TV on. It was Robert who always turned it off.

Sunday morning Hannah woke up relieved that the dream had not made an encore appearance. She glanced at the clock. It beamed 8 a.m.

"I'll start on the laundry early," she said cheerfully.

Christy called just as Hannah was finishing her second cup of coffee. The day was shaping up well. Hannah was grateful she had avoided an interrogation by Margo.

"Have you heard from your dad?" Hannah asked.

"Yeah, yesterday. He was beat. Said he's glad he's coming home. He'll be back tomorrow. Speaking of tomorrow, can I come by your office in the afternoon so you can read through my stuff?" Christy pleaded.

"Tomorrow's not so good. How about this morning?"

"I can't. I have a date with Eric and Kay to hang out. Couldn't I just come by for a teeny bit tomorrow? My report isn't very long. It's the creative writing thing. I really need your professional opinion."

"You know I can't give you much time in the office. What's it about?" Hannah said, reluctant to give in to Christy too quickly.

"It's hard to explain. You have to read it. It won't take long. I promise," Christy said laughing at herself. They both knew she was a con artist. "I'll come by after three and be gone before four!"

"Don't be late." This time, Hannah didn't really mind Christy's manipulation. She actually missed her stepdaughter, even with her frequent crises.

With Christy's call out of the way and the laundry in the works, Hannah congratulated herself. "I'll easily make it uptown by lunchtime, as promised."

3

"PROMISE ME, IF WE don't like living in America, we will leave and go to Palestine," eight-year-old Hannah begged.

"Yes, yes, I promise," her father said just to stop Hannah's constant badgering. "If we don't like living with your uncles in New York, we can go to Palestine." But he was certain it would never come to that.

At the time, they were still Hershel, Malka, and Hannah Stein, living in Zeilsheim, a displaced person's camp, outside of Frankfurt, Germany. The U.S. Army had appropriated the German village to make room for the thousands of Jewish refugees who were flowing into the American sector. The refugee families were billeted in houses set up like barracks on an army base.

Dr. Hershel Stein was recruited to be a medic in the camp clinic, and life took on a welcome normalcy for the family. Each morning Dr. Stein put on his Army-issue Eisenhower jacket under his white lab coat, took the briefcase packed with his medical paraphernalia, and went to work, happy. Malka kept their living quarters gleaming, and busied herself making clothes for Hannah from parachute material she'd gotten from one of the American soldiers on the base. At school Hannah slowly began to interact with other refugee children. The high point of her day was hearing the teachers tell stories about life on a kibbutz in Palestine, and the promise of Israel. Unlike her parents, who longed to resettle in the United States, she was convinced that living on a kibbutz in Palestine was where they all belonged. Tasked with studying Hebrew and English, Hannah eagerly applied herself to tackling Hebrew, but she refused to learn English.

There was great camaraderie among the survivors in the DP camps. Evenings her parents socialized with fellow refugees and shared delicacies like canned peaches and chocolate bars that Harry brought back from the PX. While the grown-ups talked, Hannah sat in the corner doing homework, always keeping one ear glued to the adult conversations. But having heard stories from camp survivors, she'd flee the moment anyone mentioned Auschwitz, Dachau, or any other concentration camp. When Hannah encountered a person branded with a number, she instinctively covered her wrist. Not having a number tattooed on her forearm was a reminder of how lucky she was. She felt guilty for having no visible scar. What she had experienced during the war was nothing compared to the suffering of those who had a tattoo.

Most of the talk Hannah overheard seemed to concern overcoming immigration obstacles.

"You were lucky the Red Cross got you in touch with your brothers."

"How can we find a sponsor if we don't have family in America?"

"I have no documents, no birth certificate, no marriage license. How do I prove who I am?"

But what the refugees feared most were medical exams. According to rumors flying around the camp, even if they were lucky enough to find a sponsor, and managed to secure proper documents, a medical condition like TB could automatically make anyone ineligible for immigrating to the U.S.

After listening to several such sessions, Hannah interjected herself into the adult conversation. "Why do you only talk about going to America?" she asked. "Maybe it's so hard to go there because they just don't want us! What about Palestine? We could start our own kibbutz!" Hannah insisted.

"Aren't you the little Zionist?" David Kruger said as he affectionately pinched her cheek.

Nothing she said could alter his preference for emigrating to the U.S. Her proselytizing fell on deaf ears.

"Family, that is what is important," her father told a dejected Hannah. "Don't you ever forget that!"

Being reunited with his brothers was key, but Hershel Stein also looked forward to his life as a doctor in New York. He knew it would take some time to establish a practice in a new country, but he imagined life in America would be the way it was in Poland before the war, only better. They would be safe, in a country where everything was possible. Going to another war zone like Palestine was out of the question. Hannah never considered how war-weary her parents were.

Her father was sure of their future as they walked up the gangplank of the SS Marine Flasher, a former troop transport, on May 11, 1946, to set sail for New York from the Port of Bremen. While Hannah was sure they were going to America on a trial basis only.

The sky was clear and the ocean not too choppy for most of their nine-day passage. Ideal weather for crossing the Atlantic. The mood on board the ship was festive. Having survived the war, the nearly seven hundred expatriates from Poland, Germany, Latvia, the Soviet Union, Hungary, Yugoslavia, Czechoslovakia, and Rumania, breathed a communal sigh of relief now that they were headed to a country where the streets were paved with gold. During the day, almost everyone stayed on the promenade deck. People sang, sunbathed, and played cards. Mother and daughter played bridge. Hannah taught herself solitaire.

Women and children were billeted on the upper decks. Men, housed below, slept on hammock-like berths, stacked one on top of the other— their quarters, hot and airless, the equivalent of steerage.

Many passengers fought seasickness. Those who were able took their meals in the cafeteria-style mess hall. Eating in shifts, they waited in line for food, which they then carried on metal trays to long metal tables arranged in rows. The decor of the mess hall was battleship gray.

Hannah only felt queasy at mealtime. A finicky eater, she was reluctant to try the foods offered. She insisted Wonder Bread tasted like cotton. The sight of powdered eggs, scrambled and covered with ketchup for breakfast, and chipped beef for lunch made her feign seasickness. But

Hannah loved desserts. Actually, she would have been content with a steady diet of chocolate pudding and chocolate bars.

By the time her mother woke Hannah up on May 20, 1946, the ship had already docked in New York Harbor.

"Hurry up and get dressed! Your father is waiting for us on the deck," she told Hannah.

Her mother's anxious tone of voice made Hannah uneasy. She dressed quickly, closed her small suitcase, and grabbed her mother's skirt as she followed her topside. On deck, seeing the welcoming throng on shore, Hannah held on tight. She remembered her panic when she had playfully spun around and lost sight of her mother in the crowded Warsaw Central Station, where they had been squatting for days along with hundreds of women and children, waiting to be transported in sealed boxcars to the countryside after the Germans had leveled Warsaw. She thought she had lost her mother forever then. Now, in this foreign country Hannah feared being separated even more. But she needn't have worried. Just like baggage, each refugee had an identification tag around the neck and was destined to be turned over to a waiting sponsor.

Clutching her mother's skirt, Hannah stood at the railing, her eyes and mouth open wide. She was stunned by the sight of the New York skyline. It seemed as if they had landed on another planet. Everything was larger than she had imagined, and more frightening.

Hannah watched her father scan the crowd on shore looking for familiar faces he had only seen in photographs. His two brothers, Joseph and Jake, who were coming to greet them, had left Poland before little Hershel was born.

Having arrived in the Promised Land, the refugees on board were eager to disembark. Walking as fast as the crowd would allow, Hannah followed her father and mother toward the gangplank. Once off the ship, the line of refugees moved at lava speed through several immigration checkpoints. When they were cleared, Hershel, Malka, and Hannah Stein had morphed into Harry, Molly, and Hannah Stone.

Waiting in the crowd, Harry thought he recognized his oldest brother, Joseph. Standing next to him, someone was waving a placard with STONE spelled out in huge block letters.

"Follow me. I see them!" Harry signaled. With a battered suitcase under each arm, he rushed toward them. Molly and Hannah trailed behind, dragging their own bags.

"Joseph! Jake! We're here!" Harry yelled in Yiddish.

Only Joseph, his son Michael, and Jake were there to collect the refugees. Sam, brother number three, a manager of a pajama factory in North Carolina, hadn't come up North because it was the middle of his busy season. Harry was disappointed. Sam was the one brother he actually knew.

As she and her mother stood off to the side, Hannah watched her father. She was surprised to see tears well up in his eyes as he embraced his brothers.

Hannah coolly scanned Uncle Joseph from his shoes up. When she finally reached his unsmiling face, Hannah was amazed at how much her uncle resembled his father, minus the long beard. Joseph was just as tall and seemed just as stern as the grandfather she had always feared. Uncle Jake, who had no children, seemed more welcoming. He picked Hannah up and swung her around till she felt giddy.

All around her on the dock, Hannah heard snippets of conversation she did not understand. People were speaking English faster than any language she was used to hearing. She was amused, watching their mouths move rapidly. When her cousin Michael spoke to his father in English and she could not figure out what was being said, Hannah stopped being amused. She realized she had made a mistake refusing to learn English in Zeilsheim. Hannah resolved to remedy that as quickly as possible. For now she was forced to speak German to her relatives, and they, Yiddish to her. The Stone family in New York did not speak Polish.

Joseph hustled them into a Checker cab for the trip to the North Bronx where he and his family lived. Sitting on one of the folding seats, Hannah trembled anxiously when she looked through the sunroof and saw a train speeding by on the elevated train tracks. She prayed to the Black Madonna to keep the train from crushing them. As soon as she saw the open sky, Hannah breathed easier. Everything seemed to be bigger and faster than she had imagined.

It had been decided that Joseph and his wife Beverly would make room for the arriving relatives since they had the largest apartment. Their two-bedroom, fourth-floor walk-up, in a residential section of the

North Bronx, was part of a large complex. The neo-Tudor buildings were connected by a common courtyard, with well-tended hedges along the walks. The nearby park, complete with a children's playground, was in full bloom. To Hannah it felt as if they had moved to the country.

In that apartment Joseph and Beverly had raised their two sons. David was in the Navy but Michael, the oldest, three years younger than his Uncle Harry, still lived at home. Since his bedroom had been appropriated by the refugees, six-foot-tall Michael had to sleep in the living room on a small foldout cot from the Army & Navy store. But he didn't seem to mind. As he heard his uncle's war stories, Michael felt embarrassed that his flat feet had kept him out of the army.

For several weeks Aunt Beverly's floral living room couch, protected with clear plastic, was occupied by a steady stream of visitors. They were eager to hear first-hand what happened in the war. During the day the wives came and Molly, sitting in Uncle Joseph's overstuffed easy chair, presided. Husbands arrived in the evenings after work. Harry took center stage.

Whenever guests came, Hannah positioned herself off in the corner of the living room. As they talked, she struggled to translate the spoken Yiddish into German and then into Polish. Some subjects were too painful to hear. As Molly tearfully began talking about what happened to her parents, Hannah bolted from the room.

The female visitors often talked about the wartime hardships they had to endure.

"Believe me, it was no picnic here!"

"Everything was rationed. I had to wait on long lines to get some sugar."

"Our married daughter is still living with us. They can't find an apartment."

It was clear to Hannah that the visitors wanted the refugees to know that they too had had to struggle because of the war. Life in America was harder than they had dreamt, Molly and Harry realized. Once he found out he could not practice medicine without going back to medical school, Harry's initial optimism turned into paralyzing sadness. Financially, medical school was out of the question, even if his English had been good enough. They had arrived in America with only the two new one-dollar bills that a soldier had given Hannah in Germany.

One night, some weeks after they arrived, while they thought she was asleep, Hannah heard her parents whispering in their bed next to hers.

"Coming to New York to my brothers was a mistake," Harry confessed. "I should have taken the Army's offer. If I had joined the U.S. Army and stayed in Germany, I'd still be a doctor. Now I'm nothing."

Hannah saw her mother squeeze her father's hand. "We agreed we didn't want to stay in Germany," Molly said. "Remember, we decided that everything was worth giving up to come here to your brothers. That's why I went to that doctor to end my pregnancy once the papers came for you, me, and Hannah. We have to make this work!"

Hannah didn't fully comprehend what she overheard that night, but she remembered how sad her mother was after seeing that German doctor.

In those early weeks, Molly helped Beverly in the kitchen after dinner, and Hannah watched her father often disappear into their bedroom. Peering into the room, she saw her father sitting in the dark at the foot of the bed staring into space, his stethoscope hanging around his neck, clutching his medical bag. Hannah knew that that bag was all that was left of his life as a doctor. She wanted to comfort him, but never did.

Hannah made herself believe that no matter what her mother said about their making things work, they would soon be heading for Palestine. She kept her suitcase packed, ready to leave at a moment's notice. Aunt Beverly complimented Hannah for using the suitcase as a substitute bureau in the cramped apartment.

In spite of his deepening depression, Harry had never considered leaving the U.S. and the only family they had left. But it didn't take long for the general atmosphere around the apartment to become tense. Joseph and Beverly did not have the space or the financial means to support another family.

The brothers said all the right things to each other about blood being thicker than water, but the distance between Joseph and Harry seemed to widen with each day. Joseph did not understand what being a doctor meant to his younger brother. Harry's expressed disappointment at not being able to practice medicine made Joseph impatient.

"When I came to America I had no family to take me in. I got any job I could. So you can't be a doctor! You'll be something else," Joseph said.

"I've never done anything else. What can I do here? If I'm not a doctor, who am I?" he said to his brother. Harry was actually asking himself those questions.

After one of their chilling conversations, Harry always reminded himself that he felt close to Jake and to Sam, who phoned often. Whenever Jake and his wife Leah visited, Jake managed to cheer Harry up.

"You're a smart boychick," Jake teased Harry. A tailor who'd never finished high school, he was very proud of his kid brother, the doctor. "You'll do okay here. First you'll learn English and then you'll go to medical school. You'll be a doctor again!" Jake predicted. "For now, rest a little!"

Harry wanted to believe Jake's prediction, but rest was the last thing on his mind. One thought consumed him: How will I support my family?

The source of Molly's sadness was different. Not only were Joseph and Beverly not her blood relatives, they made her feel like an indentured servant. Beverly expected Molly to clean the house, do the dishes, haul the laundry to the Laundromat down the hill, then iron every piece to perfection. What Molly dreaded most was being upbraided in front of her daughter whenever Beverly was displeased. Timidly Hannah took her mother's side, but that never stopped her aunt's tirades. When Molly complained to Harry, expecting some verbal support at least, she got none.

"We have to be grateful they took us in," Harry said, dismissing her complaints. "You want Beverly to thank you for living in her apartment and making her son sleep in the living room on a cot? It's a good thing David is in the Navy and not living at home!"

Molly felt trapped. During the war she clung to the hope that at some future time things would go back to prewar conditions. Now she knew that was not to be. There was no brother to comfort her, or father or mother. Molly didn't even have Harry in her corner.

She remembered hearing stories as a child about some of her father's relatives emigrating to the U.S. Desperate to improve her situation, Molly called every Landau listed in the New York phone book. When she connected with Harold Landau, who turned out to be a distant cousin, everything changed for Molly. Harold, his wife Lee and their teenage daughter Marion gave her a new perspective on life in America. She not only had her own family again, but Harold looked so much like her father that *the sight of him made Molly happy. A hug from Harold wiped away a week of Beverly's taunts.*

The Landaus often took the newcomers out for a Sunday ride in the country in their black Buick sedan. A favorite destination for Hannah was The Log Cabin, in Armonk, New York, where she got to eat apple pie with vanilla ice cream, topped with chocolate syrup, until her stomach was about to explode.

Ironically, since she had had no expectations about life in America, Hannah was not disappointed. The remoteness of her aunt and uncle seemed natural. To her they were strangers, family in name only.

Gradually the idea of leaving the U.S. and going to Palestine began to fade from Hannah's consciousness. She could not pinpoint the exact moment when the prospect of living on a kibbutz in Palestine stopped being her dream. It could have been shortly after eating pizza became a treat she looked forward to rather than something that turned her stomach. Or once she taught herself to blow bubbles with the Double Bubble gum cousin Marion Landau gave her. The gum and her prowess at blowing bubbles remained a secret pleasure. Harry had forbidden Hannah to chew gum.

By the beginning of July, the household had settled into a regular routine. Joseph got Molly a job as a seamstress in the children's coat factory where he was a foreman. While the work was hard, she preferred toiling in a sweatshop to being under Beverly's thumb. Besides, she was bringing in a sorely needed paycheck. Though it was meager.

Monday through Friday after washing the breakfast dishes Molly went to work with Joseph, grateful she didn't have to make the long subway trip into Manhattan alone. She returned with him in time to help Beverly with dinner. As tired as she was, Molly continued to do whatever chores Beverly assigned her. Before she went to sleep, Hannah gently massaged her mother's newly callused fingers with soothing Jergens lotion from Aunt Beverly's secret drawer. Hannah loved its almond scent.

Harry spent his days pacing in the Stones' living room, or sitting with his Polish/English dictionary on his lap, trying to read the newspaper or a basic medical text that Jake bought for him. He spent his nights brooding. For the first time in his life he saw himself as unemployable and a financial

57

burden. While Harry was grateful Joseph had gotten Molly a job, it was humiliating for him that his wife was now the family breadwinner. Instead of applauding her for earning money at a job she had never done before, Harry rewarded his wife with indifference. No sign of affection passed between them.

Hannah managed to stay out of her father's way. Her main focus was learning to speak English. Her teacher was the radio Aunt Beverly had on all day in the kitchen. Sitting at the kitchen table, Hannah softly repeated the words she heard, without knowing what they meant. She practiced, determined to become perfect.

Whenever Aunt Beverly encouraged her to go down to the courtyard to play with the youngsters her age, Hannah resisted. She preferred watching from the safety of the apartment. One day as she peered down from the fourth-floor kitchen window, Hannah, her mouth opened wide, was fascinated by what she was witnessing. Three girls were gliding around the concrete walks on shoes that seemed to have wheels attached. She leaned out farther than was safe. Hannah managed to grab the window frame in time and trembling, she pulled herself back to safety, relieved Aunt Beverly had been busy cooking and did not notice her near fatal mishap.

When she saw two girls standing several feet apart twirling a rope, as a third girl jumped in, Hannah looked to her aunt for clarification.

"What are they doing?" she asked in German. Hannah was now adept at translating Aunt Beverly's Yiddish answers into German. It wasn't ideal, but they understood each other.

This time Beverly opted for English. 'They're jumping rope," she said. Seeing Hannah's blank expression, she added in Yiddish, "You could be jumping with them and having fun."

Hannah bit her lip. "Nein," she said shaking her head violently. "I cannot speak to them," she answered in German. But in truth the language barrier was only part of it. Hannah didn't know how to be a kid. Comfortable taking part in a conversation with adults, expounding on world politics, she didn't know what to say to her American peers even if she could speak English fluently. Also, they could play games she had never tried. Hannah preferred keeping her shortcomings a secret. Then there was the way she looked. Her hair and her clothes made it crystal clear she was not one of them.

Before she rushed off to work with Joseph each morning, Molly carefully braided her daughter's hair, anchoring the braids with two large navy taffeta bows on top of her head, as was proper for young girls in Poland. In America, wearing childish handmade dresses with smocking and puffy sleeves, instead of shorts and polo shirts, only emphasized her being different.

One day Aunt Beverly insisted Hannah accompany her to the market. But when she spotted two girls playing jacks on the stoop of the building next door she pulled a reluctant Hannah by the hand toward the girls.

"This is my niece Hannah," Beverly said. "She doesn't speak English, but I'm sure you can still teach her to play jacks."

Both girls nodded and waved to Hannah. She managed a weak smile and waved back. Hannah started to follow her aunt as she was walking away. Aunt Beverly shook her head. "Stay," she ordered in Yiddish, and pointed to the girls on the stoop.

At that instant, with the two girls staring at her, she was almost as panicked as she'd felt years ago when Aunt Emma had left her alone in the apartment in Warsaw. Hannah wished her mother had not put those big bows in her hair that morning.

At Aunt Beverly's urging, grudgingly Hannah began to venture downstairs to the courtyard. She soon understood enough English to know they called her "four-eyes" because she wore glasses, and made fun of her hair and her clothes. But she was determined to learn the games they played, and never let on that she understood what they were saying about her.

In Poland being Jewish made Hannah an outsider. Now in America, in a neighborhood that was primarily Jewish, she was still an outsider.

Slowly things did change for the better. As Harry's English improved, so did his spirits. For Molly the anticipation of weekend visits with the Landaus made the hard work endured during the week bearable. And Hannah, masquerading as the fly on the wall, found solace in her special secret. She now understood everything. Although she still had not uttered a single word, she was pretty sure she could. Hannah was unwilling to let an English word escape her mouth until she was absolutely certain she could speak like a native. No Mistakes Allowed. She was waiting for the right moment to spring it on everyone.

* * *

When it came, Harry briefly considered an offer from Sam to move to Asheville.

"We have a big house and you can work for me in the factory. You won't be a doctor, but you'll make a good living. I'll see to that," Sam said.

Harry was tempted by the prospect of earning money and once again being the family provider. But he was not ready to give up being a doctor. He turned Sam down. However, when Sam sent train tickets for them to visit Asheville, it was decided that before Hannah started school in September the three of them would make the trip to the South. Harry was euphoric at the prospect of finally being face-to-face with the brother he had not seen since they were children. But the euphoria was mixed with a great deal of apprehension about their making the trip alone.

Michael took them to Grand Central Station. Before they boarded their train, he handed Harry a fistful of change and a stack of three-by-five index cards. To lessen Harry and Molly's anxiety about their not being able to speak English, he had written out questions they might need to ask. WHERE IS THE BATHROOM? WHERE IS THE RESTAURANT CAR? WHICH WAY TO THE INFORMATION BOOTH? WHERE IS THE PUBLIC PHONE? One side of the card had the questions in English, and the Polish translation was on the other. All could be answered by pointing.

The train was packed. Michael helped them onto the next-to-last car where there were still some seats available. Hannah spotted two together and a single, several rows behind.

"You two should sit together," Hannah said, hoping her parents would agree. "You can always look back and see me."

The vacant single was next to a lady. Her parents agreed. Hannah was pleased. She had a plan. It was so important it overshadowed her usual fear of being separated from her parents.

After Michael left, Molly and Harry became uncharacteristically calm. So much so that after the conductor had punched their tickets, the motion of the train lulled them into a sound sleep.

The woman sitting by the window greeted Hannah with a smile, which she returned. "Do you live in New York?" the woman asked after a while.

Hannah nodded. The word "Yes" got stuck in her throat.

60

"Are you on holiday or going for a visit?"

Hannah wasn't sure how to answer. Both were true. Finally, very slowly, she said, "We . . . are . . . going . . . to . . . visit . . . my uncle." Hannah took a deep breath. Her palms were damp, but she'd done it and she was pleased with herself.

"Where does your uncle live?"

"In Asheville," Hannah answered without hesitation. And their conversation began.

As soon as Harry opened his eyes, he reached for one of his medical books.

When Molly woke up, she saw Hannah talking animatedly to the well-dressed woman and assumed that woman was Polish.

"The woman sitting next to Hannah looks like an American but she must speak Polish," Molly told Harry. After a moment she added, "Maybe she knows German."

Harry and Molly both turned and waved. Hannah and the woman waved back.

"Read your book, Harry," Molly said. "I'm going to talk to Hannah and her new friend!"

When she reached them, Molly stuck out her hand and said in Polish, "I'm so glad to meet you. I'm Hannah's mother."

Confused, the woman took Molly's hand, and addressed Hannah, "What language is she speaking?"

"Polish," Hannah answered, in a whisper.

"Is this your mother?" she asked.

Hannah nodded.

In a loud voice, as if she were talking to someone who was hard of hearing, Hannah's traveling companion said to Molly, "I'm Janey Everett. You have a fine daughter!"

Molly let go of Mrs. Everett's hand, and asked Hannah. "Is this woman an American?"

Hannah bobbed her head up and down.

Puzzled, Molly asked, "Does she speak Polish or German?"

"No. She doesn't." Hannah sighed.

Mrs. Everett patted Hannah's hand, warmly. "You talk Polish, too! Good for you!" she said. "Please explain to your mother, that unfortunately I do not speak anything but American. And I must admit when I visit

New York, I often think I speak a different American than y'all do." She grinned, waiting for Hannah to translate.

Hannah abridged her translation. She repeated that Mrs. Everett did not speak Polish or German.

"Then how were the two of you talking?" Molly demanded.

"In English," Hannah answered, sheepishly.

"You speak English? You speak well enough to have a conversation with an American?"

"Tak."

A mixture of feelings washed over Molly. "Why didn't you tell us? You knew how worried we were about making this trip and not being able to speak English!"

"I'm sorry. But before I said anything to anyone, I had to make sure I spoke perfectly, like a real American." Hannah defended her deception. "Talking to Mrs. Everett was my test."

"You can't always expect to be perfect, Hannah," Molly said. But her daughter's explanation was totally in character. As her anger ebbed, it was replaced with relief. Molly hugged her daughter. "I'm proud of you. Now we won't need Michael's cards. We have you to speak for us."

For the rest of their journey, Hannah spoke for her parents.

She earned her stripes as a translator in North Carolina. There was no problem with Sam. He could speak Yiddish and Polish. But his wife, Melanie, a convert to Judaism, spoke only English, and with a deep southern drawl. She and their two-year-old daughter, Josie, were only able to talk to Hannah. But in spite of the language barrier, Melanie made them all feel welcome. Sam had been a widower for many years before he and Melanie got married. She was glad to finally meet Sam's family from up North.

Home for Sam and Melanie was a comfortable redbrick colonial on the outskirts of town, with a screened-in porch and two spare bedrooms for guests. The quiet suburban life in Asheville, North Carolina, was a surprise to Molly, Harry and Hannah. They had assumed all of the United States was like New York City. Everything in Asheville was slower. People didn't talk as fast, and they weren't eager to do much in the hot August sun.

Sam, who had to be at the factory before the first shift of workers arrived each morning, took Harry with him to work. The brothers were long out of the house by the time Molly and Hannah got up for breakfast. Mother and daughter stayed close to home with Aunt Melanie and Josie. Molly didn't seem to mind not having anything to do nor that Hannah was the only one she could speak to during the day. She reveled in her leisure, she wrote letters, read and even creamed her face and callused hands with the lotion Melanie had given her as a present. Unlike Beverly, who expected Molly to do chores, Melanie treated her like a welcomed guest and wouldn't let her do any housework. Molly was grateful. Hannah was happy listening to country and western music on the radio, carrying Josie around the house and practicing her English.

When Melanie needed to do some shopping, they drove into town. Both Hannah and Molly were impressed with Melanie's driving skills.

"I drove practically before I could walk," Melanie said when Hannah asked how long she'd been driving. "Of course, it wasn't a car, it was my daddy's tractor," she chuckled.

During one of their trips into town, Melanie insisted they stop at her sister's beauty salon.

"You have beautiful hair," Melanie told Molly. "You shouldn't always tie it back like that."

Hearing Hannah's translation, Molly blushed. She wasn't used to compliments.

Molly not only got her hair done, she also had her hands professionally massaged and her nails painted.

"You pick the color," Molly told Hannah.

Carefully studying the many bottles, Hannah finally selected "Dither," a dramatic purplish red that was brighter than what her mother might have picked. With her new hairdo and painted nails, Molly felt like a movie star.

"Thank you. Thank you so much," she said to Melanie in Polish, and hugged her.

Hannah didn't have to translate.

Melanie made sure they were back home in time for her to have dinner ready when Sam and Harry walked through the door. That night, Molly and her new look were the sole topic of conversation.

Usually a poor eater, Hannah became addicted to Aunt Melanie's specialty: southern fried chicken, black-eyed peas, and cornbread. To her *delight, her father temporarily relented and allowed Hannah to wash it all down with 7-UP.*

In Asheville Hannah never lost sight of her major objective—perfecting her English skills. Even setting the table became a learning opportunity. Hannah thought Aunt Melanie's bright-colored Melamine plates were more festive than the green Depression glass dishes Aunt Beverly favored in New York, but helping her aunt set the round dining room table was secondary to Hannah's higher purpose. It was an easy way for her to practice translating her Polish thoughts into English sentences.

After taking the stainless flatware out of the top drawer of the mahogany breakfront in the dining room, Hannah asked, "How must I arrange the knives, forks, and spoons?" She enunciated each word perfectly.

"I think what you meant to ask was, 'Where should I place the knives, forks, and spoons?' Right?" Melanie said, eager to help her niece improve her English.

Grateful, Hannah nodded and restated her question correctly.

"The forks go on the left of the plate. The knives, then spoons on the right," Aunt Melanie instructed cheerfully.

And the lesson continued.

"These pretty napkins, where must I put them?" she asked, then quickly corrected herself. "Where should I place the pretty napkins?"

"Next to the fork!" Melanie pointed, and showed Hannah how to turn a napkin into a flower with the help of a plastic napkin ring.

While Sam, Harry, and Molly talked in Polish during meals, Hannah continued to practice her English chatting with Melanie and baby Josie, who sat in a highchair between the two of them. All the practice paid off. Intermittently Hannah found herself actually thinking in English. By the time they left Asheville, her role as her parents' translator was firmly established, and she now spoke English with a slight Southern drawl.

They arrived in New York the Friday before Hannah was to start school. On Monday morning Uncle Joseph went with Hannah to register her at the grade school both of his sons had attended. Biting her lips, Hannah walked alongside her uncle in silence. The closer they got to their destination the faster Hannah's heart raced. She wanted to run back to Aunt Beverly's kitchen, but Joseph held her small hand in a tight grip until they entered the school building. In front of the administration office her uncle told Hannah to wait on a wooden bench in the reception area. She sat, eyes focused straight ahead, but out of the corner of her eye Hannah saw several of the girls she knew looking at her and laughing. She pursed her lips and waited.

Hannah sprang up as soon as Uncle Joseph came out of the office with Mrs. Reiner, the assistant principal.

"Don't worry, dear, you'll be fine," she said, just as a loud bell sounded. Hannah relaxed a little. After she said goodbye to her uncle, she followed Mrs. Reiner to meet her class. As they entered the classroom Hannah felt all eyes on her.

"Class, I want you to welcome a new student who came all the way from Poland to America!" Mrs. Reiner announced. "Say hello to Harriet Stone."

"Hello, Harriet!" the class said in unison.

Hannah started to shake her head frantically.

"No! No! No! That's not my name, that's not my name," Hannah kept repeating. "My name is not Harriet. I'm Hannah."

Until that dreadful moment when Mrs. Reiner introduced her to the class as Harriet Stone, Hannah had no inkling her uncle had planned to change her name. When Mrs. Reiner left, Hannah once again insisted to Miss Banks that she wanted to be called by her real name, Hannah, not Harriet. But her teacher shook her head and dismissed the request.

"You're in America now, Harriet, dear. You need an American name," Miss Banks said emphatically. "Harriet is a much better name for an American girl than Hannah."

Without any warning, she was metamorphosed into a person to whom she felt no connection. During the war, Hannah understood it was necessary to become Zofia Nowakowska to stay alive, but this name change was unnecessary. She had accepted the translation of Stein, to Stone, but losing her given name was different. Hannah was who she was. She knew she had to get herself back.

That afternoon, when she recounted her first day at school, she was disappointed by her father's response. Harry, who had had no problem with Hershel Stein becoming Harry Stone, was not sympathetic.

"We all have to make sacrifices to become Americans," her father told her.

"If we can't be who we really are, what's the point of staying here?

We could have stayed in Poland, and you would still be a doctor," Hannah argued.

"You're acting like a spoiled child, Hannah," Harry reprimanded. "Harriet is a fine American name. It should be enough for you that to us you'll always be Hannah."

That was the end of the matter as far as Harry was concerned. But not Hannah. She didn't know how, but she was determined to get her name back. Until that time, every morning, a dispirited Harriet faced Miss Banks and her second-grade class, where each day she fell further and further behind the rest of the class. Because she spoke English flawlessly, no one suspected she could not read. Hannah was ashamed to reveal she couldn't. She was terrified whenever Miss Banks said: "Class, open your readers!" That was a cue for Hannah to sink into her seat and take cover behind her textbook, hoping to avoid being called upon. The words she feared most were: "Harriet, please stand up and start reading the homework assignment out loud!"

Red-faced and in a cold sweat, terrified Hannah stood trembling beside her desk. She tried to guess at the words. The ordeal always ended with Miss Banks saying, "Sit down, Harriet. You must do better!"

School became a place of torture. At home Hannah tried desperately to teach herself to read. She'd stare at the letters through the blur of her tears, trying to sound out words in her school reader. She did better with the Wonder Woman comics her cousin Marion gave her. The pictures helped her guess at the words. But her feeling of incompetence washed away all the years Hannah had felt smart. The precocious child who could recite poetry at an age when other children were still making gurgling sounds was gone. In her eyes she was now a dummy. It never occurred to Hannah someone should be teaching her to read. She thought she was supposed to do it without any help.

Although Hannah didn't feel smart anymore, being of help to her parents made her proud. She dutifully accompanied Harry and Molly when they registered for night school and went with them in the evenings to the very place that was her torture chamber during the day. But after three weeks, Harry and Molly became night school dropouts. Molly was too tired after a full day's work to go to school and Harry found a better way to improve his English after Harold Landau gave him a set of recordings of an English/German Berlitz course. While Molly was at work, Harry sat in the living room in Uncle Joseph's chair and diligently practiced his English. By the middle of October, with the aid of Berlitz and his Polish/English dictionary, Harry was able to translate all the medical books he'd gotten out of the library. And as soon as he felt his limited verbal skills were adequate enough, though he spoke haltingly, and with a thick accent, Harry volunteered at Montefiore Hospital. Within weeks he landed a paying job as an orderly. Surprisingly, Harry did not view his demotion from doctor to orderly as demeaning. It was a way of getting back to medicine, which was what he wanted.

Once Harry started working, he was nicer to Molly and generally more pleasant to be around. But he had few kind words for his daughter. There were nights Hannah cried herself to sleep trying to block out Harry's litany of complaints about her.

"Why does your daughter think her little problems are so important?"

"Your daughter thinks she knows everything."

"Your daughter expects everything to be the way she wants."

The coldness in her father's voice as he enunciated, "your daughter" made Hannah question, "Does he think I'm not his daughter?" In the morning, seeing her reflection in the bathroom mirror while brushing her teeth confirmed the undeniable fact that Harry was indeed her father. Puzzled why everything she said or did seemed to irritate him, Hannah wished she could talk to her mother about it. But she didn't want her parents to know their secret conversations had an uninvited audience.

Helping her parents with English continued to be a source of pride for Hannah. But seeing an unexplained flash of anger cross her father's face took away some of that pride. To avoid his wrath, Hannah kept to herself as much as possible. But in the overcrowded apartment there were few places for her to hide. The only room that had a lock on the door was the bathroom, which always seemed to be in use. Hannah wondered how long Uncle Joseph and Aunt Beverly would put up with the inconvenience of living with another family.

Several weeks after Harry received his first paycheck, Hannah got her answer. During their Friday night supper Joseph brought up the possibility *of making other living arrangements.*

"It won't be easy, but we need to start looking for a place for you to live," Joseph said in one breath, and then complimented his wife on her gefilte fish.

With Yiddish the language of choice at the table, at first Hannah wasn't absolutely sure she had understood what Uncle Joseph had said. When her mother squeezed her hand under the table, Hannah knew she had translated her uncle's words correctly.

"How can we afford a place of our own?" Molly asked. "It would be nice," she added wistfully. The mere possibility of living somewhere else made Molly happy. Mother and daughter smiled at each other between bites. But not Harry.

"We can't pay for an apartment. Even with Molly's salary and mine we make next to nothing," Harry said in Yiddish.

"You can't afford a palace, but we'll find you something. If not an apartment, then maybe a rooming house. Jake, Sam, and I have talked about it. We will help you," Joseph said calmly, but firmly.

It was obvious that Harry had nothing further to say in the matter.

Joseph, Harry, and Molly started the difficult search the following Sunday. Uncle Joseph would not travel on Saturday. The Sabbath had to be observed. When the three of them returned at dinnertime, Hannah could tell that her mother had been crying. Harry went into their bedroom and closed the door. No one said anything about what they'd seen.

Armed with a list of addresses, and directions for what trains or buses to take, the next time Harry and Molly went apartment hunting, Hannah, their translator, went along in place of Uncle Joseph.

"This is the best we've seen so far," Molly said as Mr. Rossetti, the building's superintendent, showed them around the dingy flat.

"Take your time. Look around," Mr. Rossetti said. "The next people be here in ten, maybe fifteen minutes. I wait outside," he said, giving them privacy to make their decision.

The ground-floor brownstone apartment on East 186th Street between Washington and Park Avenues was small, dark, and smelled of exterminator spray. Harry and Molly huddled in the kitchen, where a sliver of afternoon light streamed in from the courtyard. Hannah explored the empty icebox in the hall. "The iceman delivers once a week," she heard Mr. Rossetti tell Molly.

Hannah heard her mother say, "I can do it. I can make this place home for us!" just as Mr. Rossetti returned to tell them the next people were waiting outside.

Harry wasn't so sure, but he went over to Mr. Rossetti and said, "Ve vant to take it." Mr. Rossetti said nothing until Harry handed him a crisp one-hundred-dollar bill.

Hannah was overjoyed. She knew that once they moved to their new apartment she would be going to a new school and that meant she'd be escaping from Miss Banks and her torture chamber. But even more important than that, she was determined to get her rightful name back, and to leave Harriet behind with Miss Banks. The week before they were to move Hannah approached Mrs. Reiner's assistant after school.

"Miss Swanson, what do I have to do to get my real name back?" Hannah asked tentatively.

"I'm not sure I understand, Harriet, dear. Tell me exactly what you mean." Miss Swanson looked perplexed.

Armed with a copy of her birth certificate, and practically hyperventilating, Hannah poured out her story. Miss Swanson listened intently, and once Hannah finished pleading her case, she had her sit and wait while she went to see Mrs. Reiner. When Miss Swanson came out smiling a few minutes later, she knew she was officially Hannah again. That afternoon her smile never left her face. But Hannah never told anyone what put it there.

The refugees relocated to their new home in mid-December, with the help of Michael, Joseph, and Jake. Molly bought the furnishings they needed at the nearby Salvation Army Thrift Shop. The one extravagance she insisted on was hiring a mover to transport the upright she appropriated from one of Beverly Stone's more affluent canasta players.

"If you can take the piano out of here, it's yours," Mrs. Mandelbaum offered cheerfully. They were getting a new one, paid for with green stamps, so their little Marlene could practice and one day she would

become Miss America, just like Bess Myerson.

For Molly the piano, draped with an embroidered silk shawl, and topped with her mother's silver candlesticks they'd brought from Poland, was a symbol of better times. It provided a touch of class to the largest room, which served as living room by day, and Hannah's bedroom at night.

Even with their limited resources, Molly transformed the small, airless railroad flat into a pleasant home, but she could not eliminate the smell of roach spray. Each week Molly experimented with different air fresheners to hide the oppressive smell. For Hannah the scent of air fresheners and roach spray remained forever fused.

When they lived with Uncle Joseph and Aunt Beverly, most of their neighbors were Jewish. In this new neighborhood, they were the only Jewish family. There were many Italians, a few Irish, and other assimilated American families living in the shabby brownstones off the tony-sounding Park Avenue. Their working class neighbors, still trying to acquire a piece of the American dream for themselves, were not particularly sympathetic to the plight of new refugees.

Hannah's first day at her new school was uneventful. But not what she did before. After Harry and Molly left for work, Hannah removed the taffeta bows from her hair, undid the braids and tied her hair back at the nape of her neck. Determined to change the way she looked, she pulled a few hair strands in front, and with her mother's nail scissors gave herself wispy bangs.

"That's better," she said to the person staring back at her from the mirror. Hannah couldn't do anything about her clothes, other than to cover up her embroidered blouse with a cardigan sweater. Changing her hairstyle was enough. Feeling more confident, she walked to P.S. 85 on Marion Avenue by herself, along the same route Hannah had taken with her mother as practice the day before.

She presented her transfer papers to Miss Winters, the woman sitting outside of the assistant principal's office.

"Sit down, dear. I'll find out what class you're in," Miss Winters said. She seemed glad to see her. Hannah was just another transfer student she was welcoming.

Nobody had checked Hannah's records carefully enough to note that she had arrived in the United States seven months before. They looked at her test scores. Her I.Q. was low enough to rank Hannah mildly retarded. No one explained her situation, and her own preference for keeping her refugee status a secret placed Hannah in a Special Education class. That turned out to be a blessing in disguise.

In a class with physically and mentally handicapped students, Hannah became the star pupil. Her teacher, Miss Mullens, took a liking to the sad little girl and made a special effort to teach her to read.

The first time Miss Mullens called her to her desk, Hannah's stomach churned so loud she was sure her teacher could hear it. She held her breath and rubbed her clammy hands.

Hannah finally exhaled when Miss Mullens said, "This is going to be fun. I have some books that you and I can practice reading together in class. Then you can take them home and practice some more."

She proved to be an apt pupil. After several weeks of tutoring, Hannah no longer feared being asked to read. Buoyed by her improved reading skills, she soon looked forward to reading out loud in class. Miss Mullens was very proud of both of their accomplishments, until Parents' Day.

Molly and Harry got all dressed up to meet Hannah's teacher. When they entered the class, Miss Mullens was talking to another parent. Hannah showed her mother and father her desk and some of her work that was displayed on the bulletin board. She brought them over when Miss Mullens was free.

"Ve arre verry glad to meet you alrready," Harry said and extended his hand to the teacher. "Until yourr class ve vere afrraid Hannah vould never learrn to rread. It vas strange because she learrned to talk so fast. Ve came in May und by Au-gust Hannah vas speaking like a born Amerrican."

As Harry spoke, Miss Mullens realized Hannah's inability to read was not because she was retarded, no matter what her test scores indicated. She felt deceived by Hannah. Why didn't the child tell me that she was a refugee? Miss Mullens wondered.

The following Monday, Hannah was confused by her teacher's sudden coldness to her.

"Have I done something wrong, Miss Mullens?" Hannah asked after she cancelled their regular tutoring session.

"No, Hannah, you did nothing wrong. I just can't be spending so much time with you. It is just not fair to the others. I have to teach them, too," Miss Mullens explained.

"I could help you," Hannah said.

"That is a very sweet offer, dear," she said, and smiled in spite of herself. "Actually, you are going into another class. Now that you read so well, you don't belong in this class anymore."

That was Hannah's final gift from Miss Mullens. She had her transferred out of Special Ed. and into a regular second-grade class, where Hannah had to start fending for herself. The switch into Class 2B went smoothly. Now that she could read, Hannah felt almost normal. But she wouldn't feel smart again for a long, long time.

Hannah liked not living with Uncle Joseph and Aunt Beverly, but there were some things she missed. There was no longer celebration of the Sabbath. After working overtime most Fridays to earn extra money, Molly was now too tired to prepare Shabbat dinner. Harry was happy to eat a sandwich while he studied his medical books. Hannah missed the ritual.

When Nora Florio, who lived a few doors down on 186th Street, asked Hannah one Saturday if she wanted to go to church with her and some kids from her Catholic school, Hannah decided it would be okay and she went.

Our Lady of Mount Carmel, on Belmont Avenue and 187th Street, was not as grand as the church she attended with Aunt Emma in Warsaw, and it did not smell of incense. But Hannah knew what to do. She kneeled, crossed herself with holy water and said the same prayers she had said in Poland. After confessing a minor sin, she went up for the wafer and Communion along with her friend. Hannah knew she was Jewish, just as she had known during the war. She didn't see any harm in being blessed by a Catholic priest in New York. She liked being part of the group, and the ritual. The priest was very welcoming.

"It's nice to see a new face," Father Dominic said the first time he gave Hannah the wafer. By the fourth week he urged her to bring her parents.

"I know you like to come with your friends. Your parents could come to a different service. We like to have the whole family be part of our parish. You should suggest they come! Just to try it."

Hannah didn't want to lie, especially to a priest. She just shrugged.

The next week when Father Dominic asked her what church her family normally attended, Hannah told the truth.

"My family doesn't go to a church, Father," she said, without elaborating further.

"Maybe if you brought them here, they would want to start coming, just as you do," Father Dominic said.

"No. No they wouldn't," Hannah insisted, still not revealing the truth.

"Next week, you bring your family," Father Dominic said firmly.

"They won't come. We're Jewish," Hannah blurted out.

After hearing that confession, for a moment Father Dominic stared at Hannah without saying anything. Then he blessed her, as he had all the other times. But they both knew that she would not be back. Her new friends didn't understand why Hannah stopped coming to Communion.

Hannah enjoyed the freedom she had being on her own. When she didn't want to eat the breakfast her mother laid out for her before leaving for work—two hard-boiled eggs and a glass of milk—Hannah flushed the milk, but heeding her mother's admonition against wasting food, she hid the eggs throughout the apartment. Molly only discovered her daughter's deception later when they packed to move. She never told Harry. Amazingly the eggs did not smell up the apartment. Hannah's other secret: on alternate days, she put aside the money her mother gave her to buy milk and cookies in school, and when she had enough saved, treated herself to a verboten Milky Way bar.

Elani Zographos and Hannah started walking home together from school once they realized they lived on the same street. They were in different classes, and Elani was younger than Hannah, but that didn't matter to the girls. Her family owned the dry-cleaning store around the corner on Washington Avenue. After school, under the watchful eye of Mr. Zographos, Hannah and Elani did their homework on the floor

73

next to the front counter of the store. Seeing how her father supervised
everything Elani did, Hannah was alternately envious of his constant
attention and relieved that she herself had more freedom. Elani cautioned
Hannah that her father had a bad temper, but he did not scare Hannah.
Although Mr. Zographos shouted a lot, Hannah decided he didn't do it to
berate anyone, he just had strong opinions. Particularly when he talked
about politics. Elani was not interested. But Hannah was.

"You know everybody pretends that President Roosevelt was a saint.
He did many bad things nobody wants to mention," Mr. Zographos told a
surprised Hannah.

She remembered that in the DP camp when people mentioned
President Roosevelt's name it was in tones usually reserved for a deity. But
Mr. Zographos could not forgive President Roosevelt for dumping Henry
Wallace, his Vice President.

"He replaced him with Harry Truman because Henry Wallace is too
close to the people," Mr. Zographos said. To rectify Roosevelt's mistake, in
1948, Mr. Zographos supported Henry Wallace, the third party candidate
for President, instead of Harry Truman or Thomas Dewey.

"If Truman or Dewey become President, wait and see, you'll have
soldiers running the country," Mr. Zographos warned Hannah. She
wasn't sure how it could happen, but she knew she didn't want soldiers
running her life again. Although Hannah had reached the point where
she might approach a policeman for help if she were lost or in trouble,
uniforms were a source of fear, not safety for her. Even when Martha
Kavanaugh, a girl in her class she greatly admired, assured Hannah she
would really like being a Girl Scout, it was their uniforms that kept her
from joining. Uniforms reminded her of the Hitler Youth groups she had
heard about in Poland. And feared.

In an effort to keep soldiers off New York streets, something
Mr. Zographos warned would happen with Truman reelected, ten-year-old
Hannah took the Wallace for President buttons Mr. Zographos had given
her and stood outside the Third Avenue El train station handing them
out to people returning home from work.

One night at dinner, trying to impress her father, Hannah proudly
mentioned her campaigning efforts on behalf of Henry Wallace.

"Are you trying to get this family deported?" Harry shouted, his face beet red.

Hannah was bewildered by her father's response. *"Of course not!"* she insisted, and looked to her mother for support. But Molly eyed her plate of food and refused to take a position. *"Mr. Zographos told me if Harry Truman becomes president, soldiers will be everywhere,"* Hannah said, trying to explain her entrance into U.S. politics. She could not understand why her father had misinterpreted her actions.

"Vat you are doing is putting dis family in jeopardy by supporting a communist for President." When Harry became angry or anxious, his accent was more pronounced.

"Mr. Zographos said Henry Wallace is for the people. Is that being a communist?"

"Everything he told you . . . sounds to me like he's a communist. Having friends like that could put us in big trouble!" Harry shouted. The fear Hannah heard in her father's voice frightened her.

It was simpler during the war, she thought. Obviously, there were things that could harm them in America that she did not understand. Harry insisted Hannah limit her contact with the Zographos family. Although he didn't object to Molly's patronizing their cleaning store.

A contrite Hannah told her father she would give the Wallace for President buttons back to Mr. Zographos. Her promise to stop spending afternoons with Elani at the cleaning store was more difficult for her. But she did it. No Mistakes Allowed!

Hannah decided the only election that was safe for her to actively participate in was electing the next Miss Rheingold. Standing outside the Bartello grocery she campaigned for her favorite Miss Rheingold. Hannah always wanted the brunette to win.

When Harry Truman was reelected and the soldiers didn't come, Hannah was relieved. But the possibility of another war breaking out that could reach the United States always hovered in the back of her mind. The day President Truman announced he was sending American troops to protect South Korea, Hannah remembered what Mr. Zographos predicted, and worried. As she waited for her parents to come home that evening she tried to reason herself out of her panic. Korea was not near

New York, she told herself. To temper her panic, she did what she had done during the war when Aunt Emma left her alone. Hannah paced back and forth from the kitchen to the front door of the apartment, counting to a hundred, over and over again. As soon as she heard a key in the door, she rushed back to the kitchen. Her father found her, sitting at the table, doing her homework. Until President Eisenhower declared it was over, Hannah listened intently to the news on the radio, hoping the police action in Korea was not about to reach her front door.

On Sundays, if Harry decided he could take a break from studying his medical books, they often went to Times Square. Usually they ended up at the Stanley Theater, but only if a foreign film was playing that Harry wanted to see. Unfortunately for Hannah, her father was only interested in war movies. From the opening credits, Hannah sat in the darkened theater, her eyes closed, her fingers in her ears, trying to drown out the awful sounds of gun battles and exploding bombs. But her fingers could never block out enough and when she couldn't stand it anymore, a tearful Hannah would run into the lobby. Mr. Rosoff, the theater manager, a balding man with eyeglasses perched on the tip of his nose, and a cigarette dangling from his mouth, befriended her. He not only let her in for free, knowing she would never watch the movie, but had a comic book and a candy bar for her whenever she raced out. It was Mr. Rosoff who introduced Hannah to Archie Comics and Almond Joy.

Except for the prospect of seeing war movies, Hannah looked forward to their trips to Times Square. She liked the bright lights of Broadway and enjoyed watching the parade of people streaming in and out of arcades holding gigantic ice cream cones. But on the subway ride home her mood darkened. Besides war Hannah hated night.

Once she no longer shared a bedroom with her parents, being alone in the dark before she fell asleep set off a sense of dread Hannah could not control. Almost like clockwork, as the sun went down, she complained of stomach cramps. As bedtime approached Hannah became more and more anxious. But she got no sympathy from her father.

"There's nothing wrong with you." Dr. Stone stated coldly once he ascertained she had no medical issues. "You're not a baby anymore. Stop behaving like one," Harry chided a distraught Hannah.

The nightly ritual was always the same. After Harry pronounced his daughter fit for bed, she dutifully brushed her teeth, and, fighting panic, hugged her mother good night. Harry usually turned in after studying his medical books. Molly did her best to mediate between stern father and scared daughter. Without openly going against her husband, she made excuses to stay up and keep the light on.

Molly would tell Harry some version of, "I'll be in soon. I just have to finish hemming Hannah's skirt." Then she'd settle in a chair in the living room where Hannah slept, until her daughter fell asleep. Some nights Molly stayed up pretending to be reading long after her eyes closed. When during the night, she heard Hannah scream, "No, No!" she'd rush in to quiet her before Harry woke up.

"Dreams can't hurt you," Molly assured her daughter, and stroked her hair. With her mother sitting on her bed, Hannah usually fell into a dreamless sleep. She never discussed her recurring dream. By the time Hannah was twelve her fear of the dark miraculously stopped. But the dream continued.

The possibility of war never totally went away for Hannah. Nor did her fear of being separated from her parents. As an adult watching President Kennedy address the nation on TV about the Cuban missile crisis, Hannah's first thought was to reach her parents. If war broke out again, she wanted them at least to be together.

Hannah often saw menace in behavior that others did not find threatening. At a peace demonstration in 1968 against the Vietnam War, near the United Nations, the crowd cheered each speaker, but particularly Bobby Kennedy. The rally started out peacefully, but soon the frenzy of the crowd increased. They began chanting, "Hell, no, we won't go," which led to repeated shouts of:

"What do we want?"

"Peace!"

"When do we want it?"

"Now!"

Suddenly Hannah thought the angry crowd was no longer part of a peace demonstration. Yelling with one voice, clapping rhythmically, instead of goose-stepping, she felt her fellow demonstrators had turned into a mindless mob. She found the mob as scary as the war itself. Under the right leadership, Hannah thought, they could easily be shouting, "Sieg Heil!"

CHAPTER

4

ON SUNDAY WHEN HANNAH walked through the cobblestone courtyard of her parents' building it struck her how much it resembled the limestone apartment building in Warsaw where she had lived with Aunt Emma.

"Amazing. In all the years I've walked here I've never noticed the similarity. I block a lot better than I realized," Hannah chided herself. For a split second, she wondered if her parents had noticed the similarity. She laughed at her own blindness. Of course. That's probably *why* they moved here!

Waiting for the elevator, Hannah closed her eyes and made a wish. "Please God, let it be like it was yesterday."

When a smiling Molly greeted her daughter at the door, Hannah was convinced her wish had been granted.

"Glad to see you in such good spirits, Mom," Hannah said.

"Did you finish all the work you had to do?" Molly asked, gently pulling her into the apartment.

Hannah didn't know what her mother was referring to, until she remembered her white lie. "Oh yes," she answered, feeling a bit guilty.

"Good. Now you can relax and enjoy today," Molly said, cheerfully. Without complaining that her daughter had arrived too late to join them for lunch, she added, "We just finished eating. Would you like some blintzes?"

Hannah shook her head. "I had a big breakfast."

When no badgering followed, the tension that usually resided at the back of her neck seemed to dissipate. "It's a miracle!" she thought.

Hannah held her breath as she walked toward the living room. Seeing Harry sitting in his favorite spot on the couch reading the Sunday papers, she exhaled into a smile. He looked healthier than he had the day before. It was shaping up to be a good day.

She hugged each of her parents in turn, but the hug was not enough for her father. Reluctant to let go, Harry squeezed Hannah's hand. His warm touch made her eyes well up. When he released her hand, she settled into a comfortable easy chair near him. She took a recent issue of *New York* magazine out of her bag and laid it on the coffee table.

"When you're finished with the papers, Dad, you might want to read the excerpt of the John Ehrlichman novel about Watergate," Hannah said, pointing to the magazine. "I know it's supposed to be fiction, but he was a special assistant to the President. Reading it might make you see Nixon differently."

"I'll look at it," Harry said from behind his paper.

Not yet used to their non-combative status, Hannah had to force herself to stay relaxed. She took her copy of the Sunday *New York Times Magazine* and, pen in hand, started in on the crossword puzzle.

"Have you followed the Patty Hearst trial?" Harry asked Hannah, after a few minutes of silence had passed.

"Yeah. What about it?" Hannah felt her body tense up.

"It's amazing how people who have never been in such a harrowing situation are willing to condemn that poor child for doing whatever she could to survive. Do you think she should go to jail?"

"No. She's a perfect target for brainwashing. A malleable, privileged kid. If she'd been kidnapped by Martians, she'd have become a Martian."

"You never know what you're capable of until you are tested," Harry said, almost to himself. "People did things during the war they never thought they would do. Things they'd rather not remember." This time Harry looked to Molly for agreement.

But she didn't respond.

Molly was sitting on a side chair, a magazine resting on her lap, rubbing her hands as if she were massaging in hand cream, and periodically looked at her wristwatch.

"Is it time for Dad's medicine?" Hannah asked after she noticed her mother checking her watch for the fourth time.

"No. Why do you ask?" Molly's response was guarded.

"You seemed to be watching the time," Hannah replied.

"A nervous habit." Molly forced her cheeks into a half smile.

"No reason why you can't go play bridge," Harry said. "Hannah's here. I'll be fine."

Having Harry's permission, Molly sprang up. This time a genuine smile lit up her face. Hannah was right. He is different now that we're in New York, Molly thought. Within five minutes she had changed her clothes, put on some lipstick and was gone.

"So what are we going to do?" Hannah asked. "It's too late to watch *Meet the Press* or *Face the Nation*, but there might be a movie on TV," she offered, and reached for the TV listings in the paper. "If you're up to it, we could go for a walk in the park. It's really a beautiful day."

Harry shook his head. "No. Let's sit here and talk." He put down the paper and patted the cushion next to him. "Come sit here."

Hannah sank into the soft down of the sofa, but she felt her anxiety level rising. She hoped her father was not bracing for another tour down memory lane.

"What should we talk about?" Hannah asked with trepidation.

"I'm glad we can have this talk, just the two of us!" Harry stroked Hannah's hand.

Every muscle in Hannah's body tightened.

Oblivious to her discomfort, Harry continued. "I know what I'm about to tell you will come as a shock. But . . ."

"Stop! Please," Hannah insisted. She didn't want to kill the new good feelings between them, nor did she want to hear what her father was about to tell her. She wasn't going to allow herself to be pulled into this quagmire no matter who was doing the pulling.

"It's between you and Mother, I don't want to get in the middle of this!" She could not suppress a hint of anger in her voice.

Harry was mystified. "What are you talking about?"

"Look. I know. That's all I'm going to say," Hannah answered cryptically.

"Really? Your mother talked to you about this?" Harry seemed surprised.

"Yes!" Hannah said forcefully. "Can't we talk about something else, please?"

But Harry wouldn't be stopped. "You should have really said something. We could have talked about it."

"I don't want to talk about it. It's none of my damn business!" Hannah insisted.

"How could that be? Exactly what did your mother tell you?"

"You just won't stop, will you? Okay. You win. She told me about your girlfriend in medical school. And I don't want to hear any more about her!" Hannah stood her ground.

Harry started laughing. "You think I want to talk to you about a girlfriend?"

"I can put two and two together. I can figure things out," Hannah said. "You want to talk to me about Lena. Right? Wasn't she your girlfriend?"

"Yes. I want to talk to you about Lena." Harry was relieved that at last he had said Lena's name out loud. "But no! She was not my girlfriend."

Hannah was surprised but now curious. "If she was not your girlfriend, who is she?"

Harry took a frayed photograph out of his wallet and handed it to Hannah.

"Oh, my God!" she cried out once she focused on the faded

image of two little girls. Hannah immediately recognized herself as the child with dark hair. But the other one, a curly-haired blonde, she only knew as someone who for years had haunted her dreams.

For a moment she was speechless.

"That's Lena?" Hannah finally asked, pointing to the blonde child in the photo.

Harry nodded. He seemed to be having trouble breathing.

Hannah still looked puzzled.

"Do you remember her?" Harry asked.

"I dream about her. Who is she?"

"Your sister! She's your sister."

"My what?"

"Your older sister!"

"Oh my God! She's my sister! She's my sister!" Hannah kept repeating. "My dream was real. I had a sister and I lost her!"

Stunned and angry in equal proportion, Hannah watched Harry's mouth moving, but his words receded into the background. Barely aware of his presence, she thought about the many plausible interpretations of her dream offered by Dr. Kahn. She wanted to scream at the good doctor, "My dream was a memory not a metaphor. Not a symbol. It was the simple truth. I had a sister and then she disappeared!"

Harry reached for Hannah. He wanted to comfort her, and himself as well, but she stood up out of his reach, and paced around the room. Harry's words were overshadowed by the thoughts spinning around in her head. Why don't I remember her? Why didn't I recognize her in my dream? How could I forget my own sister? I thought I remembered everything. Why did they keep Lena a secret?

"Where is she? Where is Lena?" Hannah finally asked out loud. "Did I hurt her?" she asked, solemnly.

"Of course you didn't!" Harry said, shocked by Hannah's question.

"Tell me what happened to Lena," she demanded, and distanced herself at the opposite end of the sofa.

"Remember the day we sent you away, Mother dressed you in our bedroom instead of yours?"

Hannah nodded.

"That was because Lena was asleep in the next bed and we didn't want to wake her," Harry started to explain. "She'd been on a farm for a month recuperating from a bad case of whooping cough."

"I don't remember that," Hannah said under her breath. "After you sent me away, did Lena notice I was gone?" she asked.

"Of course! She looked for you when she woke up. We told her you were visiting friends in Kielce."

"Why did I go to Kielce, not Lena?"

"The couple chose you. You were healthier and younger. They thought you'd accept them as your parents more quickly."

Hannah rolled her eyes, remembering how relieved they were to be rid of her when Ela came to take her back.

"What happened to Lena? Where is she?" Hannah asked again.

Harry could barely speak. "We decided to send her to an orphanage outside of Radom, run by the Grey Ursuline Sisters. I figured, if we survived the war, we knew exactly where to go to get her back. Once she was completely well, I managed to get fake travel permits and took her to the nuns myself. On the train I explained the reason for our trip."

* * *

In an empty compartment he felt free to talk without being overheard.

"You know there's a war on?" he began. Lena nodded, her lips pursed, her blue eyes open wide. He kissed the top of her head.

"I am taking you someplace very special where there are other children for you to play with. You will be safe there. We are sending you away to protect you, because we love you so much," he continued.

Lena tried to understand.

"But you cannot tell anyone anything about your life before today. Nobody can know that I am your father. That has to be a secret."

Four-year-old Lena was puzzled by what she was hearing but she knew she could keep a secret if her father wanted her to.

"Do you understand what I am telling you?"

Lena shrugged. When he hugged her she tried to smile, and wrapped her small hand around his thumb.

"I know your mother and I taught you not to lie. So I want you to hide all your memories deep in your mind where nobody will know about them. Just for a while forget about us. I promise I will come back to get you once it is safe."

*   *   *

As he told Hannah about their train ride, Harry relived every agonizing moment. Occasionally, he paused to wipe his glasses that were fogged up by his tears.

"I wasn't sure she understood my explanation but little Lena was such an obedient child, I was confident she would do what I told her. When we sent you to Kielce we didn't know how you would take it." Harry sighed and moved closer to Hannah. As he reached out to touch her, she jumped up again and started pacing. He followed her with his eyes as he continued his painful story.

"Lena held my thumb so tightly it nearly went numb. At the convent, I told the Mother Superior she was the daughter of one of my patients. That before the mother had died, she made me promise to find a home for her child, until her husband, who was in the Underground, made other arrangements. I made up the part about the father being in the Underground. I was carefully laying the groundwork for getting Lena back. I thought I'd made it clear I was arranging for the nuns to care for Lena until someone from her family came to get her. I thought my scheme was foolproof. I never told the Mother Superior Lena was Jewish. She never asked. If she had wanted some documents, like a birth certificate, I could have gotten a false one and sent it to her. But Lena's blonde hair and blue eyes were enough for her to pass easily as a Gentile child. I was sure I'd thought of everything!" Harry winced at his own hubris. "I even gave the Mother Superior a box with some money and a few family mementos, as a way to identify Lena later when we came back for her. I had promised her I'd be back. I'm sure Lena believed me," he said, almost talking to himself.

She could see her father was in pain, but Hannah was not

interested in comforting him. She said nothing. Stone-faced, she sat down again at the far end of the sofa, and turned Harry's words into pictures in her head. Hannah thought about the years of pain that dream had wrought.

Harry paused only to catch his breath. He continued filling the silence, hoping to make Hannah grasp the extent of his agony.

"Your mother and I used to say that Lena was so eager to please she would follow anyone who took her hand. The last time I saw my little Lena one of the young Sisters was leading her into the garden to join the other children. Lena looked back at me and waved goodbye. I relive that moment every single day of my life." Harry's tears fell unabated.

"All this time, I've wondered what Lena remembered of her first four years. I hoped she could forgive me for abandoning her," Harry whispered.

Suddenly Hannah yelled, "You abandoned her? You didn't go back after the war to get her as you had promised?"

"Of course I went back. But she wasn't there." Harry said, almost inaudibly.

"What do you mean she wasn't there? Where was she?" With each question her voice grew more strident.

"I don't know."

"You went to the orphanage and there was no Lena?"

"That's right. I went back but she wasn't there," Harry repeated and sighed. He groped for the right words to make Hannah understand what happened. "Remember when I found you in Koslow, after the Russians came?"

Hannah remembered that day vividly.

* * *

The war was supposedly over. The Germans were gone. Still the deception continued. No one suspected Zofia Nowakowska and Marta Wilakowa were Jews. Only Aunt Emma, an authentic Christian, was who she really was. They were viewed as Polish heroines, having been banished from Warsaw by the Germans.

The sunlight streaming in through the window gave the farmhouse kitchen an amber glow. When he came through the back door, she thought he was a mirage. She dropped the dish she was wiping as their eyes met. Throwing herself at him, she was careful not to call him Tata. She remembered. Nobody was to know he was her father.

* * *

The deep lines around Harry's mouth stretched into a smile as he thought about the day he walked in on them in Koslow. "Luck was with me then," he said. "For three weeks I searched for you. I walked from town to town, where the Germans had relocated the women and children from Warsaw. I kept asking if anyone had seen an old woman named Emma with a young child. I didn't know if your mother would be with you. Think how lucky it was that Tuesday, the day the Uprising started, was her day off. It's why you were together. And I found you both. Luck was with me then," he said, his voice cracking.

Hannah closed her eyes and pictured that warm August afternoon in Warsaw.

* * *

Completely by chance both her parents had been visiting that day. She was very happy! After a lunch of kopytka *and compote at Aunt Emma's apartment, the four of them strolled along the promenade by the Wisła River. She was happy because they were together. It didn't matter to her that her left hand was holding onto Bronisław Bieliński and her right onto Aunt Marta.*

There seemed to be an unusual number of beggars asleep on the sidewalk. One of the bedraggled men motioned them over, but instead of asking for money he whispered, "Get off the street!" Realizing these men were part of the Polish Underground and that the rumored Uprising was about to start, Harry instructed the three of them to return to Emma's apartment and stay together. Then he ran off.

* * *

"After I found you, I thought getting Lena back would be even easier. I expected to see the Mother Superior at the orphanage and tell her that Lena's father had been killed and now her aunt, her dead mother's sister, was ready to raise her niece. I suspected it might take some time to actually get her back, so we moved to Radom to be close to the orphanage." Harry stopped talking briefly. He needed to weigh his words carefully so that Hannah would know exactly what happened that frigid January day in 1945.

On the sofa, Hannah remained expressionless, and listened.

"Any other cold day, with the same freezing temperature, I would have been shivering. But as I trudged through the frozen snow on the way to the convent, I didn't even feel cold. The anticipation of seeing Lena kept me warm. As soon as I saw the iron gate off in the distance, I quickened my pace." As Harry paused to wipe his fogged-up glasses, he managed a weak smile recalling how happy he was as he approached the convent.

"My heart was racing at the thought of seeing Lena in a matter of minutes. The young nun who greeted me at the gate led me to the Mother Superior's office. I smiled remembering the sound Lena and I had made walking these same glistening hardwood floors years before. Once I was inside the office, rather than the kindly Mother Superior I'd met years before, a much younger woman with a stern expression sat behind the desk. Seeing this stranger unnerved me. I told her I was there to see the Mother Superior. She assured me that she, Sister Marianna, was the new Mother Superior, and told me to take a seat. I sat down, clutching the arms of the chair to steady myself and I told her, 'I've come to get Lena!' I made it clear to this new Mother Superior that her predecessor had understood I had only brought Lena to the orphanage temporarily, until someone in her family could care for her. Her aunt was now ready and able to do that, I explained, since Lena's father had been killed in the war. When I finished, I relaxed a little. They had to give Lena back to her family. And Sister Marianna was now smiling. She didn't seem as stern as she had when I entered her office. I expected to be told how many days it would take before Lena was returned to her aunt. Instead Sister Marianna announced, 'I'm sorry, Lena is not here! There are no children here and have not been for many years.'"

Harry reached out to touch Hannah's hand. "You cannot imagine the shock I felt hearing those words," he whispered, and closed his eyes.

Noting the anguished look on her father's face, Hannah did not recoil from his touch.

"I was stunned. I thought about the last time I saw Lena, her sad little face framed by her cascading blonde curls. All I could think of was that I had come back for her as I had promised, and *she* wasn't there. 'Where is she?' I asked, barely able to get the words out. Sister Marianna insisted she didn't know. She said all the children had been moved before she got there, and the orphanage records had been destroyed in a fire. She assured me Lena would have been placed with a fine family. That was of no comfort to me. As she was ushering me out, Sister Marianna offered me a promise to try to find out what happened to Lena. I gave her our address in Radom and asked her in the name of the family to try her hardest."

Harry felt his voice getting hoarse. He stopped his monologue to take a sip of tea. But there was more to his story he was desperate to share with Hannah.

"Sister Marianna seemed sincere but as the gate shut behind me, I decided I had to talk to somebody other than the nuns. I had to be absolutely sure that Lena really was no longer inside. I waited across the street in the freezing cold, the howling wind blowing snow in my face, and watched. By five o'clock when a man wearing overalls and a warm sheepskin coat came out, I decided he could tell me what was actually going on in the convent. I followed him into a nearby tavern. After gulping down several drinks, I gained enough courage to approach him."

* * *

"I don't like to drink alone. Can I buy you a vodka?" he asked the stranger.

"I can sure use another drink in this bitter cold," the man gratefully accepted.

After many shots, when the two new drinking buddies had their arms around each other, he finally asked his question.

"How many children are there at the convent these days, Jerzy?"

"No children. Only nuns. Not an orphanage anymore. Hasn't been for years. Not since I started in '43," Jerzy said.

Hearing that, he realized that if Sister Marianna did not provide him with further information, he had no way of knowing where to start looking for Lena.

That night for the first time since his college days, he got so drunk he nearly froze to death when he fell asleep on a bench outside the train station. The next morning a porter woke him up and put him on the train to Radom.

*   *   *

"All during the war I was comforted knowing that she was safe in the orphanage. I had outwitted the Nazis, but if the nuns did not know where Lena was, how could I find her?" Harry said softly.

"But Sister Marianna did promise to find out what happened to Lena," Hannah said.

"Yes. She said she would do her best. But did she care about reuniting Lena with her aunt? All I could hope for was that she did actually try to find out what happened to Lena and let me know. I couldn't tell the Mother Superior the truth. I couldn't tell her that Lena was my daughter. That I'd brought her to the orphanage to keep her safe because we were Jewish. The Russians liberated Poland from the Germans, but the end of the war did not mean an end to anti-Semitism. It was still open season on Jews in Poland in 1945."

Hannah remembered.

*   *   *

They never went back to their old life in Krakow. There were rumors going around that some Jews who returned from the camps or from hiding were not welcomed back, some even killed. It was decided that it was safer to remain in Radom living as the Bieliński family.

With Emma part of the family, the four settled into a large but partially bombed-out apartment. Many of its windows were boarded up, and some rooms with collapsed walls were sealed off, but the plumbing and heating worked. One of the rooms was turned into an office. Dr. Bronisław Bieliński started seeing patients immediately. Because payment was often eggs, chickens, and bread, they had plenty to eat. Money was scarce.

* * *

"What about Lena?" Hannah demanded.

"What could I do? I waited and hoped Sister Marianna would locate her. I couldn't force her. I had no proof that I had brought Lena to the convent in the first place."

Hannah shook her head in disbelief. "You just gave up!" she said contemptuously. In spite of their disagreements, Hannah always saw her father as a fighter. His defeatist attitude shocked her.

"When I got back to Radom and told your mother the bad news she almost lost her mind. She wanted to go directly to the Archbishop! The Pope! What a joke! We'd have to tell him why we left Lena with the nuns. The Holy Father wasn't much help to the Jews against Hitler. I was sure the Church was satisfied knowing Lena was being raised as a good Catholic. She didn't need to be found and returned to a Jewish family. It was a very bad time for us. You probably don't remember. . . ."

Hannah remembered.

* * *

Life in Radom had a veneer of normalcy. Once again as exiles from Warsaw, they were treated as heroes by their neighbors. Zosia started attending a Catholic school. She adored the nuns who taught her. Fully aware that the girls who vied to sit next to her in class might not want to play with her if they knew she was really Hannah Stein, Zosia continued to keep the family secret.

Now reunited, the Bieliński household was not a happy one. While her mother always looked as if she were about to burst into tears or had just stopped crying, her father, when he wasn't seeing patients, seemed to be angry with everyone, but especially with his daughter.

"Why are you always listening at keyholes?" he'd yell if he opened a door and found her standing there. His scowl frightened her. Even when she didn't know what she'd done to displease him, she always said, "I'm sorry." Fortunately, her mother showered her with affection, so she shadowed her wherever she went.

On their first outing, as the front door to the apartment building slammed behind them, Hannah asked, "Where are we going, Mommy?"

"It's such a beautiful day, we'll go to the square and walk around," her mother said cheerfully, and she squeezed her gloved hand.

They were both bundled up for their outdoor trek. Although the bright sun glistened over the snow, it was bitter cold. As they strolled, she playfully jumped over mounds of snow and laughed when her breath formed circles on meeting the cold air. No matter the temperature, Hannah was happy holding her mother's hand. When her mother abruptly let go, she stood frozen. Bewildered, she watched her mother approach a little blonde girl a few feet away, sucking a lollipop.

Crouched down to be eye level with the child, she said, "You're such a pretty girl. My name is Marta, what's yours?"

Frightened, the child grabbed her mother's skirt and Marta quickly stood up to face an unsmiling mother.

"You have a lovely daughter," she said, hoping to pierce the woman's icy stare.

"Thank you," she said curtly.

Once Marta said, "This is my daughter Zosia. What's your daughter's name?" both Hannah and the child's mother were visibly relieved.

"Maja," the woman answered, more amenable now, seeing this stranger was a mother herself.

"Maja is a big girl. How old is she?" Marta asked.

"She just turned five. Yes, she is big for her age. She takes after her father!"

They moved on once it was clear that the girl was younger than Zosia.

That scene was repeated countless times whenever the two ventured out. Although puzzled by her mother's attempt to engage every blonde girl she saw, Hannah was careful not to make any critical comments. She didn't want her mother to be angry with her, too. Hannah convinced herself her mother was merely searching for suitable playmates for her.

* * *

"I felt there was something strange about our life in Radom . . . besides still pretending we were Gentiles." Hannah said. "Mother cried a lot and you frowned whenever you looked at me. I thought you were either going to hit me or send me away again."

"Why would you think that?" Harry asked, shocked.

"You seemed angry whenever you saw me, you never hugged me. Mother and you were always whispering and stopped talking if I was nearby. You spoke German so I wouldn't understand." Hannah chuckled. "That's why I learned German. I had to know if you were plotting to send me away again."

"Oh, my God! Sending you away was the last thing in the world I wanted. I wanted us to be together and happy."

"That's a laugh!" Hannah could feel her nostrils flaring the way Harry's did during their frequent shouting matches. "I was sure I had done something wrong. Just couldn't figure out what," she said almost to herself.

"I'm sorry, Hannah. So sorry. I'm the one who did something wrong." Harry's voice was quivering. "I didn't get Lena back. Your mother expected me to pull off a miracle. I was fresh out of miracles."

"Did you at least go back to the convent?" she asked coldly.

"No. What good would that have done?"

"Maybe if you'd gone back, the nuns would have tried harder to find Lena. Maybe they thought the aunt didn't care that much? How could you have given up so easily?" Her voice grew louder with each question.

The louder Hannah shouted the quieter was Harry's response.

"You don't understand how difficult it was."

"I do! I was there! I would not have given up so easily!" she insisted.

Lamely, he tried to defend himself against her accusation. "You were a child, the country was in chaos. We were helpless. Who could we appeal to? The government the Soviets installed in Lublin was not functioning. Where could we possibly start looking for a child who was now part of someone else's family? We had no trail to follow without Sister Marianna's help. We had no proof she was our child. Sometimes giving up is all you can do," Harry said softly, and closed his eyes.

Hannah kept shaking her head. Her father's passivity was unacceptable to her. And at odds with her long-held view of her father as the family protector in spite of their troubled relationship.

After a brief pause Harry tried again to describe their

predicament. "Lena was not the only one we were trying to find. There was your Uncle Leo and his wife, and other relatives who were hidden in Warsaw. The big question was what happened to my father and . . ." Harry's mouth felt dry. He gulped down what was left of his cold tea.

"Do you remember the train trip you and your mother took to Krakow?"

Hannah nodded.

* * *

She had begged her father to let her go with her mother. On the train her only thoughts were about Grandma Sonia. She bypassed the Black Madonna, her designated patron saint, and spoke directly to God. Over and over she pleaded: "Please, please let Grandma Sonia be alive!" In her childish mind it seemed possible that her prayers could make that happen. She was sure her prayers had kept her father alive during the war, when everyone else thought he was dead.

As they got off the train in Krakow, her mother ordered, "Hold my hand, and don't say anything to anyone." Hannah obeyed, until they were outside the Landau Bookstore. Then she let go of her mother's hand and ran inside. The familiar smell of new pencils welcomed her. She smiled as she headed to the counter where Sonia usually stood, fully expecting to find her grandmother there.

"Stop running!" she heard a man shout. "This is a store, not a play-ground for children!"

She ignored him. Nothing was going to keep her from her grandma. Tackled by the man, she felt his fingers dig into her shoulders.

"Where do you think you're going, young lady?" he yelled.

"I'm looking for my grandparents!" she answered. The man loosened his grip and she ran behind the counter. He chased after her. This time when he caught her, he held on even tighter.

"I'm looking for my grandmother," she yelled at him.

"If you mean Sonia Landau, she's dead," he said coldly. "This is my store now!"

Hearing that, she ran crying into her mother's arms. "I want to go back to Radom."

"We can't go yet," her mother said, and tenderly stroked her hair until her sobbing stopped.

Their next stop was the house where they used to live. Hannah did not want to go inside. Her mother had to push her through the front door. While Molly went into the parlor with the woman who now lived there, Hannah remained in the hall next to the front door and closed her eyes. Suddenly a girl about her size stood in front of her. With her hands pressing her shoulders, she pinned Hannah to the wall and shouted, "You can't come back here. This isn't your home anymore! It's mine! It's mine now!"

Hannah threw the girl's arms off and put her small hands around her throat.

The two mothers pulled them apart.

* * *

"It was devastating when Mother learned that my father and her parents were definitely dead. We couldn't even find out what happened to their bodies," Harry said in a whisper. "I should have forced them to leave and go into hiding . . . they might have survived instead of being herded into the street and shot. Ela told mother they were killed soon after I took the train to Warsaw." A profound sadness overpowered him as he recalled his risky exit. "Luck was on my side then."

* * *

As soon as he had his false papers Hershel Stein set about transforming himself into Dr. Bronisław Bieliński. Over several weeks he grew a mustache, which he meticulously trimmed each morning until it was the pencil-thin shape he desired. He bought an expensive leather attaché case for his medical tools and had the initials BB embossed on the front flap. He purchased a fedora to coordinate with his camelhair overcoat. Although he was anxious, Harry was eager to start his journey to Warsaw.

Medical bag in hand, Dr. Bronisław Bieliński walked out of the Jewish Quarter under the cover of darkness and made his way to the main railway station just as a train was pulling in. He saw two Gestapo officers standing on the platform. His shirt collar was wet with perspiration, but he took a deep breath and headed toward the train. When he reached the officers, he tipped his hat and said, "Good Morning," in crisp German. Both officers clicked their heels and let him board without even asking to see his papers.

* * *

Silent. Seemingly unmoved, Hannah remained at the opposite end of the sofa and listened.

"With no word from Sister Marianna, I believed we would never get our Lena back. We had to start a new life. I wanted us to go to America where my brothers were. But your mother could not give up hope of finding Lena. She insisted Lena was nearby. She could feel it. Mother prayed. Once I believed our Lena was lost, it was no longer possible for me to pray. By the end of April, it was clear there was no future for us in Poland. Owning up to who we really were was not a safe option. It was so difficult to live that lie, laughing at anti-Semitic jokes so no one could suspect we were Jewish. Your mother finally agreed to leave Poland when we found out that her brother and his wife were dead. They were hidden in the last building in Warsaw the Germans torched. No one survived that inferno." Harry wiped his eyes. He glanced at Hannah, who refused to look at him. Yet she seemed to be listening. Harry hoped his words were making her understand their dreadful dilemma.

"Leaving Lena behind was horrific, but we needed a safe haven for the family that was left," he said. In a halting voice he asked, "Do you remember how difficult it was for us to leave Poland?"

Hannah felt her body stiffen as she remembered.

* * *

The Russians had sealed the borders. Only people who had to be repatriated were permitted to leave the country. Once again her father had arranged for a set of false identity papers. They were to be Hungarian refugees trying to get home. Back in full war mode, this time they were protecting themselves against the Russians.

Old and frail, Emma refused to go with them. She wanted to be buried next to her husband. Harry took her to stay with a distant cousin in Lodz.

Hannah was overjoyed that Emma had decided to remain in Poland. In Radom, Emma was more attentive toward her, but Hannah was sure it was only because her parents were watching. Teaching her to tell time on the old mahogany clock did not make up for the hundreds of terrifying hours she had spent waiting alone in Warsaw until Emma came home.

They sold most of their possessions except for a few things Grandma Sonia had left with Ela: her silver candlesticks, a tablecloth she'd embroidered, her silk shawl, and some random pieces of silver. Her father converted the money from the sale into gold coins.

They left Radom by train and crossed into Czechoslovakia in the middle of the night. On the train Harry thrust the coins into her hand. "Put them in your mouth." Startled, she obeyed. When the train stopped in Bratislava, a Russian guard approached Hannah and, smiling, led her away from her parents. She was terrified. When the guard offered her candy, she refused. She kept her lips tightly closed and the gold coins safe.

Still smiling, the guard said in Russian, "You're a nice little girl. I have a daughter your age in Moscow."

Hannah could hear her heart pounding.

"Govarish po Russki?" he asked, pointing to his mouth.

As she'd been coached, Hannah pretended not to understand. She was supposed to be Hungarian, not someone who could speak Russian.

Actually the Russian soldiers who liberated them in Koslow had taught Hannah Russian. Billeted in the barn while she, her mother and Emma lived in the farmhouse, they seemed less menacing than the German officers who terrified her. Still she kept an eye on them, determined to figure out what they were plotting.

"Govarish po Russki?" one asked the first day she brought them food. She shook her head.

"I teach you!" he said in Polish and grinned.

Hannah's head bobbed up and down. And her Russian lessons began! Most Poles were not so friendly with their Russian liberators.

* * *

Once the Russian border guard was satisfied she was Hungarian as her identity papers indicated, he brought her back to her parents, and the three of them were allowed to re-board the train. They were careful *not to speak Polish onboard until they found an empty compartment and settled in. Then Harry told Hannah to spit out the gold coins, which he put in the money belt strapped around his waist. Though her father never complimented her for a job well done, Hannah was happy just to have the coins out of her care.*

"Go to sleep," her mother said as the train clanked south. Wrapped in the down quilt they had brought along to keep her warm, Hannah quickly fell asleep with her head in her mother's lap, and dreamed of the courtyard for the first time. Her own screams of "No! No!" woke her up.

"It's only a dream. It can't hurt you," her mother reassured Hannah. Exhausted, she fell asleep without ever describing her dream.

After two weeks of staying in safe houses in Czechoslovakia and Hungary, they finally arrived in Frankfurt, Germany, in the American sector. Off the train, her father surprised Hannah when he scooped her up in his arms, and spun her around. "We are very lucky. We survived the war, and we're still a family. We must be very happy from now on," he said. Sadly, there was no joy in his voice.

* * *

"After all these years, why did you finally decide to tell me about Lena?" Hannah demanded.

"You're a reporter. If anyone can find out what happened to Lena, you can."

"What?" she shouted. Hannah was almost as shocked by his answer as she was to learn she had a missing sister.

"Hannah, you're like me," Harry said. "Or rather, the way I used to be. You can do anything."

She glared at her father. Still unaccustomed to hearing such praise from him, at this point Hannah didn't much like the comparison.

"Before I die I want Lena to know that I came back just as I promised," Harry said. "I need her to forgive me for leaving Poland without her."

"That's just great! You expect me to fix something you screwed up years ago? You expect me to find her? After all this time?"

"Yes. You're the only one who can do it."

"So the only reason you're finally telling me about Lena is because you want her to forgive you."

"We wanted to tell you many times. But decided to spare you."

"Spare me! What did you spare me besides love and affection, Dad?" Hannah's rage was boiling over.

"Don't be angry. Try to understand," Harry pleaded. "It wasn't easy for me. Every time I looked at you I saw little Lena waving goodbye to me at the convent. I didn't mean to shut you out. But holding you at bay somehow made not having Lena with us bearable."

"I understand perfectly. You abandoned both of your daughters, just in different ways," Hannah answered coldly. "I was the only child left. You should have loved me even more!" she screamed.

"I always loved you. I just couldn't show it."

Harry closed his eyes, and whispered, "I did the best I could. I'm so sorry I hurt you!"

He could never forgive himself for his failure to get Lena back. But now he was desperate to undo the damage between Hannah and himself, which he'd caused.

"I couldn't hold you close because I couldn't hold her, " Harry said softly, his voice a stark contrast to Hannah's shouts.

"You punished me for something you did!"

"I punished us both. I saved you and not her."

"Remember when I told you I never asked to be saved, and you slapped me?" Hannah shot back, her body rigid, her nails almost drawing blood in her clenched fists.

"It was a reflex. I didn't mean to slap you. It hurt so much to hear you say such a thing to me. All I ever wanted was for us to be a loving family."

"Great! Wanting it is not the same as making it happen, is it? Your defense is you couldn't be a loving father to me because you failed to get Lena back?" Hannah mouthed each word carefully, in the same dreaded tone her father had used to admonish her over the years.

"Forgive me, Hannah. Please. Please," Harry begged. "I wish I could go back and change everything." His breathing labored, Harry could barely speak. "I am . . . so sorry that Lena . . . was always between you and me . . . that I never told you how proud I was to be your father."

But Harry's *mea culpa* did not lessen Hannah's anger.

"All those years wasted! If she is alive, Lena never benefited from my pain or your guilt!" Hannah yelled at her father.

"What's going on here?" Molly shouted as she walked into the living room.

Without realizing it, Harry and Hannah were both standing and from Molly's perspective it looked as if they were locked in physical battle. She stepped between them, and made Harry sit back on the sofa.

The blood had drained from his face.

"He's having one of his fibrillation attacks! Get some water and the pills on the dresser," Molly ordered.

CHAPTER

5

"HOW IS HE?" Hannah asked as Molly came out of the bedroom. Her own voice sounded raspy and unfamiliar.

Hannah had been pacing around the apartment like a caged animal looking for an escape hatch. She wanted to run, but had to make sure Harry was not dying.

"It'll take time for the medicine to take effect. But I think he'll be okay," Molly said solemnly.

"Good. I've got to get out of here." Hannah reached for her bag and field jacket.

"Don't go!" Molly said and planted herself in front of the apartment door.

"I don't want to fight with you, Mom." Hannah shook her head. "I need to be by myself."

Molly didn't budge.

"Mom, get out of my way! I mean it. I'm too mad. I can't stay here another minute!"

"Does being mad solve anything?"

"Maybe not, but at least it's an honest feeling. Until now, I've been living a lie. We all have."

Molly tried to embrace her daughter.

Hannah put her two hands in front of her, keeping her mother at bay.

"Why didn't you tell me the truth, Mom? Instead of telling me not to fight with Dad? Why didn't you tell me what the fights were really about?"

"I wanted to tell you but I couldn't. We decided it would be better for you not to know."

"We decided or Dad decided?"

Molly cast her eyes down to avoid her daughter's angry stare. She was relieved their secret was finally out. That secret had caused so much damage between Harry and Hannah. Many times Molly had considered telling Hannah everything. But long ago Harry convinced her that if Hannah knew it would only make matters worse.

"It's not always easy to know what to do," Molly said. "We thought we were protecting you. That it was best to say nothing about Lena."

"Best for whom? You were protecting Dad's image. You were never protecting me. It was always about him. You didn't want me to know that my father was the kind of man who would leave Poland without his child!" Hannah's tone was bitter.

Once she realized she couldn't temper Hannah's anger, Molly stepped aside and let her daughter leave. Let it all sink in, she thought. There was time to talk about this later.

As the elevator hit the lobby, Hannah rushed out. She zigzagged around the children playing in the courtyard, but once out on the street, Hannah slowed down and was jostled on either side by parents wheeling strollers two abreast along 86th Street heading east toward Central Park. They were chatting, enjoying the warm, sunny May afternoon while anger oozed out of Hannah's every pore. Tears streaming down her face, she searched for memories of Lena.

But all she had was the dream. Was I so jealous of her that I erased her from my memory? What were we like as sisters? She wondered. Hannah couldn't trust her parents to provide the answers.

She needed to talk to someone who would tell her the truth. Hannah decided to start with her cousins, Leah and Helena. She searched for a public phone along Central Park. After running for twenty blocks in her high-heeled platforms, a huge tote slung around her shoulders, Hannah was out of breath and about to give up her search when she reached the Mayflower Hotel at 62nd Street. Inside the hotel lobby, she found a phone booth and called her cousin Helena in Queens. Hannah let the phone ring and ring and ring before finally hanging up.

"Why don't people have answering machines?" she muttered angrily to herself. Her displeasure was pointless. Whether Helena had an answering machine or not was immaterial. Hannah's aversion to talking into a mechanical device would have prevented her from leaving a message. Frustrated, she decided to try Helena's sister Leah in California.

Hannah didn't have enough change for a long-distance call and wasn't about to call her cousin collect after passing up her daughter's UCLA graduation last June. She rummaged through her tote for her rarely used AT&T phone card and dialed, after she got Leah's number from information.

Hannah checked her watch. It was only 11:30 California time. Hope it's not too early to call, she thought. Hannah knew Leah would most likely still be sleeping. She and her husband owned a bowling alley in Torrance that stayed open late on Saturday night.

The phone rang almost ten times before a sleepy female voice came on.

"Haaloo," Leah said in her deep voice that was often mistaken for a man's.

"Sorry for waking you up, Leah," Hannah apologized.

"Who is this?' Leah sounded annoyed.

"It's Hannah."

"Hannah! Has something happened to your father?"

"No, nothing like that. But it is about my father."

"What about him?"

As she blurted out what she'd learned about Lena, Hannah was crying so hard, her cousin could barely understand what she was saying.

"Calm down, please, Hannah. What can I tell you? You really know everything already. You once had a sister, and Hitler took her away."

"Please, please, tell me what she was like! Tell me how I used to play with her. Did we like each other? Tell me why I forgot all about her!"

"Oh, Hannah. You poor child. Don't beat yourself up because you forgot Lena. You were just a baby. Did your father tell you how sick Lena was? That they sent her to stay on a farm because the air was better," Leah said.

"He told me. But that was only for a month. What about before? I don't even remember playing with her. What was she like?" Hannah asked.

"You want to know what Lena was like?"

Hannah could almost hear a smile in her cousin's voice.

"She was a doll. Always happy. You were younger but Lena did whatever you wanted. She always let you be the boss."

"Why didn't anyone tell me about her? I can understand not telling me when I was a child. But later?"

"It was not a subject your father could talk about. He never forgave himself for leaving Poland without her."

"Why didn't he try to find out what happened to her once we left Poland? The American authorities would have helped, wouldn't they?"

"When we crossed into the American zone, we filled out papers. Your father never listed Lena as a daughter he left. He was ashamed. Later he was afraid if he admitted he lied he wouldn't be allowed to come to America. Do you understand? Things were not as simple as you think."

"They're not so simple now either. My father thinks I can find Lena after all these years. After he muffed the job, he's sticking me with it. Thirty-one years later he expects me to find Lena!"

"I'm sure it's more a wish than an expectation, Hannah. If anything, he just wants you to try. He loved her very much. Not getting her back almost killed him. Your father has carried a very big weight on his heart all these years."

"He made me carry a lot of it."

"What are you talking about?"

"Nothing. Just babbling. How is Marvin? And Jennifer? I'm sorry I didn't make it to her graduation."

"That's okay. We didn't expect anyone but my sister to come. We're fine. Graduation seems so long ago. Jennifer moved in with some friends in Santa Monica a few months ago. We haven't seen very much of her since."

"But she's okay, right?"

"We hope she hasn't turned into a hippie."

"Do you think her roommates are druggies?"

"Jenny says no. But we're parents, we always think the worst."

Hannah actually laughed and promised her cousin to keep in touch.

Hearing someone else's perspective made her calmer. Outside the hotel it was still a beautiful sunny afternoon. She decided to walk to clear her head. As she strolled along Broadway, no longer out of step with everyone around her, Hannah remembered how the bright lights and the circus-like atmosphere of Times Square had made her spirits soar when she was a child. But this day Times Square and all its action did not cheer her. Hannah hailed a cab home.

She ignored the flashing red light on her answering machine when she walked into her apartment. Hannah dropped her tote by the door, kicked off her shoes and headed straight for the bedroom. Lying on her bed, she mindlessly watched the abstract images on the ceiling as the afternoon sun flickered through the blinds. In a few minutes she was in a deep sleep.

Her mother's voice, yelling into the answering machine, woke her.

"Hannah, if you're there please pick up! I've been calling you and calling you. Where are you? Hannah, please call. Please come back. Your father needs you."

Hannah almost reached for the extension next to her bed, but stopped herself.

"My father needs me. Isn't that great? Where was he all these years when I needed him? Tell me that, Mom. I've been the obedient daughter long enough. Running whenever you call. I'll come back, if and when I feel like it. Right now, I don't feel like it," Hannah shouted. Hearing herself addressing the machine made Hannah break out laughing. "I've finally flipped out!"

She didn't pick up the phone, but now fully awake, Hannah leaned against her upholstered headboard and started to re-examine her rollercoaster day. She struggled to understand the mixed emotions she was experiencing. Why am I not as angry with Mother? She had kept the same secret. She'd left Lena in Poland, too. But Hannah realized she never felt abandoned by Molly. Annoyed yes. Never abandoned. If anything, her mother wanted to be too close. The more Hannah analyzed her feelings, the clearer it became that her overwhelming rage toward Harry was not due to his keeping Lena a secret, or for leaving her sister in Poland. Hannah was furious with Harry for all the years he'd cut himself off from her. Once she realized that her anger toward her father totally crowded out any sense of loss of Lena, Hannah felt ashamed. She was my sister and I never missed her!

Time away from her parents brought some clarity, enough so that she realized she could not avoid dealing with them. She checked her watch. It was nine o'clock. Still she decided to go back uptown.

"Oh, I'm so glad you're here! Thank you. Thank you for coming back," Molly said when she opened the door.

Hannah sighed and without saying a word walked past her mother into the kitchen. She started to boil some water and selected an herbal tea bag from Molly's collection.

"I was afraid your father wouldn't get through the night," Molly said, trailing after Hannah. "Would you like something with the tea?"

Hannah shook her head, still refusing to speak. But she knew she couldn't keep the silent treatment going much longer.

"How is he?" she finally asked.

"He's been napping fitfully. Waking up every few minutes asking for you," Molly said in a whisper. "Now that you're back, I know he'll be better." She nodded her head for emphasis.

Hannah and Molly both heard Harry's weak voice, calling out, "Hannah? Hannah, is that you?"

Molly rushed into the bedroom. Hannah remained in the kitchen, sipping her cup of tea. She was not going to make anything easy for Harry. Not after all the misery he had put her through. She could hear her mother reassuring him, "Yes, Hannah is here."

Molly came back into the kitchen smiling.

"He says he has to talk to you. I told him I wouldn't let you see him until his heart is back to normal. He's going to nap for a while. Your father hopes you're not planning to leave again."

"I'm not the one who leaves," Hannah said. She couldn't resist the jab. But the time away from them served its purpose. She was in a more forgiving mood. But not toward herself.

How could I have forgotten that I had a sister? she continued to question herself.

"Why don't I remember Lena, Mom?" Hannah asked. "I've only thought about her in my dream and that felt like a nightmare."

"Losing Lena was a nightmare," Molly said. "I'm glad you didn't remember her. You remember too much. This way you didn't have to grieve all these years."

Molly went over and put her arms around her daughter. This time Hannah did not resist. She let herself be hugged, but she didn't hug back.

"We did get to keep you—that was a miracle," Molly said, her tears soaking Hannah's silk blouse. "Don't be angry with your father," her mother said, for once defending her husband to her daughter. "When he first told me he couldn't get Lena back, I was furious. I thought there was no limit to what your father could do. I was devastated when he failed at something so important. We didn't get Lena back because it was *bashert*, it was meant to be this way," Molly said. "Your father has punished himself enough all these years."

"He punished me too, and I didn't do anything," Hannah said coldly. She was not ready to absolve Harry of his shortcomings as a father.

Hannah went in when Molly decided Harry's heart was finally beating normally. Seeing how frail he was, lying motionless on the bed, staring at the ceiling, shook Hannah. Now, not sure what she wanted to say to him, she walked slowly toward his bed. As he saw her approach, Harry tried to push himself up into a sitting position, but his arms couldn't hold him and he fell back onto the pillow. Without saying a word, Hannah sat down on the chair next to his bed. He extended his shaky hand to touch her. She did not pull away, and Harry started to cry. He motioned for her to come closer. As she sat on the edge of his bed, and he stroked her hand, Hannah felt a bond between them that had seemed unlikely a few hours earlier.

"I never realized how much I was hurting you," Harry said, his breathing labored. "I don't know why keeping my distance from you made not having Lena with us bearable." He spoke in bursts, between heaving breaths. "I wish I could redo the last thirty years. I didn't want to punish you for my mistake. Forgive me, please . . . I didn't mean to hurt you," he repeated over and over.

"That may be true, but it still hurt. A lot, for a very long time," Hannah said with some bite to her voice, but the anger was gone. When she had stormed out of the apartment, she had expected to hold onto that anger forever. Now, surprisingly, she no longer wanted to extract a pound of flesh from her father. She thought about how good she had felt on Saturday before he told her about Lena. Hannah wanted to believe there was still time for them to love each other, as they should have all these years.

"I was afraid I'd lost you, too," Harry whispered.

"I'm not that easy to lose," Hannah shot back.

"I wanted us to be close, a loving family," Harry said. "But Lena was always there separating you and me."

"It would have hurt less if I knew the reason for our screwed-up relationship," Hannah said.

"I'm so sorry. We should have talked about Lena."

It was clear both father and daughter wanted to repair their relationship. With Lena out in the open, they now had a chance to make up for the past. Hannah could stop being the mirror for Harry's guilt.

"Things may be different now," she told her father. But while Hannah seemed ready to accept his heartfelt apology, she wasn't ready to pardon herself. "I don't understand how I could have forgotten that I had a sister," she said, giving voice to her own guilt. "You don't forget something like that!"

"You were a child," Harry said. "Besides, your mind can do strange things to protect you, to help you survive. Sometimes that price is too high," he added almost inaudibly. Hannah knew Harry was thinking about leaving Poland without Lena.

"Instead of torturing yourself and hurting me all these years you should have been furious with the nuns and the Catholic Church for not helping you find her!" Hannah said trying to numb his guilt. "Think about it. What was your mistake? You sent Lena away to save her life. And when you went back to get her, as you promised, she wasn't there."

But his guilt was all Harry had left of Lena. He couldn't let it go so easily.

"Before I die, I must know if she's alive," Harry said, hoping God could hear him.

"She's alive. I know she's alive," Molly said, standing in the doorway to the bedroom. "I left Poland without her because I knew we did what God wanted us to do. We saved her life by sending her to the nuns. If we were meant to get her back, we would have. God had a different plan. She's alive and she's had a good life. I feel it in my heart," Molly said.

"That's not enough for me," Harry insisted. "I want her to know I tried to get her back. I kept my promise! Losing Lena was unimaginable, not knowing what happened to her is even worse. I know you can find her, Hannah. You'll think of a way. Please, please try," Harry begged.

This time when Harry asked Hannah to find her sister, instead of rage, she felt pride and terror in equal measure. Knowing that her father thought her capable of such a feat somehow softened his years of criticism and rejection. Hannah knew the task was next to impossible. But failing was not an option.

"After all this time, where do I start looking?" she said, mostly to herself. But as she spoke the words, the reporter in her kicked in. Pretend it's a story, she told herself. If Lena is alive, there has to be a way to find her. Begin with what you know and see where it leads! Hannah hoped to keep the knot in her stomach from growing larger.

"You'll find a way," Harry said wistfully.

Hannah watched the color return to his sunken cheeks. "I'll do my best," she said, praying it would be enough.

"I love you," Harry said. "Please don't ever doubt that."

"I love you, too," Hannah said and rested her head on her father's bony chest.

Free of the anger that had fueled her day, Hannah remained at Harry's bedside for a time, holding his almost skeletal hand. His rhythmic breathing reassured her he was alive. Silently, she vowed to do everything she could to make sure he stayed that way. First find the right doctor! Then figure out how to find Lena. If she's still alive . . .

Harry reached over to stroke Hannah's hair. The prospect of seeing Lena again not only lifted his spirits, but also seemed to improve his physical well-being. He closed his eyes and fell into a restful sleep for the first time in months. In his sleep, he rocked forward and back as if he were praying in a synagogue. The man who in the past refused to talk to God now was asking for His help. "I have to know what happened to her."

PART II

CHAPTER

6

Poland, May 1976

AT THE GRAVESITE, holding onto her son Stefan's hand, Lena stood ramrod straight. It was cold for May. The wind was blowing with such force through the weeping willow near the open grave she could feel the low branches lash her back with every gust. Her black suit jacket was appropriate for the occasion but not warm enough to stop her shivering. As she stoically watched two men lowering the casket into the ground, Lena wished she had the power to stop them and bring Stefan Jankowski back to life. He had been her loving father for all but her first four years and she longed to see his cheerful face again. The idea that in a month she would celebrate her thirty-ninth birthday without him was unbearable.

Trembling, Lena mouthed the words to the 23rd Psalm along with all the other mourners, but her mind wandered back to another, much warmer, May day when she saw Stefan Jankowski for the first time.

* * *

Lena had been at the orphanage for some months when, as usual, Sister Janina found her charge alone in her room.

"I don't know why you would rather be off by yourself than playing with the other children," Sister Janina said with mock anger in her voice.

Lena shrugged. She preferred watching the magpies out of her window perched on the edge of the water fountain in the courtyard. Lena amused herself by translating their chatter into conversation.

Sister Janina shook her head and sighed. "But never mind, child. It's not important now. Put on your best dress, Lena," she said. "There's someone special waiting to see you downstairs."

My father must have come back to get me, Lena thought. She took her favorite dress out of the chest where she kept the few things she'd brought with her. Lena had worn that navy-blue velvet dress, with a white lace collar and smocking around the capped sleeves, the day she'd arrived. When she finished dressing, Sister Janina said, "Let me see now, we need something to dress up your lovely curls," and she pinned a big navy taffeta bow in her hair. "Now you're ready," the Sister said and led her charge to a part of the convent where children were never allowed uninvited.

Sister Janina pushed open the heavy carved wooden door to the visitors' room, and Lena followed a few steps behind.

Almost as imposing as the chapel where they recited morning prayers, the room was bathed in sunlight streaming in through the large stained glass window. It took Lena a few seconds to adjust her eyes. Many paintings adorned the walls, but the biggest was of the Madonna, her golden halo shimmering in the sun. Lena had to stretch her neck back, until it hurt, to see the ornate chandelier in the center of the high ceiling.

The rhythmic sound of their footsteps on the highly polished wooden floor was muffled once Lena and Sister Janina reached the Persian rug that covered most of the room. Lena heard her heart thumping. She wondered if Sister Janina could hear it, too. The Sister steered her toward a man and a woman sitting on a bench at the far end of the room. The woman's straw hat, slightly askew, over her blonde curls, and her bright yellow sundress, were a sharp contrast to the nun's dark habit.

As she sat very straight, her legs crossed at the ankle, she seemed to be studying her painted fingernails. The man was throwing his hat in the air with one hand and catching it with the other. As they approached, Lena could hear him whistling softly.

Who are these people, Lena wondered. Why did Sister Janina think they were special? They did not look familiar. Disappointed at first, Lena consoled herself. They must be here to take me to my family?

The man stood and rushed toward them before Sister Janina and Lena reached the bench. He bent down so his eyes and Lena's were almost at the same level.

"You look like a little princess," he said. "Are you a real princess?"

"I don't think so," she said, and stepped closer to Sister Janina, trying to hide in the folds of her black habit.

"I can still call you Princess," he said, trying to tease her into a smile.

Lena shook her head. "No. My name is Lena," she told him emphatically.

"So glad to meet you, Lena," the man said and stuck out his hand for her to shake. Reluctantly, she took it after Sister Janina nudged her with her elbow.

"Lena, this is Mr. Stefan Jankowski. He and his wife, Helga, would like you to go home with them. They want you to be their little girl," Sister Janina announced cheerfully. By then Helga had come over and she offered her hand as well.

"No! I can't go with them," Lena whispered to Sister Janina, shaking her head frantically. She wanted to remain at the orphanage until her father came back for her. "I must stay here. I have to wait for my family," Lena insisted.

"I'm afraid that's not possible, dear." Sister Janina was firm. "All the children are being moved. Mr. and Mrs. Jankowski have a place for you in their home."

"No! Please, no!" Lena argued, still in a whisper. "I have to stay here so my family will know where to find me."

"If . . . when your family comes, we'll know where to send them," Sister Janina assured the child.

"Do I really have to go with these people?" Lena was close to tears.

"It would be for the best," Sister Janina said solemnly.

Sister Janina was right. It was for the best. I could not have picked a better father for myself than Stefan Jankowski, Lena thought as she watched his coffin being covered with clumps of earth.

Stefan had been totally devoted to her. Helga, however, was another story. At the gravesite service, she had to be restrained by her son Rudi from throwing herself onto her husband's casket. A gesture the handful of mourners accepted as an expression of true grief, a sharp contrast to Lena's restraint, which she suspected they saw as unfeeling. She thought Helga's gravesite behavior was a performance. Today, Helga, the widow, was center stage, and determined to make the most of that role.

Lena felt estranged from the other mourners. Although she had known them most of her life, once she'd gone away to university, everything had changed. Being a doctor in Warsaw put more than geographical distance between them. Lena hoped Stefan would forgive her for feeling so removed from his friends and neighbors. It wasn't that she felt superior to them, that would have been out of character. But whatever they had had in common evaporated over the years of her absence. There was a chasm between them that Lena had no desire to fill. And she thought they now saw her as a curiosity.

"How are you doing in the big city?" Mr. Kukolowicz, the stationmaster, asked Lena whenever she visited Sandomierz.

"Fine," was all she could offer. Lena hoped she didn't seem standoffish but she didn't feel comfortable sharing her life story with someone who was essentially a stranger.

"I'm sorry about your father. We all are," he said when she came back to Sandomierz for the funeral.

His concern seemed genuine. Lena was touched. "Thank you. Thank you," she said appreciatively. "Please give my best to your wife and to Janka. I hope they are both well." Lena and Janka had been schoolmates years ago. But time and the distance between Sandomierz and Warsaw separated her from the whole Kukolowicz family.

After the Mass, Lena had warmly greeted the people who'd come to pay their respects to her father. She was glad for Rudi and Helga that so many of their neighbors were there, but their presence was of no comfort to her. With Stefan's death her center was hollow. How will I recover from this loss? First no Ryszard, now no Stefan.

Lena had had almost eight years to adjust to her widowhood, but she was unable to shed her grief. It seemed like only yesterday that the policeman had brought her the shattering news.

* * *

She remembered that young officer clutching his hat as he told her, "Dr. Malińska, there's been a terrible accident. Your husband was shot."

"Oh, my God!" Lena crossed herself. "How did it happen?"

"There was a student demonstration that seemed to be on the verge of violence. To stop the advancing students, one of the policemen aimed his weapon. He tripped, the gun went off. The bullet hit your husband."

"My husband was in a demonstration? That's not possible. There must be some mistake. Ryszard is not political. He cares about equations, not politics. He wouldn't be in a demonstration!"

"No. He wasn't one of the demonstrators. The bullet went wild. Your husband was just walking in the street, reading a book. They told me it was a book about mathematics. He didn't seem to be paying attention to the crowd growing around him."

"How could such a thing happen?" Lena screamed. "Where is he? What hospital? I must go to him."

"I'm afraid he's not in the hospital." The policeman cleared his throat. "He's dead."

Lena slipped to the floor. The next thing she knew she was lying on the couch, the policeman bending over her.

"Are you part of a bad dream?" she asked.

"I'm afraid not."

* * *

After the others had left the cemetery, Lena and her son lingered. He watched as she walked closer to the pit to say a private goodbye to her loving father. Still shivering from the cold, Lena crossed herself, and threw a single purple-and-white iris onto the dirt-covered casket, finally letting her tears flow unabated.

"I love you, Tata. My life will be impossible without you," Lena whispered. She knew he was proud that she had become a doctor, but what was the point of having a daughter who was a doctor if you didn't even tell her your symptoms and you didn't listen to her advice? Why in heaven's name did you ignore my warnings?

She looked skyward, hoping for a sign that he could hear her. She saw dark clouds massing in the sky, and thought about their frequent phone calls.

"Tata, I don't like the way that cough sounds. Stop smoking!" she urged for the umpteenth time.

"It's nothing. Just a cold," he insisted. "Bad weather makes my throat raspy. Don't you worry about me." Stefan never wanted to burden Lena. He longed to see her happy again.

"It's not fair, Tata," Lena lamented whenever they spoke. "How could a mathematics professor at the University of Warsaw who had no interest in politics be killed during a student demonstration he wasn't even aware of?" She was still in shock over Ryszard's death.

Stefan had worked to ease her pain. Now with him gone, there was no one to even try.

* * *

From the moment he set his eyes on her, Stefan's thoughts had always been for Lena's welfare. At the orphanage both Stefan and Helga marveled at how lovely she was. Her pale skin and delicate features made Lena look more like a porcelain doll than a flesh-and-blood child. Since Helga didn't think that she could have a child of her own, she agreed to take Lena in.

"She has my blue eyes. Her hair's the same as mine, and almost as curly," Helga said proudly the day they brought Lena home. On the basis of their looks, Helga and Lena easily passed for mother and daughter. At first, she seemed to enjoy fussing with Lena's clothes, and braiding her hair, but as Stefan lavished attention on the child, Helga became critical.

"Don't spoil her," she admonished her husband. "If you get her used to having everything her way, she'll expect life to be like that, and be really disappointed," Helga warned.

* * *

Helga's father had doted on her the same way Stefan doted on Lena. When Helga was a child, every day her father came home from the Gymnasium where he taught Romance languages, and German literature, the two of them played a game of hide and seek.

"Where's my little Duchess? I can't see her anywhere. Where should I look for her? I hope she didn't decide to run away. I would be so sad if she left. I have to find her," her father would shout as he vainly searched under the table and behind a door, under a pillow. "She has to be here to get the special present I have for her!"

As soon as he mentioned a present, the game was over. Helga would come out of her hiding place and jump into her father's arms, asking, "What did you bring me, today, Tata?" Actually, it never mattered what the present was. It was only important that her father was home.

When she was seventeen, her perfect world blew up. One afternoon when she arrived home from school her mother was crying.

"They took your father to the hospital. He was coughing up so much blood," her mother told Helga. Three weeks later, he was dead. It was TB that killed her father, and it killed the life Helga cherished, as well. While she, her mother and ten-year-old brother still had their house to live in, now there was no money coming in. Rudolf had no life insurance and her mother had no profession to return to. But after years of making all of Helga's clothes, she was an experienced seamstress and secured a job in the tailor shop next door to the bakery where Stefan worked. She was grateful to Abraham Rothman for giving her the job, but Helga thought it was demeaning for her mother to be working for a Jew. With her brother too young to work, the family struggled to make ends meet for the year Helga stayed in school. But Helga's mother insisted she finish high school, just as her father would have wished. Once she graduated, there was no talk of her going to the university. Helga became the cashier in the bakery Stefan's uncle owned.

Long before he had the courage to say anything to Helga beyond, "Good morning," and "Good night," she became the unattainable goddess of Stefan's dreams. He was awed by her. She was beautiful, but also a high school graduate whose father had been a respected teacher. No one in his family had even finished high school.

"You don't need to go to school to bake bread," his father told him. Stefan didn't disagree with his father. But now he feared that his lack of education would keep him from someone as fine as Helga. How could such a person of high quality become interested in me? Stefan asked himself. So for a time, he worshiped Helga from afar without any hope of anything more. She was aware of Stefan's interest and enjoyed seeing the power her smile had over him.

When Stefan finally summoned enough courage to ask Helga to tea, she happily agreed. From her perspective, Stefan wasn't a bad catch. His financial prospects were good. His uncle had no children, so ultimately the bakery would belong to Stefan. As the owner of a business he could take care of her and her family. And he wasn't bad to look at either. Stefan was tall and straight, with an athletic body. But best of all, he obviously adored her. Helga's mother encouraged the match.

"He is a wonderful man, Helga. He may not be a dreamer like your father, but he's a hard worker and will take good care of you," she told her daughter. Helga agreed with her mother's assessment, but she always believed that Stefan was below her station.

They were married three days before Helga's twenty-first birthday. She would have preferred a trip to Düsseldorf where her father had family, but Stefan and Helga settled on a brief honeymoon at a small hotel overlooking the mountains in Zakopane. When they returned home, the newlyweds moved in with her mother and brother, and Stefan became the head of their household. Her mother willingly vacated her bedroom so Helga and Stefan could have the largest room. Helga still worked at the bakery, but now she felt like an owner's wife, even if she wasn't one yet. Since they no longer needed the meager wages her mother earned as a seamstress, she stopped working at the tailor shop. When Uncle Józef died, Helga was certain her life would finally right itself.

But instead of the bakery going to Stefan as everyone expected, it had to be sold to pay off Uncle Józef's gambling debts. Helga was inconsolable. It wasn't enough for her that Stefan still had a job with the new owner who promoted him to head baker. She had counted on Stefan owning the bakery. There was no prestige in being the wife of the head baker. From then on Helga's disappointment tainted their marriage. But Stefan continued to think he was the luckiest man in the world, because a woman like Helga had taken him as a husband. The only thing he still wanted was to become a father. That proved to be an elusive dream until Lena came into their lives.

After Lena had been with them for six months, Helga became pregnant. Stefan was delighted at the prospect of being the father of two. But not Helga.

"Stefan, we can't afford two children! Now that we're going to have a child of our own, we have to send Lena back to the nuns," she insisted.

Not wishing to upset his pregnant wife, Stefan reluctantly went back to the convent to explain their new situation to the Mother Superior. She was not happy and urged him to reconsider.

"Stefan, Lena is a lovely child. She deserves a caring family. I saw the love in your eyes the day you and Helga took her. How can you take that love away now? It would absolutely break her poor little heart to lose another family."

"Believe me, Holy Mother, I don't want to give Lena back. It's Helga. Now that she's finally pregnant, she doesn't think we can afford two children. I don't make that much in the bakery."

The Mother Superior bowed her head and she folded her hands as in prayer.

"You remember when I first told you I had a little girl for you, I said she was special?"

Stefan nodded.

"I know you're a religious man, Stefan. I think God sent Lena to us, to test us. We have to protect her. I think that's what God wants us to do."

Stefan nodded in agreement, but he didn't really know what he was agreeing to.

"The man who brought Lena here was a doctor. He told me Lena's mother was his patient. As she was dying, she asked him to find a home for her daughter, because Lena's father was in the Underground and could not care for her. I didn't ask for any more information than he offered. I didn't want to force him to tell me lies. But I suspected that Lena was Jewish and that he brought her to us to save her life."

"Oh, my God!" Stefan exclaimed. "Lena is a Jewish child?"

"I don't know anything for sure. I only have my suspicions. Lena has never mentioned her family. She never said a word about her life

before she came to us. It was probably good that she did not dwell on the past. We tried to provide a happy life for her. You can give her the future she deserves. Of course it is possible that at some point someone from her family may come looking for her. But the way things are going in this war, that's not very likely. I think God wants you to take care of her, Stefan."

He already loved Lena and he wanted to keep her, but Stefan also knew the danger was real. It was common knowledge that the penalty for harboring any Jew was death. For him, saving Lena was worth the risk. He knew Helga would not feel the same way. More than likely Helga would say, "What have their kind done for us? Why should we stick our necks out for a Jewess?"

"I want to keep Lena. I really do. But what should I tell Helga? I can't admit we've taken in a Jewish child. Helga will fear being arrested. She didn't want to keep her even without the danger."

"You don't have to tell her about my suspicions. After all, that's all they are. Tell Helga I've convinced you to keep Lena temporarily, until her family tries to get her back. Nothing more." She smiled deviously.

"What if somebody was to report us to the authorities claiming we are keeping a Jewish child?" Stefan asked.

"Why would anyone suspect that Lena is anything but what she looks like—a perfect Polish girl? Nobody could prove that she wasn't. It would be different if she were a boy. Girls don't get circumcised," Mother Superior said, shocked at her own candor.

Stefan mulled over the pros and cons as he rocked in his chair. While he didn't like the idea of deceiving his wife, he wanted to keep Lena. He finally decided that withholding the truth from Helga was all right since he was doing it with the Church's blessing.

"We'll keep her!" he announced forcefully to the Mother Superior.

The Holy Mother breathed a sigh of relief, crossed herself and kissed her rosary.

To seal their clandestine pact, Stefan lurched across the desk to shake her hand and in the process almost knocked over an inkwell.

"I think overall Helga has enjoyed having Lena around," Stefan said, trying to reassure himself that he'd made a wise decision. "Once the baby comes, Lena will be a great help. I'll remind Helga how responsible she is.

Besides, having two children is twice the blessing. God will take care of us," he said with a new assurance.

Once he agreed to keep Lena, the Mother Superior brought out the inlaid mahogany box left with her for the child.

"I decided to hold onto this until I was sure you were keeping Lena," the Mother Superior explained.

Not a Pandora's box but it did hold some treasures: a gold pendant encrusted with garnets and a matching bracelet, several gold coins, and five hundred złotys. Also in the box were two photographs, one of two little girls, another of the same two girls with a blonde woman in her late twenties who looked very much like Lena. But nothing inside to identify her family, no names, no address.

Stefan realized the inlaid box and its contents—minus the photographs— was the perfect carrot to win Helga over. He put the two photographs in his shirt pocket before he returned home.

Knowing how much Helga loved getting presents, as he opened the front door Stefan called out, "Helga, I have something for you." He set the elegant box on their rickety kitchen table and waited for her reaction.

Helga stared at it for a moment, then wiped her hands on her apron before gently stroking the smooth surface.

"It's so beautiful. Where did you get it?"

"From the Mother Superior. Open it. What's inside is even better."

"Why? Why did she give it to you?"

"For keeping Lena."

Helga glared at her husband. "You were supposed to tell her we can't keep her," Helga said angrily. "We have our own child . . ." Her voice trailed off as she started to examine the contents of the box.

Stefan said nothing. He watched Helga survey each treasure separately. She held up the antique pendant, put it against her neck, and checked her reflection in the window.

"Very beautiful. Where did the Mother Superior get this?"

"The man who brought Lena to the convent left it with her."

"This jewelry is Lena's! That's hardly a gift for me," Helga said bitterly. "She must come from rich people."

"I don't think four-year-olds wear such fancy jewelry. It's for you for being her mother. At least until someone from her family comes to get

123

her. That's all I agreed to," Stefan assured his wife. "We keep Lena until someone comes for her."

Helga seemed to be mesmerized by the contents of the box. As she sat at the kitchen table fondling the pendant, Stefan could feel her coming around.

"If we keep Lena until her family shows up, all this is ours?" Helga said, when she finally spoke.

"Yes."

"Okay, then, we'll keep her until they come. I'll try to be a good mother to her 'til then," Helga said. Tapping the smooth surface of the box, she added, "Maybe her rich relatives will reward us when they come?"

Almost against her will, Helga grew fond of Lena. At night when she put her to bed, she'd read the same stories her father used to read to her. She even taught Lena the poem, "My Little Duchess," that her beloved father had written for her sixth birthday.

When Lena recited the poem after she'd memorized it, Helga was so pleased she rewarded Lena with a green velvet dress, which she had made herself, carefully duplicating the lace collar and smocking of the dress Lena had outgrown, but now stored in the bottom of her clothing chest.

Lena's eyes lit up when Helga unveiled the new dress.

"Thank you so much . . . Mama." As grateful as she was, it was still hard for her to call Helga "Mama." She knew that was expected, even without Stefan's prodding. When she modeled the dress, he applauded.

Everything changed between Helga and Lena once Rudi was born. His was a difficult birth, and he was a sickly child. Helga had named her son after the father she adored, hoping he would grow up to be the image of his namesake. When it became evident that Lena would always outshine him, Helga took her disappointment out on Lena.

Rudi is our flesh and blood; Lena is only another mouth to feed, Helga told herself to justify withdrawing from her. Still, she never mentioned sending Lena away again.

Stefan's devotion to Lena only grew. He more than made up for what his wife withheld. He encouraged Lena to study hard and urged her to do something important with her life. He made it possible for her to think she could become a doctor.

* * *

While Lena appeared to be fully functioning, grief heaped upon grief numbed her senses. As she and her son walked silently toward the cemetery gate, a young boy approached them.

"Dr. Malińska, I have a message from Father Tadeusz. He would like you to stop by the Rectory on your way home."

"Thank you," Lena told the boy, but hearing the priest's request made her wince. It intensified her feeling of guilt for not attending church regularly.

"Go back to the house and tell Grandma I've gone to see Father Tadeusz," Lena told her son, and briskly headed up the hill to the church.

CHAPTER

7

New York, May 1976

BACK IN HER OWN APARTMENT, Hannah looked around almost expecting to see some evidence of the turmoil stirring inside her. So much in her life had changed in the course of one weekend, it was hard to believe there was no visible sign of the sea change she'd undergone. Nothing seemed different, yet everything was different.

Hannah wished she could talk to Robert. Calculating he was airborne somewhere over the Pacific Ocean, west of California, she knew he was out of her reach.

It was late. She only had time for a quick nap before the alarm would go off at 7 a.m. But her mind was reeling. Good feelings and bad memories kept colliding in her head. Her father's new tenderness was coupled with a fair amount of sadness when she thought about the special moments they had missed out on. Her wedding was a case in point.

Hannah remembered how distraught she had been the week before the ceremony. She'd been standing in front of the mirror trying on her tulle veil when Molly called.

"I don't think your father will be able to come to the wedding, Hannah. And I can't leave him alone."

"He won't come because Robert is not Jewish. Is that it? When did he become such a rabbi?"

"It has nothing to do with Robert's religion, believe me."

"Then why won't he come?"

"It's . . . it's his heart," Molly said.

"Maybe the great Dr. Harry Stone should get a second opinion," Hannah yelled into the phone. She would have cried if her rage were not in full force. "It's my wedding for God's sake! I should be able to count on my parents to come to their only daughter's wedding!"

"Calm down Hannah, please. He may be better by next Sunday. We'll see. . . ." her mother said softly before hanging up.

The morning of the wedding as she was getting dressed, Hannah still didn't know if her parents would be there to give her away. She never told Robert.

If they don't show up, I'll tell him my father had a stroke. Who knows? Maybe it will be true!

Hannah finally breathed a sigh of relief when she arrived at The Arts Club across from Gramercy Park and spotted her parents talking to the judge who was to officiate. She could see Harry was out of sorts. His face was drawn. He tried to smile as Hannah approached, but he avoided her eyes.

"I'm glad you could make it, Dad," Hannah said, her tone of voice more appropriate to welcoming a casual acquaintance. Instead of hugging his daughter, Harry took her hand briefly. Molly, teary-eyed, embraced Hannah.

The ceremony went off without any further snags. Twenty-five guests and the bride and groom enjoyed a delicious lunch. But Hannah often relived that agonizing week she'd spent wondering whether her parents would make an appearance. Even now recalling that her father never hugged or kissed her on her wedding day brought tears to her eyes.

Hannah shook her head to dislodge the painful memory. That was then, she told herself. At least now I understand why it happened.

Lying in bed after a relaxing hot shower, Hannah flipped through an issue of *People* magazine with a smiling Goldie Hawn staring out from the cover. Candy for the brain, she laughed. "Life doesn't have to be serious all the time," Robert's voice echoed in her mind. For a change, Hannah found herself in agreement with that sentiment.

Nice! Goldie's going to have a baby, and then she's going to get married. Maybe if I'd tried it in that order I'd have gotten pregnant, too, Hannah thought, but quickly pushed that disturbing subject out of her mind. The past weekend had re-jiggered a lot of her feelings. Even with the daunting task Harry had set out for her, Hannah felt her life was on a better trajectory. Admittedly, Harry's health was a problem, but she expected the right cardiologist would resolve that issue. Hannah took several cleansing breaths and congratulated herself on how well she'd been tolerating all the turmoil. Her road map was clear. First find the perfect doctor for Harry, then start looking for Lena. For the moment she convinced herself that tracking down her sister, even after thirty years, was not impossible for an experienced reporter.

Hannah slept through the alarm that Monday. Still groggy, she got to the office mid-morning, without any edibles for her co-workers, or even coffee for herself. She usually appeared at the magazine early, and energized, with a container of black coffee in one hand and in the other, a bag filled with croissants, doughnuts or brownies (her personal favorite) to share. Always on the hunt for the best edible delights, she'd proudly advertise her success.

"Believe me, you're in for a special treat," she'd announce as she distributed her goodies on the way to her cubicle.

While Hannah felt guilty for not bearing gifts as usual, her co-workers were too occupied to complain. When she reached her desk, she called Robert in Amagansett. The phone rang five times before the answering machine came on. She started to leave a message, but instead hung up without saying a word. She hadn't changed that much. Two hours later Robert called.

"You rang?" he asked cheerfully.

Hearing his voice, Hannah fussed with her hair, as if Robert were watching. It cheered her that he knew she had phoned even though she had not left a message. We may be physically apart, but we are still bound together, Hannah reassured herself.

"I confess. I called and left no message."

"That's not news! What's up?"

Her initial instinct was to blurt out everything that had happened, but she stopped herself. Hannah wanted to be face to face with Robert when she told him about Lena and her new relationship with Harry.

"You first. How was the trip?" she asked instead.

"God, I'm glad it's over! No more junkets for me. I'm going to enjoy thinking small for a while. Feels great to be back," Robert said. "What's going on with you? You sound different."

"A lot has happened," Hannah said, not wanting to reveal too much. "Are you coming into the city this week?"

"Turns out I have to go in today to pick out some hardware and fixtures," Robert said. "You free for dinner tonight? I'll cook. I should be finished by six or seven."

"Perfect! Meet you at the apartment." Hannah grinned.

As she cleared her desk from the previous week's work, Hannah found herself first humming, then singing: "It's a great day for singing a song, it's a great day for moving along . . . ."

Before she got to the next line Josh yelled from his cubicle: "Everything okay, Hannah?"

"Yes. Why?"

"No doughnut, no croissants! Only your dulcet tones in our future?"

"Sorry. I overslept! Forgive the singing," Hannah yelled back, embarrassed. She hadn't realized she'd been singing. A few minutes later, a more serious Hannah appeared at Josh's desk.

"Since you are our resident medical expert, I need help finding a heart specialist for my dad. A *mensch* who knows his stuff. My father's been treating his own heart condition until now. I have to find someone who will treat him like a peer, not just a patient."

"No problem. I'll make some calls," Josh offered.

Hannah was grateful, but she wasn't about to leave such an important search to only one source. She intended to make many calls on her own.

A little after three o'clock Christy arrived, carrying a single red rose.

"It's a peace offering for helping me in your office."

Hannah sniffed the flower. "Thanks for the thought. But you don't need a peace offering. We're not at war, are we?"

Christy flashed her Chiclets smile, just like Robert's.

"How've you been, kiddo?"

"Good, I guess."

"Not sure?"

"Teenagers are supposed to be full of angst. If I'm good, then I'm not cool."

"Being cool isn't so cool, believe me. Better to be good," Hannah said and mussed Christy's bangs. "Let's get down to business. Your paper, please."

Christy anxiously perched on the edge of the guest chair as she handed over her folder. Reading the opening sentence, Hannah tensed up. In the form of a diary, Christy had written an alternative ending for Anne Frank. In this version Anne had survived the war and was now living in New York. Christy portrayed a grown-up Anne Frank as Hannah.

"I'm really not the right person to advise you on this. I'm one of the few people on the planet who has neither read *The Diary of Anne Frank* nor seen the movie," Hannah confessed.

Christy was surprised. It never occurred to her that Hannah would not have read a book that was so close to her own experience. She grimaced and pleaded. "Take a look anyway, please!"

Hannah nodded and as a precaution swiveled around in her chair, turning her back to Christy. She didn't want to be seen crying. When Hannah finished, she dabbed her cheeks before facing Christy again.

131

"God, Hannah, I didn't want to upset you. I just need this to be a good paper."

"It's very good," Hannah said. "I'm sure your teacher will agree."

Christy reached for her folder. "Thank you for reading it. Anything I should change?"

"No, nothing. Except the typos I circled. Congratulations," Hannah said. Under her breath she added, "It would have been really something if Anne Frank had survived to write her own sequel." As she said those words Hannah thought about her lost sister and the muscles in her face sagged.

Noticing the change in her demeanor, Christy apologized. "I'm so sorry. I didn't realize reading this would upset you."

"Maybe now I'll read the book," Hannah said to reassure Christy.

A relieved Christy checked her watch. Beaming she said, "I told you I'd be out of here before four."

"Your word is good. I'm proud of you on both counts," Hannah said and got up to give Christy a big squeeze. "I've missed you," she admitted and kissed the top of her head.

That evening Hannah left her office early—for her. On the way home she stopped to pick up flowers and a bottle of Robert's favorite Chardonnay. When she got off the elevator at 7:30 p.m., she heard music coming from the direction of her apartment. As Hannah opened the door, Robert shouted in his most melodramatic voice, "Honey, you're home!"

In the best B-movie tradition, Hannah rushed into his outstretched arms. Holding the wine in one hand and flowers in the other, she let herself be twirled around the room to Frank Sinatra singing "Come Dance With Me!"

Hannah closed her eyes. The dizziness she felt was slightly intoxicating. She didn't want the music to stop, nor to let go of Robert. But when the timer went off, their dance was over.

"M'lady, you have exactly twenty minutes before making an appearance at the dinner table. Now the chef has to go to work." He brushed her nose as he reached down to kiss her, then headed for the kitchen.

Hannah looked around and saw the dining table was set, with candles ready to be lit for a romantic dinner. Robert had thought of everything. She felt like Cinderella on her first real date with the Prince after he'd returned her glass slipper. With Robert in the kitchen preparing dinner, she was able to sideline her usual fear of his abandoning her. At that moment she accepted their separate living arrangement as temporary.

In the bedroom, giggling at her reflection in her full-length mirror, Hannah reprised their dance. She whirled herself around the room, and collapsed on the bed. He still loves me!

Hannah took a bite of Robert's spectacular sole *almandine*. "Mmm, delicious!" she said, then sighed and dropped her fork. "I've got to tell you what's been going on!"

Robert kept shaking his head as Hannah replayed her weekend with Harry and how she found out about Lena.

"That's a hell of a story! Would make a great book," he said. "You could have a best seller. Maybe even a movie."

"Not much to write about yet," she said, dismissing the book idea as premature. "I'd have to find Lena to give the story a happy ending." But Hannah knew that even with a happy ending she would not want to write about her family's troubled history.

After they had polished off the bottle of wine, Hannah finally felt brave enough to bring up their situation.

"I've been thinking a lot about us," she started timidly. What about you?"

"Sure. I always think about us. I want us to have a good life together."

"But I'm living in New York and you're in Amagansett!"

Robert laughed. "Right now, after all this wine, it does seem weird." He reached for her hand and squeezed it. "Hannah, I was miserable. Everything was wrong. I had to do something."

"Why such a major change? Why did you have to move out?"

"Oh, God! I was blaming us for what I was feeling about myself and my career. I'm a lot happier now. I like my work. I like being in

Amagansett. I think it would be a great place for you to write your book." Robert grinned. He raised his eyebrows several times à la Groucho Marx and moved his fingers along the edge of the table, as if he were typing. Hannah just shook her head.

"I do miss you, Hannah. I miss us. I wish we could be together, have a kid and live like normal people."

"What normal people?"

"Okay. Happy people!"

"I'd be happy if we were living together right here," Hannah said, as she got up from the table and plopped herself down on their living room sofa.

Robert followed and sat down beside her. "I can't come back yet. I have to be in Amagansett for work. Let's just finish our three month experiment."

Hannah bit her lip. "I don't like waking up without you. I don't want to lose you."

"Who said anything about losing me?" Robert said and pulled her to him.

"Losing you would ruin my life the way losing Lena ruined my father's," Hannah said, resting her head on Robert's shoulder. That brought their conversation back to Harry.

"You know, he didn't have to torture himself or you all these years. There were other ways to deal with losing Lena," Robert said, being uncharacteristically critical. "Don't you think he could have started looking for her himself?"

Hannah found herself in a strange new position: defending her father instead of enumerating his slights.

"No. Actually he couldn't. Harry had lied to the American authorities in Germany about having another daughter. Once we were in the U.S., he kept his secret because he was afraid he'd be deported for his lie," Hannah explained.

"Why isn't he afraid of being deported now?"

"I'm sure on some level he is. But what's important to Harry now, is that Lena knows he came back for her. That he kept his promise. He needs Lena to forgive him for leaving Poland without her. Just as he wants me to forgive him."

"For what? Not loving you?"

"He loved me in secret, the only way he could."

"Wow! You've forgiven him then, for all the pain he caused?"

"Not totally. But I know he couldn't help it. Harry did not survive the war unscathed. None of us did," Hannah said, her eyes clouded with tears.

"We have another chance, my father and I," she said.

Robert kissed her trembling lips. She hoped the kiss was a prelude to his spending the night. But then Robert looked at his watch.

"I wish I didn't have to go," he moaned.

"Then stay, please. You can take a train in the morning," Hannah coaxed.

"I can't. I've arranged to meet a contractor tomorrow by 7 a.m. at the house. If I'm not there, I'll lose him. I've got to take the last train back tonight." He looked at his watch again. "Which means I have to leave now!"

Their blissful evening came to an abrupt end. Hannah was crushed.

"When are you coming to visit me?" Robert demanded in mock anger, as he headed for the door.

"Friday! I'll take the day off!" Hannah was surprised to hear herself offer to ditch work on a closing day.

"Great. Take an early train. I'll treat you to a special country breakfast. Then we'll make some new plans."

Loath to see him go, Hannah walked Robert to the elevator. As they waited they held each other close. She was glad management had not yet repaired the slow elevator she had so often railed against.

The next three days had an edge of unreality for Hannah. She got up early every morning as always and went to work. But she was on autopilot as she did her interviews and wrote her stories. In between, she made endless calls looking for a doctor for Harry.

By Wednesday she'd arranged for him to see Dr. Harold Martin, a cardiologist who came highly recommended. He actually knew Harry and was delighted to take him on as a patient. Harry had treated Dr. Martin's father years ago.

Before she booked the appointment, Dr. Martin told Hannah, "Your father made me want to study medicine."

Wonderful, Hannah told herself as she hung up. He's the right doctor.

Now Lena could come front and center. Hannah began her search for her sister the same way she prepped for her writing assignments: Research. In between chasing down a doctor for Harry, she sneaked off to the library on Fifth Avenue to photocopy newspaper and magazine articles about hidden children and family members who'd been searching for lost relatives. Hannah was ready for lots of reading. But before attacking all the material on her office floor, she phoned Malcolm Taub, a college friend who knew about her refugee past. He had worked for five years as the Warsaw Bureau Chief for *The New York Times*. Hannah was sure he would be able to help.

"Up for lunch? I'm buying," Hannah said.

They met at Bryant Park and shared hot dogs from a street vendor.

"Where should I begin?" Hannah asked after she'd laid out her dilemma.

"That's a tough one," Malcolm said between bites of his hot dog. "It would be easier for Lena to find you, if she were looking. There are Jewish organizations that would help her."

"But she doesn't have much to go on either," Hannah said. "If she was adopted by a Gentile family, she may not even know she's Jewish. Harry said he left pictures but no names."

"Big problem," Malcolm said. Sorry not to be more encouraging, he also did not want to give Hannah false hope. "I knew several Jewish families who tried to find children they had hidden with Christians during the war. In one case the family refused to return a little girl, and, like your father, the family had no proof that they were her rightful parents. Since Lena was put in an orphanage, no doubt by the time the war was over, she was being raised Catholic."

Malcolm did promise to contact people he knew in Poland on her behalf. She was grateful for whatever he could do. Hannah remained on the bench in Bryant Park feeding the pigeons what was left of her hot dog bun and plotting her next gambit. I knew it wouldn't be easy. I can't let myself be discouraged. She took out her clipboard and studied the list of organizations that tracked refugees.

For a fleeting moment Hannah toyed with Robert's suggestion that she keep a journal and ultimately write about her search. The journalist in her warmed to the possibilities. A great suggestion, thank you, Robert. My search could be the story, even if I can't find Lena. She knew she could sell her editor on such an article. Or even a book publisher. But ultimately Hannah cooled on the idea. It was not in her nature to expose her own life. Still she decided to keep a journal.

Hannah had no problem arranging to take Friday off, since both her stories were scheduled to close on Thursday.

Early Friday morning before taking the train to Amagansett Hannah stopped in to see her parents. She was surprised when her father came to the door. Harry still moved slowly, but the color had returned to his cheeks. He seemed less frail.

"Glad to see you looking so well, Dad. Where's Mom?" Hannah said as she noticed that the ever-hovering Molly was nowhere in sight.

"She went next door. Only been gone a few minutes. Come sit down," Harry said, as he steered his daughter toward the living room.

"So how is your work going?' Harry asked, trying to appear casual. But before she answered that question Harry asked, "Have you made any contacts that could lead to Lena?" When he saw Hannah's startled look he added, "I don't mean to push. I was just wondering."

Hannah wished she had some encouraging news. "I've made calls, gathered research on how other people have found their missing relatives," she said. Knowing Harry had hoped for more, she added, "I'm just starting, Dad. But I am working on it."

Harry cupped Hannah's face in his hands. "Thank you," he whispered.

I have to get over being surprised every time he touches me, she told herself.

"I do have some good news, Dad," she said. "I got you an appointment with a heart specialist. He comes highly recommended. And it turns out, you treated his father."

"What's his name?"

"Dr. Harold Martin."

"Jerrold Martin's son? Little Harold is a doctor. Isn't that something?" Harry said out loud, but really to himself.

"He remembers you very well."

"I bet he won't recognize me when he sees me. When did you make the appointment for? I'm actually feeling better now. Maybe we can wait a while?"

"Uh-uh, the appointment is for next Monday. Don't back out now, Dad, please. The sooner we get your meds changed, the sooner you'll get well."

"Don't you worry, he's not backing out of anything!" Molly yelled into the living room from the foyer. "That's why we came back early from Florida."

"Okay. Mom, you're in charge of getting Dad to the doctor's office at 11:30 Monday morning."

"You're not coming with us?" Molly asked.

"I wasn't planning to, but I can."

"It's not necessary," Harry said.

"Yes. It is. Please come, Hannah," Molly insisted.

"Sure. No problem. I'll pick you up and we'll go together." Hannah looked at her watch. She had barely enough time to make her train. "I've gotta go," she said, and got up to leave. Her mother raced after her.

"Where are you going?"

"To Penn Station. I'm going to the beach."

"You can't go out of town. Your father needs you."

Hannah looked back into the living room and saw Harry reading the paper.

"Mom, Dad looks fine. We're going to the doctor on Monday. There's nothing for me to do here."

"What if something happens?"

"Nothing will happen. But if it does, call me. You know the number."

"Why do you have to go away?"

"To be with Robert. My husband." Hannah squirmed. She hadn't told her parents about their quasi-separation, only that he was away working. The truth was too complicated.

"Who works on the weekend?" Molly asked.

The cab let Hannah off at the entrance to Penn Station. She had enough time to buy her ticket, rush down the stairs and step inside the last car as the doors closed behind her. Hannah was relieved the car was empty. Packed trains brought back bad memories. Her sweaty neck was the residual Pavlovian response to her body reliving the trauma when years ago she had lost sight of Aunt Emma and her mother in the crowded Warsaw Central Train Station. The panic had lessened, but discomfort hung on. She wondered, Will my life be dominated by what happened in my first seven years? Until the day I die? Ultimately, Hannah decided those early years played havoc with everybody's life.

After changing trains at Jamaica, Hannah stretched out over three seats and watched the landscape blur by through the unwashed window. As the train picked up speed, she began to imagine the ride Lena and Harry took to the orphanage outside of Radom. Before long, Hannah fell asleep, lulled by the jostling motion of the train.

She began to dream in Polish. The mood of her dream was light hearted. Once again two little girls were playing in a court-yard. The blonde, she recognized as Lena, was dressed in a flowing white dress, had a crown of garlands in her hair and was holding a shimmering silver wand. She circled Hannah and pointed the wand in her direction.

"Come, we can play again," Lena said. "Follow me!" Without waiting for Hannah to respond, she took her hand and gently pulled her toward a carousel some distance away. As they got closer, the girls watched the brightly painted horses bobbing rhythmically up and down. Hannah stood frozen, afraid to move.

"Come," Lena repeated as she jumped on to the carousel. With trepidation, Hannah followed. Once onboard, each selected a horse and held on laughing, as the carousel picked up speed.

"Tickets please! Tickets please!" shocked Hannah out of her dream. She sat up, slightly embarrassed by her disheveled state.

"How long before we get to Amagansett?" she asked as she handed her ticket to the conductor.

"We're on schedule," he said under his breath, and walked on.

That momentary discomfort aside, Hannah was relieved her dream was not a nightmare. It feels good to have a pleasant dream about Lena for once. Hannah took it as a positive sign. For the rest of the trip her thoughts were a mixture of fanciful daydreams coupled with concrete plotting. She mused, Does Lena remember me? Does she know she has a family looking for her?

CHAPTER

8

Poland, May 1976

AS SHE ENTERED, grown-up Lena still felt small inside the imposing Gothic cathedral, just as she had when she was a child. The dampness made her shudder, but the familiar whiff of incense brought back fond memories of the many Sundays she spent there with her father. She missed those days. Lena remembered how proud he was of her at her first communion, and then her confirmation.

She crossed herself with holy water at the door, then went to light a candle for Stefan. Momentarily blinded by the light shimmering through the stained-glass windows, Lena tried to shed her guilt for not attending church regularly. Why do I have to go to church with strangers to talk to Him? God is everywhere, she reasoned. But Lena had to admit, being inside a church felt special.

Seeing her kneeling at the side altar, Father Tadeusz walked toward her. Startled, Lena jumped up when his pudgy hand tapped her on the shoulder.

"I didn't mean to frighten you, my child," Father Tadeusz said. He made the sign of the cross and touched her forehead as he blessed her.

"Thank you, Father," Lena said, keeping her head down to shield her tear-filled eyes.

"Your father loved you very much, Lena. He will continue to look after you."

Lena nodded and wiped her wet cheek with the back of her hand. "It's hard for me to believe he's gone."

Father Tadeusz gently put his arm around Lena's shoulder. "Come," he said, and led her toward the Rectory. They walked in silence. The sound of her high heels on the stone floor echoed throughout the empty church.

"I have known you a long time and your father even longer. I hope you think of me as someone you can depend on. Not just as a priest but as your good friend," Father Tadeusz said once they were in his office.

Lena was surprised. She had always viewed him as the pious sermon giver who granted communion. Not someone with whom she had a personal relationship.

"You're very kind, Father. You needn't worry about us. Stef and I will be fine. But I had planned to talk to you about Rudi before I left. I'm worried about him. Helga can't expect him to take care of things for her. Maybe you can make her understand," Lena said.

"I'll keep my eye on them. Don't you worry," Father Tadeusz assured her.

Lena was relieved. She didn't want to abandon her brother, but she had no way of taking care of him either. Rudi's limitations were a source of disappointment for his mother. For him they were a cause for sadness. With Stefan gone, Helga and Rudi had no buffer to protect them from each other. Lena hoped Father Tadeusz would help. Rudi had a steady job on a construction crew, but he could not step in for his father and take care of Helga.

"Rudi wasn't the reason I asked you here," Father Tadeusz began. "When I gave him the Last Rites, your father asked me to give you this." He handed Lena a brown envelope tied with a ribbon.

"Your father made me promise that if you needed help, I would provide it," he said as he walked off into a corner of his office to give her privacy. It was obvious Father Tadeusz knew what the envelope contained. That made Lena uncomfortable.

She carefully untied the ribbon. Inside Lena found two photographs, and a handwritten letter in Stefan's uneven scrawl. She heard her father's voice as she read the opening salutations and smiled.

My Darling Lena,

Please believe me that everything I did, I did because I loved you. I know that is not much of an excuse. I have already asked God to forgive me. Now I'm asking you to forgive me, too. I hope after you read this letter, you can find it in your heart to understand and forgive me.

When we found you at the orphanage, I knew you were our miracle. When Sister Janina introduced me to you and at first you did not want to come with Helga and me, I was heartsick. I wanted to take you in my arms and beg you to be our little girl. I didn't do that because I was afraid I would scare you even more. I have loved you from the moment I first saw you. I could not have loved you any more if you had been our own flesh and blood. But when Helga became pregnant, she thought that it would be better if a childless couple adopted you. She thought we should take you back to the orphanage. It was not something I wanted to do, but I went to the convent to see the Mother Superior because Helga believed it would be best for all of us.

The Mother Superior told me then that she suspected you were the child of a Jewish family, who had sent you to the convent to keep you safe from the Germans. You know what happened to the Jews in World War II. Many Jewish children were saved by the nuns. Mother Superior told me she thought God had sent you to us to be saved. As soon as she said it, I knew she was right. God had entrusted you to my care, and I was not going to disappoint him. I never mentioned to Helga that the Mother Superior thought your people were Jews. Only that it was possible that someone from your family might try to get you back sometime later. But I never thought about that. From then on you were my daughter. I decided having two children was better than only one. I was sure Helga would ultimately agree with me.

After the war was over, I got a letter from a Sister Marianna asking about you. She wanted to know how you were getting on and then she told me the person who brought you to the convent had returned. He told her your real family wanted you back.

That's where I need your forgiveness. By then I couldn't give you up. I lied to Sister Marianna. I told her you had been sick and had died. My darling Lena, I kept you from your real family, and I lied to Sister Marianna because I couldn't let you go. I did the best that I could for you. But I know it was selfish of me to keep you. Your real family must have suffered a great deal and they deserved to get you back. But I was too weak and selfish to let you go.

I don't know who they were or where they were from. Sister Marianna said a Dr. Bronisław Bieliński who came looking for you was the same man who brought you to the convent. You never talked about your people. You were so young I always assumed you did not remember them. I hoped that you thought of me as your father. I certainly felt like your real father. Sometimes I completely forgot how you came into our life.

The only clue we have to your people are the two photographs and the jewelry that Helga keeps in the beautiful inlaid box, which was also left for you. I hope you don't mind that I let her have the jewelry. You couldn't wear it and it did give her pleasure and made her happier to have you with us.

Please remember that I always loved you, and wanted the best for you. I know I may have deprived you of your family, but no one, not even your real family, could have loved you any more than I did. Forgive me.

Always,
Your loving father

After she finished, Lena sat motionless on the edge of the straight-backed wooden chair, staring into space. She clutched the letter and the photographs to her chest, and her thoughts went back to a day years before when she was playing with Rudi.

* * *

Eight-year-old Lena had been chasing her four-year-old brother around the room. Rudi was so intent on avoiding capture, he kept looking back to see where she was, and he crashed into a wall. The sound of his head hitting the wall frightened him and he started to cry. Lena rushed over and tried to tickle him to stop his crying just as Helga came into the room. Seeing her son in tears and thinking Lena had somehow harmed the child, she pulled Lena away with such force her hand left an impression on her arm.

"What have you done to my child?" she yelled.

Before Lena could explain, Helga whacked her hard across her face. Lena's shocked cry made Rudi cry harder. When Stefan walked in, the two children were screaming.

"What happened here?" he asked Helga. She glared at Lena and whisked Rudi, still crying, out of the room without answering Stefan's question.

Stefan bent down to wipe Lena's tears, and held her in his arms until she calmed down.

"Rudi is very lucky," she said, after a while.

"Why is he lucky?" Stefan asked.

"He has parents who love him. Who wouldn't send him away."

"Lena, your parents loved you very much. That's why they sent you away. There was a war. I know they sent you to the nuns to keep you safe. They wanted God to watch over you. If they could have kept you safe themselves, they would have."

"But the war is over now. They never came back to get me."

"There were reasons . . ." Stefan's voice trailed off. "Just remember, Lena, I couldn't love you any more if you were my own flesh and blood."

"You won't send me away?"

"Never!"

* * *

Remembering that day Lena finally understood what Stefan had been trying to tell her. Long ago she had given up hope of ever being reunited with her parents, still the pain of having been sent away remained a festering wound. Now she knew her father had come back for her, as he'd promised. Her family had not abandoned her. Even if she wasn't with them, she now knew they wanted her.

Lena had always felt out of place, but when she looked in the mirror she always saw the face of a Polish Christian. Indeed her blue eyes and blonde hair were proof of her Gentile heritage. How could my parents have been Jews? Lena wondered. Even Helga told her the two of them looked so much alike she could have been her real daughter.

Growing up Lena had heard people say that Jews were the killers of Christ, and general troublemakers. As a child she decided Jews possessed special powers to be able to cause so much trouble. While Helga had no fondness for Jews, Stefan and Aaron Rothman, the tailor's son, were good friends. Lena recalled how upset Stefan was the day he told Helga the Rothman family had been sent to Treblinka. She thought they were moving to another town, and Stefan was upset because he would miss his friend. She did not understand until much later that being "sent to" Treblinka meant going to a concentration camp and certain death.

Stefan's letter brought Lena both solace and shock. Her only visible response was the steady stream of tears cascading down her cheeks. Her body stayed rigid, her face emotionless, but her thoughts swirled around at lightning speed.

In Poland you were either a Catholic or a Communist. Am I still a Catholic? Does having Jewish parents negate my communion and confirmation? How would people treat me if they suspected my parents were Jews? Lena remembered that at the university a rumor that a student had any Jewish blood met with an avalanche of derision. She thought about the recent firing of some Communist officials rumored to have Jewish ancestry. She knew not many Jews remained in Poland after the war. What happened to my family? she wondered.

Lena felt lightheaded. She leaned forward to get blood flowing to her brain. As she began to fall, Lena heard Father Tadeusz coming toward her. Slowed by his portly frame he reached her just as she touched the floor. Through her tears she could see the concern on his craggy face.

"Are you hurt?" he asked, and helped her back onto the chair.

Lena shook her head. She couldn't find her voice. Lena knew he expected her to say something, but there was nothing she wanted to say to him. Lena didn't love Stefan any less now that she knew his secret. In any true meaning of the word, he was her father. It was because he loved her so much that he couldn't give her up. Lena loved him and understood. He didn't need to be forgiven.

"You must be very confused," Father Tadeusz said, breaking the awkward silence. "Talk to me, child, please. You need someone to sort this out with."

I do need to sort all this out, Lena thought, but not here. She wanted to bolt out of the Rectory, but didn't want to be rude. "Forgive me, Father. I'm not ready to talk now. I need time to think." Lena stood up to leave.

"Stefan asked me to help you, child, and I will, if you let me," he said, trying to engage her.

"I appreciate that you want to help. But right now I don't know what kind of help I need," Lena said. The air felt close, she could hardly breathe. She started for the door.

Resigned to letting her go, he said, "Remember, I'll be here whenever you need me." And blessed her again.

Inside the church Lena took several deep breaths of incense-laden air and walked toward the front door. As always before leaving, she dipped her hand in holy water next to the entrance, knelt facing the altar and crossed herself.

Outside in the cool air she began to breathe normally. Lena forced her mind back to her first day with the nuns. Running a film in reverse through the sprockets in her brain, she saw herself meeting the other children in the courtyard, Sister Janina's welcoming face, and finally her small fingers clutching a man's hand, not really his hand, but his thumb. No matter how hard she tried, Lena couldn't see his face, but she knew that the man who brought her to the orphanage was her father. My father came back to get me, just as he said he would, Lena told herself. She said his name: Dr. Bronisław Bieliński. Am I really Lena Bielińska?

With his letter, Stefan had reached out from the grave and had given Lena back her real family. She was grateful, still the tears flowed. It's a miracle! I don't feel as alone as I did at the cemetery, she thought.

Lena studied the two pictures she held in her hand. She recognized herself as the blonde child, wearing the same dress she wore the day she first met Stefan and Helga. The picture of the two girls with the young woman brought more tears. The woman has to be my mother, Lena reasoned. Was the other child a playmate or my sister? No matter how hard she tried, she couldn't retrieve any memories of her life before the orphanage.

In those early months with the nuns, thinking about anything related to her life before, left Lena sobbing. To stem the tears she buried her memories, and focused on the day when her father would come back for her. She held on to that hope for some time, but gradually gave up all expectation of ever being reunited with her family once she went to live with Stefan and Helga.

Unfortunately, because of what Stefan told Sister Marianna, Lena knew that they were no longer looking for her. It's up to me to search for them. But first I have to find out who they are. When she saw the name of the photographer and his Krakow address stamped on the back of both pictures, Lena thought optimistically, I have a place to start looking!

She rubbed the face of the woman in the picture. "Mama," she said. "At least I know what you looked like." She looked exactly like Lena.

It was windy and getting colder, but Lena seemed oblivious to the dropping temperature. If anything, the chill felt good. She wasn't ready to go home and started walking aimlessly towards the center of town. Along Żeromskiego Street Lena found herself searching for signs that Jews existed in Sandomierz. She suspected her roots were elsewhere. But suddenly Lena felt part of a group that had been invisible. She needed to affirm their existence.

There were few people along Opatowska Street. But as she passed through the gate to the town square she joined an overflowing crowd of shoppers at the farmer's market. In a dreamlike state, Lena made her way around the stalls and headed for the small museum on the ground floor of Town Hall devoted to the history of Sandomierz. She had not visited the museum for years, but thought she might find some mention of Jews in the area. Inside, she found nothing, and asked the guard, "Have there been any exhibits about Jews living in Sandomierz? Where they worked?"

"Not that I've seen," he said, genuinely apologetic.

Lena felt foolish and headed for the door.

"Wait a minute," the guard yelled after her. "Guess they did live here once. When I worked in the registry office on Żydowska Street, someone mentioned the building used to be a synagogue. Isn't that a Jewish church?"

"I think it is, thank you," Lena said and waved goodbye. The registry wasn't far. Even though it no longer functioned as a synagogue, Lena decided to take a look. She briskly made her way back through the stalls, and turned left onto Oleśnickich Street. On Żydowska, clutching Stefan's letter and the two pictures, Lena stood in front of the imposing red brick 18th-century structure that once housed a synagogue, and tried to conjure up Jews walking into worship. Sadly, she could not summon any Jewish faces.

When she got back to the house, her son and his uncle Rudi were playing cards at the kitchen table. Lena went over to kiss Stefan, but he pushed her away, embarrassed.

"You can kiss me," Rudi said.

"Where's your mother?" Lena asked as she hugged her brother, and kissed the top of his head. Rudi pointed to the bedroom. Lena put the precious envelope she'd been holding into her purse, and knocked on Helga's door.

"Can I come in for a minute?" Lena said through the door.

"If you want," Helga answered guardedly.

Lena entered the room and closed the door behind her. She leaned against it, reluctant to invade Helga's space.

"Are you feeling okay?" she asked.

"I'll manage. I always have," Helga said, resting on her bed, still dressed in her widow's weeds.

Lena's eyes wandered around the room, and settled on the inlaid box her father mentioned in his letter. It was on top of Helga's chest of drawers. As Lena started to walk toward it, Helga jumped off the bed and picked up the box.

"So that's what he wrote about to you in that letter he gave Father Tadeusz," Helga said. "Well, I deserved the jewelry. It's all I ever got for taking you in. I suppose you want it back?"

"No. I don't. The jewelry is yours," Lena said without any rancor. "But I would like to look at it and the box."

Helga grudgingly handed the box to Lena. Although she had seen it many times before, this time Lena looked at it differently. She tenderly stroked the box. As she touched it, she felt as if she were connecting with her real mother.

CHAPTER

9

AS THE TRAIN PULLED into the Amagansett station, Hannah spotted Robert off in the distance. With his hands jammed into his jean pockets, his blue work-shirt collar sticking out of a bulky Irish knit sweater, he looked as if he'd stepped out of an L. L. Bean catalogue. The gray flecks in his hair shimmered blond in the sunlight.

Fooled by the cloudless blue sky she saw through the train window, Hannah expected to be embraced by a warm breeze. Wearing only a khaki safari jacket over her poor-boy turtleneck and her bell bottoms, the cool air surprised her as she stepped off the train in her signature three-inch platform shoes, which raised her to the desired five-foot-seven height. Robert's quick embrace shielded Hannah from the unexpected chill.

She felt warm and welcomed, until he said, "I see you brought your work with you!" as he carried her heavy tote to his car. Hannah wanted to shout, "No! I didn't bring any work!" The mountain of research she had stuffed into her bag was there to ease her guilt for not staying at her desk and furthering her search for Lena. Instead she let out a nervous giggle. Some residual guilt washed over Hannah. It wasn't true this day, but she remembered other times when her work did take over their time together. No squabbling, she told herself. Nothing is going to spoil this weekend. I won't let it.

On the short drive to the farmer's market along Montauk Highway, Hannah relaxed as she let her body sink into the familiar soft-leather front seat of Robert's 1963 turquoise Rambler. Long ago Hannah had christened his station wagon "The Rust Bucket."

"Call it anything you like, for me it's perfect. Starts right away, and gets me where I want to go. It's transportation," he countered every time Hannah suggested it was necessary for them to think about an upgrade.

At the market Robert quickly went about filling his wire basket with edible delights for the meal he'd promised her. The smell of fresh bread made Hannah hungry.

"Don't touch anything in the basket," Robert yelled, and gently slapped her hand when she tried to break off a piece of the still-hot croissant. "You can hold out a little longer. Exercise your famous willpower," Robert said in mock anger.

As she watched him go from stall to stall, Hannah lamented her own lack of interest in cooking. Maybe it's not my fault. I've got Harry's genes instead of Molly's. She liked that explanation.

As Robert pulled into the driveway, Hannah stiffened. She knew that seeing the cottage under their new circumstances would be hard for her. Surrounded by dune grass and other modest beach houses, the small, two-story, gray-shingled A-frame was on a lane just behind the dunes. From the deck off the upstairs bedroom Robert and Hannah often watched the ocean waves undulate on the sand. In the late afternoon they'd sit sipping wine and congratulate themselves for being fortunate enough to have such a spectacular view. Seeing the sun set was a perfect coda to any day.

When the front door slammed behind her, the familiar smell of damp pine embraced her. Hannah closed her eyes and recalled the happy times she and Robert had spent there. Her memories cheered her until she walked into the living room that now doubled as an office. The drop-leaf dining table they found at a thrift shop and she'd waxed to a hard luster finish was folded and relegated to a sidewall. Robert's large drawing table, piled high with blue prints, T-squares, rulers, and other architectural paraphernalia, now dominated the room. The gray-ticking couch, along with a white sale-cloth easy chair and glass coffee table were shoved to the other side of the room. Tacked on the walls, with pushpins, were huge renderings of the two houses now in mid-construction. It was still the same beach house, but now it was officially Robert's. Deep down, Hannah had always considered the cottage to be his.

She had been out of town on an assignment when Robert first saw it and he couldn't reach her. The house was exactly what they both wanted and at a price they could afford. He put down a deposit that very day. "I couldn't risk losing it," he explained. It was the only time Robert ever made a major decision without consulting her. Until now.

"We'll be ready to eat in no time. Just relax," Robert said, as he took his cache of food into the kitchen. Grinning, he added, "If you can figure out how to do such a simple thing."

"I'll do my best," she said with the utmost seriousness. "Do you have anything cold to drink?"

Just as the question fell from her lips, Robert handed Hannah a mimosa before disappearing into the kitchen. She looked around trying not to feel displaced. Hannah was surprised to see the staircase leading to the master bedroom now had a railing. For years she had pressed for one. Seeing the change unnerved her.

"The house looks very different," she said.

"It's only temporary," Robert yelled back.

Unlike Hannah, he attached no significance to the changes.

Robert had not considered his move a break in their relationship. But he had to admit that their living apart did create a distance between them that was greater than the 107 miles from Manhattan to Amagansett. Robert liked living away from New York City even more than he thought he would. He wished he could persuade Hannah to move to the cottage, but he had not ruled out moving back to the city once his two houses were finished. Having Hannah at his arms' reach made Robert realize how much he'd missed her.

The noonday sun streaming through a wall of windows made Hannah squint. While Robert cooked, she sank into the comfortable down couch, sipped her drink and consciously tried to purge all negative thoughts from her mind as she tracked a parade of puffy clouds being chased by the forceful wind.

In exactly eighteen minutes Robert came out of the kitchen to show off his beautiful French omelet.

"Where shall we eat, inside or out?" he asked.

"I'm tempted to say on the deck, but maybe it's too windy," Hannah said.

"Fine. We'll enjoy the sun inside, without the need for sunscreen." In one motion of his left hand, Robert transformed his workspace into a dining table by shoving everything that was on top into a cardboard box.

Hannah quickly set the makeshift table, and they dug in.

"Delicious! My compliments to the chef," Hannah said after her first bite.

"And you didn't even have to tip the delivery guy."

"I'd be happy to give some serious compensation to the chef."

In half the time it took to prepare, the two of them devoured an omelet meant for four, along with marmalade-laden croissants, and berries topped with *crème fraîche*. They laughed, toasted, and happily ogled each other, both avoiding serious talk.

Their playful eating orgy was reminiscent of the meal shared by Albert Finney and Diane Cilento in *Tom Jones*, one of their favorite movies.

Finally, over coffee, Robert said: "How is Harry holding up? More important, you and Harry?"

"Better than I would have imagined a week ago."

"Have you any idea how to go about looking for your sister? I take that back. Knowing you, you're probably only days away from finding her."

"I'm afraid that's what Harry thinks. I know he's disappointed that I haven't made more progress. I suppose I should feel proud that my father thinks I could find her after all this time." Hannah sighed and shook her head.

"He waited thirty years to tell you about her. Even he can't expect you to miraculously make her reappear."

"Forget pulling off a miracle, the truth is I'm not sure where or how to begin. I'm trying to locate a thirty-nine-year-old Polish woman who was called Lena as a child. That is really all I have to go on."

"Harry is right about one thing, if anyone can do it, it's you."

"I wish . . . I've been reading up on hidden children, hoping that would lead me somewhere. All the stuff I've gathered so far is in my tote."

"Is that what you planned to do all weekend?"

"No. It's an old trick to eliminate guilt. I used to carry my books everywhere in college. Having them with me was my guilt protector, even if I didn't do the reading. I stuffed my bag and came to be with you. I want this weekend to be about us. I've really missed you," Hannah confessed. Feeling vulnerable, she cast her eyes down.

"Me too," Robert said as he reached to squeeze her hand.

Reassured by his touch, Hannah asked her burning question: "How much longer will you have to stay here?"

"You mean when will the houses be finished?"

That wasn't what Hannah meant, but she wanted the answer to that question as well, so she nodded yes.

"Should be done by the end of August at the latest."

"How's the work been?" She expected to hear all about the difficulties of finding qualified workers, and meeting the demands of irrational clients.

"So far, it's been great. It couldn't be going any better. I have a great crew and the clients and I are on the same page about everything. Hannah, I really like working for myself. And living out here, that's been great, too. All except the fact that you're there and I'm here."

"Yes, I know," Hannah said in a whisper.

"This summer will be wonderful. I won't be spending my Friday nights rushing to an overcrowded train or sitting on the Hampton Jitney for hours on the L.I.E. You will!" Robert grinned and offered a toast, "To no commuting! *Cin Cin!*" He raised his wine glass, and clicked Hannah's. "Of course the winter is another story. I know it gets pretty cold here. This house needs insulation."

Hannah's jaw went slack. Oh, my God! He intends to stay at the beach permanently! She felt Robert still loved her, but Hannah feared that might not be enough to keep their marriage on track. Would she be forced to choose between their marriage and living in New York?

As soon as he noticed Hannah's troubled gaze, Robert asked plaintively, "Don't I at least get a peck on the cheek for slaving over that hot omelet pan?"

"You deserve more than that," Hannah said and playfully plunked herself down on his lap.

Robert held her face in both his hands and looked into her tear-filled eyes for a few seconds before kissing her quivering lips. The force of their kiss made it clear how much they'd missed each other. She would have liked to be carried up to the bedroom in his arms, like Scarlett O'Hara was by Rhett Butler, but settled for being led upstairs, holding on to the newly installed railing.

They embraced at the top of the stairs. Their six-week hiatus made them hungry for each other. Still clinging, one to the other, they landed on the bed. Their lovemaking was feverish. They satisfied their lust. Both realized what being apart had cost them.

"It always should be like this with us," Hannah whispered.

Robert agreed. When they finally broke apart, they fell asleep contentedly. Robert woke up when he rolled over and hit his head on the edge of the night table. His eyes caught a glimpse of his note pad—scrawled in block letters was an appointment he'd made to meet an electrician. He checked his watch, and reached for his jeans.

Hannah woke up as he was putting on his sneakers. "Where are you rushing to?" she asked, wistfully.

"I have an appointment with the electrician. He's at the house by now. I gotta run. Promise, I'll be back in an hour, two at the most. He's waiting for the new specs. Damn! I'm sorry. I'm so sorry," Robert said.

"Now who's letting work interfere with our life?" Hannah said laughing. "Go! I'll clean up. In two hours you won't recognize the place."

Early the next morning Hannah and Robert were awakened by a beam of sun shining through the skylight over their bed. Neither wanted to budge. Instead they made love like newlyweds. Afterwards they held each other close. Hannah wished she could melt into Robert's body, to make it impossible for him to ever leave her. They were both hungry. Robert decided to go out for fresh rolls and the newspaper. Reading the paper in bed on the weekends used to be their ritual when they lived together. Of course, in their New York apartment they had the convenience of having the paper delivered to their door. Reluctantly, Hannah let Robert go.

"Hurry back," she said. Hannah couldn't remember the last time she'd felt this good. She was sure Robert felt the same way.

When he returned armed with a breakfast tray, they ate their still-warm rolls with jam, drank freshly brewed English Breakfast tea in bed, and read the paper in comfortable silence just the way they used to. Later, bundled up against the cool breeze, they walked along the beach. Hannah had almost forgotten what a good time they used to have doing nothing special. She was almost afraid to breathe. Hannah didn't want anything to change. As they approached the house on the way back, Robert heard the ringing phone and rushed in to answer it.

"Where have you been? I'm here at the station. I have been waiting for you for more than twenty minutes!" Christy's voice blared through the phone. Robert held the receiver at arm's length to protect his eardrum.

"Oh, my God. I forgot you were coming. I'll be right there." Robert hung up and looked around for Hannah.

"Hey, Hannah, where are you?"

"Upstairs. Getting out of these clothes. Come and join me."

"That was Christy. It's her weekend. I completely forgot. She's

157

waiting at the train station. I've got to pick her up. See, you make me forget everything."

"So sorry." Hannah's tone was flat, serious.

"Not your fault," he laughed, "I'm the jerk who forgot."

When Hannah didn't respond, Robert knew her silence was not a good sign. He rushed up the stairs two at a time. When he reached her, he saw she was throwing her stuff into her overnight bag.

"What are you doing?"

"Packing. You can leave me at the station."

"Don't be ridiculous!"

"This is your weekend with Christy. I shouldn't be here." Hannah saw herself as an uninvited guest. She felt she had to leave. "I'll take the next train back to New York."

"You're not going anywhere! Christy will be very glad you're here. She's always telling me how boring I am," Robert said. Determined to make her stay, he playfully tried to force Hannah's lips into a smile with one hand, as he emptied the contents of her bag back onto the bed with the other.

"I know you're disappointed. I'd rather we had the entire weekend to ourselves. But the three of us will have a great time. We'll have other weekends, just the two of us," he assured her.

Finally, after admitting to herself she didn't want to leave, Hannah said, "Okay. I'll stay. It won't be the same. But I have to admit I've missed Christy."

Robert kissed the top of her head, and they both rushed to the car.

Christy was the only person at the deserted Amagansett train station. When she saw Hannah, she ran toward her.

"My teacher was very impressed," she whispered in Hannah's ear.

"What are you two females plotting?" Robert feigned displeasure.

"Nothing." Christy sported her best Cheshire grin as she let herself be hugged by her father. She enjoyed sharing a secret with Hannah.

Later, back at the house, just as Robert started to unpack the groceries for their planned barbecue, the phone rang.

"Can you get that?" Robert yelled to Hannah. "Whoever it is, I'm not available."

But the call was not for Robert.

"You have to come back right away!" Molly said, as soon as she heard Hannah's voice. "I can't take care of your father alone." By her tone Hannah assumed Harry had taken a turn for the worse.

"I'll be there as soon as I can," she said.

Robert could see the tears in her eyes. "Who was that?"

"My mother. I have to go."

"What's going on?"

"Mother didn't say. She just said I had to come back right away."

"Hannah, you're not a doctor. If Harry's really sick, only a doctor can help him. Call her back and tell her you'll be there tomorrow."

"He's his own doctor. He won't let her call anyone."

"But he let her call you."

"I have to go. You didn't hear the desperation in her voice," Hannah said.

A cheerful Molly let Hannah into the apartment. It was not what she had expected. She was further startled to see her father at the piano picking out tunes and looking better than he had on Friday morning before she had left for the beach.

Harry was obviously surprised to see her.

"Weren't you going away for the weekend?"

Hannah nodded. "Something came up," she told her father, and glared at her mother who refused to make eye contact.

"How are you feeling?" Hannah asked her father as she walked into the living room.

"Good. Not great but better."

"You're looking better, too," Hannah said. While she smiled at Harry, Hannah was seething. She suppressed the urge to scream at Molly. Hannah didn't want to make a scene. Her mother was counting on that.

"I'm in need of a cup of tea," she said, when she saw her mother going into the kitchen.

"Where's the medical emergency you got me back here for?" Hannah demanded.

"Quiet. I don't want your father to know I called you. I never said there was a medical emergency. I said I couldn't take care of your father alone."

"What do you expect me to do?"

"Be here to spell me. That's what a good daughter does."

"What about what a good mother does?" Hannah shot back. Out of frustration, her anger had turned to tears. "You called me away from a wonderful weekend with my husband for no reason at all."

"No reason! I had a whole winter of reasons you didn't want to hear about. All you ever think about is your own life. Think about me for a change. I'm the one who's been in prison," Molly complained.

10

ON MONDAY MORNING the Stone family arrived twenty-five minutes early for their appointment with Dr. Martin, a trademark move for Harry and Molly.

As they sat in the empty waiting room, Molly tried to show her motherly concern. "Hannah, I hope you had a good breakfast," she said.

Still furious about her ruined weekend, Hannah ignored her mother. She shielded her face with the morning paper, pretending to be reading, until the nurse announced, "Dr. Martin will see you now."

Inside the doctor's office, Molly pulled her chair closer to Harry's. Hannah sat off to the side, a spectator to the ensuing drama. She watched Dr. Martin take notes as he listened to her father's meticulous description of his symptoms. When he finished, Harry and Dr. Martin went into the examining room across the hall. Hannah went back to pretending to read the paper.

"Dr. Martin doesn't seem a bit worried about your father. He'll know what to do," Molly said confidently. Hannah said nothing. She hoped her mother was right.

A pale and drawn Harry came back into the room after the examination. Hannah held her breath as she waited to hear what the doctor had to say.

"There's a limit to what I can do here. More tests would be helpful," Dr. Martin said, adding, "The best place for that is the hospital."

Molly stiffened in her chair.

"No! Absolutely not! I'm not going into the hospital," Harry said forcefully. "I have congestive heart failure. I need to have my medication changed. I don't need to be in a hospital for that!" Harry's strong response demonstrated a vitality not supported by his wan appearance.

Dr. Martin didn't argue. "As you know, Dr. Stone, the trick with congestive heart failure is finding the cause. Best place for doing that is in the hospital," he repeated.

Harry continued to shake his head.

"What I have in mind is not the usual hospital stay. It's part of the Medical Center, but feels more like a three-star hotel. All the tests are done at the hospital, but you and your wife stay in a private room. You'll take your meals in a pleasant dining room. Think of it as a vacation," Dr. Martin said and leaned back in his chair. "It's up to you, Dr. Stone. You could stay at home and come in to the hospital for the tests. Your call!"

Harry deliberated. He weighed the doctor's reassuring words against his own almost pathological fear of becoming a helpless patient, at the mercy of attending physicians. In the end what Dr. Martin described sounded manageable. Harry agreed.

"I'm in your hands," he said. By the time he reached out to shake Dr. Martin's hand to seal their bargain, the color had come back into Harry's face.

"Are there doctors around . . . in case we need them?" Molly asked, nervously.

"Of course," Dr. Martin assured Molly.

Sounds okay, Hannah reassured herself as they left the doctor's office. But the possibility that something could go wrong stayed with her. No Mistakes Allowed. I'll will him back to health the way I willed him back to life during the war. Hannah thought about that day when a tearful Aunt Emma announced, "*Pan Bronisław nie żyje!*" All the men in his building were executed, she said.

"No. No, he can't be dead!" Hannah had insisted. That night she knelt in front of the framed image of the Black Madonna on the table next to her bed and begged her patron saint for a miracle. The next morning when she awoke she was sure Bronisław Bieliński was still alive. "I know he is alive. I feel it," she told Aunt Emma, who had dismissed Hannah's feelings as wishful thinking. But the child turned out to be right.

On that particular day a waiting room full of patients kept him working later than usual at his office across town. By the time he returned to his apartment, he'd missed the mass execution.

Nobody ever found out why the men were executed. It was rumored they were rounding up members of the Polish Underground. Worried he might be suspected of being a collaborator as he was the only man not killed, Harry immediately found another place to live. While he added that narrow escape to his running tally of all the times dumb luck had saved him, Hannah childishly believed she and the Black Madonna had kept Harry alive.

Still relying on Harry's luck, and her power to will him back to health, instead of the Black Madonna, Hannah now put her faith in Dr. Martin.

By the following Thursday, her anger toward her mother finally dissipated. Hannah went along with Harry and Molly as they checked into the Co-op Care unit of the N.Y.U. Medical Center on First Avenue. Although Hannah wheeled him into their private room, Harry didn't feel like a patient being admitted into a hospital. With a view of the New York skyline, a well-appointed sitting area, complete with a comfortable sofa, coffee table, an easy chair and a huge TV set, their spacious room could pass for a tastefully decorated hotel suite. But what made Harry particularly happy was that Molly would be staying with him.

"You were trying to get me to go for a vacation to Miami Beach this winter. Pretend this is Miami. We're on vacation," Harry said. "The only thing missing is a wet bar," he joked.

Molly squeezed her husband's hand. It looked good to her, too. "I'm going to check out the dining room and see if we need to make a reservation," Molly said, rushing off.

"Hurry back," Harry yelled after her. In that moment, Hannah saw how dependent her father was on her mother. She had always assumed it was the reverse.

Hannah returned the next morning. She had taken the day off from work to be with her parents before going to the beach, this time for an uninterrupted weekend.

While Molly remained in the room, Hannah wheeled Harry to the hospital for a series of tests. The last test, an echocardiogram, which was a simple non-invasive procedure, inexplicably had to be redone several times.

"I'm sorry it's taking so long," the technician apologized when Hannah cornered him as he came out of the room without Harry. "We're having a problem with the equipment. Been getting a strange noise. We've called for the supervisor," he explained.

When Harry was finally wheeled out, he was so weak, he looked as if he was about to slide off the chair. Uncharacteristically docile, he didn't say a word about being inconvenienced for three hours.

A glum Hannah wheeled her exhausted father back to his room.

"What's happened? He looks terrible," Molly said.

Hannah shot a stern look at her mother who immediately softened her assessment.

"What you need, Harry, is something to eat. You must be starving," Molly said.

Seeing Robert sitting on the sofa, Hannah's mood brightened.

"When did you get here?" she asked.

"I finished my errands about an hour ago," he said and rushed over to help get Harry out of the wheelchair.

Molly checked her watch. "The dining room is open. I'll get some food." Preparing food was how Molly made things better.

The best she could do now was to bring it from the dining room.

"Yes. Yes. You go," Harry whispered. Going anywhere was not an option for him. Leaning on Robert, Harry pulled himself up and almost threw himself onto the bed. His face drained of all color, Harry stretched his skeletal frame out on the bed, and closed his eyes.

Robert put his arms around Hannah to steady her.

With Molly out of the room, and Harry seemingly asleep, Hannah whispered to Robert, "This is not working the way I thought." Besides the problem with the echocardiogram, Hannah didn't like the churning in her stomach. That usually foreshadowed something bad was about to happen.

"I hope I didn't make a mistake pushing Harry to see a specialist. He seemed better when he was his own doctor."

"Hannah, cut it out. You're not responsible for your father's condition. Harry's a grown man, and a doctor. He realized he needed help."

"But what if this doctor I forced on him doesn't help him?" Hannah said, and continued to berate herself. "Maybe I didn't look hard enough? He counted on me to find the right person."

"Give it a chance. It's only been a day," Robert said.

Molly returned with more food than anyone wanted. Harry barely tasted the broth she tried to feed him before he fell asleep. Hannah and Robert drank their coffee and picked at their sandwiches.

As Harry slept, Molly watched TV, nervously changing channels. Robert and Hannah leafed through magazines. When Harry woke up and asked for tea and toast, everyone was relieved, especially Molly. By the time Robert and Hannah were ready to say goodbye, Harry was able to sit up to watch the evening news.

"Remember if you need the nurse during the night, you can call her," Hannah told her mother as she kissed her goodbye.

"I know what to do," Molly assured her daughter.

"Have a good weekend, you two," Harry said and insisted on hugging both of them. The fact that being hugged by her father felt normal cheered Hannah.

When she called her mother on Saturday morning, Molly picked up the phone on the first ring. Hannah detected strain in her mother's "Hello."

"How is everything?" Hannah asked.

"Your father is still very weak. And his ankles are swollen worse than yesterday. I don't know why he's not getting any medication," she said. "They won't tell me anything."

"I'll call the nurse," Hannah offered.

When Hannah finally got through, the harried nurse on duty was not helpful.

"Your father is getting the treatment his doctor prescribed. If you have questions, talk to him," she said, and hung up.

Hannah called Dr. Martin, but he was away for the weekend. The doctor on call did not answer his page.

"They probably stopped Dad's medication as a way to determine what works and what doesn't," she told her mother, trying to reassure her. "They know what they're doing," she added, but that was not how she felt.

Molly called on Sunday at the crack of dawn. The panic in her mother's voice roused Hannah quicker than a piercing alarm clock.

"You have to come right now," Molly pleaded. "The nurse says she can't do anything and I can't find a doctor to talk to. Maybe you can make them help him."

Hannah started getting dressed even before she hung up the phone. She checked the train schedule. When she was packed and ready to go, Hannah woke Robert to take her to the station.

"Why are you going back? He's in a hospital, for chrissake!"

Hannah shook her head. "I put him there."

Hannah gasped when she walked into the room and saw Harry lying motionless on the bed. She could hear her heart pounding as she tiptoed to his bedside. Hannah held her breath as she put her hand in front of his nose to see if he was breathing. When he slowly opened his eyes, she exhaled. He stared at her, but she wasn't sure her father recognized her. With his bony hand on his chest he whispered, "The pain, the pain. I can't stand the pain."

Hearing Harry's voice, Molly, who was asleep in the next bed, shot up.

"Thank God you're here," she said, and grabbed her daughter's hand.

Hannah pulled it away and reached for the phone.

"My father, Harry Stone, is in great pain," she heard herself say in an unfamiliar shrill voice, when a nurse finally picked up. "You've got to give him something for the pain!"

"I can't. I told your mother. I can't even give him a Tylenol without a doctor's okay. I'm really sorry," she said.

It shocked Hannah that the nurse on duty was just as helpless as she was.

"Please. Please, get him a doctor then," Hannah begged. "He has to be seen by a doctor."

"Believe me, I've been trying," she said, "but we're short-staffed because it's a weekend, and they are dealing with several emergencies."

Hannah called Robert.

"If he was at home, I could call 911 and somebody would come. Here I can't get a doctor and the nurse can't do anything. He's in pain and I can't do anything to help him. Should I go to a drugstore and buy some aspirin?"

"Don't! Don't do anything that could make things worse," Robert counseled.

For the rest of the day, while Molly slept, Hannah sat beside Harry's bed and stroked his cold hand, as he went in and out of a restless sleep. Stoically, she pleaded with God. "I can't lose him now! I can't lose him now!"

Early Monday morning Dr. Martin appeared.

"Let me examine him and then we'll see what to do," Dr. Martin said, calmly. When he finished, he ordered the nurse to give Harry pain medication. Within minutes, Harry drifted into a more restful sleep, and Dr. Martin motioned Molly and Hannah out of the room.

"The pain is not angina. The sac around Dr. Stone's heart is filling up with water. That water is now pressing on his heart. All we have to do is puncture the sac and get the water out," Dr. Martin said.

"That sounds like an operation," Molly said. "Harry won't agree to an operation."

"It's not major surgery, more like a procedure. Once that's done Dr. Stone should be fine," he said.

This time Dr. Martin's assurances did not convince Hannah or Molly.

"Why did the water fill up around his heart?" Hannah demanded. "He never had that problem before!"

"We don't know what's causing your father's congestive heart failure. That's what we were hoping to find out," Dr. Martin said, his voice marked with irritation.

As soon as the doctor left, two attendants moved a sleeping Harry to a semi-private hospital room. When he awoke, Harry Stone knew his worst fears were now realized.

I managed my congestive heart failure better on my own, Harry thought, although he was grateful they had lessened his pain.

When an unfamiliar doctor in a lab coat appeared holding a clipboard and pen, Harry looked disdainfully at him.

"Dr. Stone, I've come to get your signature for the procedure," he said.

Harry glared. "I'm not signing any form for any procedure."

Rattled, the doctor left. Only to be followed by a succession of other doctors, clipboard in hand, each pressing Harry to sign the consent form.

"You have to find a way to get rid of the water without cutting me open. Use your miracle pills!" Harry mocked. "Start playing doctor, instead of butcher!"

To Hannah he said, "This is a teaching hospital. To them I'm just a guinea pig."

Harry was blaming the doctors, but Hannah felt responsible. No matter what Robert said, she could not be dissuaded from the notion that Harry's present condition was her fault. Her mistake. The doctor she had selected to make him better had only brought him pain. During visiting hours, when the medical staff tried to enlist her help in persuading Harry to sign the consent form, Hannah refused. She couldn't side with those she no longer trusted.

When Molly left the room briefly, Harry motioned for Hannah to move closer.

"Remember, Hannah, I don't want to end up a vegetable attached to a machine. I won't be anybody's experiment. Promise me you'll make sure of that," he said. "I want to live, but only if I'm really alive. I agreed to all this, against my better judgment. I wanted to buy myself more time with you." He reached for her hand. "And to give you enough time to find Lena. I must see her before I die."

"You're not going to die!" Hannah insisted and squeezed Harry's hand. She wished she had some hopeful news about Lena to keep Harry fighting. Having made no headway, she felt she was failing her father on all fronts.

The medical stalemate was finally broken the evening Hannah and Molly saw Dr. Caulder leaving Harry's room waving the consent form in the air like a victory flag.

"Your father has finally signed, and it is not a moment too soon," Dr. Caulder said, convinced his prodding had paid off. With his pain now contained by the morphine, in his lucid moments, it was his desire to stay alive long enough to see Lena that had made Harry agree.

A combination of disbelief and relief washed over Hannah. At that moment she chose to believe the doctors would pull off her much-needed miracle. "When will you operate?" she asked.

"As soon as I get a slot in the O.R.," Dr. Caulder said. "Probably tomorrow afternoon."

Hannah put her arm around her mother's shoulder. "Once this is over, Mom, you should take Dad on a real vacation."

"I'll be happy if he just comes home." Molly was uncharacteristically somber.

After they said goodnight to Harry, without thinking, Hannah said to Molly, "Come home with me." As soon as the words were out of her mouth, she was sorry. Being in her own apartment she could pretend her life was normal, at least for the night. She knew with Molly there that would not be possible. Hannah felt guilty for her momentary wish to be rid of her mother.

Outside the hospital, First Avenue was still busy with the tail end of rush hour traffic. On Second Avenue Hannah hailed a cab downtown. In the taxi, neither of them spoke. A grateful Molly held onto Hannah's hand as if she were the child.

Ignoring the flickering red light on the answering machine, Hannah called Robert as soon as they entered the apartment. Hearing Hannah's "Hello!" his agitated voice bellowed out of the receiver. "Why do you bother having an answering machine if you don't call in to check your messages? I've been leaving messages since early this morning!"

"It's been a trying day."

"What's going on?"

"Believe it or not he's agreed to the surgery."

"Want me to come in?"

"No. It's just a procedure." Hannah repeated what she'd heard from the doctors. But she was glad Robert had offered to come in.

Hannah went into the kitchen after she hung up. She found Molly sitting at the counter staring blankly into space. In a role reversal, Hannah cut two pieces of Molly's homemade strudel she kept in the freezer and put them in the toaster.

"Do you want tea, coffee, or milk?" Hannah asked.

Molly shook her head.

"Eat, Mom," Hannah said, as she placed the warmed piece of strudel in front of her mother. "It's what you tell everybody."

As Molly was taking her first bite, Hannah licked the jam from her fingers and headed for the shower.

When she came out of the bathroom, Hannah heard the unrelenting whistle of the teakettle and rushed to turn it off. She found her mother now sitting stone-like at the dining room table, oblivious to the piercing sound.

"Were you making tea, Mom?" Hannah asked. Molly seemed startled by the question, even though she had obviously put the water up to boil.

"No. I'll just go to sleep," she said.

"I left you one of my night shirts and a new toothbrush, on Christy's bed."

Hannah walked over and gently touched her mother's shoulder. As soon as Molly felt Hannah's presence, she leaned her head against her daughter's body.

That night, tossing in her bed, Hannah was visited by a distraught Aunt Emma who announced Harry was dead. Hearing her own voice shouting, "He can't be dead! He can't be dead!" Hannah bolted upright in bed. The room was dark except for the light from the TV. "He can't die, not now!"

Hannah no longer had the Black Madonna to appeal to, so she talked directly to God, "Please, please, don't let him die!"

Now wide awake, she went in to check on her mother. She found Molly curled up in Christy's bed, sound asleep.

Hannah reached for the still unopened box of Marlboros in her bag, but changed her mind. Instead she opted for a bowl of mint chip ice cream, and got out her LENA folder. She knew her search for her sister was the only way she had to keep her father fighting to stay alive. Hannah resolved to accelerate her efforts to find Lena.

The next morning Hannah dropped her mother off in front of the hospital.

"Tell Dad I'll be back long before he goes to the O.R.," Hannah called out to Molly, standing on the sidewalk. As the taxi lumbered along First Avenue, she made a mental list of all the things she hoped to accomplish before Harry's surgery.

No time to shop for special treats, Hannah stopped at the corner deli, picked up some Drake's crumb cakes and a coffee for herself.

"Morning, Erica. Any messages?" she asked the receptionist.

"You have a pile!" She handed her a batch of pink slips.

As soon as Hannah entered the editorial area, there was a lighter spring to her steps. Glad to be at work, she distributed the crumb cakes with an apology. "Better something, than nothing," Hannah said sheepishly. She reached her cubicle, put the coffee container down on her desk, just as the phone rang.

"Hannah Stone," she said in her best business-like voice.

"They're going to operate this morning!" Molly yelled. "Please come! Your father wants to talk to you before they take him."

She dashed out of the office without saying anything to anyone.

By the time Hannah reached the hospital, Harry was being wheeled out of his room. He'd been sedated and wasn't making much sense. His eyes open slits, he reached for her hand as she walked alongside while the orderly steered his bed to the patients' elevator.

"Lena, you're here," he whispered. "I knew my Hannah would find you."

She didn't correct him. Hannah held on to her father with both her hands.

CHAPTER

11

Poland, June 1976

IN A WARSAW CLINIC on a rainy Friday morning in late June, Dr. Lena Malińska stood with her arms folded in front of her elderly patient, and, in mock anger, admonished her.

"I can't make you better unless you do your part," the doctor said. "You have to take all the pills I give you. If you stop as soon as you feel a little better, the infection will come back. These pills may not work the next time. Understand?"

"Yes. Yes. I do understand! I will take everything just the way you told me to. I promise, Doctor. I bet your mother must be very, very proud of you, like I am of my lovely Ewa here," the old woman added.

Lena nodded her head. "I'd like to think that my mother is proud of me," she said. And that she's still alive, Lena thought to herself.

"You can make another appointment at the desk as you go out," Dr. Malińska told Ewa, handing her a bag with medication. "Make sure your mother does what she has promised to do."

"I will," Ewa assured the doctor. As she gently put her arm around her mother to steady her wobbly gait, Lena watched with envy.

Before the two women left the tiny examining room, the old woman turned, grabbed Lena's hand, pumped it firmly with both hands. "I can see you are not only a good doctor but a fine lady. You must be a wonderful daughter," she said.

"Thank you," Lena said to her patient. Silently hoping she would soon have the opportunity to prove that she was.

Lena glanced into the packed waiting room, and braced herself for an exhausting day. A nurse walking toward her was holding a cup of tea in one hand and a stack of patient folders in the other.

"If you won't take time to eat, the least I can do is make you drink," she said and forced the cup of tea into Lena's hand. Touched by the nurse's concern, she took the tea. Luckily the folders were destined for another doctor. Thank God, Lena thought, and breathed a sigh of relief. She checked her watch. It was only 11:45, but her feet already ached.

She returned to her cramped office just off the examining room, and put the cup of tea that the nurse brought her down on her desk, next to a cold cup that was almost full to the brim. She looked at the stack of folders and sighed. The pile on the left represented the patients she had already seen that morning. The taller stack on the right, she had yet to see.

Reaching for her next patient's folder, Lena knocked over the framed picture of her son and his father taken just weeks before Ryszard was killed. Lena's eyes always welled up at the sight of five-year-old Stefan in his soccer shirt proudly standing in front of his father with one foot resting on a soccer ball. The photo served as a reminder of what she'd had, and had lost. As she restored it to its rightful spot on her desk, Lena noted the piece of paper she'd been staring at for weeks, with the phone number of the Krakow photo shop. She kept putting off making the call, afraid it might prove to be a blind alley. Lena took a deep breath. No better time than now! she thought, and dialed.

When a man's voice answered, Lena wasn't sure how to start. "Um . . . I'm . . . I'm Dr. Lena Malińska. I live in Warsaw," she began. "I'm trying to locate a Z. Turowski who used to take pictures in Krakow around 1939. Are you Z. Turowski? Are you the Z. Turowski who took pictures in Krakow then?" she asked.

"The answer is 'Yes' and 'No.' I am Zygmunt Turowski, but I couldn't have taken any pictures in '39. I wasn't born until '40."

Lena slumped down into her chair.

"Sorry to have bothered you," Lena said, after a moment of silence. She was about to hang up, when the voice on the other end said, "The person you are probably looking for is my father. Does he still have pictures you're trying to find?"

Lena's heart was racing. "No. I have the pictures. I'm trying to find the people." Realizing this photographer was her only link to her real family, she asked tentatively, "Your father is alive and well?"

"He is alive, but not so well."

"I'm sorry. But would it be possible for me to see him even for just a few minutes?"

"He doesn't work anymore. He's retired."

"Does he still live in Krakow?"

"Yes. He still lives here."

"I hope he is well enough to see me. I promise I won't take much of his time."

"Why do you need to see him?"

"I need him to tell me if he took the pictures and if he remembers who the people are."

"That may be a problem. He's pretty old and doesn't remember things."

Lena refused to focus on that possibility. "If he'd be willing to see me, I'll come to Krakow on Saturday," Lena said.

"I'm sure he'll like the company. He doesn't get many visitors," Mr. Turowski said. "Come to the shop first. Maybe if I see the pictures I will know if they are his."

For the next two days Lena could barely concentrate on her patients. Early Saturday morning, after she delivered her son to a friend's house where he was to spend the night, Lena took the two-and-a-half-hour train ride to Krakow. Settled into her seat, her mood seesawed between fanciful optimism and total despair. The idea that in three hours she might finally find out who she really was made her spirits soar. But the thought that Zygmunt Turowski might not name the woman in the picture brought tears. Lena took out her pictures and stroked the face of the woman she believed to be her mother. Help me, Tata, just as you always have, Lena begged her deceased father.

She emerged from the Krakow train station, and was greeted by the bright noonday sun. Lena looked around hoping the mere sight of the city would evoke some childhood memories. But nothing seemed familiar. She was about to ask the woman walking toward her for directions to the photo shop, when she spotted the Tourist Information Center directly across the street. A helpful young woman behind the counter provided Lena with a map of the city and pointed her in the right direction.

It was a short walk from the station to the address Mr. Turowski had given her. Lena strolled along the cobblestone streets, looking for anything that might remind her of her early years. No images from her past materialized. She stopped in front of the storefront with large gold letters that identified it as Z. Turowski & Son. Lena tried to picture herself as a little girl walking in to be photographed. When she opened the door, a bell announced her entrance. The man behind the counter was dealing with several customers at one time.

Lena waited anxiously, fondling her two photographs. When it was her turn, the man she assumed to be Mr. Turowski walked toward her. She thought he looked older than the thirty-six years he would be if he were born in 1940, as he had told her.

"How can I help you?" he asked cheerfully.

"Mr. Turowski, I'm Lena Malińska from Warsaw. We spoke on the phone."

He nodded. She placed her treasured photographs on the counter in front of him.

"Have you ever seen these photos?"

He studied them carefully and shook his head. "But they look like the kind of pictures my father used to take."

"Even if he didn't actually take them, at the very least he must have developed the film. Isn't this his stamp?" Lena asked as she turned the photographs over. "He would still have to know the name of the people. That's really all I need. I'd like to show him these pictures."

"When I told him you were coming, he was very pleased. He likes company. I'm afraid I don't have much time to spend with him. But I must warn you not to expect too much. My father's memory is foggy these days. He doesn't always make much sense either. I hope you didn't make this trip for nothing."

Zygmunt Turowski gave Lena his father's address, and on her map of Krakow indicated the route of the tram she needed to take to Nowa Huta, the section of Krakow where his father now lived. She left the shop, and instead of rushing to the tram, Lena found herself walking almost in slow motion. On the one hand she was eager to meet the elder Zygmunt Turowski and show him her photos. But if he did not hold the key to her identity, she feared her search might be stymied by the old photographer's lapsed memory.

From the time she boarded the #5 tram at the central train station until she got off, Lena could not control her mood swings, from hopelessness to elation and back again. Off the tram at Plac Centralny, she was shocked by how different Nowa Huta looked from the rest of Krakow. The soaring Gothic churches, medieval town square and narrow winding streets were a stark contrast to the wide boulevards and the heavy Stalinist structures that dominated Nowa Huta. With the statue of Vladimir Lenin at the center of the Avenue of Roses, Soviet influence was hard to miss.

As she rang the buzzer to the fourth floor apartment where the senior Mr. Turowski lived, Lena cast a furtive glance skyward and crossed her fingers. An elderly woman wearing a soiled white apron opened the door a crack.

She squinted at Lena through very thick lenses. "Are you the doctor from Warsaw?" she asked.

Lena nodded.

"Maybe you can give me some medicine for my cough," she

said, as she opened the door to let her in.

"Sorry, but I don't have any medicine with me."

"Too bad," the woman said, and showing no further interest in Lena, led her into a small, darkened room that smelled of mildew. "The old man's in there," she said. "I think he's sleeping. You can wake him up. He's always falling asleep."

For a moment Lena looked around what appeared to be the parlor. She could identify no human form, asleep or awake until she realized that what she thought was a mound of pillows resting on an upholstered chair seemed to be breathing. Hoping not to frighten him, Lena gently tapped the shoulder of Mr. Zygmunt Turowski.

His eyes opened slightly, but he wasn't sure he was really awake, or that he wished to be.

"Mr. Turowski, my name is Lena Malińska. I have come from Warsaw to talk to you. I have some pictures that I believe you took a long time ago."

The elderly man studied Lena as he tried to reassure himself that she was real.

"I took a lot of pictures," he said once he decided she was worthy of a conversation. "I make good pictures. People came to Krakow from all over so I could take pictures of them and their whole family."

Lena sat down on the edge of the chair about an arm's length from Mr. Turowski and handed him the two photographs. First the one of the two little girls, then the two girls with the blonde woman.

"Do you remember taking these pictures? Please, please try to remember." Lena was almost begging.

He stared at the photo of the two girls for a time, then shook his head.

"You don't remember them?"

"I can't see them! Kaja, where are my glasses?"

Lena ran out to find the elderly woman. "Are you Kaja?'" she said when she found her in the kitchen.

"Yes. What does he want?'

"His glasses. He can't see without his glasses."

"He could be sitting on them. They are never very far away from him."

Lena rushed back into the parlor. Mr. Turowski now had his glasses on and seemed to be studying the photographs.

"These could be my pictures. But my mind is not so good anymore."

"Look very carefully. Is the woman familiar? Can you remember her name? Or the two little girls?"

"Such happy children. I took many pictures of children."

"Did you take these pictures of these two little girls?"

"Maybe. Yes. Yes."

"You do remember them!"

"Who?"

"These two little girls."

"They were lovely little girls. I took pictures of lovely little girls."

"Their names! What is their name? "

"I don't know."

Mr. Turowski seemed bewildered. Lena realized that while he might have actually taken these photographs, he was incapable of identifying the girls or the woman.

"Mr. Turowski, does the name Bieliński mean anything to you?"

Lena hoped hearing the name would jog his memory.

He shook his head. "I don't think I know anybody by that name."

"What about your records? You know, the names of people you photographed? Do you know where your records are? What about your old negatives?"

"I used to keep very good records. People would come and order more pictures. Long ago I had very good records. Now I have no records. You should ask my Zygmunt. My son, he knows where everything is."

My God, he should have told me he had his father's records! Why didn't he? Lena wondered.

She thanked the old man and rushed out of his house. Lena ran to the tram stop and caught one about to pull away. For the entire trip back, she prayed that Zygmunt Turowski Jr. still had his father's negatives and records.

The disappointed look on her face as she entered the store told

Zygmunt what he had suspected.

"He couldn't help you? I'm not surprised." He seemed genuinely concerned.

"I think these are his pictures," Lena said excitedly. "But he couldn't remember the names. He said you had all his old records! Where are his old files? I must find them!" Lena was practically shouting.

As her voice grew louder, Zygmunt Turowski became less sympathetic.

"Listen, I'm getting ready to close," he said. "I am not about to start rummaging in the basement for old files that I probably threw away years ago."

Realizing her anger showed, Lena quickly softened her tone of voice. "I'm so sorry. I don't mean to burden you with my problem. But these pictures are my only link to my family."

Zygmunt became more receptive. "I would like to help you. On Monday, I will check out the basement. If I find anything still there from before the war, you could come back, and look through the stuff yourself. But I must warn you, a lot of what once was stored there got damaged when we had an electrical fire. I did throw most of it out."

On the train back to Warsaw, despite Mr. Turowski's warning, Lena remained hopeful. On my next trip to Krakow I will discover the information I need to find my family. That mere possibility was enough. Lena was grateful to Stefan. "Thank you, thank you, Tata, for getting me this far." As she drifted off to sleep, she thought, Even if my parents are not alive, at least I want to know my real name.

In her Warsaw apartment on Sunday morning, Lena woke up early, before Stefan returned from his friend's house. She decided to visit Ryszard at the cemetery by herself. Lena wished she could discuss everything that had happened with him, but she was willing to settle for a one-sided conversation.

As she approached the gravesite, Lena saw a bouquet of fresh flowers in a ceramic vase resting against his tombstone, and she knew that Pola, Ryszard's mother, had paid him a visit. I guess I'm not your only visitor, Lena thought, as she knelt and crossed herself. It saddened her that she and Ryszard's parents had grown even further apart since his death. Roman always seemed glad to see her, but Pola maintained a coldness that Lena could not penetrate.

Lena sat down on the stone bench at the foot of Ryszard's grave and looked around to make sure she was alone before she started talking. "I didn't bring you flowers," she said apologetically, then added, "but I have lots to tell you." Her soliloquy was mainly about her trip to Krakow. Lena ended her one-sided conversation puzzled. When should I tell our son about Stefan's letter? She wished Ryszard could advise her. Talked out, Lena sat silently on the bench for a time, hoping for a sign that he heard her. Alas, there was none.

Back in the apartment, Lena was still debating whether to tell her son about her father's letter, as Stefan walked in carrying his overnight bag.

"Did you have fun?" she asked.

"I guess," he said, and started for his room.

"I went to see Dad at the cemetery this morning."

"You should have waited. I would have gone with you." Stefan sounded disappointed.

Lena tugged at her son's free arm as he walked by. "Sit down, Stef. I want to talk to you."

She decided it was time to tell him what she already knew. She didn't want to keep her search a secret. After all it was his family, too.

"Anything wrong?" he asked, and dropped his bag.

"No. Something is right."

Lena laced her fingers with his, and started talking.

"What are you saying, Mom?" Stefan jerked his hand away and became agitated. "You didn't have to go to Krakow to find out about your family! You and me! Uncle Rudi and Grandma Helga. Papa Roman and Grandma Pola! That's our fam . . ." Stefan stopped mid-sentence as he remembered the heated exchange he'd witnessed between his mother and Grandma Pola outside the church before his father's funeral.

181

"You don't have to find out who you are," he said, his voice less strident now.

As Lena tried to embrace her son, he stepped out of her grasp and kept talking.

"It's not like you just found out you were adopted. You always knew it. Why does it matter now? Grandpa told me many times he felt like you were his real daughter. He loved you." Stefan was close to tears.

"And I loved him. But Grandpa wanted me to know who my people were. That's why he left me these pictures and wrote the letter. I guess I can't expect you to understand. You're only twelve."

"I'm almost thirteen," Stefan shot back.

"I know you feel grown up. But there's much you can't understand. Growing up, I never felt like I belonged in Sandomierz. I want to know where I was born and to whom. Maybe then I'll find out where I belong."

"You belong here with me. You're my mother!" Stefan shouted, his whole body shaking.

Lena reached out to hug him. This time he let her. Once he calmed down, she decided to tell him the rest. "Grandpa thought my family sent me to the nuns to keep me safe, because they were Jews. You remember studying about the Holocaust in school? How the Germans sent Jews to concentration camps?"

Stefan pulled away. "No! Your parents can't be Jews!" he shouted. "You don't look anything like Marek's mother. She's a Jewess."

"Grandpa thought they were, and that was why they sent me to the nuns. That would mean that I am Jewish by blood and . . ."

"No! No! No!" Stefan wouldn't let her finish. "It doesn't matter if your parents were Jews! You're not Jewish anymore. I don't want any more changes!" he yelled, and ran out of the apartment.

Oh, my God. What have I done? How could I have been so thoughtless? I told him too much, too soon! Being reunited with her family was paramount for Lena. Their being Jewish was of little importance. She was annoyed with herself for not knowing that what she considered good news would upset her son. She should have realized that for a twelve-year-old boy in Poland there was no upside having a mother with Jewish blood, even if she had been confirmed and had lived her life as a Catholic.

He'll come back once he's calmed down. Then we'll talk, she tried to reassure herself. I'll bake his favorite chocolate babka. Lena checked her cupboard. Happily, she found all the ingredients. No shopping on Sunday.

Both Ryszard and Lena had considered themselves apolitical. While the anti-Jewish propaganda had been swirling around her while she was growing up, it had no direct impact on Lena's life. The rabid anti-Jewish campaign which had erupted in Poland in 1967 after the Six Day War was not something she even thought about until Ryszard mentioned the firings at the University of people with Jewish ancestry. Lena recalled reading newspaper articles about the thousands of Jews suspected of being Zionists who left Poland in 1968. Now, she felt guilty for her own insensitivity to the plight of the Jews in Poland.

Lena was distraught. The sun was beginning to set. Stefan had not returned. She had been calling his friends most of the afternoon, but no one had seen him. The beautiful chocolate babka she'd made for him had cooled and was waiting to be eaten. By nine o'clock, when she was ready to phone the police, there was a knock on the door. Relieved, she thought, he must have forgotten his keys again. Lena flung open the door and said, "Stef, you had me really worried!"

She was surprised to see her mother-in-law.

"Don't worry," Pola said. "He's fine."

Where is he?"

"At our house. With Roman."

"Why didn't you call to tell me he was with you?"

"I'm sorry. I should have," Pola said. "I'm very sorry!"

"Did he tell you why he was upset?" Lena asked.

"It's why I'm here," Pola said, and put her arms around her daughter-in-law.

Lena was taken aback by her mother-in-law's sudden warmth.

As the two were walking into the living room, Lena decided to tell her mother-in-law the whole story. Before she got a word out, Pola asked, "Remember how upset I was when you insisted on having a church wedding?"

Lena nodded, confused. That was years ago. Why is she bringing that up now?

"I should have explained then," Pola said. "I should have told Ryszard. But Roman convinced me there was no point."

Lena remained on the edge of the sofa. She turned her head from left to right, as if she were watching a tennis match, as Pola nervously paced back and forth.

Puzzled, Lena wasn't sure what her mother-in-law was trying to tell her.

When she heard Pola say, "I couldn't tell my own son that I was Jewish!" Lena jumped up.

"What? What did you say?" she yelled. She grabbed Pola with both hands to keep her still.

"I couldn't tell my own son I was Jewish," she repeated.

Shocked into silence, Lena forced Pola onto the sofa. With the two of them sitting side by side, Pola continued with her story.

* * *

Pola Malińska, née Friedman, grew up in Lublin in a secular Jewish family. She was the youngest of four children, the only daughter. Her father, Jakub, a jeweler by trade, liked to joke that he was a devout Socialist by religion. He and his best friend, Karol Maliński, were both active in local politics. When Karol, a Catholic, fell in love with a Jewish girl, Jakub encouraged their relationship. Rebekah Neuman and Karol Maliński were married in a civil ceremony and had one child, a son. They named him Roman.

Roman and Pola had played together as children. So it was no surprise when they started dating. After she graduated from the Gymnasium, instead of going on to the university Pola worked for her father in his jewelry store. Designing rings with semi-precious gems was her specialty. In 1935, just before her twenty-fourth birthday, Pola and Roman were married in a civil ceremony. Both families saw their union as a blessing. And for a time it was. With Hitler on the march things changed.

＊　＊　＊

"My father expected bad things to happen," Pola said. "With a heavy heart he watched the news. In September '38 when Great Britain, France, and Italy signed the agreement with Hitler that allowed Germany to annex the Sudetenland, he thought that was just the beginning. So before the Germans marched into Poland, which is what he expected to happen, he sent my brothers to Russia. Being a Socialist, he trusted the Soviets. They had not signed the pact with Hitler until '39. My brothers died at the siege of Leningrad, fighting the Germans." Pola dabbed her eyes with her sleeve, but kept on with her story. "My father had a different plan for me, Roman, and Ryszard, who was just a toddler. He wanted us to relocate to Warsaw where nobody knew us. I didn't want to leave my family, but my father insisted. It wasn't forever, he assured me. Luckily Karol had a friend in Warsaw who arranged for Roman to get a job working for a printing company, and another friend helped us find a place to live. My father suspected that things would be bad for Jews, even those who were not religious. He arranged to have my papers and Ryszard's altered to list our religion as Catholic, same as Roman's. That was our passport to safety."

Listening to Pola, Lena wondered if her own family story was similar to hers.

"From the time I left Lublin, I stopped being Jewish," Pola said.

Why didn't she go back to being Jewish after the war? Lena wondered. Her unasked question was soon answered.

"I promised myself as I watched the Warsaw Ghetto burn that if the Germans were defeated and we survived the war, I would proudly go back to being Jewish. Absurd isn't it? Adolf Hitler's determination to rid the world of Jews made me feel Jewish." Pola laughed nervously. "It was hard to forget that in '41 a Catholic mob murdered all the Jews in Jedwabne. And nobody objected! Still, after the war, we considered going back to Lublin, even though we knew our family was gone." Pola's voice was almost a whisper. "They died when the Germans liquidated the Lublin Ghetto—even

Karol. Somebody had reported Rebekah was a Jew, and she was forced into the Ghetto. Although he was born a Catholic, Karol insisted on going with her."

Lena wanted to say something comforting, but no words came.

"I didn't go back to being Jewish because Poland was not safe for Jews after the war. Those who returned from camps or from hiding, were not welcomed back by their former neighbors. After forty-two Jews, including a baby, were murdered in Kielce on July 4, 1946, and there was no outcry from the Catholic Church, I knew I couldn't live safely in Poland as a Jew."

Lena heard a mixture of anger and resignation in Pola's voice.

"So we stayed in Warsaw and continued our charade. It was best for Ryszard, we told ourselves. But my secret burned a hole in my soul. We considered emigrating to Israel after Ryszard died. With all the anti-Jewish feeling starting up again in '68. But it was too late for us. I couldn't leave Stefan . . . or not visit Ryszard's grave.

Pola took a deep breath. She wanted to explain her coldness to Lena.

"It gnawed at me that Ryszard had fallen in love with a practicing Catholic. That you and he were married by a priest. And that my only grandchild was being raised as a Catholic. I had betrayed the vow I made to the Jews I watched die in the Warsaw Ghetto. I couldn't tell my son the truth. All I could do was freeze you out, Lena. I'm so sorry," Pola said.

"I'm sorry, too," Lena heard herself say.

Pola grabbed her daughter-in-law's hand. "Being Jewish in a country that doesn't like Jews is difficult. It's safer to be a Jew in private. But I don't have to keep my secret from you. You and I can help each other be who we were supposed to be."

Lena was overwhelmed. So much to take in. But now that she understood better who her mother-in-law was, she could empathize and embrace the woman she thought had rejected her all these years. Lena welcomed a chance to repair their frayed relationship.

At the clinic, even while she was examining a patient, Lena listened for the phone and quickly rushed to answer whenever it rang, always hoping it was Zygmunt Turowski on the line with some good news. By Wednesday her spirits were visibly dampened. I'll give him until the end of the week. Then I'll call.

Thursday afternoon, when she no longer expected his call, it came.

"I couldn't start looking until yesterday. But I have good news for . . ."

"You found the records!" Lena interrupted. "Thank God!" She instinctively crossed herself.

"It's too early to thank God. But if you are still willing to come back and look for yourself, there's a big pile of junk in boxes in the basement that might have what you're looking for."

"Oh yes! Yes! I'll be there on Saturday. I'll take the first train in the morning."

Zygmunt ushered Lena down the steep steps to the basement. A lone, naked light bulb illuminated the corner where cardboard boxes filled with his father's files were haphazardly stored. Some were blackened and smelled of smoke, others had water stains. Knowing what could be inside, Lena stared at the heap some might categorize as garbage and saw a potential gold mine.

With a gentlemanly flourish, Zygmunt wiped off a wooden stool. "You can sit on this. I hope it's okay," he said apologetically.

"Thank you," she said gratefully. "I brought a flashlight, in case you had no electricity down here."

"Don't worry about keeping things in order. You are the only person who cares about what's here. We were planning to throw it all out," he said as he left her to her task.

"So glad you didn't," she said under her breath.

Full of anticipation, Lena reached for the nearest box.

After an hour, Zygmunt came down offering her tea and a biscuit.

"No, thank you," she said, and shook her head. "I can't stop. I've hardly made a dent!" Lena pointed to the mound of boxes she still had to go through before he closed the shop for the day.

When she'd gone through more than half of the cartons, Lena opened a box with a series of negatives and some photos stamped "PROOF" that looked eerily familiar to her. Examining the negatives carefully, Lena found the one from which Mr. Turowski had developed the picture of the two little girls. Stunned, she swallowed hard and opened the yellow envelope that was attached to the side of the carton. Inside, a receipt named Hershel Stein as the person who had ordered the pictures. On another scrap of paper in the same envelope a Krakow address was jotted down in pencil.

Within minutes of her discovery, Zygmunt had come down to check on her, and she jumped into his arms. Embarrassed, Lena quickly let go, and shouted, "You have no idea what this means to me! Now I may be able to find my parents!"

Zygmunt was pleased. His wife had been nagging him to clear out the basement. He was glad he had ignored her.

"Would you be willing to sell me these pictures and negatives?" Lena asked, handing him the batch she had selected.

"They're yours if you want them." He repacked the photographs and negatives into a tidy bundle she could easily carry, and wished her well with her search.

It was still light when Lena exited the photo shop. With the time she had left before catching the train back to Warsaw, Lena decided to visit the address she'd found scribbled on the slip of paper, assuming it was the house where Hershel Stein had once lived.

Her heart pounding, Lena stood across the street looking at the red brick building with gray wood trim around the windows. After a few minutes, she summoned enough courage to knock on the door and face the current occupant.

"Yes. What do you want?" the woman asked suspiciously as she peeked out the door. Her salt-and-pepper hair was more salt than pepper. Lena thought she looked to be in her early forties.

"I'm trying to find someone who used to live here. Hershel Stein."

"Nobody by that name lives here. No Jews in this neighborhood," the woman said and slammed the door.

"Did you know him or his family?" she yelled at the closed door.

"No. Go away!"

"That was pointless," Lena said out loud. As she continued her walk, she felt someone was following her. Lena looked around and saw an elderly woman staring at her, shaking her head. When their eyes met, the woman seemed to want to say something to her.

"Good evening," Lena said when the woman reached her.

"Are you looking for someone?" she asked.

"Yes, I am. Do you live on this street?"

She nodded and pointed. "Just over there."

"Did you live here before the war?"

"Yes."

"Did you know Hershel Stein?"

The woman crossed herself. "I thought you were a ghost. You look so much like Malka."

"Like who?" Lena asked.

"Like Malka, Malka Stein!"

Lena fumbled for the picture of the blonde woman with the two little girls. "Is this Malka Stein?" she asked.

"Yes! Yes! With her daughters!"

"They had two daughters?" Lena was almost shouting. I have a sister! She looked skyward and mentally thanked Stefan.

"Do you know where Hershel and Malka Stein are today? Did they live here after the war?

"Sorry. I don't know what happened to them," the woman shook her head. "It was a bad time."

"I should introduce myself. I'm Lena Malińska."

"Nadia Rustycka," the woman identified herself.

They shook hands. Neither wanted to let go.

"You want to find the Steins?" Nadia asked, still holding Lena's hand.

"Yes. I believe they are my parents. I was adopted as a child. I never knew who my parents were. Now I'm trying to find my real family."

"You certainly look like Malka," she said. "You live in Krakow?"

"No. Warsaw. I came for the day."

It was getting late. Lena knew her time was limited. "I want to talk to you about the Stein family, but I can't now. I left my son alone," she explained. "I will come back another time. Then you can tell me everything you know about them."

Nadia shook her head. "The person you should talk to is Ela

189

Wyszyńska. She was good friends with Malka. If anyone knows what happened to them, she does."

"How do I get in touch with her? Does she still live here?"

"No. Not anymore. I may be able to find her. I know her daughter. Might take some time. Ela has been ill. Not sure she's still alive. But if anyone knows what happened to Malka and Hershel Stein, it would be Ela," Nadia repeated.

The two women exchanged phone numbers and embraced.

"Call me if you find out anything." As she ran off, Lena yelled, "If Ela will see me, tell her I'll come back to Krakow whenever she wants."

Racing to make her train, Lena repeated over and over, Hershel and Malka Stein are my father and mother. When she settled into her seat for the trip back to Warsaw, Lena took out the photograph of Malka with her daughters. Without any tears flowing this time, she stroked her mother's cheek and thought, I still don't know where you are, but finally I know who you are!

PART III

12

New York

THE DOCTORS WERE RIGHT. It was not major surgery, and Harry's operation was a success. But seeing her father wrapped in a shroud-like sheet when she was finally allowed into the recovery room, Hannah felt herself slipping to the floor. A nurse caught her halfway and made her lie on a nearby gurney.

"He looks worse than he is," she assured her.

"Is he in a coma?" Hannah asked once her light-headedness had passed.

"No. He just hasn't come out of the anesthesia yet. You better stay here a few minutes. I don't need you as a patient, too!"

Lying on the gurney watching Harry's motionless form under the sheet, Hannah thought about his fear of ending up as a vegetable.

When she reported her father's condition to Molly, she said, "He's resting comfortably." Hannah left out the morbid details. Her mother, who had been praying silently in the visitor's lounge, grabbed her hand and kissed it.

"Help me! Somebody, help me!" Harry was screaming when Molly and Hannah came in for their ten-minute visit once he was moved to the surgical ICU. He looked like a mad character cavorting in *Marat Sade*. Shocked, Molly stopped dead in her tracks. Hannah ran to the nurse attending another patient, who seemed oblivious to Harry's cries for help.

"Please help my father," Hannah begged. "He's screaming for help."

"I have patients here who've just had heart transplants. Your father is in much better shape than they are," was the nurse's answer. Not bothering to hide her annoyance, her nostrils flared as she spoke. Hannah thought she looked like a horse braying.

"He's cold. He's shivering. At least give him a blanket," Hannah pleaded.

"We're out of blankets," she snarled. "If you can find a blanket, by all means bring it in," she said, challenging Hannah.

Leaving Molly waiting outside the ICU, Hannah ran to the recovery room and begged the nurse who'd helped her onto a gurney for a blanket. Within minutes she returned with two blankets. As she covered her father, Hannah was shocked to see that his arms had ballooned to twice their normal size.

"No!" she blurted out. Hannah felt impotent. Harry's cries for help reverberated in her head long after she'd left the ICU.

Twenty-four hours later, with him back in a regular room, Hannah regained some optimism. He's alive! But Harry's recovery did not go as planned. Nobody had predicted that post surgery his arms would continue to fill up with water.

When visiting hours were almost over, Hannah bent down to kiss her father. She thought he seemed warm, but ascribed it to the heat in the room. The air conditioning was off and it was a hot day. The nurse making her rounds came in as they were about to leave.

"What's my most demanding patient griping about this evening?" she asked, sounding playful. When Harry didn't open his eyes, she checked his vital signs. After charting his pulse, temperature and breathing, the nurse left without saying anything. Hannah rushed to read his chart. Harry's fever had spiked to 103 degrees.

She ran out to talk to the nurse and crashed into her and the intern-on-duty just outside Harry's room. The young doctor looked uncomfortable seeing Hannah.

"You have to leave now," he said.

Hannah ignored his words. Molly, who was still sitting next to Harry's bed, did as she was told, but hovered in the hall.

"Why is my father's temperature so high?" Hannah wanted an answer.

Ignoring her question, the intern nervously read the chart. Without making eye contact with Hannah, he cautiously approached Harry, whose face was now covered with red blotches. His lips were dry and cracking, his breathing labored.

"Do something!" Hannah demanded, still hoping he could work magic.

"You have to go now," the intern repeated. "It's past visiting hours!"

Hannah stayed put.

Once he realized she wasn't going anywhere, he left. Hannah followed. "What are you going to do?" she yelled as he walked toward the nurses' station. When she saw him reach for the phone, Hannah went back to her father and tried to calm herself. Harry was burning up and she was sure he was drifting into unconsciousness. Twenty minutes later Dr. Russo, the resident-on-duty, arrived.

"Don't worry. It may look bad to you, but it's nothing we can't fix with some antibiotics," Dr. Russo said confidently, and ordered some medication. He was reassuring. Hannah wanted to believe him.

"Go home now. I'm on all night. I promise you I'll keep an eye on your father."

She agreed to leave but not before she hired a private duty nurse to stay by Harry's side for the night. Hannah wasn't going to lose her father to carelessness.

The next morning when Hannah and Molly walked into his room, Harry was asleep. His fever was down slightly, to 102, but his Popeye arms were still waterlogged. When he awoke, Harry begged to be taken home.

"Can't you see they're trying to kill me? Get me out of here," he whispered conspiratorially.

Hannah was afraid they were killing him with incompetence, but she didn't know how to reverse that course. Two days later when she and Molly came into Harry's room and found another man in his bed, she thought her fear had been realized. Hannah ran to the nurses' station.

"What happened to my father? Where is his private-duty nurse?" she asked the woman at the desk she hadn't seen before.

"Who's your father?"

"Harry Stone."

The woman calmly checked the patient roster.

"Oh, he had trouble breathing. He was taken to the ICU last night. Private nurses are not allowed there. The night nurse must have sent her home."

Hannah grabbed her mother by the hand and the two raced to the ICU.

Hannah went in to see Harry alone. Her father was now breathing with the help of a respirator.

"Oh my God," Hannah cried out, then covered her mouth. She thought Harry's fear of ending his life attached to a machine was close to being a reality. And it was all her fault. When she touched his cold hand, Harry opened his eyes briefly and tried to form a smile.

"How are you feeling?" Hannah asked without thinking.

Unable to speak, Harry squeezed her hand several times, and drifted back to sleep. In his drug-induced haze, Harry communed with the daughter he was so desperate to see again. He told Lena about his life and how much he missed her.

For as long as Harry remained tethered to the respirator, Hannah vowed to stay close, hoping her presence would keep him alive long enough for his body to repair itself. Her normal routine stopped. She didn't go to work that day, not the next, nor the days after that. She did not act like herself, nor look like herself. She had no interest in her appearance and shunned make-up entirely. Even ChapStick never touched her dry lips. The person who carefully picked out just the right outfit each morning now pulled on the first thing she grabbed.

Between visiting hours both Hannah and Molly stayed in the lounge near the ICU. Nursing a container of black coffee, Hannah sat close to the door, ready to pounce if she spotted one of Harry's doctors who might give her an update on his condition. She tried to distract herself by reading the newspaper. But the news paralleled the disorder in her own life. A car bomb injured a reporter in Arizona, eleven people were killed when the Teton Dam collapsed in Idaho, and on the international scene, the U.S. Ambassador to Lebanon was assassinated in Beirut!

With Harry now unable to talk, Molly and Hannah kept their conversation simple during their visits. Hannah was reminded of the bad old days when Molly instructed her not to say anything that might aggravate her father.

Harry responded to their prattling about the weather by closing his eyes. When Hannah brought a pad and colored markers so Harry could jot down his thoughts, he gripped the pen forcefully, but the shaky letters he formed were illegible.

"We need a pharmacist to decode your writing, Dr. Stone," Hannah said, hoping for a smile. She got a cold stare, and the word LENA scrawled in large block letters across the pad.

As she said "Lena" out loud, Hannah felt her cheeks turn red.

"I'm working on it, Dad," she lied.

Consumed with the state of Harry's health, Hannah had done nothing regarding Lena except feel guilty. The books and clippings about hidden children languished alongside folders of letters she'd written to government agencies in Washington, Jewish organizations around the world, the Red Cross, even the Catholic Archdiocese of New York. Everyone she had reached had been polite, even sympathetic, but no one had gotten back to her with any useful information. Even Malcolm's leads in Poland led nowhere.

As a reporter, Hannah prided herself for being able to figure out a plan of action in pursuit of any story. But she usually had more to go on than a frayed photograph and a first name. Still, failure was not an option, she told herself.

Seeing Harry's eyes fill up with tears, the tightness in Hannah's stomach hardened. Desperate to lift her father's spirits she said, "I should know something soon."

For Hannah there was an upside to the present crisis. Every Friday, as soon as he could get away, while hordes of New Yorkers headed to the beaches in the Hamptons, Robert made the reverse commute into Manhattan. Hannah did not even have to ask. He usually found her in the hospital lounge waiting for a chance to visit Harry or on the lookout for one of his doctors.

On the down side, even after Harry was breathing on his own and out of the ICU, Hannah showed up at the magazine between hospital visiting hours only to do the minimum. The yellow legal pads usually filled with future story ideas were blank. She felt guilty for letting her work slide and worried about losing her job, but she couldn't help herself. Hannah had fought to get herself accredited to the Democratic Presidential Convention to be held in Madison Square Garden in mid-July, but her press credentials on top of her inbox were now of no interest to her.

When Robert was in New York, as soon as the three of them returned to the apartment from visiting Harry in the evening, Molly would run into the room she had co-opted from Christy, to be out of their way. Hannah knew her mother felt like an intruder. She was sorry she didn't make her feel more welcomed. Something else I can feel guilty about, Hannah thought. Having Robert next to her in bed at night made life bearable.

Robert tried repeatedly to bring some needed diversion into their life.

"Hannah, you can't stop living because your father is in the hospital!" he said for the umpteenth time.

Hannah's guilt kept her tethered to her father's hospital room. "You don't understand," she argued. "I put him there, thinking they'd make him better!"

In spite of her protestations, Robert finally forced Hannah to take a real break on July 4th. The whole city was geared up for the bicentennial celebration and Robert had accepted an invitation to a black-tie party. When he told Hannah about it, she automatically said, "No. I can't go."

"Hannah, I'm dragging you away from the hospital this Sunday, kicking and screaming, if necessary. Not out of town. Just downtown," he said. "We're going to the new Windows on the World Restaurant on the 107th floor of the World Trade Center. We'll have a great meal, watch the Tall Ships sail by and the Grucci fireworks fill the sky. I promise you're going to love it."

"I can't," Hannah insisted. "Harry needs to know I didn't abandon him," she said. For her there was nothing worse than feeling abandoned.

"Hannah, you're not helping your father by suffering along with him!" Robert shot back. "Besides, you're the history buff. You can't ignore the bicentennial!"

"That's what television is for," Hannah insisted.

"Not this time. You're coming with me and that's that. I don't want to see you end up in a bed next to Harry. Or in a padded cell," Robert added sarcastically.

"My father's body is filling up with water. Nobody knows why, and I'm supposed to go on with my life as if nothing was wrong?"

"No. But you're not supposed to stop living either."

Hannah relented.

Sunday morning on July 4th, while Robert was in the shower, Hannah turned her attention to getting ready to go out in public. She took a look at herself in the full-length mirror in the bedroom and barely recognized the reflection that stared back at her.

"What a mess!" was her assessment.

Hannah's hair hung, straggly and limp, just below her shoulders. Her face was drawn and she had dark circles around her sunken green eyes.

Although she hadn't weighed herself, Hannah knew she had lost weight. Her bell-bottom pants now rested on her hips instead of at her waist. Hannah guessed she was probably down a couple of dress sizes. As she searched through her closet looking to find something appropriate to wear, it shocked her that after three months, her clothes still smelled of stale smoke. While lighting up always remained an option, Hannah was proud that the sealed box of cigarettes in her bag remained untouched even with everything that was going on.

She was pleased when she found the bright orange silk Missoni dress she had not worn in years. "I can wear it now," she said, laughing at the stranger in the mirror. It did not smell of stale smoke and was a perfect fit.

Robert and Hannah joined the crowd of revelers in the lobby outside the huge stainless steel elevator doors waiting to be taken to Windows on the World. It only took fifty-eight seconds for the express elevator to "fly" up to the 107th floor.

She cringed a little on take-off as she felt her ears pop. "Are you sure we're not being beamed up into the Starship Enterprise?" Hannah said and squeezed Robert's hand. But once the door opened, she instantly decided the breathtaking 360-degree view of the Statue of Liberty and the illuminated bridges to Brooklyn, Queens and Staten Island were worth the scary trip. Looking through the forty-foot windows that encased the room, it was easy to forget the chaos below.

Robert immediately got into the spirit of the occasion. As they maneuvered through the crowd to reach their host, Jack Lawry, and his wife Annabelle, Robert pulled Hannah from one guest to another, exchanging pleasantries.

Hannah happily mingled with Robert's colleagues. She knew many of them by name only, rather than by face. Jack and Robert had both studied architecture at Yale. Now Jack was trying to convince Robert to come back to New York once his Amagansett projects were completed to join the small firm he and several of their peers were forming. For that reason alone, Hannah was predisposed to like Jack. She thought bubbly Annabelle might take some getting used to. But she listened attentively as Annabelle described life with their newborn baby.

"I love her to pieces, but she sure makes me tired," Annabelle said, whipping out a picture of adorable Laura sucking on a teething ring. "I guess those exhausting days are long gone for you since Christy is a teenager."

Jack shot Annabelle a stern look. She seemed perplexed.

"Christy is my daughter. I was married before," Robert explained.

"Oh, sorry. I just run off at the mouth. Please forgive me," Annabelle said, giggling nervously. "Jack never made that clear. He just told me you had a teenage daughter," she said to Robert.

"It's no big deal," Hannah said. "Robert does have a lovely teenage daughter and maybe someday we will have a child together."

To cover their momentary discomfort, each took a sip of their drink.

For almost six hours Robert was able to pull Hannah back into the real world. After a few drinks she found herself talking easily to people about something other than Harry's illness. During dinner, as they watched the awe-inspiring Tall Ships sail around the tip of Manhattan and applauded the splendiferous Grucci fireworks bursting across the evening sky, it surprised Hannah how much she was enjoying herself.

I'm so happy. It feels good to be alive! she mused, squeezing Robert's arm.

Afterward, Hannah and Robert joined a sea of celebratory New Yorkers and hand-in-hand slowly walked home. Hannah thought about her father only intermittently.

On Monday when Hannah and Molly visited Harry, he was sitting up in a chair talking animatedly to a Catholic priest.

"Father Murphy! I didn't know you knew my husband," Molly said. She herself had often spoken with the priest in the visitor's lounge.

"We met when I came by to see Mr. Hughes," he said, pointing to the now empty bed across from Harry's. "Your husband is a very interesting man."

Molly beamed.

Hannah was surprised to see her father talking to a clergyman of any religion.

"Have you converted my father yet?" she asked.

"Not yet, but I'm trying." Father Murphy grinned.

"Listen, this priest has a better chance with me than that rabbi who stuck his head in, gave me his card and left. I haven't seen him since," Harry said. "Hannah, I told Father Murphy all about Lena. He has an idea for how you might be able to find out what happened to her."

"That's great. We can use whatever help you can give us, Father," Hannah said. But she was skeptical. She had already contacted the Archdiocese of New York.

"You need to write a letter, explaining the whole story to Karol Wojtyła, the Archbishop of Krakow. If anyone can find out what happened to your sister, he can. I'll give you the address and help you with the letter, if you wish."

"Oh, my Hannah doesn't need help. She's a published writer," Harry said.

Slightly embarrassed, Hannah was nevertheless warmed by her father's obvious pride.

"I would really appreciate your help," she told Father Murphy, and immediately took out her note pad.

Hannah and Father Murphy huddled in the corner of Harry's room while Molly fluffed her husband's pillow and combed his hair. Having sketched out the letter, Hannah cut her visit short and rushed back to her office. She wrote and rewrote. At that moment Hannah viewed the letter to the Archbishop of Krakow as her most important writing assignment. It had to strike just the right tone. The carefully crafted final draft enumerated everything the Archbishop and Harry had in common. They'd grown up in the same city, both played soccer, were both Polish patriots before the war, and both of them had suffered under the Nazis. She explained how Lena was left with the nuns, and that Harry was unable to find out what happened to her when he tried to get her back after the war. Hannah made the urgency clear. Harry's health was failing, and he desperately wanted to find his long-lost daughter before it was too late.

Hannah rushed to the post office. Seeing the clerk stamp the letter "Special Delivery" gave her a reason to feel optimistic. For the first time since her father asked her to find her sister, Hannah actually felt they had a shot at tracking Lena down.

While Harry's congestive heart failure was now better controlled, the underlying cause was still a mystery. Hannah had considered taking him to another hospital by ambulance for a second opinion until Robert ran into Dr. Frederick Baines, a friend from Yale who was an internist at the hospital. He was willing to offer a second opinion.

After examining Harry and studying the echocardiogram the technician had had so much trouble administering when Harry first arrived, Dr. Baines was certain the problem was inside Harry's heart. He recommended an angiogram. Admittedly an invasive procedure, but Dr. Baines insisted it was worth the risk. It would finally provide an answer. Surprisingly, Harry agreed.

While the angiogram was in progress, Hannah and Molly awaited a diagnosis in the visitor's lounge. As her mother chatted amiably with a group of her lounge pals, Hannah mindlessly flipped the pages of an old magazine. When Dr. Caulder motioned for her to come into the hall, she ran out and braced herself against the wall.

"Your father has a tumor inside his heart," Hannah heard the doctor say, and she reached into her bag for the unopened box of Marlboros. Dr. Caulder pointed to the yellow and black sign that clearly said: "No Smoking."

Overnight, Harry became the hospital's star patient. Dr. Martin admitted that in all his years of practice he had never treated any-one with a tumor inside his heart. Harry has always been unique, Hannah thought. Doctors from all departments came to peer at his chart. The med students, the surgical team, they were all looking forward to an unusual operation. Harry again resisted. Until one evening, in the middle of August, he agreed to sign the consent, even before Dr. Caulder finished making his pitch. Harry told Hannah, "I need more time. With Father Murphy's help, maybe I'll be lucky and live to see Lena. It's worth a shot."

The operation was scheduled for the following day. After almost three months, the hospital visits with her father were her new normal. He could be touched, stroked, kissed. He was alive. She needed him to stay that way. Were Harry's chances of surviving heart surgery as great as advertised? Hannah prayed Dr. Caulder could deliver on the miracle he'd promised.

Harry made it through the surgery. The staff was jubilant. His heart was strong, with a new mitral valve in the place where the tumor had been. There was no mention of the biopsy results or need for further treatment. Harry's scar was healing rapidly. The doctors reassured him he was on the mend and would be out of the ICU as soon as he started breathing normally. Harry practiced diligently. Both Molly and Hannah took turns timing his breaths off the machine.

He did it again, Hannah thought. Just like his close calls during the war.

Hannah was on her way to getting her life back. She came to the hospital only in the evenings. The yellow pads on her office desk were once again filled with future story ideas. No longer limited to talking to subjects on the phone, Hannah arranged in-person interviews. Possible subjects: Lee Radziwill, about to start an interior design business, eighteen-year-old Sandra Irwin, now a midshipman at Annapolis since women were admitted in July, Jane Pauley, a transplant from Chicago, scheduled to join the *Today Show* in October, and Françoise Sagan was about to visit New York to publicize a book about Brigitte Bardot. But the story that interested Hannah most had haunted her since before Harry's operation. The .44 Caliber Killer who was terrorizing New York City had killed Donna Lauria and wounded her friend, Jody Valenti, as the young women were sitting in Jody's mother's 1974 Cutlass Oldsmobile after a night of dancing at a disco. Hannah wondered how Jody was dealing with being a survivor, and how Donna's family was coping with the loss of a daughter.

"What are you going to do once your life doesn't revolve around visiting hours with your father?" Robert asked when Hannah announced Harry was about to leave the hospital.

Although he was laughing when he said it, Hannah thought Robert's question was an implied complaint.

"I'm sorry. I know the last few months haven't been easy on you . . . on us." She hoped he understood how important he was to her very existence. "I couldn't have made it without you," she said solemnly.

"Hey, lighten up," Robert said, as he put his arms around her. "Freud's assessment aside, it was just a stupid joke. We're okay!"

Intellectually she believed Robert loved her and wasn't about to leave, but there was still the problem of getting pregnant.

"Maybe we can work on making a baby?" Hannah said.

Robert grinned, and with his index finger and thumb he lifted Hannah's lips into a smile. "I like the way you think," he said.

CHAPTER

13

Poland

THE MOMENT SHE HAD GOTTEN off the train from Krakow, Lena vowed to educate herself about being Jewish. Even before launching her search for her family. Since then, as exhausted as she was, Dr. Malińska still spent her evenings reading into the night. Subject of choice: Jewish history, past and present.

One Sunday while Stefan was playing soccer, Lena decided to visit the Jewish Historical Institute at 5 Tłomackie Street. With trepidation, she walked up the five front steps and through the mahogany door into what in pre-war days had been the Main Library of Judaica. Inside the boundary of the Warsaw Ghetto, the building had been damaged on May 16, 1943, when the Germans blew up the Great Synagogue next door. Miraculously the Library building survived. Thirty-three years later, parts of it were still under renovation.

There was much for Lena to see and learn. Reading all the testimonials from Holocaust survivors made her weep, which she expected. But as she meandered from exhibit to exhibit, she was surprised to learn how expansive Jewish life and culture had been in Poland. As if by osmosis, Lena felt herself borrowing other people's history to make up for the lack of her own.

Scanning the other visitors, Lena noted they looked very much like her. Still whenever she made eye contact, instinctively, Lena shielded the gold crucifix around her neck with her hand. It was a treasured gift from her proud father after her first communion.

Before she headed for home, Lena decided to take a walk along Plac Grzybowski and wandered over to the Nożyk Synagogue, the only Jewish house of worship in Warsaw that had survived the war. Damaged during an air raid in '39, it had been used afterward by the Germans as a stable. Surveying the work that had already been done to the neo-romantic structure, Lena mused, "It still needs serious restoration. Just as I do!"

Lena periodically checked in with Nadia Rustycka in Krakow. But as the days became weeks, she feared Ela Wyszyńska might not be found, or worse, could be dead. Nadia called with good news at the end of August. Ela was back in her apartment and ready for a visit. Lena was overjoyed. This time when she took the train to Krakow, she brought her son along.

"Lena, Lena, my baby," Ela said as she welcomed her and Stefan into her tiny apartment.

"You knew me?"

"When you were a baby. You're the spitting image of your mother now," she said and touched Lena's cheek with her gnarled hand. "And you're a doctor, just like your father!"

The pleasure of seeing Lena seemed to illuminate Ela's wrinkled face. The joy of having made a connection with someone who knew her parents made Lena weepy. The two women embraced. Leaning on her cane, Ela, tentatively, led the three of them into her living room. The women sat, side by side, on the tufted red loveseat. Stefan picked a chair opposite them. He was there as a witness.

Ela tried to engage the boy. "I knew your mother since she

was born!" she told him, expecting to answer a flood of questions about his mother's early years. Stefan nodded, then sat quietly and listened. There was nothing he wished to ask.

"Lena, my dear, you're so like your mother. It's hard to believe you're not your mother," Ela said.

Looking at Lena brought back memories of the days before the war when she was young and life was good. Widowed for many years and hobbled by arthritis, Ela missed her friend and pined for the life they once shared.

"My God, there is so much I have to tell you," Ela said, and sighed. "I wish Janek was still alive," she added, as she explained how she and her husband had taken her younger sister, Hannah, to live with a childless couple in Kielce. "When that didn't work out, I brought your sister to Warsaw. Once your father got false papers for her, I took her to live with an elderly woman. In those days traveling for me was easy. No arthritis. I didn't need a cane then to get around." As she remembered her former self Ela's face brightened.

"I was going to bring you to the nuns at the orphanage near Radom, but your father thought it would be less suspicious if he, a doctor, made the arrangements. He expected to get you back after the war. But they wouldn't tell him where you were!"

"I know!" Lena said.

For a split second she allowed herself to think about the life she might have had if Stefan had told Sister Marianna the truth. Not wanting to be disloyal to him, Lena quickly banished all thoughts of what might have been.

"Your parents didn't know where to start looking for you!"

Lena cleared her throat, then nodded. She could not bring herself to reveal Stefan Jankowski's deception to Ela.

"Tell me about my parents," she begged. "What were they like?" Lena hoped Ela's stories could reawaken some childhood memories.

"They were wonderful people. You come from wonderful people," Ela assured Lena. "I have pictures to show you." She reached for the leather-bound photo album resting on the end table.

"They had such a beautiful wedding!" Ela said as she opened the album.

As soon as she looked at their wedding portrait, a torrent of tears flowed down Lena's cheeks. She immediately recognized her mother. Now finally she saw her father's face.

Until that moment, the only memory Lena had of her father was of his thumb.

She listened intently as Ela regaled her with stories about her family. Although eager to recapture her past, Lena hoped to get help with the present and future. The two questions she needed Ela to answer were: "Do you have any idea where my parents went after the Soviets arrived? Where do you think they might be now?"

Ela's answer to both questions was, "I wish I knew." She dabbed her eyes. "I saw your mother only once after the war was over. She came back to Krakow with Hannah for a few days. They were all living in Radom, still as Christians."

Lena felt a pang of jealousy. She took out her picture of the two little girls and fingered Hannah's face. They got you back!

"I gave your mother some things your grandmother left with me. . . . It was a bad time. A very bad time!" Ela said, remembering.

Lena recalled that Nadia had used exactly those same words.

"We lost touch soon after that. I don't know what happened to them." Ela pressed her eyes closed to keep her tears in. She only knew that Hershel and Malka had hoped to smuggle themselves out of Poland after the Russians closed the border.

"They wanted to go to America to be with Hershel's three brothers," Ela said. "But I don't know where in America the brothers lived. I don't know if they ever got there. How could I know? We lost touch." She sighed.

For several hours as Ela and Lena talked, Stefan watched their emotional reunion. He was relieved this woman could not tell his mother where her parents were, or even if they were still alive. She said she wanted to find out the name of her birth parents and where she came from. Now she knows, he told himself. That should be enough. Losing his father and grandfather was traumatic enough.

Suddenly being told he has Jewish blood was hard to deal with. Stefan didn't want his life upended any further.

When her guests stood to leave, Ela asked, "Lena, would you like to see where you used to live?"

Lena pulled the piece of paper she found among Mr. Turowski's negatives from her purse. "Was this the address?"

Ela nodded.

"When I went there the woman who answered the door wouldn't even talk to me. She won't let me inside."

"Don't be silly, child," Ela said with a chuckle. "I'll make sure she lets you in."

With the top of her cane, Ela banged forcefully on the massive front door. The same woman who had slammed the door on Lena stuck her head out. Ela pushed the door wide open.

"Your mother must be turning over in her grave knowing you wouldn't let Dr. Stein's daughter in to see where she once lived," Ela shouted.

"I didn't know who she was. She could have been from the secret police," the woman whispered to Ela. "Come in," she said to Lena, and lowered her eyes.

As she looked around, Lena tried to picture herself as a small child running through the rooms. But there were no familiar smells or feelings to awaken her dormant memories. Only the wallpaper in one of the bedrooms seemed vaguely familiar.

"Do you want to see the courtyard? Ela asked. "It's where you and Hannah used to play."

Lena nodded. She held her breath as Ela opened the back door. What she saw was a cobblestone courtyard that meant nothing to her.

"It was a long time ago. In another life," Lena said to no one in particular. She reached for her son's hand.

Lena had reserved a first-class compartment in a non-smoking section for the train ride back to Warsaw. That entitled them to a meal, but Ela had insisted on packing them a snack.

"What you get on a train is nothing like home cooked food," she said, as she forced the picnic basket into Lena's hand.

As soon as they entered their empty compartment, Stefan stretched out and promptly fell asleep. Too excited to sleep, or even eat, Lena used the two-and-a-half-hour train trip to recover from her emotional visit by savoring the memories that Ela had provided. Lena consciously forced her neck muscles to relax as she replayed Ela's stories in her head. The hardest part is over. With what Ela has told me, I can now start my search for Hershel and Malka Stein. Unfortunately, what Ela couldn't tell Lena was that Hershel and Malka Stein were now Harry and Molly Stone.

14

New York

ON THE WAY TO THE HOSPITAL one Friday evening, as Hannah approached the Metropolitan Synagogue on East 35th Street, she stopped and watched people arriving for the Shabbat service. She had thought about going in to pray for her father many times before. This time she actually considered buying tickets for the upcoming High Holy Days. It would be a formal way for her to ask God to inscribe Harry in the Book of Life. Hannah was sure her father would be shocked if he knew she was considering a visit to a synagogue.

The run-up to Harry's departure from the hospital went very well. Molly was back in her own apartment, getting everything ready. Adella, his private duty nurse, was ready to come with them. When Hannah told her mother that Harry was scheduled to leave on Saturday, September 25th, Molly was delighted.

"That's wonderful," she said. "It's the first day of Rosh Hashanah. Your father will be starting a new life for the New Year."

That Thursday evening before Harry was scheduled to go home, Hannah almost confessed to her mother that she planned to attend Rosh Hashanah services on Friday evening. Knowing Molly would assume Harry's life was in peril, that Hannah knew something she was not telling her, she stopped herself. Instead, Hannah casually mentioned that she'd be arriving late for visiting hours on Friday night.

In the office, every time Hannah looked at the envelope that held her tickets to the High Holy Day services, her anxiety level soared. She last remembered being in a synagogue when she was twelve years old. Her parents had insisted she go with them to a Bar Mitzvah in Vineland, New Jersey. It was an Orthodox congregation and the service was in Hebrew. She remembered how impressed she was when Harry was called to the *Bimah* and read from the Torah. She was ashamed she couldn't read the Hebrew prayer book. Hannah had forgotten all the Hebrew she'd learned in the DP camp in Germany.

Given her history, The Metropolitan Synagogue seemed like the ideal place for her to beg God to extend Harry's life. The congregation shared the red brick building with a church. Being Reform, she would be able to follow the service in English, and Hannah was reasonably sure she'd be more likely to fit in there rather than at an Orthodox congregation.

The dress code required among ultra-conservative sects remained a puzzlement to her. Where in the Old Testament, she wondered, is it written that bearded men with long curly *payot* over their ears, must wear black suits, long black coats, with their black fedoras or homburgs covering black skull caps? Women wearing comfortable shoes, and long sleeves as a concession to modesty, made some sense to her. But the need for a wig to be worn over a full head of hair, she found baffling.

As she approached the entrance to the synagogue Hannah checked her watch. Services were not due to start for another thirty minutes. "Good. I'm early. I'll go in, sit down and melt into the background," she reassured herself. Hannah planned to be safely in her seat, before people who knew each other arrived.

Hannah showed her ticket to the elderly woman sitting at a folding table near the door.

"*Gut yontiv*," she said, "go right in."

"*Gut yontiv*," Hannah repeated. She walked past the young boy and girl giving out prayer books, into the empty sanctuary.

Hannah looked around. A man was seated at the organ, and off to the side a group of people in white robes, obviously part of the choir, were studying sheet music. The austere decor lacked any of the trappings she associated with a traditional Jewish house of worship. The pews reminded her of her church-going days with Aunt Emma during the war, but without the smell of incense.

She sat down, tenth row from the back, third seat in. People streamed in, took their seats. As the room began to fill up, Hannah tensed a little, hoping she hadn't chosen a seat belonging to someone else. Once the rabbi greeted the congregation, and the service was about to start, she decided she was safe.

Being surrounded by strangers, Hannah expected to feel like an outsider. It surprised her how quickly she seemed to bond with the congregation. Especially when she suddenly found herself singing along with the choir in Hebrew. While she enjoyed feeling part of the community of worshipers, Hannah never lost sight of her real mission. At the end of every prescribed prayer she spoke directly to God. "Please let Harry live! Inscribe him in the Book of Life," she begged.

As soon as the service ended, Hannah rushed out and headed for the hospital. On Park Avenue she almost collided with a panhandler asking for change. She put her hand in her jacket pocket and gave him the two crumpled dollar bills she took out.

"God will reward, young lady," the man yelled in her direction as Hannah ran off.

"God, I hope you're listening," Hannah said.

She walked into Harry's room sweaty and out of breath. Molly didn't notice. Harry appeared to be asleep. He stirred when Hannah walked over and touched his hand.

"Let him sleep, he's tired," Molly said. "It's too bad you weren't here. I took your father to Rosh Hashanah services on the main floor of the hospital."

"He was willing to go?" Hannah was surprised.

"Not only was he willing. He was a star. The service was mostly in English. Harry and the rabbi were the only ones who could say the prayers in Hebrew. It's a shame you missed it," Molly said. She took out the mimeographed prayer book she'd kept as a memento to show her daughter.

Hannah grinned.

"How does it feel to be home, Dr. Stone, after all these months?" Adella asked as she walked her charge into his living room.

"I was beginning to think this day would never come," he said as he looked around the familiar apartment with pleasure. Even the lingering smell of paint did not put a damper on Harry's spirit. The sunny peach walls, once a drab beige, were the perfect backdrop for his new attitude.

Mentally, Harry had drawn up a to-do list that would reorient his life: (1) Make up for lost years with Hannah, (2) Appreciate what I have instead of mourning what I've lost, (3) Be patient. Give Hannah time to find Lena.

"Get ready for a special meal," Molly announced from the kitchen. "With plenty of sweets to make sure we have a sweet year. No more hospital food for you, Harry. You'll see, with my cooking in a month, maybe two, we'll be ready to go to Florida." Molly was prepared to finish what the doctors had started.

Harry did not argue with his wife. But he was content to stay in New York. He intended to stay near Hannah.

That Saturday morning while Harry and Molly were settling in, Hannah was at the Rosh Hashanah service, sitting in the same seat she had occupied the evening before, praying.

On Rosh Hashanah it is written,
On Yom Kippur it is sealed . . .

How many shall pass on,
How many shall come to be,
Who shall live and who shall die . . .

Just as the night before, Hannah enjoyed being part of the community of worshipers. But some Torah readings did give her pause. The section about Abraham and Sarah had left her wondering. Would Palestinians and Jews be fighting and killing each other if Abraham had not listened to Sarah and sent Hagar and Ishmael into the desert? Would the hijacking of the Air France plane flying from Tel Aviv to Paris have been avoided and the rescue in Uganda at the Entebbe airport deemed unnecessary, if God had not promised the land of Canaan to Isaac and The Chosen People, in the Torah, and to Ishmael and his descendants, according to the Koran?

She thought about the bombing on Ben Yehuda Street in Jerusalem in early May. A Palestinian terrorist killed thirty-three civilians. But Hannah was not there to question. She was there to plead for Harry's life. "Please spare my father's life, inscribe him in the Book of Life," she tagged on her private prayer to every part of the service.

After the Torah reading in which biblical Hannah pleaded with God for a son, the modern-day Hannah added, "Would it be too much to ask for Robert and me to have a child of our own?"

Hannah and Robert arrived at the Stone apartment on Saturday evening just as Adella was about to leave. She had given Harry his bath, his medication, helped him pick out a dress shirt and festive tie, and explained to Molly what was to be done until she returned.

"I'll be back tomorrow after church," Adella said, as Molly walked her to the door.

"Don't worry. I'll take good care of your patient," Molly said with great assurance.

Adella put her arm around Molly in a sideways hug with one hand, and turned the doorknob with the other.

"Happy New Year," Robert and Hannah said in unison as the door to the apartment sprang open, before they even rang the bell.

"Happy New Year to you, too," Adella said, grinning, and walked out the door.

Molly embraced her daughter. "This will be a wonderful year for all of us," she announced.

Hearing all the commotion, Harry came to greet the guests.

"Happy New Year," he said and pumped Robert's hand. His stance was tentative, but his handshake was strong. Hannah and Robert were delighted to see Harry dressed in slacks and a sports jacket, instead of the striped gown that had been his uniform for so long.

"You look very dapper, Harry," Robert said.

"Glad to shed my hospital clothes." He grinned, and turned his attention to his daughter.

"Happy New Year," he said and slowly walked with Hannah arm-in-arm into the living room.

"You've outdone yourself, Mother," Hannah said when she saw the perfectly set dining table.

"It's not just the start of a New Year but a new life for us. It had to be extra special. Wait till you taste what I've prepared."

Hannah knew her mother enjoyed entertaining and that her friends considered her a great hostess. But she could not remember the last time she used her fine china for a family meal. To complete the festive occasion, Molly also hauled out her fragile crystal wine glasses, and the antique sterling silverware that she usually kept in a hermetically sealed box to prevent tarnishing. Hannah glanced over at the piano, and noticed her grandmother's ornate candle-sticks holding ceremonial candles. As they were about to sit down, Molly walked over to the piano and lit the two candles. For a few moments she stood transfixed by the flame, then she covered her eyes with her hands and prayed silently. Hannah was reminded of Aunt Beverly performing her Friday night ritual.

When Molly finished, she motioned everyone to the dining table.

"Please say the prayer, Harry, so we can sit down to eat," she said.

Harry quickly rattled off, "Blessed are Thou, Lord our God, Ruler of the universe, Who brings forth bread from the earth."

"That's not good enough," Hannah insisted. "Let's have some Hebrew, Rabbi Stone! Mom told me you practically led the Rosh Hashanah service in the hospital."

"Tonight, the English is out of respect for Robert's feelings," Harry said, as he prepared to pour the Manischewitz wine into each glass.

"Sorry Harry, you can't use me as an excuse. Remember, I'm used to hearing a Latin Mass. Actually, I prefer listening to prayers said in a language that I don't understand. They make more sense that way."

"English is good enough," Molly said. "Let's eat!"

First, she doled out pieces of the round ceremonial challah, dripping with honey. After Harry said the appropriate prayer came apple slices dipped in honey. Then they raised the crystal goblets as Harry blessed the wine.

Molly had worked hard to prepare a special meal, now the guests had to show their appreciation by enjoying it. Robert did not appreciate the first course, Molly's specialty, sweet *gefilte* fish, which he only moved around on his plate. To make up for that, he requested a second helping of chicken soup with several matzo balls, each the size of a silver dollar. Molly was pleased.

The food just kept coming. Roasted chicken, Hungarian goulash, candied sweet potatoes, and creamed spinach. And for dessert, honey cake, lemon cookies and stewed fruit. There were enough sweets to induce a diabetic coma. Molly was doing her part to make sure they all had a sweet year.

"My mother always said, a feast at Rosh Hashanah meant there would be plenty for the year," Molly said. "I remember all those wonderful holidays with the whole family together."

"I remember that, too," Hannah said. "The big long table, covered with a white tablecloth. Everybody was sort of leaning back. Grandpa Jakob was sitting on a big cushion. And he drank wine from that cup we smuggled out of Poland!" Hannah pointed to the silver cup in front of Harry.

"That was Passover, not Rosh Hashanah," Harry said. "You

remember that? You were just a baby." He shook his head in amazement, then almost in a whisper added, "How is it that you remember that *Seder*, but you have no memory of your sister?"

"I don't know," Hannah said.

The mood around the table suddenly changed. No one spoke, until Molly jumped in. "I think I did it right this year. I've sent out New Year's cards. And I donated to charity. I did what the rabbi told us," she said.

"You think God has time to actually scrutinize your every deed?" Harry asked.

"Yes, I do," she answered, seriously. Even without belonging to a synagogue, Molly always felt she had direct access to God.

"I know Mom enjoyed the service at the hospital. But what about you, Dad?"

"It was my chance to ask God to inscribe me in the Book of Life. We'll see if he'll listen to me." Harry laughed.

"I'm sure He will," Molly said.

Since she had not mentioned praying for Harry herself, nor that she had planned to do it again on Yom Kippur, Robert decided to rectify Hannah's omission. He turned to her and asked, "What about your Rosh Hashanah . . ." but stopped mid-sentence when he felt her kick under the table. Robert lamely added, ". . . wish! Tell us your Rosh Hashanah wish!" He couldn't imagine why Hannah would not want to tell her parents that she went to services, but he knew enough not to betray her secret.

"My wish is the same as my father's," Hannah said. She wasn't sure why she didn't want to tell her parents about her prayer-fest. For the time being, she wanted it to be between herself and God. Hannah quickly changed the subject.

"I hope you're enjoying your new surroundings, Dad. Mom really worked hard to get everything done on time."

Molly took a bow.

"It's great being home!" he said forcefully.

Harry's first week out of the hospital went better than Hannah could have hoped. There were no frantic calls from Molly and no need for unscheduled trips to her parents' apartment to handle medical crises. Each night Molly filled her daughter in on the day's activities. Hannah was able to focus on her work, on Robert, and even on herself.

The Thursday evening when Hannah walked into Dr. Kahn's office, she wasn't sure why she had made the appointment. Looking around the room she noted that the faded Kilim rug in front of the well-worn couch was now threadbare, but little else had changed in the three years since she last sank into the overstuffed brown leather chair.

"It's been so long, so much has happened. I don't know where to begin!" she said.

"You know it doesn't matter," Dr. Kahn said. "Just begin."

The familiar scent of lavender candles that permeated the room was comforting. Hannah took a deep breath. "Remember my scary dream with the two little girls? And all your interpretations?"

He nodded.

"Well, it turns out the blonde girl in my dream was my sister! Her name was Lena." Hannah waited for a response to her shocking revelation. But the only sound she heard was a creaking noise as Dr. Kahn rocked back and forth in his chair.

He looked puzzled, but said nothing. He kept shaking his head, as Hannah continued explaining what had happened.

When she finished, Dr. Kahn sat back in his chair. He exhaled a deep breath and finally said, "Talk about keeping secrets! Your story takes dysfunctional to a new level. How are you dealing with this now?"

"I have it pretty much under control, I think," Hannah said.

"Then why are you here?"

"I don't understand why I don't remember Lena! Why can't I remember my sister?" This time she had come for an explanation, not an interpretation of her dream.

Dr. Kahn seemed to be searching for the right answer. "There are lots of reasons. First of all, you were a baby. Your sister and you were separated when you were very young. Second, when something terrible happens, loss in your case, you try to protect yourself. You lock away memories that are too painful. The loss of your sister was so traumatic that it was actually easier for you to eradicate her from your consciousness than to deal with the pain. It's a coping mechanism. There's even a clinical name for it, Repressed Memory Syndrome."

"Then why did I have the dream for all these years?"

Dr. Kahn laughed. "Ah, no matter how hard you try, you can't always control your subconscious. Things slip out, like your dream." He tapped his fingers on the arm rest. "You know, we could have dealt with this in your therapy," he said sternly.

Hannah remembered how often he had tried to push her to talk about the past. "I could not do it then," she said calmly. "Now I have to find Lena, or at least find out what happened to her. Not just for Harry. For all of us," Hannah said.

"I hope this is not our last session, Hannah," Dr. Kahn said. "You have a lot of anger to work through. It would make sense to do it here."

Hannah agreed.

On Saturday, Robert had a meeting in Amagansett, so Hannah came to dinner alone. After her session with Dr. Kahn, a lot of the fury Hannah was able to quell was in danger of resurfacing. Thinking about those wasted years and the pain her parents put her and themselves through made her want to scream. But Hannah decided it was more important for them as a family to hold on to the good moments than to relive the bad.

Molly again prepared a hearty meal and served it on the good china.

"You should have asked Adella to stay for dinner," Hannah said, when she saw what Molly was preparing in the kitchen. "The three of us can't possibly eat all this."

"We have to stuff ourselves. Tomorrow we fast," Molly said. "Of course, not your father. Are you going to fast, Hannah?" It was a question Molly asked her daughter every Yom Kippur. Hannah always felt, on some level, her mother was testing her Jewishness.

"Yes, Mom, I am," Hannah said, this time without a hint of sarcasm in her voice. "After this meal I should probably fast for a week," she said.

Molly again lit candles before they sat down to eat. But with just the three of them, dinner seemed less festive. After dessert, Harry turned on WQXR and the voice of Robert Merrill singing *Kol Nidre* filled the room.

"Wouldn't it be wonderful if next year we have Lena here with us?" Harry said.

"That would be wonderful, and a miracle," Hannah whispered.

"Maybe we are due a miracle," he added.

On Yom Kippur, the Day of Atonement, Hannah settled into her usual seat just as the rabbi bid *"Gut Yontiv!"* to the congregation.

Now on her third visit to the synagogue, although she had not said a word to any other worshiper, having exchanged smiles whenever she made eye contact, Hannah felt she belonged. It surprised her that she could so easily feel a part of this anonymous group she randomly joined.

One passage in the service held a special meaning for Hannah.

For transgressions against God, the Day of
Atonement atones; but for transgressions of
one human being against another,
the Day of Atonement does not atone,
until they have made peace with one another.

Now that she and her father had made peace, Hannah hoped her private prayers would get a fair hearing and Harry would be sealed in the Book of Life.

Unexpectedly, the toughest part of the service for Hannah came during the afternoon memorial service. She began to sob hysterically, as the choir and the congregation sang *Zog Nit Keyn Mol* in Yiddish. It was the song sung by partisans in the ghettos of Poland and became the anthem of the Holocaust for most survivors. Hannah cried for all the relatives she lost in the war, even though she could no longer remember some of their faces. The woman in the seat next to her gave Hannah a handkerchief and patted her back as if she were consoling a child. Her sobs stopped when the song ended, but Hannah could not control the flow of tears.

After the *shofar* sounded at the conclusion of the service, Hannah extended her hand to several people around her, and wished them, *"Shanah Tovah!"* Then she quickly made her way outside. Robert, leaning against a car, was waiting.

"Happy New Year," he said, and pulled her affectionately to him.

"Shanah Tovah," Hannah responded.

"Shanah Tovah!" he repeated, and hailed a cab to get them to Molly's breaking-the-fast dinner.

The following Saturday when Hannah arrived for her weekly visit, she was pleasantly surprised. There was a great improvement in Harry's physical condition. It was hard to believe that two weeks before, this man shuffled around his hospital room in paper house slippers.

"Dad, you look wonderful. Ten years younger than when you went into the hospital," she said, and meant it. Hannah decided God must have granted her wish and had indeed sealed her father in the Book of Life for another year.

"I'm starting over," Harry said, and put his arms around Hannah. "I'm going to enjoy the simple things I didn't let myself enjoy before."

Being embraced by her father no longer seemed unusual. But Harry's new attitude was. Seeing him in such good spirits and in obvious good health allowed Hannah to push the question of his biopsy totally out of her mind.

What put a damper on her state of elation was Harry's question, even before she took off her jacket, "What have you heard about Lena?" Hannah winced and shook her head. "Nothing yet. I spoke to Father Murphy. He's been in contact with the Archbishop's office in Krakow. He's sure they're working on it. We should hear something soon."

"We'll hear something soon," Harry repeated. Noting her pained expression, he added, "I know you're doing everything possible. I have to be patient! I'm confident. If anyone can find out what happened to your sister it's a crackerjack reporter like you!"

Instead of enjoying her father's praise, the enormity of his expectations almost choked her. What if Harry's health depends on my finding Lena? If I don't deliver will that kill him? That was Hannah's greatest fear.

Every visit she steeled herself for the inevitable, "Have you heard anything from Poland?" Unfortunately, Hannah couldn't manufacture good news. Unless the Archbishop of Krakow came through with some leads, Hannah didn't know how to proceed. The pile of correspondence on her desk was mounting, but she was not making progress. The great reporter was stumped. An admission she had trouble making to herself, let alone her father.

The Saturday she begged off seeing her parents, Hannah found a letter from the office of the Archbishop of Krakow mixed in with her usual bills and junk mail.

She held the unopened envelope in both hands, and debated her next move. Should I rush over and let Harry read it? No! What if it says something awful, something that would break his heart? I need to know what it says before I show it to him.

Hannah unfolded the letter carefully, as if it held some magical power that a wrong move on her part would destroy. The letterhead proclaimed it was official. Hannah's face muscles sagged once she realized it was written in Polish. Undaunted, she searched her bookcase for the Polish/English dictionary she'd had since her refugee days. As she tried to read it, Hannah sounded out each syllable phonetically, the way she did when she was teaching herself to read English. Surprisingly she didn't have to look up many words. A few sentences in, Hannah's spirits brightened. It was an acknowledgment of her letter, and although signed by Stanisław Dziwisz, the personal secretary to the Archbishop, it promised that Archbishop Karol Wojtyła planned to personally look into the matter. They were determined to find out what happened to Lena, and planned to pass on the information as soon as they had it.

Hannah was ecstatic. "Thank you, God!" she screamed out loud. "Now there's a chance!"

She had expected nothing more than the names and addresses of people and places she would have to contact. This was much more than she dared to hope for. But Hannah knew that retracing Lena's steps, even for someone as connected as the Archbishop, could take time. She worried that an answer might come too late for Harry. But she quickly rebounded. Harry was on the mend, she told herself. Besides, the prospect of seeing Lena would keep him fighting to stay alive.

Robert walked into the apartment just as Hannah finished rereading the letter. He saw her sitting on the living room couch, clutching a piece of paper.

"Has something happened? Is Harry okay?" he asked, expecting the worst.

"Everything's great," Hannah said, and handed Robert the letter.

He started to laugh. "Are you going to tell me what it says or am I expected to guess?"

"The Archbishop of Krakow has agreed to find out what happened to Lena. With the help of your Catholic Church we may yet get our miracle!"

"I'm delighted that my church can be of some help!" Robert grinned.

As soon as she walked into the apartment, Hannah handed the Archbishop's letter to Harry with a flourish.

"Thank you, God!" he said once he'd read the letter out loud.

It was the first time Hannah had heard her father address God in gratitude. Harry reread it silently several more times before he gave it to Molly.

Then he gripped Hannah in a bear hug. They twirled around until they were both dizzy.

With Harry recuperating at home and Robert back living at the apartment, Hannah stopped waiting for the other shoe to drop. Whenever the phone rang, she no longer assumed it was bad news. In their nightly phone calls, she happily listened as Molly rehashed everything that had transpired in the apartment in minute detail.

Hannah actually enjoyed her mother's chatter because everything she reported was good news.

"Your father is doing very well. Adella said so. The physical therapist thinks so, too. He's eating everything I make for him. I think he's gained some weight." To Molly this was the strongest sign that the worst was definitely over.

Hannah continued to visit her parents on the weekends, often with Robert. Happily, all signs indicated Harry was thriving. Between naps and Molly's forced feedings, he pored over family photos that for years had been hidden away in cookie tins and stored behind shoeboxes in the back of the bedroom closet. With his new mindset, Harry allowed his past to seep into the present by focusing on happy moments caught on film.

When the photographs became his dreams, Harry enjoyed being back with those he had loved and lost. Awake, he no longer wondered why he had been spared. Instead Harry was determined to make the most of the life he had left. His relationship with Hannah was priority one. To make up for past slights, he showered her with compliments and hoped that repeating, "I love you, Hannah!" would somehow erase past hurts. Harry wanted to earn her forgiveness. But he could not forgive himself, nor diminish his guilt for leaving Poland before he found out what happened to Lena. Harry knew there was a chance she might not have survived, but he secretly felt Molly was right. Lena was alive somewhere.

Before he drifted off to sleep every night, as he pulled the covers around himself, Harry repeated, "Hannah will find Lena! Hannah will find her!"

Molly made sure every meal she served got a thumbs up, but the food no longer graced her good dishes. Still Hannah was grateful the atmosphere around the Stone dining table remained optimistic, if not joyful.

The highlight of her weekly visit for both Hannah and Harry was a stroll they took around the courtyard of the building, usually after lunch or sometimes after an early dinner. When

Molly agreed it was warm enough outside, off they went, arm-in-arm, with Harry wearing the cashmere sweater and scarf Hannah bought for him as a coming-home present. His tweed cap tilted to the side made him look every inch the country squire he never was. On those walks they attempted to deconstruct their troubled past.

"Do you remember how you taught me to read *The New York Times*—by folding it in half?" Hannah asked. "I think of that every morning when I open the paper."

"I'm glad I've given you at least one happy memory," Harry said. "You know our fights at the dinner table. I never wanted it to be that way. I'm so sorry," Harry said, his voice cracking.

"It's okay, Dad!" Hannah squeezed his arm. "Now I know why. That makes all the difference." Hannah sighed. "We lost so much time. But at least now I know you love me."

"Of course I love you, Hannah. I should have loved you twice as much. But I couldn't."

Sometimes their conversation exposed a nerve.

"Remember the time you were playing with matches and your beautiful curls turned into a halo of flames? I put the fire out by throwing my lab coat over your head!"

Hannah put her hand to her mouth. "No, Dad. That wasn't me. My hair was never curly. It was Lena you saved from being fried. I do remember that nobody ever let me near matches."

At lunch the day Molly mentioned that she had scheduled an appointment with Dr. Martin for the following Monday morning, Hannah offered to go with them. Molly mouthed the words, "Thank you."

"You don't have to come. We're not children," Harry said.

Hannah ignored her father's mild objection.

"You're looking great, Dr. Stone!" was the cheerful greeting they got from Dr. Martin when the three of them entered his office.

Harry returned the compliment. "You, too," he said, and shook the doctor's extended hand. "I see you don't need the crutches anymore."

"We're both doing well," Dr. Martin said. He had broken his ankle in a cycling accident just before Harry left the hospital. Off to the side, Hannah noticed a silver-topped cane resting against the wall. The doctor, like Harry, was still recovering.

Molly and Hannah remained in the office. As the two doctors went into the adjacent examining room, Hannah heard her father say, "I thought I was improving, but now I don't think so." She never heard Dr. Martin's response. Harry's pessimistic assessment of his condition surprised Hannah. It doubled her determination to get the results of Harry's biopsy.

A chipper Dr. Martin returned to the office alone, after he finished examining Harry.

"Mrs. Stone, do whatever you've been doing. Your husband looks one hundred percent better than when I saw him last!" the doctor said.

Molly was pleased. From the outset she knew her cooking would make all the difference.

"You can go in and help your husband get dressed if you want," Dr. Martin told Molly. As she left the room, he reassured Hannah. "Being out of the hospital has done wonders for your father!"

That was good to hear, but Hannah wanted the results of the biopsy. She cleared her throat and asked her dreaded question. "What did the biopsy show?"

Dr. Martin started shuffling some paper in Harry's medical folder, and avoided making eye contact. "Not sure there was a conclusive report," he mumbled.

Hannah shook her head. "You must know by now. Was it cancer or not?" she asked firmly.

"That's beside the point," he said. "Your father is doing well now, which is all that matters. That's what you have to concentrate on!"

With that evasive answer Hannah realized the truth. The knot in her stomach tightened. She didn't want to press further. She couldn't bring herself to ask the obvious question: How long does he have?

In the taxi, Molly coquettishly held onto Harry's arm as he affectionately patted her hand, but Hannah read his pensive mood as clear evidence that he, too, had quizzed the doctor regarding his condition, and now both she and her father were keeping a secret from Molly.

"We should be celebrating! Why do you look so glum?" Molly asked Hannah.

"Just planning the rest of my day," she lied.

In spite of what she now knew, Hannah still clung to the hope that Harry's luck could defy the odds. She was counting on that, and her search for Lena to keep his body fighting to stay alive. Hannah vowed to enjoy the time they had together rather than focus on the inevitable.

During their strolls, when Hannah noticed that Harry's breathing had become labored, she'd suggest going upstairs. "It's a little chilly for me," was one ready excuse.

Harry accepted whatever reason Hannah gave for aborting their walk, but both of them knew he was the reason they had to stop.

Over the next month the happiness quotient in the Stone household depended on who was in the room. Molly continued to see improvement where there was none. Although Dr. Martin insisted he was doing well, Harry could tell that he was getting weaker.

By the end of December, the swelling returned to his ankles, and Harry required stronger drugs to make his aches and pains more tolerable. Since the change was gradual, everyone adjusted without much discussion. Harry never acknowledged what he sensed was coming. He was determined to hold on as long as he could.

Now both Robert and Hannah visited on Friday evenings. Molly continued to light Shabbat candles, but she stopped planning their return to Florida. Adella came earlier, stayed later, and joined them at their family dinners. There was little optimistic talk at the table. It was the banter between Harry and Adella that lightened the mood.

"You spend entirely too much time here, Adella," Harry chided his nurse.

"You know I can't leave you, I'm addicted to your smart-aleck remarks," she shot back.

"Molly, you have to find her an interesting young man."

Molly played along. "I'll do my best."

"Don't make him too young. I prefer older more distinguished gentlemen," Adella said, and nudged Harry with her elbow.

Periodically, in mock anger, Harry insisted she needed to go and take care of some sick people. But they both knew he was grateful that she stayed.

Now Harry was spending most of each day stretched out on his bed, disoriented by the drugs he needed to kill the pain. He lay there fully dressed, propped up by pillows. When he tried to read, he'd often sink into a deep sleep with a folded *New York Times* in his hand. Instead of their courtyard walks, Hannah now sat at Harry's bedside during her visits. Sometimes she watched him drift in and out of sleep. With his eyes open, he appeared to be talking to his mother or to Lena. Seeing Hannah at his bedside seemed to anchor Harry in the present. He looked forward to their talks, although those talks often took place in his dreams.

In his weakened state the only visitor besides Hannah that Harry welcomed was Father Murphy. His presence seemed to invigorate Harry's body. Especially when he had good news.

"They finally located Sister Marianna," Father Murphy eagerly reported. "Unfortunately, she is very old and may not remember much. I'm sorry to say, Harry, a lot of the records are not so easily found," Father Murphy's voice trailed off.

"But they are still trying, right?" Harry asked.

"Oh, yes. I've been assured it's been a priority for the Archbishop."

"Then they'll find her. I just have to stay alive until they do."

Father Murphy couldn't help himself. On his way out, he blessed Harry as he would any of his parishioners.

"If it works, you've got an easy convert," Harry said grinning.

Occasionally Molly talked about the future, but it was obvious her husband was failing rapidly. As Harry felt himself slipping away, there were moments he was glad his fight was almost over. Only at the mention of Lena's name did he even try to cling to life.

Watching her father's pained face as she sat by his bed, Hannah almost wished he would let go.

"Promise me, Hannah, you'll take care of your mother. She's more fragile than she lets on," Harry whispered to a tearful Hannah. She nodded and bent down to kiss him goodnight. As always, she left hoping this would not be the last time she saw her father alive.

Then one day, Hannah came home and found the letter from the Archbishop they had been waiting for stuffed in her mailbox. Her hand shook as she ripped it open, anticipating good news. After carefully mouthing the first sentence in Polish, the muscles in her face tightened and tears gushed.

Lena was dead.

They were sorry to report she had died soon after being adopted by Helga and Stefan Jankowski, a couple from Sandomierz. For a long time Hannah sat frozen on the edge of her living room sofa, the letter pressed to her chest. She wept. She didn't even hear Robert opening the door.

The apartment was dark. He called out: "Hannah, what's happened?"

She did not respond. When Robert sat down beside her, Hannah rested her head on his shoulder, and handed him the letter.

"How bad is the news?" he asked.

"She's dead. My sister is dead. I can't tell Harry that," Hannah whispered.

"Just show him the letter."

"No. It would kill him."

Suddenly their visits reverted to the bad old days when Hannah had to watch every word. Only this time she wasn't trying to avoid a fight. She was in agony. I can't tell my father his Lena is dead!

When he asked if she had any news from the Archbishop, Hannah felt trapped.

Harry grew short-tempered. "Have you called Father Murphy? The Archbishop should have gotten back to us by now," he insisted.

"I have nothing I can share," she said. That was the truth!

"Hannah, I don't have much time left!" he shouted, "You can't just go about your business and wait. Write another letter, call them! They must know something."

Hannah started to hyperventilate. She knew she couldn't keep Lena's death a secret much longer. But seeing her distress stopped Harry's rant. He pulled her toward him.

"I'm sorry, I'm so sorry, forgive me," he said. "I know you're doing everything you can. . . . I need to see her . . . There isn't much . . ." He never finished his sentence, just gently rocked Hannah in his arms.

Her secret was safe for another day.

CHAPTER

15

"THANK GOD YOU'RE THERE. Your father is back in the hospital. In the emergency room!" Molly's anguished voice blared through the phone.

Hannah scribbled a note for Robert and rushed to the hospital.

When she saw Harry moaning on a gurney, Hannah went in search of a doctor. She spotted Dr. Martin attending another patient. "Doctor, doctor, you have to help my father! He's in great pain!" she pleaded.

"I'll take care of him, Hannah. We'll move him to the hospital," Dr. Martin promised.

Hannah sat at Harry's bedside wringing her hands. Now heavily sedated, and without his glasses, he saw only an outline of her form. He reached out to touch her hand.

"My angel, Lena, you have come to save me," Harry whispered in Polish.

As he looked lovingly at Hannah, she knew he was seeing his firstborn.

In a morphine haze, a semi-conscious Harry explained to Lena how he had tried to get her back after the war, just as he'd promised, and how much they missed having her with them all these years. Peppered throughout his monologue, Harry repeated, "I love you so much. Please forgive me!"

The old Hannah might not have been so willing to pretend to be Lena. The circumstances demanded it.

At 5:49 that Saturday morning Harry Stone died.

The last words Hannah heard her father whisper were: "I knew Hannah would find you. You have an amazing sister."

When the doctors came in for their morning rounds, a disheveled Hannah was still sitting there.

"You shouldn't be here!" one of the doctors admonished her.

Hannah looked up but did not budge. The resident immediately checked for Harry's pulse. The doctors left. But Hannah remained. She finally let go of her father's cold hand when the nurse ushered in Molly and Robert.

Molly walked over to the bed, smoothed Harry's hair and stroked his cheek. She could not believe he was gone. To her, he looked like he was asleep. Hannah was surprised that her mother did not cry.

Since Harry died on the Sabbath, Molly was at peace. "Your father's soul will go directly to heaven," she told Hannah. That seemed to be of some comfort to Molly. To Hannah, Harry's death meant she was cheated a second time.

Once Harry passed that Saturday morning, Hannah went into overdrive. Jewish tradition mandated that the funeral be held the next day, Sunday. She actually welcomed the short deadline. Having so much to do left little time to think. Hannah was determined to give her father a funeral befitting the son of a rabbi. She thought Harry would appreciate her effort. She knew that, for him, it was the tradition that was sacred. Hannah felt that maintaining the ritual connected him to those he'd lost.

After she arranged to have Harry moved to the funeral chapel,

Hannah made sure her father's lifeless body would be watched and prayed over until the interment. Then she and Robert took Molly home to her apartment. In the cab, she closed her eyes and rested her head on Hannah's shoulder. As they waited for the elevator, Hannah took her mother's keys and emptied the overstuffed mailbox. No one spoke. As soon as the three of them walked into the apartment, Molly disappeared into the bedroom without offering to make tea or food.

Hannah peered into the familiar living room. Everything in the apartment was the same, but it felt like a very different place now that Harry was not sitting in his customary spot.

Robert embraced Hannah. "We'll get through this," he told her.

"I know," she said.

While Robert stayed with Molly, Hannah went to the funeral chapel on Amsterdam Avenue. She picked out the pine casket without any nails, chose the blue and white prayer shawl and the simple white linen shroud for Harry to wear after his body was washed.

Finding a rabbi to officiate could have been a problem. Hannah did not have time to make her usual exhaustive search for an appropriate Conservative rabbi. She was forced to ask the funeral director for a recommendation. Luckily the rabbi he suggested turned out to be ideal. Rabbi Steinberg was himself a survivor who had come to the United States after the war.

Writing Harry's obituary notice was very difficult for Hannah, but contacting friends and family was easier than she had expected. It felt good to talk with family members she had not spoken to in years. After she and Robert had made the final phone call, Hannah mindlessly flipped through the mass of mail she had dumped on the hall table hours before. Then she remembered the Archbishop's letter she'd been carrying around. Mouthing the words, she reread the letter: Lena died in 1944 soon after she was adopted by Helga and Stefan Jankowski. "Now it's really over," Hannah said out loud. With Molly out of earshot, she asked Robert, "What do I do about this now?"

"Nothing," he said, and put his arms around her.

"You think I should keep this from Mother for the same reason Sister Marianna didn't tell Harry the truth thirty years ago?"

Hannah asked. In the letter, the Archbishop explained that when Sister Marianna found out Lena had died she thought it best to keep that knowledge to herself and spare Lena's family the sad news.

"Just wait awhile. Letting Molly know now that her daughter did not survive doesn't ease her current loss. Maybe you could contact the Jankowski family and find out how she died," Robert advised.

"That makes sense. I should know more before I tell mother anything."

Robert cradled Hannah in his arms until Molly came out of the bedroom. She looked so small. Hannah had been totally focused on Harry and had not noticed how frail her mother had become. Now we're the only ones left, Hannah told herself.

"We have to be there for each other," she said.

"Don't worry about me, Hannah. I'll be fine," her voice lowered to a whisper. "Your father is here."

Hannah looked at the empty sofa, and sighed.

"Come help me decide what I should wear tomorrow," Molly said.

In the bedroom Molly laid out a couple of suits and a dress.

"What do you think? Which should I wear?" Molly asked. What she meant was, "What would your father want me to wear?"

"Dad always liked that dress," Hannah said.

"Yes. Harry would prefer the dress," Molly agreed. They both still wanted to please him.

Hannah was amazed to see the large turnout for Harry's funeral. She stationed herself next to the memorial book and thanked everyone for coming. Some were strangers, others she had not seen since she was a child. Hannah listened as people told her how important her father had been to them. She felt jealous but also proud that Harry had so profoundly touched many lives.

Periodically, she glanced over at her mother who seemed to be buoyed by friends and relatives. Molly's support group, people she'd bonded with during Harry's stay in the hospital, arrived in force and stayed by her side. Including Father Murphy.

When Hannah saw Robert motion to her, she went over to him.

"The funeral director said before they close the casket, someone from the family has to make sure the right person is being buried," Robert reported.

Hannah froze. The last time she had seen her father, he was seemingly asleep in his hospital bed. She didn't want her last memory of him to be in a casket, wrapped in a shroud. "I can't do it," she said.

"You want me to. Or Molly?"

"Ask her. I just can't do it," she repeated, "Mother may need to. She never got to say goodbye," Hannah said, almost to herself.

As she went back to greeting late arrivals, Hannah saw Robert take Molly over to the casket.

The memorial chapel was filled beyond the allowable number. Hannah thought her father would have been astounded. Many asked to say a few words. She wished he could hear the tributes.

Seated in the front pew, holding Molly's hand for the duration of the service, Hannah heard what was being said but it seemed to be happening far away. She was jolted back to reality when the rabbi started to cut the black ribbon pinned to her suit lapel. The symbolic ribbon was meant to be a reminder of her loss. As if she needed one!

After the funeral, the festive atmosphere in the packed Stone apartment was a sharp contrast to those final months of Harry's illness. Molly actually let out a laugh, something her daughter had not heard from her mother in some time. Friends and relatives were telling "Harry" stories, as they feasted on bagels, lox, and sturgeon. And rugelach for dessert. They talked about him as if he were in the next room. In her head Hannah replayed their court-yard walks the way families show home movies.

Molly Stone looked around her apartment and watched the revelers. "This is the way it should have been when you were here, Harry," Molly said, then added, "You wasted so much of your life. And mine."

PART IV

CHAPTER

16

A WEEK AFTER HARRY'S FUNERAL, Hannah returned to work. Glad to be back, even the sight of her desk piled high with unopened mail felt welcoming. Normally, she would have cursed under her breath and pushed the pile of mail onto a ledge to be dealt with later. But the junk littering her desk was actually a useful diversion. Hannah had no deadlines, an unfamiliar situation for her, and opening letters and reading through countless press releases was something to focus on other than the loss of her father and sister.

And Molly. What to do with Molly? Of course, it would be best if in a couple of months she decided to go back to Florida. But it was not something Hannah was able to suggest. She didn't want her mother to feel she wished to be rid of her.

Hannah spent her first week back cleaning up her office. As co-workers came in to chat, several asked her if she was planning to leave.

"Why do people think I've taken another job? Or am I about to be fired?" Hannah asked Ariel, her friend who had just been named Features Editor.

"People think you're leaving because nobody has ever seen the bottom of your desk before," Ariel said laughing.

"The last thing I want now is to change jobs. I've had all the changes I can deal with for a while. I hope no one is thinking of firing me," Hannah said seriously.

"Not to worry," Ariel assured her.

Hannah was free to resume her normal life, but Harry's death left her with a void she didn't know how to fill. Whenever she recalled the feel of her father stroking her cheek, she had to wipe away tears covering the spot that had welcomed his touch. She especially missed their Saturday walks and, even toward the end, sitting at his bedside when the only subject that seemed to bring him back to life was Lena.

If he had died while Hannah viewed him only as a factor in her birth, his death would have had a decidedly different impact on her.

But for a short time he was the father she always wanted. It's not fair, she thought. I lost him twice.

Deceiving her father had been painful, but Hannah felt it was better he died believing Lena was at his bedside. I gave him that, she thought.

By Friday, the only folder left unfiled was labeled LENA in big block letters. Hannah was about to put the last letter from the Archbishop inside the folder, when she remembered that Molly had still not seen it. I'll show it to her tonight. No! Robert is right, I should find out how Lena lived and died before I show Mother the letter.

Hannah put it back in her tote.

She was concerned about her mother, but not worried. Unlike Harry, Molly was in good health, loved playing bridge, and Hannah knew she had a circle of friends she enjoyed palling around with in the city. That first week, the two had talked on the phone just as they had while Harry was alive. Their calls were shorter. Molly had less to report. When Hannah called and her mother didn't answer, she was glad. Hannah assumed Molly was out with a friend.

Friday evening when she arrived at her mother's door, Hannah rang the doorbell repeatedly before a rumpled Molly let her daughter in. The apartment was in total darkness. Hannah switched on the hall light as she closed the door behind her. Molly brushed her mussed hair off her face. Her dress was wrinkled. It looked as if she'd been sleeping in it. She had obviously missed her long-standing Friday appointment with her hairdresser.

"Are you feeling all right, Mom?" Hannah asked.

"Of course," Molly answered, without any force to the statement.

"I rang the bell a long time. Were you sleeping?"

"Yes. Yes, I must have dozed off."

"Didn't you expect me? I told you I was coming for dinner," Hannah said, a tinge of annoyance in her voice.

"The day just got away from me," Molly said, as she looked at the hall clock. "I can make you something if you're hungry," she offered.

Hannah followed her mother into the kitchen. What she saw told the whole story. Molly Stone's pristine stove was a mess. The smell of burnt coffee permeated the room. The cups and saucers piled in the sink indicated Molly was at least drinking tea or coffee. Hannah opened the refrigerator. It was fully stocked, just as she'd left it a week ago.

"Mom, have you eaten anything today?"

Molly seemed surprised by the question. "Not sure. I'm not hungry."

"Sit down," Hannah ordered.

Molly obeyed.

"I'll make us both an omelet," Hannah said.

As her daughter washed the dishes in the sink and cleaned the stove, Molly sat at the table staring into space, her hands folded in front of her as if they were resting on a desk in first grade.

"Mom, you have to eat, even if you're not hungry," Hannah said as she served the omelet she'd prepared. "Remember how you used to make Dad eat when he didn't want to?"

"It didn't do him any good, did it?" Molly said. "He's gone."

"I know. But you're here and you need to eat to stay alive."

"I don't feel alive," Molly said. "Sometimes I think your father took me with him."

Until the moment she had touched his lifeless cheek, Molly had believed that Harry would be well again. She had put her faith in the trifecta of God, Dr. Martin, and her cooking to make that happen. Once that combination failed her and Harry was gone, Molly seemed to be sleepwalking instead of living.

For forty years, when Harry Stone told his wife what to do and when to do it, she complained bitterly to her daughter. She had resented Harry's dictatorial manner. But now that he was gone, she needed him to tell her if the coffee pot was boiling over.

Hannah placed her mother's fingers around her fork. "Eat," she said.

An obedient Molly slowly ate the omelet.

That was a small victory, Hannah thought. She realized her mother could not be left alone. After Molly finished eating, she went into the bedroom, and Hannah phoned Adella.

"Any chance you could come back to stay with Molly, at least for a couple of weeks?" Hannah asked.

"I was about to start a new job next week, but I didn't tell them yet," Adella said.

"Please, please come back. She really needs you. I didn't realize how bad it was until I saw her this evening."

"Don't you worry. I'll be there in the morning. We'll fix her," Adella promised.

"Thank you," Hannah said solemnly. Relieved, she called Robert. "I don't feel comfortable leaving Mother here alone."

"Spend the night," he said. "Let Adella in tomorrow and give her a key. It may take a while, but I'm sure Molly will come out of it."

"I'm glad I didn't tell her about Lena."

"She doesn't need to hear more bad news now," Robert said.

Her search for her sister was over. But Hannah, the inveterate reporter, had many questions. How did Lena live during the war? What was she like as a child? Exactly how did she die? She needed those questions answered before she showed the letter to her mother, and before she herself could put the matter to rest.

Hannah decided she had to talk to the family that adopted Lena. Even if they only had her for a short time, they deserved a proper thank you for taking Lena in, she reasoned. And Hannah convinced herself that she had to talk to Helga and Stefan Jankowski in person.

CHAPTER

17

OVER LINGUINI AND CLAM SAUCE at Pete's Tavern, Robert listened as Hannah, the reporter, plotted her trip to Poland.

"I have a name and a place to start. Father Murphy got me the address for Helga and Stefan Jankowski. What could be easier?" Hannah said confidently.

"It would be easier if you were flying into Warsaw, Wisconsin, instead of Warsaw, Poland," Robert said. "Do you remember how freaked out you were five years ago when the guard checking your passport in Spain asked when you left Poland?"

"I don't know why that upset me so much. I guess it was the first time I'd been out of the country. I think I can do it now," Hannah said. "I'll pretend I'm on a story." Hannah often forced herself to do things as a reporter that she would never tackle otherwise. When necessary she covered riots, got on a ski lift in spite of vertigo, and took a white-knuckle ride in a helicopter.

"What will you tell your mother?"

"I'll just say I'm going away for a week for work, and not mention where to. If I told her I was going to Poland, she would definitely freak out. Remember, we left Poland illegally. Technically I'm still a Polish citizen. My mother would be afraid they might try to keep me. One of their friends was arrested and put in prison when she went back to visit her sister. I don't remember the details. But her husband paid a lot of money to get her out."

"But you're not afraid, right?" Robert said with more than a little sarcasm in his voice.

Hannah sighed and shook her head. As her anxiety level increased, her enthusiasm for the trip waned a little. They still don't like Jews in Poland, she thought. Not much had changed on that score. She bit her lip and fought off any negative thoughts about her impending trip. I have an American passport, she reassured herself. I can't be like Harry and Molly. I can't let the past cripple me for the rest of my life. Instead, Hannah challenged her grown-up self to measure up to the capabilities she demonstrated as a child.

At the Polish Consulate, Hannah felt less confident. When a dour Elka Woleńska, neatly dressed in a navy suit that looked like a uniform, asked for her passport, Hannah was glad it was in the name of Hannah McCabe and not Hannah Stone, and certainly not Hannah Stein. When she had applied for her passport, Hannah was indignant hearing she had to use her legal married name. Now, in the Polish Consulate, being seen as Hannah McCabe she felt protected. Hannah wondered if on some level she saw Robert's not being Jewish as a plus, rather than a minus. Would he know how to keep her safe if the unthinkable happened here? The way Harry had. For now, it was enough that she had his name to shield her.

Having noted Hannah's place of birth, in a lilting Polish accent, Elka Woleńska asked, "When did you come to America?" Her friendly tone indicated real interest.

Hannah responded as she always did, with evasion: "I was pretty young."

Undaunted, Elka continued: *Pani mówi po polsku?*

Hannah shook her head no. Her being able to speak Polish, without anyone from Poland knowing that, gave her an edge.

"Do you remember much of Poland?" Elka continued.

"No," Hannah shook her head. "That's why I want to go back."

"To see family?"

"Yes. To see family," she nodded. Almost the truth. Always best to stay close to the truth, she thought.

As Elka reached for an application form, Hannah said, "I'm pretty sloppy, can I have a few just in case I make a mistake."

"Of course. Have a good trip," Elka said, and handed her the forms, which Hannah accepted with sweaty palms.

The form was straightforward, Hannah thought. Until she had to list her maiden name. Why do they need to know that? She wondered. Suddenly Hannah was back in war mode. Ostensibly there was no need for secrecy. But even with the protection of an American passport, Hannah preferred to keep part of her true identity secret. She considered writing BIELIŃSKA. It seemed like a minor alteration in light of a greater truth. That's who I was the last time I was in Poland, Hannah thought.

She wondered if they could put you in jail if you lied about your maiden name on an application form. The mere suggestion aroused a sense of panic. Hannah was shocked by what she was feeling. She furtively looked around the large room, which suddenly took on a dangerous aspect. There was absolutely nothing to be afraid of, she told herself. I am standing in a building on East 37th Street in New York City. Nobody wants to hurt me, deport me, or put me in prison. Still, she was having trouble breathing, and every muscle in her body tightened.

Hannah filled in all the blanks on the application form truthfully. As she finally wrote STONE in block letters, she was relieved that she did not have to write STEIN.

As she imagined disembarking the airplane at Okęcie Airport in Poland, her mounting anxiety almost derailed her plans. At that moment, Hannah realized there wasn't much difference between her and her parents. She may have learned to speak

English without the trace of an accent and easily passed for being American-born, but the past controlled her present, just as it did theirs. With one difference. Unlike her parents, Hannah was not going to let her fear keep her from going back to Poland. She had to find out first-hand what happened to Lena. She owed it to her. She was the one who survived.

CHAPTER

18

Poland

THE FLIGHT ON LOT AIRLINES was uneventful. Robert had plied Hannah with enough wine before she boarded that she fell asleep almost as soon as she strapped herself into her seat. The pilot's voice announcing their descent woke Hannah up. Her breathing became labored and her palms began to sweat. To keep calm she repeated, I'm an American citizen, I'm an American citizen. Once on the ground, Hannah was prepared to be grilled by a hostile immigration officer. Instead, her American passport evoked a smile from the man behind the Lucite partition.

"Speak Polish?" he asked when he noted that Poland was her place of birth.

Hannah shook her head. "Sorry," she said sheepishly.

"What city?"

"Krakow."

"Beautiful city. Much history. Your husband is American?" he asked, noting her marital status.

"Yes." Hannah nodded. She was eager for his questioning to stop. But if he asked when she'd left Poland, she was prepared with, "I was a child." He couldn't blame a child for leaving Mother Poland illegally! If he were to ask her maiden name, Hannah was buoyed by the fact that Stone, unlike Stein, didn't scream, "She's Jewish!" Hannah hoped her green eyes would again aid the deception. But no other questions followed.

"Welcome back to Poland!" he said, returning her passport.

"Thank you," Hannah said and wondered whether he would be welcoming her back knowing she was Jewish. In the eyes of the West, the Polish Communist party was viewed as responsible for the recent government purge of anyone with a drop of Jewish blood. But Hannah believed distrust and dislike of Jews was part of the Polish DNA.

As she looked around the small arrival terminal, Hannah relaxed. No wartime memories to summon here, she thought. Yet she knew that at any moment the fear that she'd been suppressing could overpower her.

Outside, Hannah walked toward a line of parked taxis. Should I splurge on a taxi or take the bus? She weighed her options, keeping in mind the warning in her travel guidebook about unscrupulous Warsaw cab drivers. The driver at the head of the taxi line was leaning against the hood of his car, reading a newspaper. Hannah made her decision once she saw the "Taxi" sign on the roof had a number. According to her trusty guidebook, that meant this was a legitimate cab. When Hannah reached him, the driver folded the newspaper and tipped his cap.

"Jarek Tarnowski, at your service," he said. As he gallantly opened the passenger door, he added, "I luff America," and then put her luggage in the trunk.

"I have aunt in Chicago. I go see her someday," Mr. Tarnowski said, sliding behind the wheel.

"Don't go in the winter. It's very cold," Hannah advised, happy to be making small talk.

"Like Poland?"

They both laughed.

Though she didn't feel the need to keep it a secret, Hannah wondered what gave her away as an American even before she said a word.

Hannah sat back in her seat and pretended there was nothing unusual about her trip. When she looked out the window what she saw held no meaning for her. After studying the train schedule she'd picked up at the airport, Hannah realized she had most of the day free before taking the afternoon train to Sandomierz. She considered doing some sightseeing.

I'm an American tourist. That's what tourists do! At that moment Hannah wished she had let Robert come with her.

By the time the taxi pulled up in front of Hotel Polonia, Hannah had decided to ask her driver to be her guide. "Do you have time to show me Warsaw?" she asked. "I will pay you."

"*Tak, tak*. Yes, yes. I have time," he answered eagerly.

"I have to register at the hotel. Do you want to come back later?" Hannah asked, as Jarek Tarnowski opened the door of the taxi.

"No. No. I wait," he said, and carried her bags into the lobby.

As she followed him, Hannah stared at the entrance. Nothing seemed familiar except the name. But this was the same hotel where Ela and three-year-old Hannah had spent that one night when she had slept through a bombing.

While Hannah was checking in, her soon-to-be-tour-guide parked his taxi on Jerozolimskie Avenue and waited. When she came out, he gallantly held the passenger door open for her, and proudly announced there was much to see in Warsaw. He also assured his American passenger that he loved everything from America, but especially Coca-Cola and Humphrey Bogart.

Though he seemed to understand English pretty well, he struggled to form sentences. Still, Hannah did not let on that she spoke Polish.

"Is all new!" Jarek Tarnowski said pointing to the skyline. Obviously proud of the rebuilt Warsaw, he asked, "What you want to see first?"

"Let's start our tour with the Old Town. *S-ta-re M-ias-to*," Hannah enunciated each syllable very carefully, as if she were trying to read it phonetically in the guidebook she was holding in her hand. Jarek smiled his approval at her attempt to speak Polish.

Left in ruins by the Germans, the Old Town had been faithfully restored. The Market Square with its pastel buildings and cobblestone streets looked like a movie set to Hannah. According to Jarek, the restoration of the Royal Castle, dynamited by the Germans, had only been completed recently.

To augment Jarek Tarnowski's enthusiastic, yet inadequate, narration Hannah tracked their route on the map she had picked up from the concierge at the hotel. As they drove past the Monument to the Ghetto Heroes, Hannah stared at the modern apartment complexes that now stood on the ruins of the Ghetto. "Are there many Jews in Warsaw today?" Hannah asked.

As soon as the words left her mouth, she was sorry. Seeing him turn to look at her, Hannah squirmed. I bet he's thinking, "Is this American a Jewess?" Even thinking the word "Jewess," commonly used by Gentiles to refer to Jewish women, made her cringe.

To rehabilitate her image in his eyes, Hannah quickly said, "I meant did many of them come back after the war?" She emphasized the word them.

Hannah could see his head turn from side to side. But under his breath, in Polish, he muttered, "For what? There's nothing here for them." Hannah did not let on she understood his words. He simply reinforced what she had suspected. Gentiles in Poland did not miss the Jews. To change the subject, she pointed to a building that towered over the city skyline. "What is that?" Hannah asked, as they headed back south.

"Is Palace of Culture and Science. A gift from Stalin to the people of Poland. Looks like Russian wedding cake, no?" he said with a laugh. Then he added proudly, "Rolling Stones gave concert there nine years ago."

Hannah thought it looked a lot like the Empire State Building in New York.

As they drove around, Hannah got to see more churches and palaces than she knew had existed in Warsaw. She was enjoying the tour, but it wasn't until they passed the Blikle cake shop on Nowy Świat that something registered with her personally. Hannah thought about the times she opened a box from Blikle filled with *pączki*. Whenever he visited, Harry, as Bronisław Bieliński, used to bring Emma her favorite treats from that bakery. While *pączki* looked like jelly doughnuts, they tasted much better. Hannah had almost forgotten how surprised and disappointed she was when she took a bite of her first jelly doughnut in America.

A very different Warsaw whizzed by the car window than the one Hannah remembered. The last time she was there, the city was ablaze and the unforgettable stench of burnt corpses permeated the air. As Jarek pointed out the new Soviet-style architecture mixed in with the beautifully restored Gothic churches and neoclassical palaces, the new Warsaw did not feel frightening. Passersby did not look much different from people she might encounter in Cleveland or Chicago. Still, Hannah couldn't help wondering what was in their hearts.

At the completion of her guided tour Hannah offered to pay Jarek Tarnowski in U.S. dollars. He was ecstatic. When he dropped her off in front of her hotel, they shook hands.

"Have a safe flight to Chicago," Hannah said, and waved goodbye.

She had just enough time to order a snack from room service before heading to the train station for her trip to Sandomierz. As she walked briskly along Jerozolimskie Avenue to make the train, Hannah congratulated herself on how well she had acclimated to being back in Poland after touring Warsaw with Jarek Tarnowski. Until she stopped at the curb in front of the newly redesigned Warsaw Central Train Station.

Hannah knew the Germans had blown it up after crushing the Warsaw Uprising. But the futuristic exterior shocked her. It had no connection to what she remembered. Having seen how faithfully the Old Town was restored, she was unprepared for this replacement.

Inside the station was crowded. As she entered, Hannah blinked and suddenly she was back on a packed platform in October '44.

* * *

The Uprising had failed. She, Aunt Marta, and Emma had been squatting on the floor of the station for many days. Along with hundreds of other women and children, they were being expelled from Warsaw.

Watched over by German soldiers pointing their guns, they waited. But no one knew where they were going. Or when.

As a diversion she had been spinning herself around like a top. When she stopped, and saw no sign of Aunt Marta or Emma, she was sure she'd lost them forever.

By the time they found her, she had started to hyperventilate. But she did not cry.

* * *

Now, more than three decades later, standing in the new Warsaw Central Train Station, the same feeling of panic Hannah felt then resurfaced. Again, hardened knots churned in her stomach.

A young boy chasing after his mother bumped into Hannah and brought her back to the present just in time for her to buy a ticket and make her train to Sandomierz.

Gazing out the window of the #8 bus she boarded outside of the Sandomierz train station, Hannah wondered what her sister's short life had been like. She tried to imagine little Lena skipping along the cobblestones or trailing after her "parents" in the narrow streets of this picturesque city along the Wisła River.

Hannah had timed her arrival to appear at the Jankowski house at dinnertime when most people would be home. She chose to come unannounced. As a reporter, Hannah thought surprise usually gave her an advantage. When she reached for the heavy iron knocker on the Jankowski front door, she still had not decided how she should present herself.

"Yes? Can I help you?" Helga asked in Polish when she cracked open the door. Her tone clearly indicated she was not interested in helping this intruder.

Hannah opened her mouth to speak, but no sound came out.

"What do you want?" Helga asked.

Hannah cleared her throat. "Hope you can understand my rusty Polish. I've come a long way to talk to you."

"What about?" Helga managed to inject both hostility and curiosity into her question.

"I'm a reporter for a magazine in the United States . . ."

Helga interrupted. "You are from America?"

Hannah nodded.

"Come inside!" She pulled Hannah through the threshold. Before she closed the door, Helga looked up and down the street to see if anyone was watching.

Without uttering another word, Hannah followed her into the front room. She looked around for family photos. Only a framed picture hanging on the wall, of a young couple on vacation in the mountains, caught her eye. By the time Helga motioned for her to sit on the couch, Hannah had formulated an acceptable opening.

"I'm writing a story about Polish families who adopted children during the war. Whose relatives live in the United States," she added lamely. "You and your husband adopted a daughter, Lena?"

"Yes, we adopted Lena. But why is that a story now?" Helga asked.

Hannah couldn't bring herself to tell Helga the truth. "The American family would like to thank you for taking Lena in and caring for her," she finally said.

"We gave her a good life. My husband adored her. Stefan completely spoiled the child."

Hannah felt jealous as she recalled Harry's coldness.

"It's sad that it was for such a short time," Hannah said.

"What do you mean?" Helga was indignant. "We took care of Lena always!"

"How old was Lena when she died?" Hannah asked.

"What are you talking about?" Helga shouted. "Lena is not dead. She's a doctor in Warsaw. Dr. Lena Malińska. You can ask her yourself. She sees patients at the Central Hospital on Wołoska Street. It's my husband who is dead!" Helga cried out.

Hannah was struck dumb. Her hand trembled. She could barely scribble Helga's words into her reporter's notebook.

"So sorry for your loss," Hannah finally whispered.

"You must be talking about a different Lena," Helga said.

Hannah nodded. "Yes. Perhaps the American family was given the wrong information. We may be talking about two different people."

Helga frowned. Now with Stefan gone, she could use some help from America. She would have welcomed a reward. She'd earned it.

Hannah's mind was reeling. Her heart was racing. Before Helga could ask any more questions, Hannah wanted to make a quick exit. She stood up and grabbed her bag.

"I have to do some more checking," she blurted out. "Thank you for seeing me!" And headed for the door.

Once the door slammed behind her, Hannah took a deep breath of cool air as her thoughts seesawed between thinking that her sister was still alive and the alternative, that the only thing Lena Malińska had in common with her Lena was the first name. The reporter in her wondered how the Archbishop could have made such a mistake. It is possible, she decided. The elderly nun could have passed on wrong information. Records get lost and misfiled.

For the time being, optimism won out. Unbelievable! My sister isn't dead! How fitting that Dr. Harry Stone's first born is a doctor? Without the benefit of his prodding.

Hannah felt she would explode if she didn't share her news soon. I must call Robert, was her first thought. Remembering what she'd been told by journalists about phones being tapped by the government, Hannah had second thoughts. Do I want the Polish authorities to know that an American reporter who was born in Poland, and may have left the country illegally, is now back looking for her sister?

Hannah decided the news was too extraordinary not to share with Robert! I'll be very careful. Just like during the war. Now at least I have an American passport! That must count for something. Even behind the Iron Curtain.

She started her search for a public phone in the Town Square. When she finally located one at the train station, it was broken. Frustrated, Hannah asked the clerk at the ticket counter for help. The woman rolled her eyes, realizing Hannah was a foreign tourist.

"There are three ways to make an international call in Poland," she explained. "If you are lucky enough to have a phone at home, you live in a hotel or, as most people do, visit a post office. *Poczta Polska* is where you buy stamps, send letters, receive registered mail, and make long distance calls." But no matter where the calls were placed, international calls required an appointment.

Resigned, Hannah realized her good news would have to keep till she got back to Hotel Polonia. By the time the train pulled into Warsaw's Central Station it was night. Hannah was glad she had only a short walk to her hotel. The café she'd passed that afternoon had looked inviting, now seemed menacing. Hannah quickened her pace. A group of East German tourists was milling around the lobby. She gave the concierge Robert's office number and asked her to arrange an international call, then raced upstairs to her room to wait. But it took a while before the concierge was able to get the call through.

When Hannah finally heard Robert's voice, what she blurted out made no sense to him.

"What are you telling me?" Robert asked, confused.

Hannah took a deep breath and started again. "I can't explain now. Just know that Lena did not die as a child. She lives in Warsaw." Hannah was careful. She did not mention Lena's last name. Nor who gave her the information, or any fact that could identify the person she was talking about.

"And you know this, how?"

"The woman who adopted her told me. It's amazing! Lena's a doctor. Isn't that just incredible?" Hannah was careful not to say where Lena practiced, just in case someone was listening and taking notes. She was sorry she let it slip Lena was a doctor. Too much information, she chided herself.

"Are you sure it's the same Lena? It's a pretty common girl's name, wouldn't you say?" While pointing out the obvious, Robert was reluctant to put the kibosh on Hannah's astonishing news.

"No. I'm not sure," Hannah admitted. While she had not dismissed the possibility that this was a different Lena, she tried to suppress the notion. "I'm going to talk to her tomorrow."

"Your mother misses you. She's invited herself to dinner this evening," Robert said.

"You're taking her out to eat?"

"No. She's bringing food to the apartment. She keeps asking me where you went, and I'm not as good a liar as you," Robert said.

"Unfortunately, I've had more practice."

After she hung up the phone, Hannah's anxiety quotient started to rise. The fact that the concierge had her passport, which clearly stated she was born in Poland, was worrisome. What if the Polish authorities decide to investigate how I left Poland as a child? Then again why would anybody care when Hannah McCabe left Poland? she reasoned. No one at the hotel had even asked her where she was born.

As she took a bite of her kielbasa sandwich that she'd brought back from Sandomierz, the telephone rang.

"Hello," Hannah said cautiously, wondering why she was getting a call from the front desk.

"Hannah, your mother has freaked out, she found the letter," Robert said, his voice shaky.

"What letter?"

"From the Archbishop. It was on your desk."

"What was she doing at my desk?"

"I don't know. She went in there to put her coat down, I think. After she read it she came running out of the room, screaming and yelling in Polish. I couldn't figure out what she was saying. When I finally got her to talk English, she calmed down. Now she's sitting in the living room staring into space. She keeps repeating, 'That can't be! That can't be!' Should I tell her what you found out?"

Still censoring her comments, Hannah said, "I don't think so. We should wait until I know one way or the other. Does she know where I am?"

"No. Should I tell her?"

"Absolutely not! Let me talk to her. She'll feel better if she gets a chance to yell at me for keeping the letter from her," Hannah said. "Can you take the day off tomorrow? Make her stay over. She shouldn't be alone."

"No problem. I can work at home. I'll keep her here until you sort this out," Robert promised.

When she picked up the receiver Molly's "Hello," was lifeless.

"Mom, I'm sorry we kept the letter a secret," Hannah said. "We didn't tell you because we wanted to spare you. We thought it was the right thing to do," Hannah said.

"It's not easy to know what is the right thing to do," Molly said without a trace of malice. "I was so sure Lena was alive. I thought I would feel it if she was dead."

Hannah crossed her fingers as she hung up the phone. "I hope I'll have good news for you tomorrow, Mom," she said out loud. Hearing her own voice in this unfamiliar environment made Hannah feel more alone. She was glad her room faced the street so she occasionally heard the sound of life outside. Hannah was not hungry enough to finish her sandwich and too keyed up to sleep. She turned to the routine that calmed her when she worried about a story. Legal pad in hand, she sat down on the bed and went into prep mode. She started to write a list of questions for Dr. Malińska. As she did for any important interview, Hannah rehearsed. This time she practiced asking her questions in Polish. Not out loud, but in her head. In case her hotel room was bugged.

Exhausted, Hannah fell asleep holding the picture Harry had shown her when he first told her about Lena.

Early the next morning, after she finished the continental breakfast left at her door, Hannah got directions from the concierge to the Central Hospital at 137 Wołoska Street. It was either a twenty-six-minute bus ride or a fifty-three-minute brisk walk. Eager to confront Lena Malińska, Hannah took the bus. At the hospital, when she could not find someone who spoke English, Hannah was forced to speak Polish. But locating a particular doctor in a hospital complex in Warsaw was not very different from trying to do the same in New York.

A nurse's aide who saw how frazzled Hannah was took pity on her.

"Can I help?" she asked.

"Yes, yes, I hope you can. I'm looking for Dr. Lena Malińska."

"Do you know where she works?"

Hannah shook her head no. She felt foolish. Some experienced reporter I am, Hannah berated herself. I should have asked Helga where in the hospital Lena worked!

The aide made several calls and came back happy. "I found her!" she said triumphantly. The young woman started to give Hannah directions, but gave up. "I will take you," she said, and escorted Hannah through a maze of corridors to the wing where Dr. Lena Malińska saw patients.

"Good luck," the aide said as she left Hannah in the crowded reception room.

Now forced to speak Polish, Hannah found herself actually thinking in Polish. "I would like to see Dr. Malińska," Hannah said confidently to the woman collating papers at the reception desk. "I need to speak . . ."

The receptionist cut her off mid-sentence. "The doctor is not here. She is not seeing patients today," she said without looking up.

"What about tomorrow?"

She shrugged. "I don't know. Do you wish to see another doctor?" she asked, finally looking at Hannah.

"No. I do not want to see a different doctor. I will come back tomorrow."

"As you wish," the woman said, and went back to her paperwork.

Normally, Hannah felt it best to assume the worst, and be surprised when something good turned up, but in this situation, she had allowed optimism to take root. Although she still had no proof that Lena Malińska was her sister, she had almost decided that she was. Hannah was eager to surprise Molly with the good news. This delay was frustrating, but she did not feel defeated.

Instead of wallowing in disappointment back in her hotel room for not connecting with Dr. Malińska, Hannah viewed this free time as an opportunity to do some sight-seeing on her own. The map of Warsaw and her guide book in hand, she headed for the Royal Łazienki Park. As she explored the grassy walks, in her head, Hannah replayed that special afternoon. She was there with Aunt Marta on her day off, feeding the red squirrels, pigeons, and ducks. But on Lipowa Street nothing remained of the ornate lime-stone building where she had lived with Aunt Emma. A modern, three-story concrete structure now stood in its place.

What was once here now exists only in my memory, Hannah mused. Sad. But no surprise. The last time I walked on this street all the buildings were on fire.

As she strolled over to the promenade along the Wisła River, Hannah thought about that balmy Tuesday afternoon in August, just before the Warsaw Uprising started. She still marveled at how unusual and very lucky it was that both Bronisław Bieliński and Marta Wilakowa were visiting her that day. Luck made it possible for Hannah to be with her mother for the rest of the war.

Reading the mention in her guide book that the former Library of Judaica on Tłomackie Street was now the Jewish Historical Institute, Hannah thought, I should go there! Without Jarek Tarnowski looking on, I could mourn those I had watched being annihilated years ago.

But the mere prospect of revisiting that area instantly replayed the harrowing sound of explosives ignited by flame throwers. Recalling how the buildings in the Ghetto had been set on fire one by one, Hannah could almost smell the acrid smoke as it once hovered above Warsaw. She wiped her eyes. No. I can't go there. Not alone. Maybe if Harry and Molly were with me.

Once she got back to her hotel Hannah immediately asked the concierge to place another overseas call to Robert, this time to the apartment. When the call finally came through, she cautiously explained the delay. She asked Robert to make Molly stay for another day, and quickly hung up. Whoever is listening, Hannah thought, must be bored to tears.

The next day when Hannah presented herself at the hospital, a different woman was now sitting at the reception desk. She seemed friendlier, but still a barrier.

"I'm sorry, Dr. Malińska is very busy. She is going away, and we are not scheduling any new patients for her."

"I am not a patient. I am a journalist. I need to ask the doctor a few questions."

"Is it about her trip to New York?"

Hannah was taken aback. Lena Malińska was going to New York?

"Yes. It's about her trip to New York," she lied.

The woman told Hannah to take a seat on a bench in the waiting room and disappeared down the hall. When she returned, she was shaking her head as she approached Hannah. "Sorry. The doctor doesn't wish to speak to you."

"I must talk to her. It is very important. It's a personal matter," Hannah insisted.

The receptionist sighed. "There is nothing I can do. I'll try to find her nurse. Maybe she can help you. Wait here."

As soon as the woman turned the corner, Hannah followed. She was surprised that the guard stationed in the waiting room had not stopped her. Hannah hid behind a cart piled high with medical supplies and watched. When the receptionist went back to her post, Hannah warily approached the room the woman had just exited. She took a deep breath, then ventured in.

Inside, Hannah looked around the empty room for signs of Dr. Malińska's presence. The office itself looked nothing like what she was used to seeing. The walls were bare and needed painting. No diplomas or commendations, usually on display in doctors' offices in the U.S., adorned these walls. The desk was stacked high with what she assumed to be patient files. When she approached, Hannah immediately spotted the same photograph of two little girls that Harry had shown her. Suddenly this drab room was transformed into a magical place.

"What are you doing here?" an angry voice behind Hannah shouted.

She spun around and was face-to-face with a woman who was the spitting image of her mother, thirty years ago. There was no doubt this was her sister. Oh, my God. I've found Lena. I've found her. Hannah tried to speak but her parched mouth could not form any words.

"Are you the journalist who wanted to see me?" Lena demanded. Hannah nodded.

"I told Magda I have nothing to say. Please go."

Hannah did not move. When she finally spoke, she said, "I don't want to talk to you about your trip to New York. I want to talk to you about this," and handed Lena the duplicate of the picture on her desk.

"Who are you?" Lena asked, her tone registering a mixture of shock and fear. "How did you get this picture?"

"I am the other child in that photograph," Hannah said.

She felt no need to keep her identity a secret from her sister.

Instinctively, Lena started to cross herself, then stopped. "You are Hannah, Hershel and Malka Stein's daughter? My sister?"

Hannah nodded.

"I cannot believe this!" Lena almost shouted. "How could this be? I heard my parents and sister went to America."

"They did."

"But you are here!"

Both sisters started to laugh and cry at the same time before they fell into each other's arms.

"Is miracle!" Lena shouted in English.

"*Tak! Tak!*" Hannah yelled in Polish.

While her sister completed her shift, Hannah remained in the tiny office. Having found her, she needed to stay close. Hannah felt drained. She'd made the trip back to Poland in spite of her fears, and accomplished more than she had expected. But her feeling of joy for having found her sister alive did not override her sense of guilt for not having found her sooner. In her musings she wondered, Had I shown Harry the Archbishop's letter when it first arrived, would I have found out the truth sooner? Did my mistake cheat Harry?

Lena held onto her sister's hand as they walked out the main entrance of the hospital, heading for Hotel Polonia. Surprising, this time as soon as they got into her hotel room, the concierge called with New York on the line.

"Molly is still with you?" Hannah asked when she heard Robert's voice.

"Yes. I convinced her to stay. Is the news good or bad?"

"The best."

"Then you tell her."

Hannah hoped whoever was listening would be celebrating with them. As soon as Molly picked up the phone, Hannah said, "You were right, Mom. The Archbishop was wrong. Lena did not die as a child. She's grown up. And a doctor!"

"How could you possibly know this?" Molly wasn't shouting but she was obviously angry. "Where are you calling from?"

"I'm in Warsaw. And there's someone here who needs to talk to you."

Hannah handed the phone to her sister. Lena took the receiver and sat on the bed with her back to Hannah.

"Hello," Lena whispered. "*Tak*. I think is dream, too."

As the long-lost daughter and her mother talked in Polish, Hannah could hear her sister's halting breaths and assumed she was crying. On the other end of the phone, Hannah pictured Molly crying and rejoicing.

Hannah sat dry-eyed in the corner of the darkened room.

Now it's my turn to ask you to forgive me, Dad. I'm so sorry I cheated you out of this reunion.

CHAPTER

19

HANNAH FELT LIKE A HELIUM balloon seeping air. Having traveled over four thousand miles to find her sister, she was content now to be under Lena's protective wing.

"We almost home," Lena said in English, as the tram was about to cross the Śląsko-Dąbrowski Bridge. Hannah was eager to see where her sister lived.

Lena had told her that she and her son Stefan had a modest two-bedroom apartment in a section of Warsaw where Hannah had never been. Known as Praga, it was on the other side of the Wisła River. Hannah remembered hearing during the last days of the Warsaw Uprising that the Soviet army was across the river in Praga. The Underground fighters who hoped to liberate Warsaw had expected them to come across to help fight the Germans. But they didn't.

As Lena was showing Hannah around the apartment, her son Stefan walked in fresh from soccer practice, still wearing his uniform. Hannah watched as her sister explained to her son who their guest was. Noting the troubled look on his face, Hannah decided the boy was less than pleased to see her. Lena pushed a reluctant Stefan toward his aunt.

Hannah extended her hand to her nephew.

"Say something to your Aunt Hannah!" Lena ordered in Polish.

He took her hand and whispered, "Glad to meet you." It was clear he felt otherwise.

"I'm glad to meet you, too," Hannah said, also in Polish, and wrapped both her hands around his long fingers. He had Harry's piercing green eyes. It surprised her how much he resembled her father. Heredity is destiny, she thought.

"You look a lot like your grandfather. He was a soccer player, too," Hannah said, remembering an old photo of Harry as a young boy, also in his soccer uniform.

The boy shrugged, but said nothing. He was happy to escape to his room once his mother said, "Go do your homework. I will tell you when dinner is ready."

"Stef has had a rough time adjusting to change," Lena said in Polish, once her son was out of earshot. "First his father was killed, then his grandfather died suddenly. We didn't even know he was sick. Finding out about my real parents was very upsetting for my son. Too much change . . . too fast."

"I bet it was hard for him to accept he had Jewish blood running in his veins," Hannah said in English, under her breath. Lena either didn't hear or chose not to comment.

Clearly a sensitive subject for both of them. A deep sigh was Lena's way of dealing with her discomfort when Hannah's gaze fell on the tiny gold cross around her neck. Lena still could not bring herself to take off that cherished gift from her father. She covered it with her hand, knowing it had a different meaning for Hannah.

Her sister's eyes did well-up seeing Lena's cross, but not for the reason Lena suspected. The cross reminded Hannah of the last time she saw her adored grandmother. It was then that Grandma Sonia took the Star of David from around Hannah's neck and replaced it with a gold crucifix.

"You sit, relax. I make dinner," Lena said in English, and patted her sister's hand. In the time they had been together, the sisters didn't go for very long without some physical contact. Lena needed to touch Hannah to reassure herself that she was not a mirage. After months of agonizing about how she could possibly find her family, having her sister sitting in her living room seemed like a miracle. She credited Stefan, her father, with making it happen.

Hannah settled on the couch and looked around the small but cozy front room looking for similarities to her own space. On a table in the corner, she spotted an elaborately framed picture of Lena holding a cascading bouquet of white flowers, standing next to a young man. She walked over to take a closer look.

It was obviously a wedding portrait of Lena and her husband Ryszard. But what really got Hannah's attention were the books surrounding the picture.

By carefully sounding out each syllable of the title of the first book she picked up, *Hit-ler-ow-ska Po-li-ty-ka Za-gła-dy Ży-dów*, Hannah translated it into English: *Hitler's Policies of Exterminating Jews*.

"Good God!" she exclaimed as she realized all the books stacked on the table dealt with the Holocaust, and in equal height to her own mound of research about hidden children.

A copy of *The Painted Bird*, the Jerzy Kosinski novel about a young Jewish boy's horrific experiences during the war, surprised Hannah. Unlike the other books it was in English. Hannah flipped through a few pages until she read: "I lived in Marta's hut, expecting my parents to come for me any day, any hour." Then closed the book.

"Have you read the Jerzy Kosinski novel?" Hannah called out to her sister.

"I try. Is too hard for me in English. I wait for them to permit it be published in Polish. And you, you read it?" Lena asked.

"No," Hannah answered, without elaborating. To herself she added, It's too hard for me in English, too.

The smells emanating from the kitchen attracted Hannah's attention. She positioned herself at the doorway and watched her sister prepare *kopytka*—her favorite Polish dish of fried potato dumplings, smothered in butter, and sprinkled with powdered sugar. Lena hummed as she sautéed. Hannah did not recognize the song, but the scene felt familiar.

"Thank you so much for making *kopytka*," Hannah said, clearly delighted at the prospect of tasting her favorite Polish dish again.

"I knew you would like it, too," Lena said in Polish.

Molly had stopped making *kopytka* once she decided that cooking with butter or frying anything was unhealthy.

"I bet you're a great cook," Hannah said.

"Wait till you taste. Then you say what you think," Lena said.

After they finished eating the feast Lena prepared, Stefan, who had remained silent during the meal, quickly retreated to his room, and the sisters began cleaning up.

"Now can I compliment the chef?" Hannah asked.

Lena nodded. "Please," she said in Polish.

"I pronounce you a great cook!" Hannah said as if she were offering a benediction. To herself she added, *Just like Molly.*

Lena took a bow. Pleased to be appreciated.

"Sorry we don't have dishwasher," she said, pointing to the dirty pots and pans soaking in the sink. "In America you have such luxuries."

Hannah nodded. "You are right, we do enjoy all kinds of mechanical luxuries in America. Actually, Robert ends up doing our dishes."

Anyone watching could not tell that these women had not known each other the day before. They seemed comfortable making small talk. But they were strangers, wondering how to transition to being sisters again. Both agreed that having Hannah spend the night was a good way for them to start.

Lena handed her sister one of her nightgowns, strongly reminiscent of Molly's nighttime wardrobe. Hannah wished she had thought to bring her own p.j.'s.

The first thing Hannah noticed as she walked into Lena's bedroom was the outline of a large crucifix that had once hung above the headboard. She wondered when it had been taken down.

Propped up by pillows, the sisters stretched out on Lena's double bed ready to begin their serious get-acquainted session. For Lena getting to know Hannah was a way to reclaim her missing first four years. Hannah wondered if it was possible for them to reestablish the closeness she was told they shared as children.

While eager to get to know each other, neither was sure how to start. Language was an issue. Lena's English was halting. She felt more comfortable speaking Polish. While Hannah's Polish accent was flawless, her vocabulary was limited. When she couldn't think of the Polish, she'd throw in an English word. Still, they managed. If they stepped on each other's sentences, the sisters giggled.

When Hannah confessed to a fear of flying as she talked about her LOT Airlines flight to Poland, Lena brought up her impending trip to New York.

"Some reporter I am. I never even asked why you were going to New York!"

"For World Health Conference at U.N. Doctor who supposed to go to conference got sick. Head of department decided I was good substitute because I speak English," Lena said in English, and laughed. She added quite seriously in Polish, "But I believe Stefan arranged it all."

"What do you mean?" Hannah was puzzled. She thought Lena was referring to her son.

"My father, he has been looking after me most of my life. And I believe he still is," Lena explained in Polish.

Hannah flinched when Lena referred to Stefan as her father. Lena didn't react.

Alternating between English and Polish, Lena tried to explain how Stefan had been helping her from the beyond.

"When I visited Ela in Krakow she told me my parents most likely left Poland. Maybe to New York. I must find way to go look for them there, I pray," she said in English. "And my prayers were answered," she continued in Polish.

"How does that have anything to do with Stefan?" Hannah was still puzzled.

273

"I know to you is childish," Lena said in English. In Polish she explained, "But I believe somehow he made sure my prayers were answered. He has always wanted my life to be better. That is why he left the letter and the pictures."

Lena pointed to the two original photos lying on the night table and handed them to Hannah.

"Harry carried this one in his wallet," Hannah whispered.

"Is not just picture. Look on back," Lena instructed in English.

Hannah read the name, "Z. Turowski," out loud.

"Pictures lead me to photographer who took them. That is how Stefan helped me find name of my family. Once I had name, I was sure I find you," Lena said. Reverting to Polish, she added, "With Stefan's help of course."

Hannah felt the blood drain from her face. "Stefan? No! No!" she shouted. "It was Harry who helped you. He was the one who left the photos with the nuns that had the photographer's name stamped on the back. Harry, our father, is the one who made it possible for you to know the name of your real family. All these years he blamed himself for not having done enough to find you. God, I wish he could be here!"

"Wish so, too," Lena said. Reverting to Polish, she added, "If only we had the power to go back and rewrite our history."

Each quietly pondered exactly what in her past needed undoing.

"I wish Stefan had told me he was sick," Lena said, breaking the silence. "I'm a doctor. I should have saved him, I could have, if we had caught it in time."

Silently, Hannah wished she could have found Lena while Harry was still alive.

"Why did the Archbishop think you were dead? How could he have made such a mistake?" she wondered out loud.

"I know exactly how it happened. Stefan explained it in his letter to me."

As Lena laid out what Stefan had done, Hannah was stunned.

"You must have been so angry when you found out," she said.

"No. I wasn't. How could I be angry with someone for loving me so much he couldn't give me up?"

Hannah was baffled by Lena's response.

"What do you mean? How could you not be furious?" Hannah felt such rage toward Stefan.

"How can I be angry with someone for loving me?" Lena repeated.

Hannah could not understand her sister's unconditional love for the man who caused her family so much grief.

"Stefan was a wonderful father," Lena said.

Not fair! Hannah thought. My sister had a loving father. I had a loving father for less than a year. But Hannah didn't want to blame Lena. Stefan was the obvious villain.

"Your Stefan was selfish," she said defiantly.

"You not know him. He was not selfish. He risked his life for me. He believed I was Jewish child, still he kept me, even with the danger. He saved my life."

"I'm glad he saved your life. But that life would have been very different if we had gotten you back after the war. All our lives would have been different."

Lena shrugged. "We can't change the past."

Hannah had no comeback. And she certainly didn't want to provoke an argument with Lena at the start of their relationship.

"I envy you," Hannah said. "You are so accepting."

Lena shook her head. "I feel out of place long time. Finally I learn to accept life way it is," she said. In Polish, she continued, "I believe your destiny is worked out without any input from you. Maybe the life we have is what we were supposed to have."

Molly's words echoed in Hannah's brain: "We didn't get Lena back, because it was *bashert*, it was meant to be this way."

"God planned all this? Is that what you think? If you ask me, it wasn't a very good plan!"

Lena saw no need to defend God. And she was uncomfortable talking to Hannah about her feelings for Stefan.

"Tell me about our family," Lena said to change the subject.

Her sister's request sounded to Hannah like a childish plea for a bedtime story. Her anger subsided. Hannah, the reporter, proceeded to narrate their family saga as she'd pieced it together. Starting with the courtship of Malka and Hershel.

CHAPTER

20

MALKA LANDAU AND HERSHEL STEIN grew up in Krakow. According to them it was an idyllic place to live. They cherished the old days when the family was intact. Almost eighty thousand Jews lived there before World War II.

They had known each other since childhood. Hershel was her brother Leo's best friend and a fixture in the Landau home. Malka was awed by him and the ambitious plans he shared with Leo at her parents' dining room table.

"Starting my medical practice will be just the beginning. I plan to have my own clinic and even a hospital someday. It will be a place where people come to be treated, from all over the country."

Whenever Hershel spoke to her, Malka blushed uncontrollably. She never expected him to be interested in her. Their romance came years later.

The Church may have preached that Jews were the killers of Christ, but Hershel had many close Gentile buddies on and off the soccer field. He studied hard and did well at the university, but when it came time to go to medical school, he had to go to Prague, where it was easier for a Jew to be accepted. He rarely came home. Leo heard from him only occasionally. In his second year of medical school he returned for his mother's funeral. His mother's death from pneumonia was the first tragedy in Hershel's life. He never forgave himself for not being there and blamed his father for not telling him how sick she was. Hershel was certain he could have saved her had he been home.

A week after the funeral Hershel returned to Prague to finish his studies. His father and three sisters were proud but worried for his safety. Moving into the Gentile world was not something Rabbi Moishe Stein would have wished for his youngest child. One consolation was that Hershel remained closer to home than his older brothers. Before he was born, Joseph had left for America, then Jake. Sam followed when Hershel was ten years old.

By the time he came back to Krakow to open his practice, Malka was grown up. With her blonde bob she looked like her favorite movie star, Clara Bow. Although shy and under the sway of her formidable mother Sonia, Malka was more self-assured now. She was working as the book-keeper in her parents' printing business and bookstore and saw herself as a woman of the world. To emphasize her worldliness, Malka smoked cigarettes through a long silver holder. Actually, before her marriage, the largest city Malka had visited outside of Krakow was Lodz. Her view of the world was formed by the movies she saw and articles she read in Kino Magazine. *Malka thought Hershel was as handsome as the movie actor Tyrone Power.*

Their elaborate wedding was officiated by Rabbi Moishe Stein on September 6, 1936, three years before the Wehrmacht units occupied Krakow. The newlyweds moved into a spacious house in the center of town, outside the Jewish quarter. They easily made friends with their neighbors, who were other professionals. Dr. Hershel Stein was a happy man. His practice prospered just as he had planned. As his reputation for being an able diagnostician grew, people came from other towns and villages to seek treatment.

On June 16, 1937, when Baby Lena arrived, Hershel was thrilled, if a little embarrassed at becoming a father nine months after the wedding. As the first grandchild on Malka's side of the family, Lena's every grimace, burble, and smile were celebrated. Ten months later, on April 16, 1938, Hannah made her appearance. The sisters soon became as inseparable as twins.

Hershel and Malka were not only the perfect couple but they also made an excellent team. In her crisp white uniform, Malka cheerfully welcomed his patients into the ground floor office. She also kept the books, and once the girls arrived, supervised Kaja, their nanny. On the occasions when Hershel was asked to consult on a case, Malka enjoyed telling his patients, "I'm sorry, we have to reschedule your appointment. The doctor has been called away to Warsaw." Life was good.

Everything changed when the Germans came.

Jews in Poland wanted to believe things would ultimately go back to normal, just as they had in the past. Not Hershel Stein. To avoid what he feared was coming, he wanted the entire family to leave Krakow and go somewhere where they weren't known.

"If you stay it may be far worse than you can imagine," Hershel reasoned, as he tried to convince his father and the rest of the family to leave. His Gentile friends introduced him to Polish citizens willing to risk their lives to help Jews. These people secured false papers and arranged for hiding places. While false papers didn't come cheap, Hershel had the money to acquire them.

With new papers that he would arrange for, he thought those who could pass because of their looks could live openly as Gentiles in a town where they were not known. But those who needed to go into hiding would be unable to venture out. It would be too dangerous for them and their benefactors.

For Rabbi Moishe Stein going into hiding was the only possibility. He knew with his long gray beard and classic Jewish features he could not pass for a Gentile. He equated going into hiding with being in prison. He refused to leave.

"I'm too old to live in a cave of my own making. I would be a prisoner," he said. "I couldn't go out. It would be too dangerous for anyone to come to see me. What kind of life would I be saving? I will stay here and accept what the Almighty plans for me."

Sonia and Jakob Landau also refused to leave. But Hershel's two widowed sisters, Salka, and Rushka, his sister Sara and her husband

Samuel, his nephews, Monek, Lunek, and two nieces, Leah and Helena, decided to follow Hershel's plan. Finally, Malka's brother Leo and his wife, Ada, agreed to go into hiding.

In July 1941 when rumors reached Krakow that a mob murdered all the Jews in Jedwabne, a town in northeastern Poland under German control, Hershel knew he had to move quickly. And he did.

Hershel remained hopeful that all those he managed to place in hiding, and those who were living openly with false identities as Gentiles, would be safe. If their luck did hold, and they survived the war, he expected the family to be reunited without much difficulty.

CHAPTER
21

SUDDENLY HANNAH EXPLODED!

"Stefan's lie ruined our family!" she shouted. "His lie caused such heartache. I suffered, Mother, we all suffered! You can't imagine what not getting you back after the war caused our family! You had Stefan. I lost a father. Harry never got over losing you! And he took it out on me. Father never got over his guilt for leaving Poland without you!"

As Hannah shouted, Lena jumped off the bed and closed the door to the bedroom. She wanted to keep their heated voices from reaching her son's room.

Lena couldn't renounce her love for Stefan, but she couldn't dismiss Hannah's burst of anger, either.

"I know that if Stefan had not told the nuns I had died, and had given me up after the war, I would have had a different life," Lena said. "I regret that I never got to know our father. That I grew up without you or a mother. But I don't regret having married Ryszard."

Lena picked up the framed photo on her bedside table of Ryszard holding Stefan in a bear hug and stroked her husband's face. "I wouldn't have had my son if I had gone to America. I do regret being a widow." Her voice a mere whisper.

"That was my destiny to raise my son alone," she said, fighting back tears.

The mention of Ryszard's death made Hannah focus on her sister's loss instead of her own.

"What a senseless death! Being shot the way Ryszard was. That was horrific!" Hannah said. "How awful that Ryszard's accidental death ended up shaping your destiny!"

Hannah realized they'd both suffered major losses.

"I'm sorry," Hannah said, "Being sisters now and tomorrow is what we have to concentrate on. We shouldn't be fighting over what can't be changed. What happened in our past is history."

"You know so much about our family history . . . you remember so much," Lena said, wistfully.

Hannah shook her head.

"Not so much. Only bits and pieces. I do remember everything from the morning I was sent to Kielce. Vividly. Especially Grandma Sonia." Just saying her name brought tears to her eyes.

"I don't remember you," Hannah admitted. She considered telling Lena about her dream, but didn't.

Still more comfortable asking than answering questions, Hannah said, "What do you remember?"

Lena sighed. "The train ride to the orphanage . . . holding onto father's thumb. When I went back to Krakow and saw the house our family used to live in, the wallpaper in one of the bedrooms looked familiar, but that's about it."

"You don't remember me either, do you?"

"No. I'm sorry. I'm the older sister, but I don't remember you!"

"Our cousin Leah told me we were inseparable," Hannah relayed.

Lena patted her sister's hand. She mourned the irretrievable loss of her first four years.

"You're lucky to have your son," Hannah said, switching the conversation back to the present.

"I know. What about you and Robert? Do you want children?"

"We've been trying," Hannah answered finally, although it was not a subject she wanted to discuss. "Robert already has a lovely daughter from his first marriage."

"Maybe you should think about adoption." Lena offered. "Helga and Stefan couldn't have a child of their own until they got me."

"No!" Hannah shot back and shook her head. "I remember how I felt about the people in Kielce. I didn't want them. I wanted my own parents!"

Lena was sorry she'd brought up the obviously touchy subject of adoption.

An awkward silence fell between them, until Hannah went into reporter mode.

"What was it like for you during the war? Did you know what was happening to Jews? I know you were only a child."

"Not as much of a child as you!" Lena playfully flicked her finger at her younger sister's nose. "The war didn't affect me directly, the same way it did you. I knew bad things were going on as I was growing up." Lena remembered fleeting conversations that she had overheard between Stefan and Helga. She never fully understood what was being said.

"Before the war many Jews lived in Sandomierz. I heard talk of Jews being sent to Treblinka or Belzec. I didn't know that being sent to Treblinka meant they were going to a concentration camp. I thought they were moving away. Helga didn't seem upset by what was happening. Stefan was. After the war when the Communists came, I remember hearing Helga say it was the fault of the Jews."

Lena felt ashamed. *I never thought about what was happening to Jews in Poland. I should have!* she scolded herself.

"When I visited Ela in Krakow, she told me a little about what you went through. It made me cry," Lena's voice cracked.

"It still makes me cry if I let myself think about it," Hannah said.

"Still? All these years later?" Lena was surprised.

Taking a respite from the past, Hannah said, "Warsaw looks very different now from what I remember. The trolley cars along Marszałkowska Street are gone. It's practically a three-lane

283

highway. It's a bustling business center. And no more horse and carriages, either!"

Lena kept steering the conversation back to the war years. "You were in Warsaw for the worst of it. It must have been horrible seeing the Ghetto burn."

Hannah bit her tongue. A trick she used during the war to keep from crying. She thought back to that day when Harry forced her to talk about Poland. Their painful reminiscing resulted in a closeness between her and her father Hannah didn't think was possible. She decided rehashing the war years with Lena might do the same for their relationship. *If I cry, maybe the tears will finally flush out the poison polluting my system.*

Hannah sat up, pushed herself against the headboard and hugged her legs.

"Yes. It was terrible. When it started in April, the SS had tanks, machine guns and flame throwers. All around Warsaw you could hear the shooting and things exploding. The Jews behind the ten-foot wall that surrounded the Ghetto managed to hold off the Germans for twenty-eight days even without comparable weapons."

Lena interrupted Hannah's narrative. "You knew all this—when it was going on? You were a child."

Hannah laughed and blew her nose into her soggy tissue. "I stopped being a child by the time I turned four. I had to know what was going on. I listened and watched. I knew I was Jewish. Pretending to be Gentile. You know, not everybody in Warsaw cared about what was happening to the Jews. I knew if someone suspected the truth . . . " Hannah's voice trailed off.

Lena hugged her sister.

"I was lucky. I survived," Hannah said solemnly, and started to describe the day the Warsaw Ghetto Uprising ended.

"They blew up the Great Warsaw Synagogue! The final bang reverberated throughout the city."

Lena thought about her visit months ago to the Jewish Historical Institute, next door to where the Great Synagogue stood. She'd read about the destruction of the Ghetto, and had seen pictures, but now listening to Hannah made it much more personal. More horrifying.

"All of Warsaw was gray. You could see the buildings glow as they burned, house by house. The smell of smoke lingered for a long time," Hannah said, her voice an eerie monotone. "It took the Germans longer than they had expected to liquidate the Ghetto, but they got the job done. They sent all those who survived to die in Treblinka. I had to pretend I didn't care."

Hannah paused. In the dim light she looked at the bureau opposite the bed. As if in counterpoint to her own story, she saw a photograph of a young Lena looking up adoringly at Stefan. She tried to remember where she herself could have been at that moment in time.

Tears trickled down Hannah's face. Lena reached over and patted her sister's moist cheek with a hankie. "You poor thing. You were just a child," Lena said.

"A very old child!" Hannah cracked a smile, then rested her head on Lena's shoulder. Comforted by her sister, she continued. "That was not the only uprising I was a witness to. In August of '44, when the Polish Underground tried to liberate Warsaw I wasn't just an onlooker. The Underground fighters held out for sixty-three days but the Germans, again with their superior weapons, crushed the Uprising when the Russians didn't cross the river to help. The Germans turned Warsaw into rubble."

Hannah pointed out the window. "We were just on the other side of the river. One of the last houses to be taken by the Germans. Toward the end of the fighting, many wounded fighters were huddled in our basement, too. I heard people whispering, 'If the Germans come and they find these wounded here, they will kill us all.' That's what they did in other buildings. Mother, a rosary in her hand, was leading everyone in prayers as we awaited the inevitable arrival of the German soldiers."

Lena interjected. "Mother was with you?"

Hannah nodded. "You would call it destiny! It just happened that Mother was visiting me and Emma on the day the Uprising started. She never went back to her job. As she led everyone in prayer, they treated her as if she were a direct descendant of the Virgin Mary. No one even suspected she was Jewish." Hannah chuckled. "Her blue eyes and blonde curls, just like yours, and her convincing chanting of the prayers, made them think she was one of them."

"You were together from then on," Lena said. A hint of envy in her voice. "After the Uprising you and Mother were together," she repeated, and smoothed Hannah's hair.

"Yes, we were together. But she was always Marta Wilakowa. Aunt Marta, never my mother. That's how it was."

An image of her terrified self, standing alone at a Warsaw tram stop, flashed before Hannah's eyes.

"I remember the time Mother finally came by on her day off, after not visiting for many, many weeks. She brought me a present, a coloring book and crayons, and said the two of us would be going out. It would be a wonderful day, she promised. I was ecstatic. We had lunch at a restaurant where I gorged myself on ice cream. Then we went to the park, walked around, fed the red squirrels, pigeons, and ducks, and enjoyed being together. It was a wonderful day. But I knew her visit was coming to an end when I saw her checking her watch. As we approached the tram stop for the trip back to Emma's, my stomach started to grumble, and not from too much ice cream. While we were waiting, Mother saw a couple who knew her employer. She smiled and waved at them. Looking straight ahead and without moving her lips, she explained who they were. I could tell she was nervous. I knew being seen with me was a problem. I was standing next to her, but not holding her hand. Then as the tram pulled up, she whispered, 'Stay here and wait! Someone will come for you.' And she got on board! I was left alone. Paralyzed. I don't remember how long I stayed there until my cousin Helena came to take me back to Emma. It seemed like forever."

Lena squeezed her sister's hand. She knew there was nothing she could say that would erase that frightening memory.

It was a source of pride for Hannah during the war that she kept her tears in check. Now they flowed unabated and she didn't care. She continued narrating the documentary unspooling in her head.

"While Mother prayed to God for someone to come and save us from the Germans, I childishly wanted the Germans to come," Hannah said. She got out of bed, walked to the window, and looked out across the river. "I couldn't stand the cries of pain from the wounded lying on stretchers. I covered my ears, but that wasn't enough to drown out their moaning. When all the wounded had somehow been evacuated through the sewers, just before the Germans arrived, I was sure Mother had saved us all with her prayers. They didn't shoot us. With their drawn bayonets, they herded us into the street, made us walk in the gutter."

"Forgive me! I force you to talk about such a horrendous time," Lena said, when Hannah came back to the bed.

"Probably good for me to get it out," Hannah said. She wiped her cheeks with the sleeve of her borrowed nightgown and kept on. "I remember the oppressive heat from the burning buildings. The flames glowed red and gold on both sides of the street. It was October, but it felt as hot as summer. I wanted to rip off my coat. Mother and Aunt Emma each held my hand so I wouldn't. We were walking over lifeless bodies that had been there for days in various stages of decomposition. I can't forget that dreadful smell of decaying flesh. It comes rushing back even now, when I see a dead body lying in the street on the news, or even in a movie. The German soldiers shouted, '*Mach schnell!*' I accidentally kicked a helmet lying in the road and it rolled. A head was still in it. I almost threw up. Mother and Emma dragged me by my hands to keep me moving. . . ."

As Hannah's memories poured out, Lena pulled her sister close and stroked her hair. She felt guilty. The war had only touched her obliquely. By comparison her life in Sandomierz with Stefan and Helga during that same time had been relatively blissful.

In spite of the tears, Hannah did not stop her reverie. "I remember a frail, elderly couple in front of us. They were leaning on each other, struggling to walk. I thought of Grandma Sonia and Grandpa Jakob. When I saw one of the officers aim his pistol at them, I had to protect them. I pulled away before Emma and Mother knew what was happening, and ran to the officer. 'Don't shoot them, don't shoot them!' I yelled. The only thing I could do to stop him was to kick his shiny boots."

"Weren't you afraid?"

"I must have been. Afterward, my whole body was shaking. But at that moment I was only thinking about protecting the old couple. It worked. Other people helped the old man and woman move along. Mother and Emma pulled me into the crowd and held my hands tighter than before."

Pointing to the window again, Hannah said, "The Russian soldiers might have been just around the corner from here. While Mother prayed for them to come from Praga, I wondered why God didn't make them come to save us."

That brought a chuckle from Lena. "You wanted the Russians to save you, but in Sandomierz we were afraid of the Russians," Lena said.

Hannah sighed. "By the time they came, the Germans had burned Warsaw to the ground. We were lucky they didn't kill us. Instead of packing us off to Treblinka as they had with the Jews who survived the Warsaw Ghetto Uprising, they shoved all the women and children into sealed boxcars, like cattle. Occasionally the train came to a stop. An armed German soldier would slide open the metal door and someone was allowed to get off to get water. At one stop Mother volunteered to go. She came back carrying several jugs. She was very brave."

Now Hannah proudly recounted what her mother had done. At the time, she was terrified that her mother would never return.

"We had no idea what would happen to us or where we were going. Until the heavy metal door of the boxcar slid open in Koslow. Did you know in Sandomierz what had happened in Warsaw?"

"Yes. Of course we knew," Lena said.

"The people in Koslow welcomed us as Polish heroines because we had been banished from Warsaw by the Germans. No one suspected Zofia Nowakowska and Marta Wilakowa were Jewish."

Hannah still enjoyed the fact that the Gentiles had been fooled.

When she noticed Lena was weeping, Hannah stopped talking. "Enough! I don't want our reunion to be full of tears," she said.

"Sometimes crying is a sign that you feel something," Lena said. "I want to know everything that happened to you. I know it was hard being separated from Mother and Father. But what was it like living with Aunt Emma? I hope she was good to you the way Stefan was to me."

Not exactly, Hannah thought to herself. To Lena she said, "Emma certainly looked like a kindly grandmother."

Hannah got off the bed again and walked to the window. With the moon and stars illuminating the night, she could see across the river. She tried to pick out the area where she'd lived with Aunt Emma, although she knew nothing remained of the building where they had lived.

She closed her eyes and pictured five-year-old Zosia back in the apartment on Lipowa Street. Alone. Sitting on the floor next to her bed, playing with the cutout paper doll she'd made to keep herself company.

* * *

"Kaja, be a good girl and eat your food. I made it just for you," *Zosia told her paper-playmate. Playing with Kaja only tamped down her fears while it was still light. When Emma had not returned once it was dark outside, Zosia introduced her counting game. "Let's see how many times I will count to one hundred before Aunt Emma comes home today!" she told her paper doll. At first she paced leisurely around the apartment counting to one hundred: one . . . two . . . three . . . four . . . But after many, many hours of counting, in a cold sweat, Zosia shouted out numbers in a voice she did not recognize as her own. She only stopped counting when she heard Emma's key in the door.*

* * *

Hannah shook her head to dislodge the image of a panicked Zosia. "What I remember most vividly are the scary times," Hannah explained.

"Emma often left me alone in the apartment. I worried. What will happen to me if she doesn't come back? There was no one I could call. I was told to talk to no one. Not even a neighbor. But I never cried," Hannah said proudly.

"I could almost bear it during the day. As evening approached the heavy drapes, necessary to comply with the blackout, turned the apartment into a dark cave. To stave off my panic I paced from room to room counting to one hundred over and over. Always hoping Emma would walk through the door before I reached the next one hundred. When she finally did come home, she cheerfully told me about her day. I never let her know how afraid I'd been. That was my secret."

Hannah came back to the bed. Finally talked out, she sat next to Lena for a time, thinking. Suddenly she decided to share her most terrifying secret with her sister.

"One night there was a knock on the door. I was sure it was the Gestapo. Emma went to the door. I quickly found the documents Father had left with me for safekeeping, ripped them up into little pieces and flushed everything down the toilet. But there was no Gestapo. The superintendent had come to enforce the blackout. Light was shining through the window because the drapes were not closed securely. When he left, Emma asked what I had done. I told her I had ripped up our old papers. As soon as I said it, I wished I could take my confession back. Emma's only response was, 'Go to bed!' But I knew I had made a terrible mistake. By telling her about our old papers I was afraid I had revealed our secret, that we were Jewish. From that moment on, till the end of the war, I lived in constant terror Emma might turn us into the Gestapo. If she did, it would be my fault. I had made a mistake."

"Oh my God! You poor child," Lena whispered.

Locked in an embrace, the sisters rocked back and forth for a very long time.

CHAPTER

22

WHEN SHE ARRIVED inside the LOT Airlines terminal at Kennedy Airport, Hannah felt like Dorothy returning from Oz. She had to keep pinching herself mentally to shake off the air of unreality of the last few days. But the photos of Lena and her son in her purse were proof that her trip was no fantasy. Hannah cleared customs in record time and ran toward Robert who was waiting at the gate.

"The conquering heroine returns," he said, as he took Hannah in his arms and swung her around.

"How did it feel to be back in Poland?" Robert asked.

"Strange. Half the time I felt like I was in the middle of a dream. Overall, I was not as afraid as I had expected to be. But nobody knew why I was really there. It was the same old pretense. Only now I was Hannah McCabe instead of Zofia Nowakowska. I spoke to Helga in Polish, but I never mentioned that Lena was my sister. Or why the family left her at the orphanage in the first place. She didn't ask any questions about Lena's family. And at the hotel, I was an American tourist. No one knew I spoke Polish. I wanted to know what they would say when they didn't think I could understand."

"Did you discover any of their secrets?"

"Guess not," Hannah laughed. While she had not heard any anti-Jewish sentiment uttered by the friendly Polish people she'd met, that was not enough for Hannah to believe they now welcomed Jews.

"You should have brought Lena home with you!" Molly said to Hannah as she opened her apartment door.

"Mom, you really think I'm powerful enough to tangle with the Communist power structure and win?" Grinning, Hannah hugged her mother.

"Thank you for finding your sister," Molly said, and kissed her on her forehead the way she used to when she was a child. "Your father was sure you'd find her. If only he could be here for the reunion." Molly heaved a sigh.

A week later, when Lena arrived in New York for the medical conference, Hannah went to pick her up at the Tudor Hotel on East 42nd Street. As she entered Lena's hotel room Hannah saw the various outfits on the bed and chuckled to herself.

"Mother will think you look wonderful no matter what you're wearing," Hannah reassured her sister.

"I'm very nervous," Lena said and bit her lip.

"No need to be. In this case all you have to do is show up!" Hannah said.

"Where's Molly?" Hannah asked, when Robert opened the door to the apartment.

"Getting ready to make a proper entrance," he said, and winked.

Hannah kissed him, then pulled Lena in front of her.

"Doesn't she look familiar?" Hannah asked.

"No question who your mother is!" Robert said, just as Molly stepped out of the bedroom.

Molly shouted, "*Lena! Moja droga Lena!*"

Lena spun around. Seeing her mother in the flesh made the

tears cascade down her cheeks. But these were tears of joy and disbelief. Although Hannah had told her how much she resembled their mother, Lena was shocked to be looking at an older version of herself.

Holding on to Lena, Molly turned to Hannah.

"Your father came to me in a dream last night. He told me you were bringing Lena to me," Molly said.

"I'm happy he knows," Hannah whispered under her breath.

Lena looked around the well-appointed apartment and imagined Hannah's life, growing up in this loving family, being pampered by Molly. A counter image of Helga, hands on her hips, often reprimanding her for a minor offence popped into Lena's head. Then she remembered she always had Stefan in her corner.

For the next three hours Molly stayed by Lena's side. She patted her hand and smoothed her hair trying to reassure herself her lost daughter had finally been found. As the two chatted in Polish, Hannah and Robert sat nearby and silently witnessed the emotional reunion being played out in the Stones' living room. Hannah at least understood what was being said. Poor Robert had to be content watching a foreign-language drama without the benefit of subtitles.

Molly couldn't stop repeating, "Not a single day went by that your father and I didn't think about you. Wondered where you were. Or if you survived. I was sure you were alive. I could feel it," Molly said, a smile illuminating her face. The smile vanished as she thought about Harry's anguish and sighed. "Your father never got over losing you. I'm sure it's what shortened his life!"

Hannah winced.

"But you're here now. We finally have you with us! Getting you back is the miracle we had prayed for!" Molly said, and patted Lena's cheek.

Hannah was silently mourning Harry's absence.

Lena could never condemn Stefan for what he did, even though she could feel the pain her absence had caused her family. She stayed close to her mother.

Molly brought out tins of family photos. As Lena eagerly studied the pictures, she thought about the Saturday she spent in Zygmunt Turowski's basement hoping to find a clue to her family. Silently, she thanked Stefan. When she spotted some photographs that looked like those she had commandeered from Mr. Turowski, Lena let out a howl.

"These, I have!" she shouted, then listened as Molly turned the faces of strangers into family members. As she regaled Lena with stories, Molly kept a tight grip on her daughter's hand. Feeling her mother squeeze her hand hard reminded Lena how she had gripped Harry's thumb on their way to the convent. Molly gently wiped her daughter's cheek without realizing why she was crying.

"What have you planned for dinner?" Hannah asked her mother, expecting to be told there was a feast awaiting them in the kitchen. At first shocked when Molly suggested ordering Chinese takeout, Hannah understood. The woman who relied on food to make things better decided this extraordinary reunion didn't require her superior cooking skills to make it special.

While Lena and Molly remained in the living room, it was left to Hannah and Robert to plan their dinner. Surprisingly, Molly didn't issue a single menu suggestion. But as she heard Hannah setting up the dining room table, she yelled, "Don't forget to use my good china!"

Molly's cobalt blue and gold rimmed plates were already in hand. Hannah winked at Robert, who was unpacking their food, and called out to Molly, "Will do!" Bickering is over! Hannah thought. Lena's first family meal must be special!

Once they sat down to eat, Robert and Hannah finally got to join the conversation.

"How old is your son?" Robert asked.

"He is to be thirteen on his next birthday."

"He can have his Bar Mitzvah right here in New York!" Molly announced.

Before Lena had a chance to react, Hannah changed the subject as she saw her sister put her hand over the tiny cross around her neck.

"Who's taking care of Stefan while you're away?" Hannah asked.

Ignoring the Bar Mitzvah issue, Lena quickly answered, "My brother Rudi!"

Lena was surprised to see the shock on Molly's face when she mentioned her brother.

Until that moment, Molly had never considered how her lost daughter functioned in an orbit outside of theirs. Having found her, Molly expected to pull Lena into their world unencumbered. Rudi's existence brought Lena's life into focus for Molly.

"They are good pals, Rudi and Stefan. My brother is younger than I," Lena said, trying to fill the awkward silence.

"So now you have a sister and a brother," Hannah said, cheerfully.

"But she had a sister before she had a brother," Molly shot back. Staking her claim again, she pinched Lena's cheek.

Hannah was amused. In true Stone family tradition, Molly was adjusting reality to suit herself.

After they finished their dessert of ice cream and kumquats, and each of them had opened their fortune cookie, Hannah noticed Lena kept checking her watch.

"Do you have to be back at a certain time?" Hannah asked her sister.

Molly answered for her. "No. Lena is going to spend the night here."

"I cannot," Lena said. "I would like. But I tell them I be back in evening. They are expecting me. We must prepare for tomorrow. I must make ready what I will say at conference."

"Lena is speaking tomorrow?" Molly said to Hannah. "What time? Where? I must be there."

"It's at the U. N. and it's not open to the public," Hannah said.

"I'm her mother, not the public. I always went to hear you when you spoke at school," Molly said defiantly.

"This is not school, Mom. I'll represent the family. I have a press pass."

"What about after the conference? Can you come back and stay with me?" Molly asked.

"For a short time, yes. I have not much free time here. Unfortunately, I must attend conference," Lena said. "I have obligation with delegation. Is why I come."

"But I want to introduce you to your relatives," Molly said. "Give a party for you. Show you off!"

"Perhaps a small party in evening?" she suggested. "And maybe I can spend the night." Lena wasn't sure she was up to meeting more relatives. I have to get used to being part of a new family, she told herself. But Lena had to admit it felt good to know she had other family members to get to know.

"Very good!" Molly said, and clapped her hands. "I promise you a celebration worthy of the occasion."

After she cleaned up, Hannah signaled to Robert and Lena they had to leave. At the door, Molly said plaintively to Hannah, "You brought her, and now you're taking her away."

"Yes, Mom, that's how I am," Hannah said sarcastically, and blew her mother a kiss.

Molly threw her arms around Lena. "I can't let you go!"

"I must go," Lena sighed. "Is for my work."

"You sound just like Harry. Work always came first," Molly said, more as a comparison than a complaint.

CHAPTER
23

THE NEXT MORNING HANNAH ARRIVED at the U.N. early for the opening of the conference. She signed in at the press desk and headed directly to where Lena would be speaking. Hannah walked into the empty auditorium and instead of picking a seat in the rear, as she usually did at such an event, made sure she was front and center. The two sisters exchanged waves as the panel walked onto the stage. "You must be very proud of your daughter, the doctor," Hannah said to her father, clasping her hands as if in prayer. She had total confidence that Harry Stone was witnessing this scene from somewhere in the universe.

Dr. Lena Malińska was free to leave the conference after the three-hour panel discussion. The sisters rushed out and hailed a cab along First Avenue to Molly's Upper West Side apartment. When they got off the elevator, they heard loud voices emanating from apartment 7B. Both Hannah and Lena were shocked to see the size of the crowd Molly had assembled as they entered the apartment.

All chatter stopped when a jubilant Molly ran over to Lena, took her hand and pulled her into the crowd. Hannah thought their interlaced fingers looked like one pair of hands—except for the Matador Red polish on Molly's carefully manicured nails.

"Please welcome my daughter home!" Molly bellowed, and everyone applauded.

Feeling the need to ward off possible criticism for throwing a party so soon after Harry's death, Molly added, "Harry would expect us to celebrate this special occasion even without him!"

Molly had gone all out to make Lena's welcome home party a festive affair. The dining room table now held a buffet befitting a major celebration. A huge arrangement of calla lilies in the center was surrounded by many platters of fish and fowl, as well as several plates of marble cake and strudel, next to a twenty-five-cup coffee urn.

Before Lena could catch her breath, Molly dragged her overwhelmed daughter from one person to another.

"Isn't it something, my Lena is a doctor, just like Harry," Molly repeated to every guest.

Unfortunately, few people spoke Polish. Result: While Lena generally understood what was being said, because they talked so fast, she was unable to translate the English into Polish quickly enough to engage in a meaningful conversation. She just let her mother do all the talking. Until she was cornered by her cousins, Helena and Leah. They did speak Polish and took turns telling Lena stories about her early years. She listened ever hopeful their memories would bring back some of her own. But no new images of her first four years resurfaced.

Hannah was on her best behavior. She deftly fielded complaints ("How come we never see you anymore?") and graciously accepted compliments ("We're very proud of you! We read all your articles. I tell everyone, that when you came here you didn't speak a word of English. Now look at you, a published writer!"). Hannah had forgotten how strongly her fellow refugees identified with her and took pride in her success.

As she mingled, Hannah overheard several of the guests take note of the tiny gold cross around Lena's neck.

"She's probably not Jewish anymore!" Hannah heard someone say in Yiddish.

"Who knows? Once the Catholic Church gets you, that's it," another one said.

Hannah noticed that Lena often kept one hand at the nape of her neck, shielding the cross, as her mother pulled her around the room by the other. Although she wondered how her sister felt about finding out she was Jewish, Hannah never asked.

When she saw Lena struggle to keep her fixed smile on her face, Hannah came to her sister's rescue.

"Excuse us a moment, please, I need to talk to Lena," she said, and pulled her into the guest bedroom where Robert appeared to be dozing while a golf tournament was silently in progress on the TV.

"How bad is it?" Robert asked, when he caught sight of them.

"Bad enough," Hannah answered. "She deserves a rest!" And gently pushed Lena into a chair.

"I cannot stay here," Lena said. "Your mother, I mean, our mother will be not pleased with me."

"Okay, go back in there if you must. You are obviously a glutton for punishment," Hannah said.

"I do not understand. What does that mean?"

"It means you are too nice," Hannah said, just as Molly came into the room.

"There you are," she said, "I have some latecomers you have to meet."

Lena followed her mother willingly.

By eight o'clock when the place finally emptied out, both Lena and Hannah were exhausted, but Molly could have celebrated for another few hours.

"Do you think people had a good time?" Molly, the concerned hostess, asked.

"Everybody had a great time, Mom. Now you take it easy, Lena and I will clean up."

"You prepared much food, Mom. Enough to feed Polish army," Lena joked.

Molly was happy. She kicked off her shoes and stretched out on the sofa.

As she started to pick up empty plates and glasses scattered around the apartment, Hannah said, "I'm sure Dad would have had a good time!" While she had keenly felt her father's absence from the celebration, Hannah had actually enjoyed Lena's welcome home party more than she would have suspected. And she wasn't ready to leave her sister and mother.

Hannah walked over to Robert and kissed him. "I think I want to sleep here tonight. Do you mind?"

"Nope. It's more than okay with me. But I'm taking off. You two have a fun sleepover," Robert said. He kissed Hannah, gave Lena a peck on the top of her head, and waved goodnight to Molly.

Hannah and Lena, each wearing one of Molly's nightgowns, were getting settled in what was once Hannah's room, when Molly came in to say goodnight.

"Can we have some hot chocolate, Mom?" Hannah asked. It had been her standard request years ago whenever she had a friend sleep over.

"Sure. But I only have instant."

"That's fine," Hannah said.

Lena nodded without really knowing what she was agreeing to.

After Molly delivered the hot chocolate and was out of earshot, Lena asked, "Are you and your mother close?" Embarrassed, she corrected herself. "I mean our mother!"

Hannah's palms began to sweat as she recalled an episode with her mother in Koslow, near the end of the German occupation.

* * *

Having earned a reputation as a talented singer in the Koslow community, Marta was summoned by a group of German officers passing through town to entertain at a party they were having. Afraid to go and afraid to refuse, her solution was to take six-year-old Zosia along for protection. Hyper-vigilant Zosia stationed herself at the side of the refreshment table and watched the performance. But after Marta finished singing, an appreciative group of officers formed a circle around her. When Zosia finally caught sight of her, one of the officers had his arm around Marta. Seeing the pained expression on her face, Zosia took a cake fork from the dessert table and jabbed the officer in the arm. In the ensuing commotion, Marta grabbed Zosia's wrist, dragged her out the back door, and they hid in the hayloft of their barn. Zosia was terrified, and was sure the barking dogs she heard through the night were searching for them. They stayed hidden until they were sure the German officers left town.

* * *

She wished she could tell Lena how she has felt responsible for Molly since she was a child. But Hannah only felt comfortable saying, "Mother and I have had a complicated relationship. Sometimes, we're too close . . ."

During the night, Molly went in to check on her girls. They had finally talked themselves out and were sound asleep. For a few moments she stood and watched, remembering how they once shared a bedroom many years ago. Without thinking, Molly gently rubbed Lena's cheek, the way she had when she was an infant. Drowsy with sleep, Lena opened her eyes, patted her mother's hand. "*Dobranoc, Mama,*" she said, just the way she used to, and fell back to sleep.

For over thirty years, Molly had longed to hear her firstborn say, "Goodnight, Mama."

CHAPTER

24

SUNDAY WAS THE MORNING Hannah usually slept in. But when she opened her eyes this Sunday, the clock on the night table next to her bed glowed 5:00 a.m. The entire night Hannah had been trapped in a maze. Now awake in the semi-dark room, an uneasy feeling settled in the pit of her stomach. She had been worried for weeks because there had been no word from Lena. The unveiling of Harry's headstone, a year after his death, was a week away, and Hannah was afraid her sister might not be allowed to come.

She took several deep breaths hoping to force the unspecific dread out of her body, then reached over to stroke Robert's shoulder as he slept next to her. He grunted in his sleep and patted her hand. Feeling his touch lightened her mood.

Hannah quietly tiptoed around the bedroom collecting her clothes, careful not to awaken Robert. It was unnecessary. He had the enviable ability to sleep through any kind of disturbance. The innocent sleep unperturbed, Hannah thought.

She stayed in the shower longer than usual, letting the warm water soothe her stiff neck. Hannah came out clean but hardly relaxed. She decided to go visit her mother early. Hannah kissed Robert on the forehead and placed the *Times* at the foot of the bed, with a note: Be back as soon as I can. Call me at my mother's. Love, H.

Robert seemed to incorporate her kiss into what most certainly was a pleasant dream.

On her way uptown, Hannah stopped to pick up an assortment of bagels, cream cheese and some whitefish, a delicacy that Molly particularly enjoyed. Just like her mother, she hoped the food would smooth over a potentially difficult day. When Hannah arrived at the apartment, a cheerful Molly greeted her at the door.

"Good morning. It's still morning, isn't it?" she asked. "I've been up for hours trying to decide what I should wear to the cemetery next Sunday. I narrowed it down to three possible outfits. I'd like your opinion on what would be most appropriate."

Hannah was bemused. Her mother was willing to give her a vote on what would make an appropriate fashion statement at an unveiling! She returned Molly's hug. It felt good. They both wanted to help each other through a trying time. For the past year Hannah had worked hard to improve their relationship, and for the most part she was successful.

As Molly took the bag of food from Hannah, she sniffed it, then turned up her nose. "I hope you didn't buy the whitefish at Zabar's. I'm sure they don't deliver on the weekend, and what I had seen yesterday was old and dry. Not fit to eat."

"I think I picked a good one," Hannah said, and immediately changed the subject. "How's the head count going?" She was pleased with herself, knowing that the old Hannah would have bristled at her mother's remark.

"I'm halfway through the guest list. Don't worry. I guarantee you we'll have enough people. More than enough."

"Great," Hannah said.

Having picked out the headstone, made all the arrangements with the cemetery and the rabbi, Hannah had left it to Molly to ensure that the necessary number of people required to hold a gravesite service would show up. They needed a *minyan*, the quorum of at least ten Jewish men to be present. Of course, Hannah resented the fact that only men qualified for a *minyan*.

She remembered arguing with her father: "Are Jewish women chopped liver?"

Harry's answer was always: "It's tradition!"

For Harry, Hannah was willing to follow tradition.

In the kitchen, Hannah poured herself a cup of coffee, and mother and daughter sat down to breakfast.

"They must have gotten a new delivery!" Molly said as she swallowed her last mouthful of whitefish.

Hannah said, "I'm glad you liked it."

"Ten o'clock isn't too early to call on a Sunday, is it?" Molly asked rhetorically as she headed for the phone with her guest list. "We'll deal with my wardrobe after I've made my calls," she said. "Go, read the paper!"

Hannah was happy to see her mother back in charge instead of waiting for someone to tell her what to do. Cup of black coffee in hand, she walked into the living room and looked at Harry's favorite spot on the sofa. I still expect him to walk in from the bedroom and sit down. Will it ever change? She sighed.

Hannah flipped through the Sunday *New York Times Magazine* and worried about Lena. She knew her sister would call as soon as she had secured a flight to New York. Unfortunately, no call meant no flight arrangements.

Having Lena at the unveiling was crucial. It was to be her final gift to her father. Her sister by her side at Harry's grave was the only consolation for not finding her while Harry was still alive. The powers that be in Poland could once again sabotage my life. This time by not allowing my sister and her son to get on a plane!

As Hannah agonized silently, Molly complained out loud. "Lena should be here with us now," she yelled into the living room. "Lena is back in the family. She should have come a week ago. I know she's a doctor and has patients, just like Harry, but this is different. Out of respect she should have come. Harry would expect her to be here. I need her here. I need some time to get to know my only grandchild!"

Hannah let Molly rant without commenting. Even bringing up Stefan, her only grandchild, didn't force a response. "It's her nature," she told herself. "She can't help it."

Molly was halfway through her final tally when the phone rang. Hannah rushed to answer it.

"Hello," she said in a stilted voice, expecting one of Molly's friends on the other end. But there seemed to be no one on the line.

"Hello. Hello. Is anyone there?"

"Yes. Yes," a far-off voice finally said. "We have bad connection. Is me. Is Lena here."

"Your ears must be burning," Hannah said, relieved. "We were just talking about you. We can't wait to see you and Stefan. Before you say another word, give me your flight number and time of arrival."

"That is what I call to tell you."

Hannah searched for a scrap of paper and a pencil, but froze when she heard Lena speak again.

"We have problem," Lena continued.

Hannah held her breath.

"We have not got space on plane yet."

Hannah stiffened. She closed her eyes, and forced herself to think positively.

"When will you get some good news?" Hannah asked.

"I do not know if . . ."

"You are still on a waiting list, right?"

"Of course. Is possible we be able to get on plane that comes to New York next Sunday morning. What hour is unveiling to be?"

"Three o'clock," Hannah said, and swallowed hard. "With customs and immigration, that's cutting it close." Her voice was low, emotionless. "Is there any chance you could come on Saturday?" Hannah hated sounding like Molly, demanding more than was possible.

"No. Is not possible. Sunday would be earliest. And it may not . . ." Lena's voice trailed off. "I try everything I could."

"I know. I'm just glad you're coming," Hannah said, refusing to acknowledge the possibility that it may not happen.

"Who was on the phone?" Molly asked, when Hannah hung up.

"It was Lena."

"Why didn't you let me talk to her? I would have told her to come immediately."

Hannah lied. "We were disconnected." She decided to tell her mother only the good news. "Her flight information isn't final yet. She has to call back."

The morning of the unveiling Hannah woke up at 5:30 a.m. She had showered and was fully dressed long before Robert even got out of bed.

Over breakfast, which neither ate, Robert tried to convince Hannah that he should be the one to pick Lena up at the airport.

"You take care of my mother. Please! Lena expects me to meet her," she insisted.

"For God's sake, Hannah you've never driven a car west of Southampton. How are you going to make it through the tunnel and all the way to the airport?"

"Don't you think it's about time I started driving west of Southampton? I have to do this. And I will!" It was a test Hannah set for herself.

"You're sure you're going to be okay driving on the L.I.E. by yourself?" Robert asked as he watched her nervously rummage through her cavernous bag for her driver's license.

"Yes. I'm sure. If I can drive along Montauk Highway during the summer, I can manage the Expressway early on Sunday morning," she insisted. But her bravado was fake. Hannah was terrified. But also determined.

Ultimately Robert gave in. "You're right. There won't be much traffic at this hour. You'll be fine," he said, as he pulled her close. He could feel her heart racing.

He agreed to bring Molly, the wine, and the sponge cake to the cemetery, while Hannah made her solo trip to the airport. The LOT Airlines flight with Lena and Stefan on board was scheduled to land at 10 a.m. Hannah allowed plenty of time for traffic snarls.

She was waiting at the door of the Hertz car rental on East 24th Street when the manager opened up.

"Morning, you must be real anxious to get somewhere," he said as he pulled up the metal gate.

Hannah nodded but said nothing. She thought to herself, If you knew how anxious I am you wouldn't rent me one of your cars.

She managed to fill out the necessary paperwork in the guise of a normal person, but by the time Hannah slid behind the wheel of the Mercury Marquis she was in a cold sweat. The seat was lower to the ground than Robert's old comfortable heap and the configuration of the dashboard was different. Everything added to her discomfort. She had trouble adjusting the seat so her foot could reach the gas pedal and brake. Then while fixing the rearview mirror Hannah almost pulled it off its moorings. For a moment she froze, not sure she could actually start the car. Hearing a honking horn from the vehicle behind her, Hannah put the car in drive. She gave it too much gas and it jolted forward. While she made a right out of the garage onto 24th Street without a problem, she had to jam on the brake when the light turned red just as she was about to make a left onto Third Avenue. Thank God New York has lights at every intersection, she thought. No left hand turns without a light was her mantra! A skittish driver in the country, Hannah often resorted to making a right in search of a traffic light when she needed to go left.

Waiting for the light, she took a deep breath and exhaled slowly.

"I can do this," she said out loud. Seeing the sparse Sunday morning traffic, Hannah felt more in control, even though her wet palms kept slipping off the steering wheel. When the green light allowed it, she made a wide left onto Third Avenue and for eleven blocks stayed in the right lane, ready to turn onto the 36th Street entrance to the Queens Midtown Tunnel.

"I can do this. I can do this," she kept telling herself.

After she'd given the attendant at the tollbooth the exact change without incident, and the green light welcomed her to Queens, Hannah relaxed her shoulders. She let the car in front of her set the speed limit. Hannah remained a car length behind. When she realized she was whistling, just the way her father used to when he drove, pretending to be calm, she laughed out loud. Hannah wasn't sure whether she was channeling her father's behind-the-wheel anxiety—Harry was neither a happy nor confident driver—or whether Harry's spirit had somehow invaded her body so he could come along to greet his long-lost daughter. She glanced at the empty front seat and imagined her father sitting there, nervously tapping his hand on his right thigh as he anticipated seeing Lena after all these years. The image cheered her.

Despite the stress, Hannah marveled at how well her first solo drive on the Long Island Expressway went. In the airport parking lot, once she was navigating on her own two legs, the cool breeze dried her damp brow. She inhaled the jet-fumed air, and exhaled some of her tension. Only Robert could understand what a big deal this was for her. She had passed her own test.

Her next worry—the plane was late. She now had four hours to kill. Hannah found a working pay phone and called Robert to report the delay. For three hours she paced, counting the floor tiles, the way she used to count to one hundred, over and over, waiting for Aunt Emma to return. Finally, Hannah fell asleep on a plastic chair in the waiting area. The booming voice over the P.A. system announcing that the long-awaited plane had just landed awakened her. As she hurried to the immigration area, Hannah checked her watch. We're still okay. If I can get out of the airport without making too many wrong turns, we'll get to the cemetery on time, she reassured herself.

Hannah elbowed her way past others waiting, trying to get closer to the double doors that separated immigration from the rest of the terminal. When she saw Lena looking around frantically, she yelled to her sister.

"Over here, Lena! Over here!"

Once she spotted Hannah in the crowd, Lena pulled her son by the arm and the two rushed past other arrivals. They stopped just short of colliding with Hannah. Lena and Hannah threw their arms around each other.

Stefan's light brown hair was slicked back, and he was wearing a man's suit that was slightly too big for him. The thirteen-year-old looked even more like his grandfather than he had the last time she saw him, Hannah thought. In addition to their common features, Stefan's body language reminded Hannah of her father. The way he tilted his head when he was unsure of his surroundings, but didn't want anyone to know.

"Stefan," his mother said, "don't just stand there. Give your Aunt Hannah a proper hug!"

His lips pressed closed, Stefan stepped toward Hannah and extended his hand. He knew they were related by blood, but this woman was a stranger to him.

Again, Stefan's sullen manner reminded Hannah of the cold, judgmental Harry she had feared for so many years.

She wanted to put her arms around her nephew, but stopped herself. Instead Hannah wrapped both her hands around his tapered fingers and squeezed.

"Thank God you are both here! *Dzięki Bogu oboje jesteście tutaj!*" she repeated in Polish. Then added, "Welcome to New York!"

Stefan stared blankly at her. "Don't worry," she said in Polish, "you'll learn English soon enough."

He shrugged. Again Hannah held back from giving Stefan a hug.

"I've got to get us to the cemetery as soon as possible," she said in Polish as she bent down to pick up a suitcase. "Is this all your luggage?" Hannah asked in English.

Lena nodded. "Is all we have."

"Good. The three of us can manage this. Let's head for the car."

Hannah, carrying one of the bags, led them out to the parking lot. It amused her that she felt as if she were the older sister when Lena was in New York.

"Is this really your car?" Stefan stared in awe.

"No. It's a . . . borrowed," Hannah said in Polish. She didn't know the word for "rental."

Stefan mulled that over in his head, "What kind of person would lend such a beautiful car to someone?"

When they got into the car, Hannah noted the stunned look on

Stefan's face as she watched him in the rearview mirror.

"People in America must have a lot of money," he said, seeing the sea of cars whiz by. "Everybody has a car!"

Hannah laughed. "Some people have two cars."

"Amazing!" Stefan murmured to himself.

"What's amazing is that you and your mother are here, that you were able to come!" Hannah exclaimed. "I wish your grandfather could see you."

Stefan nodded. "I'm sorry he's not alive," he said dutifully.

During their drive to the cemetery, the mood in the car was more cheerful than anyone could have predicted given the circumstances. Stefan continued to give his full attention to the traffic. To reassure herself that Lena was really there, Hannah periodically took one hand off the steering wheel to stroke her sister's hand. In Polish or English, the sisters made small talk as if their being together was nothing unusual.

The somberness of the occasion took hold once Hannah made a left turn, even without a traffic light, and drove through the iron gates of Beth Moses Cemetery.

They passed hundreds of graves on the way to Harry's gravesite.

"Why aren't there any crosses?" Stefan asked.

"There are no crosses at a Jewish cemetery," Hannah said.

Lena bit her thumbnail. She had not properly prepared her son for what to expect at a Jewish cemetery. "Only the Star of David on Jewish tombstones, see," she said, pointing out several granite headstones.

"All the people buried here are Jews? There are so many of them," Stefan said.

Neither Hannah nor Lena commented.

As Hannah pulled up behind a long line of parked cars she said, "Mother was as good as her word. She really delivered."

In the distance she saw Robert and Molly in the middle of the big crowd near Harry's grave. She glanced at her watch. Exactly four minutes to three.

"We made it. I got you here on time," she said, very pleased with

311

herself. "You two better prepare to be hugged by a lot of strangers," she said in Polish.

Lena opened the door of the car, and caught a glimpse of her reflection in the side-view mirror. She ran her fingers through her hair, just the way she remembered Helga doing hundreds of times, when she was about to meet someone she wanted to impress. Lena felt a jab of disloyalty to Molly and she tried to shake the image of Helga.

"Come, *chodź*," Hannah extended her hand to Stefan. Lena took his other hand and the three of them marched toward the assembled crowd.

Molly rushed toward them. "You're here! You're here! You're finally here!" As she put her arms around Lena, Molly looked at the sky and said, "Harry, see who we brought you?"

His mouth wide open, Stefan stared at Molly. He was shocked to see how much this stranger resembled his mother. When Molly loosened her hold on Lena, she turned to Stefan. In Polish, she said, "Come, give your poor grandmother a proper hug!"

Stefan slipped his hand out of Hannah's grip and tentatively extended it to Molly. She grabbed his hand and pulled him toward her. With Lena on her left and Stefan on her right, the three walked to the grave.

Frozen in place, Hannah saw her mother, sister and nephew merge with the gathered throng into a dreamlike tableau. She stood offstage watching, until Robert's arms engulfed her.

"Congratulations!" He kissed her. "You did it!"

Robert's praise was sidelined by her own thoughts.

"I'm not an only child anymore," she said out loud, but really still to herself. "Not sure how I feel."

"You should feel good. No. Great," Robert said. "Harry is somewhere up there bragging about his amazing daughter who did what he couldn't do."

Hannah leaned against Robert. "Come on. We've got to get this show on the road!" He gripped her shoulders with both his hands and propelled her forward.

As they approached the gravesite, Hannah thought she saw Lena glance toward the grave, start to cross herself, and then stop. Their first few months in New York, she remembered seeing Molly do the same whenever she passed a church.

"Another point of similarity," Hannah told herself.

The ceremony itself was short. The rabbi spoke briefly, "Birth is a beginning, death a destination. Life is a journey. Harry Stone's journey is over, but his life will echo in the memories of those he loved and those who loved him."

When the rabbi asked: "Who will say the Mourner's *Kaddish?*"

Lena answered, "He will!" and handed her son a piece of paper.

Stefan took a deep breath, unfolded the paper, and, without looking up, started to read the Hebrew words written phonetically in Polish. When he finished reading every syllable that was written on the page, Stefan looked at his mother. Lena squeezed her son's arm.

Once Stefan stopped, the rabbi finished the Mourner's prayer. After his final "Amen," he cut the ribbon unveiling the polished black granite headstone. Etched in block letters, the inscription read:

IN MEMORY OF
HARRY STONE
LOVING HUSBAND
FATHER AND GRANDFATHER
Forever In Our Hearts

The crowd lingered after the service. Molly, the perfect hostess, began serving her homemade sponge cake and wine that she and Robert had laid out on the folding table they'd set up near the grave.

"I'm sorry for the plastic plates and glasses," Molly apologized, knowing full well no one expected china and crystal at an unveiling.

Hannah left Robert talking to cousin Helena and her husband Gerald, and with a glass of wine in hand she walked closer to the headstone to say her private goodbye to Harry. In keeping with a Jewish tradition, she placed the largest rock she could find on top of the granite headstone. Leaving the rock was proof of her visit.

She raised her glass. "I know it's not the reunion we both hoped

313

for. I'm sorry. But it's the best I could do, Dad. I wish I could have gotten you and Lena together earlier. I should have let you see the letter. If I had, I might have found her sooner. But you did have one of your wishes granted," Hannah said cheerfully. "You told me, 'Before I die, I want Lena to know that I came back for her just as I promised.' Turns out, while you were still with us, she did learn you had come back for her! Unfortunately, not from you," she whispered and sighed. "You didn't count on having a grandson, did you, Dad? Or that your firstborn became a doctor? You were right about Lena. She is more accepting. I'm more like you, confrontational!" Hannah admitted. "But I no longer feel that's so bad!"

Hannah closed her eyes and thought about their Saturday walks and how much she'd missed them. "All the time we were fighting, Dad, I always hoped things would change between us. Then a miracle happened and they did. But we had so little time. . . ."

As she continued her one-sided conversation, Hannah vacillated between looking down at the grave, and up to the sky. "Feels strange not being an only child. Getting Lena back doesn't make up for what I lost. I now have to share the only parent I have left. She has gained a mother. But my life has changed for the better. Robert is back living in New York."

Hannah stopped talking for a moment. Then she took a deep breath and exhaled. "I want to tell you a secret, Dad. I think I'm pregnant!" She grinned and lifted the wine glass up toward the sky. "Naturally, if it's a boy, we'll name him Harry!"

She ended her soliloquy, but Hannah knew she wasn't ready to end the conversation. She reserved the right to continue talking to her father, hoping her words reached him in whatever dimension he now inhabited. Hannah could not envision a universe where Harry Stone no longer existed.

In the distance she saw the dwindling crowd. Her mother and sister stood so close they appeared to be conjoined twins. When Lena made eye contact with Hannah, she extricated herself from Molly and walked over to join her.

Looking very serious, Lena said in English, "I never said proper thank you for giving me my family back." In Polish she added, "In a way you brought me back to life."

Lena kissed Hannah's hand and put her arms around her. With tears streaming down both their faces, they remained locked in an embrace for some time. Then, holding hands, they walked back toward their mother. "Oh, it is wonderful to have a sister!" Hannah said.

With one arm firmly around her grandson's shoulder, Molly was saying goodbye to the few remaining friends and relatives.

As they approached, Hannah heard her mother say, "Yes, my Hannah can do anything. She's just like Harry!"

EPILOGUE

An exchange of post cards between Lena and Hannah.

Dear Hannah,
Time has passed very quickly these last two months.
Mother has adjusted to life in Warsaw very well. She
is teaching Pola and Roman to play bridge and Stefan
English. At meal times she speaks only English to him.
He has learned many English words about food.

Love,
Lena

Dear Lena,
Things are different here, too. The daughter we're
adopting will be arriving from Colombia a week
before Molly returns home. Mother will have another
grandchild to teach English to. By the time I give birth
in seven months she will have had lots of practice as a
grandmother. The only name Robert and I can agree on
is Harry.
It better be a boy!

Love,
H

Acknowledgments

I owe much to Joseph Heller for encouraging me to write my novel, to Lou Ann Walker for helping to get it into shape, to Jeannette Seaver for first thinking *Keeping Secrets* was worthy of publishing, then adding her editorial touch. And to Lilly Golden for guiding *Keeping Secrets* to publication.

There were others who read the early manuscript along the way whose comments influenced the final draft. My daughter Sarah Bernard made me rethink the opening, and Hugo Lindgren wisely counseled that Hannah had to return to Poland. But I cannot overstate the help of Natalia Olbinski, my adviser on all things Polish.

I am also indebted to Harriet Fier, Byron Dobell, Sheila Wolfe, Robert Loomis, Hilary Mills Loomis, Joanna Hershon, Edward Sorel, Tracy Chutorian Semler, Carole Lalli, and Melissa Osborn for their support and sage advice.

About the Author

Bina Bernard reported on political figures and writers for *People* magazine. *Keeping Secrets* is her first novel. Born in Poland, her immigrant experience remains central to her view of the world. She lives in New York, where her parents settled after World War II, with her husband, Walter Bernard, the graphic designer.

A Note on the Typeface

The text for *Keeping Secrets* is set in 10 pt. Janson, an old-style typeface created by Miklós Tótfalusi Kis 1650-1702). While living in Amsterdam, Kis became a talented engraver and master for stamping matrices for casting metal type. This typeface is based on surviving matrices mistakenly believed to have been created by Anton Janson (1620-1687). In 1954 it was proven to be the work of Miklós Kris.

Keeping Secrets:
Reading Group Guide

1. What life-changing secrets are revealed in *Keeping Secrets?* What family secrets are kept?

2. Harry Stone loses faith in God when he returns to the orphanage and the Mother Superior tells him, "I'm sorry. Lena is not here." Why is Molly Stone's faith not shaken?

3. In what way does Molly deal with the loss of her firstborn daughter?

4. How does survivor guilt affect Harry's life in America?

5. Why did Harry and Molly both keep Lena a secret from Hannah for 30 years? How did this ruse complicate the life of the family?

6. Did you sympathize with Lena's response to her stepfather's confession: "I lied to Sister Marianna. I told her you had been sick and died . . . I kept you from your real family." Or were you shocked by it, as Hannah was?

7. Lena's husband is killed, and her loving stepfather dies unexpectedly. Hannah thinks her husband wants to leave her. How does each sister deal with her fear of being abandoned? Discuss the themes of abandonment in this novel.

8. Hannah became angry when her father said, "You're a reporter. If anyone can find out what happened to Lena, you can." Why did she finally agree to search for her sister?

9. Knowing the tiny gold cross around her neck is a red flag for her Jewish mother, why can't Lena stop wearing it?

10. Given the anti-Jewish sentiment rampant in Communist Poland, what would it mean for Lena's thirteen-year-old son, raised Catholic, to suddenly be revealed a Jew?

11. When Lena asks her sister, "Are you and mother close?" Hannah answers, "Mother and I have had a complicated relationship." What secret does Hannah not reveal? Why?

12. Six months after they first took Lena in, why did her stepmother want to return her to the orphanage? What changed her mind?

13. Hannah was used to her combative relationship with her father and his coldness to her. She was stunned when she heard him suddenly declare "I love you" in Polish. What made her finally forgive her father's past neglect?

14. How difficult is it for both sisters to adapt to a new family dynamic?

15. Hannah wept as she was telling Lena about the time she, Aunt Marta and Emma were squatting on the train station platform being expelled from Warsaw after the uprising failed. "Watched over by German soldiers pointing their guns, they waited. But no one knew where they were going. Or when. As a diversion, she had been spinning herself around like a top. When she stopped and saw no sign of Aunt Mara or Emma, she was sure she's lost them forever. By the time they found her, she had stared to hyperventilate. But she did not cry." Why wasn't Hannah sobbing in terror at that moment?

16. Lena grew up with a rejecting stepmother and an adoring stepfather. Hannah's mother over-compensated for Harry's withdrawal from their supposed only child. Compare and contrast the challenges the two sisters faced growing up.

17. "I remember the oppressive heat from the burning buildings. The flames glowed red and gold on both sides of the street. It was October, but it felt as hot as summer. I wanted to rip off my coat. Mother and Aunt Emma each held my hand so I wouldn't. We were walking over lifeless bodies that had been there for days in various stages of decomposition. I can't forget that dreadful smell of decaying flesh. It comes rushing back even now, when I see a dead body lying in the street on the news, or even in a movie. The German soldiers shouted, 'Mach schnell!' I accidently kicked a helmet lying in the road and it rolled. A head was still in it. I almost threw up. Mother and Aunt Emma dragged me by the hand to keep me moving." How did Hannah's flashbacks of her wartime experience in Poland alter your perspective of World War II?

18. Why can't Hannah give up acting as caretaker for both of her parents?

19. As post World War II refugees, how was the Stone Family's immigrant experience different or similar to people seeking to emigrate to the U.S. today?

20. "No Mistakes Allowed!" Why does that phrase remain Hannah's guiding principle?